Notting Hill in the Snow

JULES WAKE

OneMoreChapter

One More Chapter
a division of HarperCollins*Publishers*
The News Building
1 London Bridge Street
London SE1 9GF

www.harpercollins.co.uk

This paperback edition 2019

First published in Great Britain in ebook format by
HarperCollins*Publishers* 2019

A catalogue record for this book
is available from the British Library

ISBN: 9780008354800

This novel is entirely a work of fiction.
The names, characters and incidents portrayed in it are
the work of the author's imagination. Any resemblance to
actual persons, living or dead, events or localities is
entirely coincidental.

Set in Birka by Palimpsest Book Production Ltd, Falkirk
Stirlingshire

Printed and bound by CPI Group (UK) Ltd, Croydon, CR0 4YY

MIX
Paper from
responsible sources
FSC
www.fsc.org   FSC C007454

For my home stars, Nick, Ellie & Matt, all so talented, you never fail to inspire me. x

Chapter 1

'Do you have to bring that thing on here at this time of day?' snapped the woman, whipping round to look at me, her spiky, spider leg mascaraed eyes shooting sheer poison as everyone on the platform at Notting Hill Gate surged forward when the tube doors opened. 'Bloody inconsiderate.' I think there might have been an F-word in there as well but I didn't quite catch it.

Taken aback by her hostility, all I could mutter was a hasty, 'Sorry,' as she gave me another outraged glare.

This time my apologetic smile was tinged with a hey-lady-I-have-to-get-to-work-too shrug. Travelling with a violin case (actually it's a viola but everyone assumes) can make you unpopular in rush hour, which is why most of the time I do my best to avoid it.

Conscious of all eyes on me, almost siding with the woman who was still muttering about it being a disgrace, I clutched the case to my chest, trying to take up as little space as possible. Even though my nose was squashed up against it, she still tutted. Then she tossed her hair, saying in a loud voice, 'This is ridiculous,' and squeezed past with a rough shove which pushed me into one of the grab rails. The case ricocheted off the metal right back into my face, hitting my cheekbone with a crunch that brought tears to my eyes. The shock of the pain, and that she'd do something like that, temporarily stunned me and, rather than say anything, I just stood there like a complete idiot.

By the time I'd gathered my dazed wits together she'd gone, swallowed up by the crowd, working her way down the carriage. My cheek throbbed but it was too difficult to manoeuvre an arm up out of the crush and hang onto my viola to give it the there-there rub it desperately needed. I blinked hard, keeping my eyes closed, aware that some people had seen what had happened. When I opened them, I caught sight of a pair of warm brown eyes softening in sympathy. He mouthed, 'You OK?'

I swallowed, feeling another rush of tears, hating the unwelcome feeling of being vulnerable and pathetic. I nodded. *Don't be nice, please don't be nice. You really will make me cry.* Despite everything, the warm smile and genuine concern made me feel a little better, a single ally in the hostile crowd, all desperate to get to work. I gave him a wan, grateful smile back. Nice man. Very nice man indeed. I'm a sucker for brown eyes. And smiles, for that matter. Smiles make a difference in life. They cost nothing and they can make a big difference to your day. Like his had done to mine. Mrs Scowly Over-made-up Face was probably destined to be miserable all day.

As he looked away, I sneaked a second look. He looked all business, buttoned-up and Mr Nine-to-Five, but nice – OK, gorgeous – and in that smart suit, with very shiny brogues and short, neat cropped hair, way out of my league. This morning I was rocking the Mafia moll look, an occupational hazard when you spend half your life toting a viola case around London. The look was completed by my long swingy bob, because it was easy to keep and suited my straight conker-brown, glossy – *thank you, God* – hair and Mac's finest Lady Danger bright red lipstick because my make-up artist friend Tilly had talked me into it and a severe black dress, because I was performing later.

Travelling this early sucked but the conductor on this show was flying out to Austria later this afternoon so had called a morning rehearsal.

I noticed my smiling man for a second time among the tide of people that changed at Holborn; he was several people ahead, striding with purpose, navigating his way through the crowd with shark-like ease, unlike me, bobbing along like a little piece of flotsam trying to stay afloat and keep my viola case to myself.

And there he was again in the same lift as me at Covent Garden underground station. As we walked out of the tube he fell into step beside me. 'Is your face all right? You took a bit of a whack.' He looked at my cheekbone and winced. 'Sorry, I should have said something to that woman, but I didn't realise what had happened until she'd gone. And she got off at Bond Street.'

'That's all right,' I said. 'I didn't get the chance to say anything either.' During the rest of the journey I'd had time to get cross with myself about that. He probably thought I was a bit spineless.

I lifted my hand to my face; my cheekbone still throbbed and I could feel it was a little swollen. Great, nine o'clock on a Monday morning and I was modelling the Quasimodo look. Embarrassment turned to annoyance. A gorgeous man and here I was being a pathetic wimp. This was not me.

'I'm guessing we might be heading the same way,' he said, letting me go first through the tube barriers, indicating my case with a jerk of his thumb that seemed oddly out of character with his suited and booted form.

'The Opera House?' I asked.

'Yes. You look like a musician.'

I gasped with wide eyes. 'What gave it away?'

For a moment I didn't think he was going to laugh and then his eyes crinkled, his mouth curved and a rich deep laugh rumbled out. 'I'm psychic,' he said.

'Of course you are.'

'Violin?'

'Ah, not as psychic as you thought. Viola, actually.'

'Ah, rumbled. What's the difference?'

I raised an eyebrow. 'You really want to know?'

He nodded, his smile a little impish now. I grinned back at him. Well, why not? What's not to like about flirting with a handsome stranger, even with an outsize lump on your face, especially when you know that there's absolutely no way he's going to ask for your number or suggest an after work drink. He was the sort of man who would be more likely to have a cool, elegant blonde on his arm. I'm no fashion expert but that suit had a sniff of the designer about it and probably cost more than I spent on little black dresses in a year.

4

'A viola is slightly bigger than a violin, its strings are a little thicker and –' I paused, adding in a dreamy tone that I just couldn't help '– it has a completely different tone. Mellower and deeper.'

We continued side by side down the cobbled street.

'You think it's far superior?' he asked with a knowing smile as we hit the throng of people wrapped up against the vicious wind that had sprung up just this morning.

'You really are psychic,' I said with a quick sidelong look at the decorations that seemed to have sprung up in the last few days, even though November had another week to run. Covent Garden was decked out in all its Christmas finery, with lots of pots and containers all around the Piazza spilling over with scarlet poinsettia and garlands of evergreens, all interspersed with tiny white lights, finished off with big gold bows.

'I think you might have given it away.'

I laughed. 'I'm probably biased.'

'Have you been playing long?'

'Most of my life.'

'So why the viola and not the violin?'

I laughed and waited a beat. 'Most people start with the violin but . . .' my mouth twitched '. . . I was destined to play the viola.' I raised an eyebrow. 'Picking up any psychic vibes now?'

He frowned, pretending to concentrate before shaking his head. 'No, psychic transmission seems to have hit a block. The network's down.'

Before I could answer, a girl stepped out in our path from one of the shops already playing Christmas carols. She held out a tray of mince pies, enticing us with the smell of rich

5

buttery pastry and fruity mincemeat. Automatically, I licked my lips at the sight of the sugar glistening on top of the egg-brushed pastry.

'Mince pie?' she offered.

Both he and I ploughed to a stop and put out greedy hands at the same time, fingers brushing. We laughed.

'Sorry, I love a mince pie,' I said with a happy sigh. The delicious scent epitomised the very best of Christmas.

'Me too,' he said as he bit into the pastry, the incisive bright white bite drawing my gaze to his mouth. Something in his eyes told me he'd noticed.

Hurriedly I took a bite and winced as my cheek throbbed.

'Are you all right? That looks sore.' He lifted a hand as if he were about to touch my face and then stalled with the sudden realisation that we really didn't know each other.

'It's OK. I really ought to get to work.'

'Yes.' He glanced at his wrist. 'And I have a meeting.'

Leaving the girl, who had probably hoped to draw us into the shop with her wares, looking a little crestfallen we turned and resumed our route.

We drew level by the stage door where I was headed and I stopped. 'This is me,' I said, pointing to the sign above the entrance. 'And that's you.' I indicated the box office entrance a few yards ahead.

'Right.' He paused.

I held my breath.

'Well, nice to meet you. I hope you fare better on the journey home.'

Damn. I let out the breath with a flat huff of disappointment.

'Thank you,' I said, slipping through the door.

'Wait . . .'

My heart jumped in hope.

'. . . you didn't say why you chose the viola.'

I stopped on the threshold and sighed. Game over but it had been nice while it lasted.

'It was inevitable.' I laughed up at him, watching in delight as he raised his eyebrows in question. 'My name is Viola.'

One quick look in the mirror in the nearest Ladies was enough to send me scurrying up four flights of stairs rather than down to the rehearsal room. I had plenty of time; I had planned to replace one of the strings on my viola before today's rehearsal but it could wait one more day.

I peeped around the door of the wig and make-up room, hoping that Tilly might be in. Phew, there she was at her messy station, surrounded by skeins of hair and the scary pin-filled head blocks used to make wigs. They looked like something out of a horror film and always gave me the heebie-jeebies.

I crept in, grateful that there was no sign of anyone else around.

'Oh, my God – what happened to your face?' Tilly's voice filled the quiet room.

I winced. 'Can you do anything about it? Cover it up for me? Put some make-up on it? I know it looks terrible.'

'I can make you look like a goddess.' She rushed over and examined my face. 'Although with that lump, a misshapen one. Did you get into a fight or something? When did this happen?'

'On the way to work.' I told her the sad story, although, for some reason, I omitted mentioning brown eyes, as if I wanted to keep that nice bit of the day to myself.

'What a bitch.' She squinted at my face. 'You should probably put some ice on it to take the swelling down.'

'I would if I had an ice bucket handy,' I said. 'I don't suppose you've got any paracetamol, have you? I've got a three-hour rehearsal to get through.' And I'd have my viola tucked under my chin on that side of my face.

Tilly beamed at me. 'I have both. There's a mini fridge in Jeanie's office and we always keep supplies up here . . . purely for ourselves, of course.' She winked.

Playing nursemaid to world-famous singing and dancing principals and making sure they were calm and collected before they went on stage was as much a part of her job as doing their make-up.

'Clearly, I underestimated how vile the tube would be at this time of day, but you're in very early too.' Our working hours were anything but regular. They varied depending on whether the production we were working on was in rehearsal or had opened.

At the moment we were in the final rehearsal stage for the annual Christmas ballet, *The Nutcracker*, and Tilly was in charge of the make-up team for the production, so our hours were quite similar. *The Nutcracker* was a nice one to work on; I'd done it a dozen times before and, muscle memory being what it was, the music always came back easily, although it didn't mean I could forgo practise.

'I've got a wig-fitting with Bryn Terfel in an hour and I had stuff to do.' I loved the way she casually mentioned his name as if he were any old Tom, Dick or Harry rather than one of the opera world's most sought-after international superstars. 'I'll just get you some ice.'

'I haven't got time. Can't you just slap some make-up on?'

She pursed her lips and studied my face, putting her hands on her hips, suddenly very professional and a touch haughty. 'Course I can, but if you want me to do a decent job, getting the swelling down with some ice would be best.'

Tilly could come across as ditzy sometimes, but when it came to her job she was very serious. Most of us were. It had taken me many, many hours of practise to achieve my level of expertise and getting a job here was not something I ever took for granted.

'OK, but I've got a rehearsal in half an hour.'

'Take a seat.' She shifted a wig, which looked rather like a sleeping tabby, onto a shelf to clear a space for me and clicked across the floor in her kitten heels, her vintage-print skirt bouncing as she walked towards her boss's office.

A minute later, her boss, Jeanie, popped her head out of the office, her mouth turned down in its usual perpetual disapproval. 'What have you been up to?'

Dressed in a severe black tunic and leggings, she looked like a hovering black crow. She and Tilly, with her vintage clothes, long pre-Raphaelite hair and armfuls of clinking bracelets, were like the proverbial chalk and cheese but they adored each other.

'Slight accident on the way to work. I had a run-in with my viola case.' I smiled weakly. Tilly always said Jeanie's bark was worse than her bite but I was yet to be convinced.

'Hmph,' she said and pulled her head back into her office.

Tilly reappeared with a handful of ice-cubes wrapped in a make-up streaked pink silk scarf and I put the bundle against my skin, flinching at the cold.

'I might as well do your eyes while you're holding that,' said Tilly, scanning my face with a gleam in her eyes.

'Ooh, would you?' I said, perking up.

'Yes, it'll distract people from the bruise,' she said matter-of-factly. 'You've got great eyes, that lovely amber colour. I've been dying to have a go at them.' She was already advancing on me with a smear of something on her fingers.

'Fill your boots; I never liked to ask before.'

'Feel free to ask any time. Next time you have a hot date, come up and see me.'

I gave her a non-committal smile. Dates had been few and far between for a while.

'I'm just putting some primer on; this holds everything in place. You'd be amazed by how many people don't use it.'

'I probably wouldn't,' I teased. 'I've never heard of it before.'

'This one's a professional use one, but Urban Decay do a great one.'

I lifted my head with a touch of excitement. 'That would be the perfect Christmas present for Bella's daughter, Laura. She's sixteen and really into her make-up.'

Tilly's forehead creased. 'Bella is your younger cousin? And she's got three girls. And Tina is the eldest and she has two girls?'

'Well done. You're learning.' My extended family was a

source of great curiosity to Tilly, who'd come late in life to a relationship with her sister.

Rather like I was a late addition to my parents' marriage. Late and totally unexpected. Mum was forty-five, very nearly forty-six when she had me. Telling everyone she was sailing through the menopause apart from the bloating, not a hot sweat in sight, it was a bit of a shock to find out that she was four months pregnant.

By that time, her sister, my aunt Gabrielle, had already had two daughters, Bella and Tina, the eldest of whom was fifteen years older than me. Consequently, at family gatherings I became the awkward one that needed to be catered for. My aunt was revelling in family outings when my cousins were starting to be self-sufficient and they could go to pubs and restaurants and then, all of a sudden, I came along and ruined it all. They were back to family friendly eateries with high chairs and changing mats.

However, I made up for these disappointments when I hit puberty and grade eight on the viola at just the right time so I was able to play at both of my cousins' weddings. Sadly, this didn't prevent me from being bridesmaid on both occasions. As a result, I developed a deep loathing for three-quarter-length dresses and tulle, rather ironic given where I work. The London Metropolitan Opera Company puts on ballets as well as operas.

'I can't imagine having a family that big. Both my parents are only children. I have no cousins. Just my sister.'

'Thank your lucky stars,' I said. 'I feel like I'm on call all the time. Next week I need to go and help my cousin Tina and her girls, one night after school. They're making the annual gingerbread house and it's a two-man job holding the roof together while the icing sugar sets.'

'Gingerbread house? Ooh, I've never made one of those.' Tilly's eyes gleamed with sudden enthusiasm as she dabbed away at my eyelids, taking a step back with an appraising look. 'Surprisingly, Marcus has got a bit of a sweet tooth; I wonder if he'd like one.'

'Seriously, don't,' I said, squinting up at her with one eye, still hanging onto the ice pack, dabbing at the chilly drips running down my face as they gradually melted. 'They're a right faff. If you don't get the gingerbread just right, the walls cave in and the whole thing collapses. Last year Tina had to make two batches. And she has to do the whole boiled sweet, stained glass window thing as well.' I groaned at the memory.

'What's wrong with that? It sounds really neat,' said Tilly.

'It is when it works. When it doesn't . . .' I shook my head. Thank God for copious quantities of gin. 'Oh, the stress! I tell you, my cousins are so competitive. They want to be the most perfect mummy and outdo each other. And they have to drag me in too. Both of them want to be the favourite cousin.

'And the flipping gingerbread house is just the start. From now on until Christmas, there'll be wreath-making, Christmas cake decorating, hanging biscuit baking, Christmas pud mixing and paperchain-making. And don't get me started on the competitive parcel-wrapping – who has the best paper, the most ribbons and the best-co-ordinating presents. And then there's the carol concerts, Christingle and two different school nativities.'

Tilly stopped and grabbed my hands to calm them; they have a tendency to do my talking for me and they'd been semaphoring all sorts of crazy messages. 'Are you OK?'

I huffed out a breath, realising my voice had risen and I sounded quite heated. 'Oh, my goodness – sorry, I don't know where all that came from. Ignore me.'

'Hey, it's OK. You can have your rant. I know you love your family.'

'I do, and I love Christmas. All this.' I pointed out of the window towards the huge Christmas tree outside on the square opposite St Mark's Church. 'But sometimes it all gets a bit much with my family.'

Chapter 2

Towards the end of the rehearsal I faltered, my bow pausing for a fraction of a second, some sixth sense drawing my gaze to the doorway, where some wag had already hung a piece of drunken mistletoe.

Him again! What was he doing here?

And no sooner had the thought whizzed through my brain than I forced my concentration back to my bow, horrified at my momentary lapse during rehearsal.

Damn, I never did that. When the passage finished and we had a couple of bars' break, I caught a surprised sidelong glance from Becky who shared the desk with me. I hadn't missed the quick glare from the conductor.

When time was called I allowed myself to look towards the door. Mr Nine-to-Five was standing by the wall with Alison Kreufeld, Artistic Director and all-round scary head honcho. What was she doing down here? She dealt with a production's staging rather than the music. We rarely saw her down here in the warren of rehearsal rooms in the vast basement of the building. And who was he? What was he doing here?

They were still there, chatting quietly as we all began packing away. After the sublime sounds of Tchaikovsky and the soaring notes of *The Nutcracker Suite*, the everyday noise of chairs scraping, music stands clattering, instrument case catches being snapped open and the dull thud of instruments being nestled back into their padded homes always brought me back to earth rather suddenly.

The immense level of concentration required of a three-hour rehearsal left me wrung out and exhausted, pretty much like everyone else in the room. We're a bit like zombies when we first finish.

'Coffee?' asked one of the other strings players, as I picked up my music and carefully arranged it back into my little black portfolio case.

'Yes, meet you up there.' As I headed towards the exit, the man from the tube nodded.

'Hello again, Viola the viola player.' Lively amusement danced in his eyes.

'We must stop meeting like this.' My mouth curved in an involuntary smile.

When his gaze settled on my cheek, he frowned. 'That looks better already.'

'I have a friend in Make-up,' I said, gingerly touching my cheek.

'You two know each other?' asked Alison, her face narrowing with suspicious interest.

We looked at each other, a little bemused, holding each other's gaze for a second too long like a pair of co-conspirators.

'No,' I denied, protesting too loudly and too quickly in that

I'm-innocent-before-you-think-I've-done-anything-wrong sort of way.

'We travelled the same route this morning,' explained the man with a glimmer of a smile. 'We both started out on the same platform at Notting Hill Gate and ended up walking the same way from the tube station.' The quirk in his mouth suggested he was remembering our conversation. 'I guessed from the case that Viola probably worked here.'

'Really?' asked Alison, as if it were terribly interesting, and while there weren't quite dollar signs in her eyes there was definitely a flare of avaricious interest.

I nodded. 'Never met before.'

'What were you doing at Notting Hill Gate?' she asked, whipping her head my way in blunt, direct detective tones that immediately made me feel guilty. Stupid really because I had nothing to hide, unless living in that particular area of London had been outlawed in recent weeks and someone had forgotten to let me know.

'I live there. In Notting Hill. Have done for a while.' I bristled in defence of my beloved London borough. The estate agents could probably employ me to wax poetical about how fantastic it was – good schools, fantastic transport links, great shops, et cetera, et cetera and if there had been a Notting Hill tourist office I'd be their poster girl.

'Do you?' Her brows knitted together and she glanced at the man again. 'Interesting,' she said before turning her back on me in dismissal and tilting her head his way. 'Would you like to see the backstage area?' It wasn't so much a question as an order and with that she led him away.

I drooped a little, watching their progress down the long corridor, and then he turned and looked over his shoulder, lifting his hand in a brief goodbye and giving me one last smile. Mmm, nice broad shoulders. Nice suit. Nice smile. Nice walk. Really, get a grip Viola. But it was a nice walk, long-legged, lean-hipped, confident, upright. Can you fancy someone for their walk? No matter, for the first time in ages I felt a flicker of interest. A little bird's wing of a flutter in my chest, either that or the start of a heart attack.

I mused for a second. I wasn't sure if it was his conspiratorial smile on the tube or the quickfire exchange on the walk from Covent Garden station, but something inside me was sitting up and taking notice. And here I was, watching him walk away, walk out of my life. A sudden start of alarm buzzed. I might never see him again.

That electric cattle prod of a thought made me start down the corridor after them with long rapid strides, instinct powering my legs. A slight sense of panic bubbled when they rounded the corner and disappeared from view.

I might never see him again.

I picked up my pace. Was I crazy, chasing after a complete stranger? For goodness' sake, I didn't know him. He was probably married. If not he was bound to have a girlfriend. How had I gone from a smile on the tube and a few lines of flirty banter to romcom, he-could-be-the-one territory? Was I mad or just desperate?

Taking the corner at a fast trot, I flew around it and then pulled up sharply, skidding to a windmill-style halt, but not quickly enough. My viola case torpedoed straight into his lower stomach, narrowly missing his crotch, and he let out a loud, 'Oof.'

'Oh, God, I'm so sorry,' I gasped as he doubled over, clutching his stomach.

Oh, pants, pants, pants. They'd clearly stopped to look at one of the many black and white photos of previous productions on the wall.

Alison raised startled eyebrows. Oh, boy. A witness to my humiliation. What was I doing? I was like some crazy woman.

I lowered my viola case to the floor and, without thinking, grabbed his arm, my fingers slipping slightly on the silky fine wool of his suit jacket. 'Are you OK? I'm really sorry. I was . . .' Was what? Chasing him down like a hound on the scent of a fox?

I ducked down towards him, our heads brushing, as my other hand had reached towards his stomach with an automatic rub-it-better instinct. As soon as my fingers made contact with the smooth, soft cotton of his shirt, I could feel the warmth of his skin burning through. What was I doing? I snatched my hand away.

He lifted his head and looked up from underneath his floppy fringe. Our eyes met for a frisson-filled second before he slowly straightened, dredging up a pained smile. 'That thing's a lethal weapon. No one needs to worry about you in a dark alley, do they?'

The romcom moment withered and died as Alison shot me a furious glare and turned to him. 'I am very sorry about this. Are you all right? I can only apologise for Miss Smith's clumsiness.'

'It was an accident.' He rubbed at his stomach in a tentative way that suggested that he was in a lot more pain than he was prepared to admit. Trying to be polite.

'Can I get you a glass of water or something?' I asked. Because that was really going to help. My brain appeared to have taken temporary leave of absence.

'I think I'll be all right,' he said gravely, although there was that slight twitch to his mouth.

I must have looked pretty mad, standing there with my mouth open, saying nothing.

His eyes twinkled, with amusement or pity – I couldn't tell which. It was the one time in my life that I really did pray for a large hole to open up at my feet and swallow me down whole.

He was still smiling and my heart was doing some kind of hippity-hoppity dance in my chest like a demented rabbit.

'Where were you going in such a hurry?' snapped Alison. Honestly, I felt like I was back at school.

'Er . . . just . . . er . . . heading to the Ladies. Occupational hazard.'

Oh, dear God, where had that come from? Seriously, that was the best I could come up with? And occupational hazard? Too much information, Viola! He did not need to know how long I'd sat cross-legged in a rehearsal.

Now Alison did stare. Hardly surprising; she knew as well as I did that the nearest Ladies was back the other way.

'Right, must be off,' I said in ridiculously jolly hockey stick tones. 'Again, I'm really sorry. I hope I haven't done too much damage.' And then I looked down at his stomach and crotch.

Oops. I raised my head, catching the quick amused lift of his eyebrow.

'I think I'll survive. I'd like to say it's nice to meet you again but . . .' He winced.

'OK, then.' I walked off down the corridor in completely the wrong direction, clutching my viola case, and slipped through the fire doors to the back stairs and sank onto the fifth step – hoping they didn't decide to take the stairs. I was going to have to wait until they'd gone to double back to the Ladies and my locker. What had I been thinking?

'Hey,' I said, collapsing into a chair Tilly had saved me at a table in the canteen, along with Leonie, who worked in Wardrobe.

'How's your cheek?' asked Tilly, reaching out and grabbing my chin. 'The swelling has definitely gone down and the foundation has held. Eye make-up still looks good too.'

'Yeah, I thought you were looking glam today,' chipped in Leonie. 'Apart from the lump on the side of your face.'

'Thanks. Tilly told me you could barely see it.'

'Tilly tells lies,' said Leonie calmly.

'It doesn't look as bad as it did,' said Tilly, shooting an evil glare at Leonie, who simply grinned; she had a habit of saying what she thought. 'Besides, everyone will be too busy looking at her eyes; don't they look great?'

Leonie tilted her head. 'Actually, they do.'

I batted my eyelashes at both of them.

'It made me feel better. How did your wig-fitting go?' I asked, reluctant to volunteer any information about my morning. The embarrassment of charging into a man who'd come closest to pricking my interest in a long time was still making me cringe.

'The wig-fitting went really well,' said Tilly, a little too enthusiastically. 'Hardly any adjustments and I took lots of photos.'

Leonie and I exchanged amused looks.

'So what went wrong?' I asked.

'Nothing.' Tilly's high pitched denial countered her claim.

'What did she do?' I asked Leonie with a laugh. Tilly was hopeless with anything technological.

Leonie rolled her eyes. 'This time it's what she didn't do. I had to upload the pictures on the system.'

'I'm getting better.' Tilly grinned.

'No, you're not,' said Leonie.

I laughed at both of them. 'What does Marcus think?'

'He's given up. He loves me just the way I am,' said Tilly with a touch of smugness as she picked up her coffee. The story of how she and Marcus had got together was legendary in the building. We weren't particular friends at the time but the story, with its elements of scandal – Tilly had been suspended for a time – had rocked the Opera House last December.

Leonie scowled at her. 'You know you make the rest of us a bit sick.'

'I know. Jeanie keeps telling me,' said Tilly, pushing her hair back, her bangles jingling as she gave us both another totally self-satisfied grin. 'But I think Fred's pretty keen, isn't he?'

Leonie beamed. 'Yes.'

'Oh, shut up the pair of you,' I muttered, tutting. 'I haven't had so much as a sniff of a date in ages. And the last one was such a disaster I'm thinking about declaring myself a date-free zone.'

Tilly laughed. 'What about that solicitor who wanted to know if you'd had any injuries at work? And how much your hands were worth?'

I shuddered. 'Yes. I am never going out with a solicitor again.'

They both laughed and then I noticed someone stalking her way through the tables. 'Oh, God.' I ducked my head. 'Don't let her see me.'

Tilly looked over her shoulder and then turned back. 'She loves me,' she said with all the smug self-righteousness of someone who had been wronged and subsequently exonerated and now had the upper hand.

'Ah, Viola, isn't it? I wanted to catch up with you.' Alison Kreufeld pulled up a chair, to everyone's astonishment, and sat down.

'Look, I'm really sorry. Was he OK? He's not going to sue or anything, is he?'

'I'm sure he won't.' She smiled as if I'd just played right into her hands. 'Although you might be able to help there. I wanted to talk to you about our outreach programmes.'

I relaxed a little.

'You know that in order to qualify for some of our funding there are a number of projects where we work within the community, to make what we do here more accessible to those in all walks of life.'

'Yes.' I nodded. I'd done a few school visits, playing in assemblies and talking to gifted music students.

'Well, the gentleman I was showing around . . .'

Gentleman. Didn't he have a name? James, I decided. There was a touch of Andrei Bolkonsky from *War and Peace,* as played by James Norton.

'Viola!'

I looked up. 'Yes?'

'Mr Williams,' Alison said with emphasis, 'is a governor at a primary school in Notting Hill. His mother-in-law is a friend of the Opera House.'

So, Mr Nine-to-Five had a name and a wife.

'We've been asked to help the school with its annual nativity.' She pulled a face. 'Although it's very short notice, it does fulfil our outreach criteria and she is a very significant benefactor.'

I nodded, ignoring the barely contained sniggers of Tilly and Leonie.

'It will be mainly mornings and possibly the odd afternoon. And you're in Notting Hill.'

'OK,' I agreed, thinking that it didn't sound terribly arduous. How hard could playing a few carols for the local school be?

Chapter 3

'Tell them you're busy,' said my cousin Bella, waving a wooden spoon at me as she took a quick rest from stirring the cake mix.

I hadn't intended to mention my new outreach role but she'd asked if I was free the next day as she was expecting an Amazon delivery. 'I need you to wait in for a parcel tomorrow afternoon for me. I promised Tina I'd meet her at Westfield to go Christmas shopping.'

She lived just around the corner from me in one those sherbet, pastel-coloured houses made famous in the film *Notting Hill*. Hers was painted a pretty pale powder-blue and was sandwiched between a sunshine-yellow house and a pale rose-pink house. Just walking along her street always made my heart lift and it was one of the reasons I loved living in this area. It was never a hardship coming here and I occasionally used her front room to practise while waiting in for her parcels. Her house was even more gorgeous inside, with its big high-ceilinged rooms decorated to within an inch of their lives with John Lewis furnishings and accessories. The extremely stylish kitchen, where I was currently sitting, had featured in several style magazines and at least one Sunday supplement.

'What time's your parcel arriving?'

'Any time between twelve and four.'

'I don't think I can fit it in. I might be able to get here for three-thirty.'

'Three-thirty, no earlier?'

'I'm taking Dad to the airport and then I've just got time to come straight back home, drop the car back at Mum's and get to the school for two.'

'What are you going to be doing?' she asked.

I shrugged. 'I'm not entirely sure. Probably just helping with the musical arrangements and the singing. I've been invited to meet the class tomorrow because they're starting rehearsals. I'd said I'd go.'

'Oh, God, poor you.' Bella cringed. 'Cue crying tots because they all wanted to be Mary. And a dozen disgruntled shepherds because who wants to wear a tea towel on their head?'

'Thanks, Bel, because that's really cheered me up.'

'Oh, well, it will be light relief after a trip to Heathrow.' Bella shook her head. 'Couldn't he have got the tube or the Express from Paddington?'

I pulled a face. 'Mum said she needed me to take him. She wasn't happy about him travelling on his own with luggage.' I shrugged. 'He is seventy-five.'

Bella snorted. 'He's travelling long haul and jaunting about the States at the other end. I think he would have managed just fine.'

So did I. My dad still runs a mile every day and you've

never met a fitter, healthier seventy-five year old – he actually looks more like sixty-five – but Mum had used the magic word on me: *need*.

'Oh, well, I said I'd do it. And I'll time it so that I pick him up to give myself enough time to get to the school.'

'Well, I think the school thing is taking the piss. Surely they can't make you . . . Sorry, Laura –' she turned to her sixteen-year-old daughter '– forget I said that. Taking the Michael.'

'It's work. I can't say no,' I said.

'Extracting the urine,' said Laura, suddenly interrupting with a cool stare at her mother before going back to her book, despite having earphones in. She sat at the opposite end of the huge island counter, perched on one of the white stools. Despite the seeming impracticality, what with having three children and a dog, everything was white: the cabinets, the composite material worktop with its touch of glitter and the tiled floors.

Bella went to say something to her eldest daughter and realised it was a waste of time. Laura, with teenage flippancy, now held the book in front of her face, while her two younger sisters, Rosa, eight, and Ella, five going on ninety-five, were both darting around the kitchen in matching lurid pink fairy costumes, throwing pinches of flour into the air and making wishes with fairy dust. At least it wouldn't show on the floor.

She turned to me. 'You can say no. Is it part of your contract?'

'I don't know but I'm sure there'll be something in there about reasonable requests to appear on behalf of the LMOC. Like I said, I don't really have much choice.'

'You always have a choice,' said Bella, groaning and rubbing

27

her shoulders. 'Here, you have a go. Rosa, Ella, stop that now.' Her mock glare just brought giggles.

I took the mixing bowl from her while she continued. 'Tell them you've got family commitments. We all need you. I don't know what I'd do without you.' She looked over at the calendar. 'Thank God Dave will be home for Christmas; this latest contract feels like it's been forever.'

Her husband, Dave, was a civil engineer who worked on big overseas projects and was currently in Finland building a new bridge.

'Keep going.' She nodded at the bowl. 'I'm really hoping I've got it right this year and all the fruit doesn't sink to the bottom,' she said, rolling her shoulders as I manfully stirred the thick cake mix.

I looked with longing over at the Kenwood Chef on the side.

'It's not the same,' said Bella, catching me. 'Christmas cake should always be hand stirred. It's tradition. And you're doing a great job.'

'I thought it should always be baked at the end of October,' I said, my shoulder twinging with a sharp pinch of pain. We were at the end of November. I pushed the bowl back over the table towards her. 'Aren't you supposed to be feeding it with brandy by now? Here, you'll have to take over; my shoulder hurts and I've got a performance tomorrow.' I wasn't going to push it for the sake of bloody Christmas cake, especially when I knew from experience that on Christmas Day both sisters would turn up with a cake each, because the recipe made enough mixture for two cakes (and no one in the entire family seemed to have the power to divide by two) which, added to the extra one Mum always gave me, meant I would end up with three un-iced cakes. I wouldn't mind but the icing was my favourite bit and I'd still be eating it by Easter.

We always had Christmas at Mum's, even though my Aunt Gabrielle's place was definitely bigger.

Bella took the bowl back and, with a calculating expression, turned to her daughter. 'Laura, do you want to have a go? You can make a wish.'

Laura sighed and shook her head. She wasn't stupid either. 'Nah, I'm all good.'

'I thought that was Christmas puddings,' I said.

'Was worth a try.' Bella grinned shamelessly at me. 'You can make yourself useful and pour us a glass of wine.'

'OK, but I can only stay for one.'

'Really? But the girls wanted you to read them a bedtime story, didn't you, girls?'

I shot her a quick cross look. Low blow, Bel.

'Yes. Yes. Yes, Aunty Vila,' said Ella. '*Jesus's Christmas Party*.' She was already waving the book in the air and had come around the island to nudge at me in my black dress with her flour-coated tutu.

Then Bella added in a quiet voice, 'I could really do with half an hour or so to myself.'

'All right then,' I said, rolling my eyes at Bella, taking the battered book from Ella.

'You've only got yourself to blame,' she said. 'You bought them the book; they love it.'

'I know,' I said with a rueful smile as I opened the front page.

I finally escaped from Bella's at half past eight, having been conned into reading several other stories while, funnily enough, Bella holed herself up in the lounge with another glass of wine to crack through her Christmas card list. I hadn't even bought mine, let alone started writing them.

Chapter 4

'Which terminal is it, Dad?' I asked as I spotted the sign for the slip road for Terminals One, Two and Three.

He began fumbling through the travel folder on his knees. 'Do you know, I'm not sure,' he said in a chatty, conversational way, completely unmoved by the fact that I needed to make a major directional decision in the next thirty seconds.

'Do you think you could find out quickly, because if it's Terminals One, Two or Three I need to come off the motorway in a minute.'

I heard the shuffle of paperwork and tried to breathe slowly – in, out, in, out.

'Any time soon,' I said, looking in my mirror, taking preparatory action by indicating and trying to get into the left lane, just in case.

'I think it might be Four. Or it might be Five. It was Four last time.'

Damn, the Range Rover in the lane next to me was speeding up; he wasn't going to let me in and the car behind me was getting closer and flashing its lights. I floored the accelerator and, to the accompaniment of the angry blare of the horn of the Range Rover, I nipped into the almost non-existent space between him and an articulated lorry as we reached the first countdown sign to the slip road.

'Dad! I need a decision.'

'Four,' he said. 'We definitely flew from Four last time. Oh, no, it was Five. It was the new one. Do you know, it's the largest building in the UK and is big enough to hold fifty football pitches?'

'That's interesting,' I said with a sigh as I put my foot down on the accelerator and sailed past the slip road.

'Well, I'll be there in perfect time,' he said, checking his watch, oblivious to the sharp manoeuvre of the Range Rover, which wheeled out from behind me to overtake and when the driver drew alongside he made his displeasure quite clear with a few choice hand gestures. 'My flight's not until three-thirty and I'm checked in.'

'Great,' I said through gritted teeth, looking at the traffic on the other side of the M4 already starting to back up. I'd planned to drop him at twelve-thirty, which would leave me plenty of time to battle the traffic back into central London, but he'd faffed about trying to decide whether to take a front door key with him and then decided that he ought to have another book on the flight, which he'd packed in his suitcase. By the time we'd left my parents' apartment, just ten minutes from my flat, it was half an hour later than I would have liked. And then the traffic was horrendous on the M4 because a lane was closed.

Just as we approached the slip road – I'd moved over in plenty of time – my dad suddenly said, 'Of course, last time I went to Atlanta I flew British Airways.'

I risked a quick glance at him as he turned an apologetic face my way. 'We've still got plenty of time. I've checked in online. I only have to drop my case.'

I gritted my teeth. I had to get back to Notting Hill, drop the car and get to the school in time for two and it was already ten past one.

'I'm flying Virgin Atlantic this time,' Dad announced, apropos of nothing. There was a silence in the car. 'Not British Airways.'

'Does that mean that it might not be Terminal Five?' I asked, my fingers almost strangling the steering wheel.

'I think –' Dad drew out the syllables as I negotiated a roundabout, following the signs to Terminal Five '– that's for British Airways flights only.'

'Oh, for . . . sake,' I ground out under my breath as I did a hasty left signal and pulled back into the main stream of traffic going around the roundabout. 'Are you definitely flying Virgin?'

'Yes,' said Dad. 'See here.' He held up the paperwork just under my nose as if I could calmly take my eyes off the road and peruse the details at my leisure.

'Dad, do you have any idea where Virgin fly from?'

'Terminal Four?'

'Do you know that or is it a guess?'

'Well, it stands to reason, doesn't it? If BA flies from Five, Virgin would fly from Four.'

'Not necessarily,' I said, driving for the second time around the roundabout, past the turning for Terminal Five. 'Is there any way you could look it up on your phone quickly? I can't keep driving round and round this roundabout.'

When I started the third circuit, I took an executive decision and took the turning for Terminal Four.

'I might have got it wrong, you know. I think Terminal Five is for all flights to America, so that would mean Virgin do fly from there,' said Dad, looking back over his shoulder at the roundabout as he lifted his phone to his ear.

'Who are you calling? I asked, glancing over at him.

'Your mother; she might know.'

I raised my eyes heavenward before I spoke. Dad was a gentle soul; getting cross with him would be counter-productive . . . but seriously.

'Mum isn't going to know. You're the frequent flyer. Just look it up on your phone.'

'Phyllis, it's Douglas. No, I just had a cup of coffee. They'll give us lunch on the plane. I know, but I didn't like to bother you.'

'Dad . . .' I ground out through gritted teeth.

'Yes, Viola's fine. Driving a little too fast.' I shot him a furious look but he was oblivious, picking at the twill on his tweedy trousers. 'No, we're not there yet. I don't suppose you know which terminal the flight will go from? No, I thought Five but then I'm flying Virgin Atlantic . . . Yes, I know, I always go BA; I'm not sure why they changed it this time.'

'Dad!' I yelled. My shoulders were level with my ears and any second steam was going to hiss out of my ears. When he jumped and gave me a mild-mannered look of reproach I felt doubly guilty, but seriously, he was driving me mad. 'Clues would be good here; otherwise we're going to be driving round and round in circles.'

'Viola needs to know which terminal it is. We thought possibly Four, but then it might be Five . . . You think it's Three? Gosh, never thought of that.' He leaned my way, any sense of urgency completely lacking. 'Mum thinks it might be Three. I don't think that's very likely, do you? It doesn't sound right to me.'

I closed my eyes for a very brief second, wheeled the car into the left lane and followed the signs to Terminal Five, my hands gripping the steering wheel like claws. I pulled up in the drop off zone and hauled the car into a space, slamming the brakes on, almost sending Dad through the windscreen, and yanked my phone out of my pocket.

'Well, we've just arrived at Terminal Five . . . I've no idea.' He unbuckled his seat belt and went to open the door as I stabbed at my phone, typing into Google.

'Dad!' I yelled, grabbing his arm as he started to get out. 'Wait, I'm looking it up.'

He turned back to me, all mild-mannered and totally reasonable, as if I were the crazy person. 'It's all right dear; I'll just go and ask someone.'

I looked through the windscreen at several stern-faced police officers, their hands resting on large black guns. 'We're not allowed to stop here; it's just dropping off.'

'They won't mind. I'll just . . .' I leaned over and tried to grab at his seat belt, catching the eye of one of the police officers who was looking at the registration plate and talking into the radio just below his shoulder.

'But,' said Dad, opening the car door and putting one foot out as the policeman advanced. God, he was going to get us arrested.

'It's Terminal Three,' I hissed as the answer magically appeared on my screen. 'Virgin Atlantic fly from Terminal Three.'

'Well, that's good,' said Dad, hauling himself back into the car. 'It must be just next door.'

'As the crow flies and if we were allowed to drive across the runway, yes. But by road it's twenty minutes back round.' Holding my phone up, I shoved it towards him to show him the map on the screen.

'You seem a bit tense, Viola. It's all right. I've got plenty of time. In fact, I could have got the tube, you know, or the Express from Paddington. You didn't need to drive me.'

I bit the inside of my cheek and didn't say a word.

'You're very late,' observed the receptionist, once I'd spent another five minutes on the laborious sign-in process, waiting for my escaped prisoner photo printed badge. When had schools become like Fort Knox?

'Traffic,' I said tightly.

'I understood you were local,' she said, reading the address on the DBS certificate I'd handed over. She didn't seem in any kind of hurry to let me through the big glass maglock doors.

Finally I breached Security and was led into the big assembly hall. The wall bars and ropes, the parquet wood floor and the blue carpeted stage with the piano in the corner immediately brought back memories of my own primary school days.

'That's Mr Williams,' said the school secretary, gesturing towards a familiar figure standing on the stage surrounded by small children. At the sight of him, my heart did its funny flutter thing again.

'M-Mr Williams?' I stuttered. I certainly hadn't expected to see him here today.

'He's our parent volunteer, also helping with the nativity. And there's Mrs Roberts, our head. I'll introduce you.'

He glanced over, just as handsome as ever, my imaginings over the last week had not let me down, but there were no smiles this morning; he was too busy gripping a clipboard with grim determination. Even so my heart did another one of those salmon leaps of recognition and stupidly I suddenly felt a lot better about this whole nativity project.

'Miss Smith.' Mrs Roberts strode over on long thin legs, looking a lot more glamorous than any headteacher I remembered, to pump my hand. 'What a result. We're so delighted the London Metropolitan Opera Company –' she pronounced the name with great delight '– is helping us like this. Our nativity is one of our biggest and best events of the year. And when our usual teacher, Mrs Davies, went down with appendicitis, we thought it was all going to be a disaster but now you're on board and can take charge . . .' She clapped her hands and beamed at me.

'Er . . . um. Right.' Take charge? Me? That wasn't quite what I'd signed up for.

'Of course, Mr Williams here, one of our dads and a governor, will be here to assist you. And Mrs Davies had made a good start. She's allocated most of the parts already and started the script. This morning Mr Williams is taking the children through the opening scene with the armadillo, Joseph, Mary and the flamingos.' She looked at her watch. 'I'll leave you to it. I've got a meeting.' And with that she hurried off.

Armadillo, Joseph and flamingos? What the . . .?

I went over to stand near the stage, feeling a touch like Alice in Wonderland. Who needed Mad Hatters when you had armadillos and flamingos?

'You're late.' He barely looked up from the clipboard at me. 'Right. Can I have Jack, the flamingos and Mary and Joseph to run through the first scene?'

The five children, two of whom were identical twins, shuffled on stage, four of them in school uniform grey shorts and skirts and green sweatshirts sporting the school logo, a golden tree. They all carried a single sheet of A4 paper which I assumed was the script. The fifth child wore a Buzz Lightyear outfit stretched lumpily over his school uniform.

'OK, do you want to start?'

The five of them looked at one another and inched closer to each other, ducking their heads down behind the sheets of paper. A reluctance of children.

'Jack, off you go.'

Jack looked up from under his eyebrows, his face full of surly suspicion. 'I am the Christmas armadillo,' he declared with stout, if stolid, wooden authority. I bit back a snigger; that sounded horribly familiar. 'I am here. To guide. You. Across the far. Vast desert. It is a very long journey.'

I looked at the floor. *Friends*, that was it. The holiday armadillo. Ross in fancy dress. I swallowed the smile because Mr Williams definitely wasn't seeing the funny side of anything this afternoon.

'Joseph, you must follow me,' continued Jack. 'Our good

friends, the flamingos . . .' The twins looked at each other and immediately, with *Midwich Cuckoos'* style telepathy, both stood on one leg, the other bent at the knee. They wobbled precariously. '. . . Will accompany us on this perry . . . perry louse journey where we will face many challenges. We have to cross the river of a thousand crocodiles . . .' There was a pregnant pause and he looked meaningfully at several children seated on the edge of the stage, who looked towards Mr Williams and then one child began to clap her hands together and the others followed suit. 'Climb the mountains of a hundred bears . . .' Cue a group on the other side of the stage to start growling. 'And navigate the shifting sands full of snakes . . .' A storm of hissing broke out which went on for a good few seconds until Jack glared at the offending group and raised his voice. 'Come. Follow. Me.' He began to march around in a circle, the flamingos hopping after him.

The boy in the Buzz outfit stood there, looking down at the floor, while Mary, less of the virgin and more of the exhibitionist, had her skirt hoicked up and was flashing her knickers quite happily at the front row.

'Come follow me,' said Jack again, doing another circuit of the stage.

Still the boy didn't move. On his third circuit, Jack gave him a sharp nudge. 'Come follow me.'

The boy started. 'To affinity and . . .' he frowned and raised one arm in classic Lightyear pose '. . . to affinity and Bethlehem.' With that he and Mary followed Jack and the flamingos, the five of them marching and hopping off stage.

'Sir, sir . . .' One of the boys in the audience had shot his hand up straight in the air. 'You forgot the song.'

'Yes,' piped up another voice. 'The crocodiles sing the song.'

Mr Williams – still no first name – peered down at his clipboard and winced. If I'm honest he looked slightly sick. Then he looked up and over at me with pure panic and desperation written all over his face.

'Miss Smith, perhaps you might be able to help with this one?'

I crossed to his side, almost immediately aware of his masculinity. His business uniform, the jacket and tie, had been abandoned, tossed casually over the back of one of the wooden chairs on the other side of the hall, and his shirtsleeves were rolled back, revealing strong forearms covered in dark hairs, something I'd never considered the least bit sexy before. I could smell the faint scent of cologne and I was horribly conscious of the fineness of his cotton shirt, the broadness of his chest and the shadow of warm skin beneath the fabric.

I gave him a professional 'of course, I've got this' smile. I could play the piano and I had a pretty good repertoire of Christmas carols, although I was intrigued as to which it might be. I read the words on the page.

Crocodile Rock

'OKaaaaay,' I said. 'Interesting choice.'

'Mmm.' His mouth twitched and I thought he was going to smile but then he went and spoiled it by saying, 'Do you think you could play it?'

I gave him the look and rolled my eyes. 'I think I can just about manage it.' What did he think I was, some amateur? I could sight-read music from the age of eight. 'If I had the sheet music.' I looked at the clipboard in his hand hopefully. He shook his head.

'Right, well, I suggest we practise the songs another time,' I said in a bright, loud, this-is-so-much-fun voice for the benefit of the children before lowering it to say to him, 'I'll try and get the music for this for another day. Why don't you carry on with the next scene?'

'I can't,' he muttered under his breath.

'Why not?'

'The teacher only wrote the first scene. She was rushed into hospital with appendicitis last week and has been signed off for six weeks. The only other thing I've got is a cast list.' He ripped a sheet from the clipboard. 'Mrs Roberts has left the rest up to us.'

'Oh, sh . . . shoot.'

'Exactly. Shoot creek. Paddle-free.' He handed me the sheet of paper. 'It gets worse – read that. There are sixty kids.'

I scanned the sheet.

Armadillo – Jack

Bears – Sophie, Emily, Theo, Charlie, Oliver

And so it went on, every letter of the alphabet was covered; there were dolphins and elephants and marmosets and narwhals through to unicorns, yaks and zebus.

'Oh, dear God and who organises the costumes?'

He looked at me. 'We do.'

The end of the rehearsal couldn't come quick enough. We managed to hook up my iPhone to the school sound system and had the children singing along very badly to *Crocodile*

Rock. Thankfully, according to the snapshot of script we had, the crocodiles only had to sing one verse but even so I cringed. The words didn't even come close to relating to Christmas.

As the children of Oak and Apple classes trooped back to their respective classrooms, I heaved a sigh. Mr Williams had slipped his jacket back on, tucked his tie in his pocket and was now shouldering into a heavy wool pea coat.

'Can I ask you a question?' I blurted out.

He nodded warily.

'What is your name?'

Relief blossomed bright and sudden. 'It's Nate. God, I thought you were about to throw in the towel.'

'Not sure I'm allowed to,' I said with a disconsolate smile. 'I'm stuck with it. Thanks to your mother-in-law, I believe.'

'I'm stuck with it too. I'm a governor and . . . I promised my daughter I'd help with something. I assumed I'd be on crowd control duty.'

'I assumed I'd be on Christmas carol duty.'

'Looks like we've both been dropped in it from a bloody great height.' He looked at his watch. 'I could murder a coffee. Fancy one? Strategy meeting?'

'Sounds like a plan.'

'We're going to need more than a plan. We're going to need a Christmas miracle.'

All week the papers had been threatening a cold snap from the east with night-time temperatures expected to be sub-zero. They hadn't been exaggerating; the light was dimming and the cold air bit sharply at my face with cruel icy teeth as we stepped onto the street. Like a swarm of ants, everyone funnelled out of the school gate and the pavement was now full of small children bobbing along next to adults, their features hidden by hats and scarves and bowed like turtles by the outsize school-logoed backpacks on their backs.

'Sorry, do you have to work later? I just realised,' he said, scanning the pavement quickly.

'I do, but I don't have to be at the theatre until seven; it's only three-fifteen . . . although I'm paranoid about being late.' Just like the first time we met, we fell into step easily, although there was none of that initial easy flirty banter. Now I knew he had a wife and child.

'Your job must be so fascinating. Doing something that you love . . .' He let out a self-deprecating laugh. 'I'm assuming you love it and that it was a passion that has become your job, but maybe not.'

'Music is my passion and I am incredibly lucky that I do something I love, but it can still be hard work.'

'I don't think I've ever met anyone that plays in an orchestra before.'

'It's still a job at the—'

'Daddy, Daddy, Daddy!'

A little girl in a sparkly bobble hat that came down to the bridge of her nose, and bundled up in a dark pink down coat like a little wriggling caterpillar, came hurtling towards us and launched herself at Nate, throwing her arms around his hips, almost knocking him over before throwing her head up to look at him. 'You're still here! Can you take me home?'

He scooped her up and kissed her on the nose, her legs,

in grey tights, hung around his waist, her little black Mary Jane shoes swinging in delight as she clung to his neck, a huge beam on her face.

'Not just now. I need to speak with Miss Smith, pumpkin.'

Her lower lip poked out in a perfect pout, which Nate ignored. 'Did you eat all your Weetabix this morning?' he asked, tapping her scrunched-up nose.

'Yes –' she gave a long-suffering eye roll and Nate caught my eye and winked '– and my badnana. I was very good today,' she said with an imperious lift of her head as she patted her father's face with her wool-gloved hands.

'Glad to hear it; then you'll grow big and strong.'

She wrinkled her nose. 'Do I have to? I don't want to be strong –' she pulled a bleurgh nasty medicine face '– but I do want to be big, like you.'

He ruffled her hair affectionately and kissed her on the cheek before sliding her down. 'I think you're a bit too big to be picked up like this, these days. You weigh as much as a . . . a camel, I think.'

'A camel!' she shrieked in disgust. 'No, a crocodile,' she shouted, snapping her teeth in exaggerated bites before collapsing against her dad's hip, giggling, and then I realised she'd been one of the group on stage.

A small, rather dumpy woman with an unexpectedly plain face came bustling up.

'Grace, don't run off like that,' she scolded in a heavy Eastern European accent.

'Don't worry,' said Nate, 'she's safe.' But he turned to the little girl and shook his head. 'She's right – you shouldn't go

44

running off, even if you do see someone you know. It's not fair to whoever's looking after you, is it?'

'Sorry,' said Grace, looking suitably contrite, and she leaned towards the woman and gave her a kiss on the cheek.

The woman's face lit up and she patted Grace on the head with a gentle, familiar touch. 'No worries, little one.'

'Can I come with you?' asked Grace, turning back to her dad and latching onto his hand, looking up at him with the most hopeful, irresistible pleading look.

I laughed and Grace looked my way, her eyes wide in innocent enquiry.

'Svetlana, this is Viola; she's helping with the nativity play. And we really need to go and talk about it.'

That was the understatement of the century.

Svetlana nodded and gave me a wide friendly smile. 'Hello.'

With her straggly blonde hair and clumpy mascara, she wasn't the cool, svelte blonde that I'd envisioned Nate with. Wife? She was quite young. Nanny? There were certainly plenty of those in this postcode.

'Can I ride the donkey this year?' asked Grace, looking between me and her father with a guileless expression.

I lifted my shoulder. Did she mean a real donkey? I wouldn't have been at all surprised. Whatever happened to having Mary, Joseph, an angel or two, three kings and a couple of shepherds?

'Last year I was a sheep and I didn't like the cotton wool.' Grace pulled a face and wiped her eyes, clearly re-enacting the problems she'd had last year. 'And Mummy was cross –' she said this with childish delight, the sort inspired by having overheard something she shouldn't '– because where do you expect to find white leggings this time of year?'

'Right,' I said, stalling for time. 'No cotton wool sheep.' And here I was, already worrying about sodding armadillo scales or whatever they had.

'And Joseph was Joseph,' said Grace conversationally now. 'We don't have no one called Mary but my friend Cassie would be a good mummy for Jesus. She's got white hair and it's really, really long but she was an angel last year, except she wasn't allowed to bring her sparkly wand. If I was an angel I'd have wings with fairy lights and a wand with sparkles that glows in the dark.'

I tilted my head to one side. 'I think if I were an angel I'd want wings too, although I'm not sure they had wands then.'

'Oh, they did,' said Grace, nodding with great confidence. 'God gave them to them.'

Nate raised a discreet eyebrow my way, as if to say, *And now get out of that!*

Good old God. Him and his sparkly wands. Another thing for me to contend with. Wings and wands. All of a sudden there was an awful lot to think about. Kitting out all those animals was going to be a huge ask. If only we could stick to flocks of shepherds like every other nativity I'd ever seen. Tea towels and toy sheep everywhere.

'I'll see you later,' said Nate, tapping her nose. 'After I've met with Miss Smith.'

'I could come with you,' suggested Grace with a decided tilt of her chin, putting her hand into his. 'I know all about the tivity.' Then she added with a sudden random tangent, 'Do you think Mummy can buy me a crocodile costume?'

Chapter 5

The Daily Grind was a smallish independent coffee shop that had opened not long after I'd moved to the area and had once been a regular haunt. This was the first time I'd been in here in months.

I was grateful that Nate had stopped outside to take a call as I ignored the small elastic ping in the vicinity of my heart when I looked over at the small table in the corner. Instead I hurried towards a table on the opposite side of the room, unwrapping myself from my layers as I went to hang my coat up at one of a bank of fancy cast iron coat hooks on the rustic panelled walls. This was posh *Borrowers* territory. The walls and floors were made from reclaimed scaffolding planks, the furniture had been upcycled and given a stylish, polished gleam, shining under the new hipster bare lightbulb lighting. A distinct retro feel had been achieved with the wooden tables and chairs, all of which were slightly different Ercol designs from over the years, so bore enough similarity to create a cohesive, homogenous overall look.

'Viola! Haven't seen you for a long time,' Sally called, wiping her hands on her barista apron. I approached the counter with a little skip in my step, feeling more than welcome.

'Hello you. What are you doing in this neck of the woods? Back for a visit?'

I bit my lip, a little ashamed. When Paul had left, I couldn't bear to come back but I should have done because Sally was lovely and I should have told her what had happened. Did I confess now I'd never left or lie and say I'd moved back? Now I'd walked in, I remembered how much I'd loved the place. Time to make new memories here. The ones with Paul had scabbed over a long time ago and the scars were almost gone.

'I still live here. Sorry, Paul and I split up and . . .' I lifted my shoulders in a helpless shrug.

Paul had been gone for eight months. We'd lived together for the grand total of sixteen months; it struck me, under Sally's sympathetic gaze, there seemed some symmetry in that. The short story, he had an affair with someone else; the long story, more complicated, picked over too many times during gin-fuelled evenings of rage and despair until one day I woke up, not so very long ago, and it didn't hurt any more.

'Oh, hon, I'm so sorry to hear that. Well, I'm glad to see you today,' said Sally. 'What can I get you? Flat Americano? Or a cappuccino?'

'You still remember.'

'Of course I do; you were one of our favourite customers. I still have that little book of poetry you gave me, the Carol Ann Duffy one about the wives. Gosh, how many Christmases ago? Two? Three?'

'At least three, but I do know I've missed your cappuccinos. I'll have one of those.'

'And anything to eat? We've got the most gorgeous lime and courgette cake.' Despite her cheery words, there was a mournful twist to her mouth.

'Sounds interesting,' I said. 'And very healthy.' I narrowed my eyes. 'Should cake be healthy? Don't you have any of that delicious coffee and walnut cake you used to make?'

'A girl after my own heart,' she said, immediately straightening up. 'And yes, we do . . . bloody fat-free muffins. Get yourself a table and I'll bring it over.' Sally's eyes slid to the old table.

'I'll go over there,' I said, pointing to where I'd already hung my coat up. 'And someone's coming to join me.'

Nate ambled in ten minutes later, after I'd exhausted reading my Facebook feed, just ahead of the scrum of mums that trailed in behind him. I tried to look at his handsome features dispassionately. Married and with a child. I needed to quash those silly fluttery feelings hard and fast. Difficult when some stubborn part of me insisted on taking surreptitious peeps at those warm brown eyes and the wide, generous mouth with the slight twist of one lip.

'Hey, Nate,' said Sally, as soon as he stepped over the threshold as she passed by him on her way to my table with my order. 'Your usual?'

'Yes, please.' He spotted me in the corner.

'In or out?'

He tilted his head my way, indicating my table. 'In, today.'

Sally's eyes widened with sudden smiling interest. 'You two know each other?'

'Not exactly.'

'Not really.'

We both spoke at the same time in quick denial.

'But we keep bumping into each other,' said Nate cheerfully. 'Viola's just been handed the dubious honour of doing this year's nativity play.'

'Er . . . shouldn't that be the dubious honour of helping you do the nativity play?' I was determined to keep it businesslike. No flirty banter.

'Well, there's—'

'Holy fuck,' breathed Sally, looking horrified.

'What the hell's that supposed to mean?' I asked. Surely it couldn't be any worse than it already was?

'Nothing. Nothing,' she said, pulling a 'God help you' face.

'Thanks, Sally,' said Nate dryly.

'Good luck,' said Sally. 'It's a wonderful school and Mrs Roberts is an amazing head. She's transformed the place. She has very . . . high standards.'

From behind the counter, Sally's small blonde assistant snorted. 'She's a crazy woman. One of those super-heads that's determined to make her school the best one in the area. Talk about competitive.'

'And that's a good thing for the children,' said Sally a touch defensively. 'My daughter's there.'

'That's not what you said when she sent the chair of the PTA in, demanding that we provide all the coffee for the summer fete last year.'

'It was for a good cause,' said Sally.

'So are our profits,' retorted the other woman.

I glanced at Nate, my eyes widening with apprehension. 'You were about to say?'

He grimaced. 'I said I'd help because Grace wanted me to come into school and I –' his lips curved in a rueful smile '– and I thought this would be a nice easy gig. A couple of hours once a week, but that was when Mrs Davies was in charge. I didn't sign up for full-on producing and directing.'

'Neither did I. I thought I'd be helping with some musical arrangements.'

We both lapsed into silence.

'Have you told her about the star of Bethlehem, the year before?' Sally butted in, bringing Nate's coffee over. 'Full-on pyrotechnics. Looked incredible. Although I did worry when I saw the caretaker on standby with two fire extinguishers.'

We both glared at her and she backed away hurriedly.

'What are we going to do?' I broke the silence, putting my elbow on the table and resting my chin in my palm.

'Isn't there anyone else at the Opera House that could help . . . someone –' he lifted his shoulders in a half-hearted attempt at tact '– you know, with the script or something?'

'I don't think anyone could help with that script.'

He shot me a quick amused smile before tapping his steepled fingers against his lower lip, drawing my gaze to his mouth. Very sexy mouth.

I waved my hands, cross with myself for noticing that totally inappropriate fact, as if to push the thought away. But of course, like a particularly pernicious thorn, it had embedded itself. *He has a wife, Viola.*

'I'm going to be tied up all weekend . . . Do you think you

could have a go at writing the next scene? You're the artistic one and we need something by Monday.'

I eyed him, feeling less than charitable towards him. 'What with me only working on Saturday night, you mean?'

He frowned. 'No, that's not what I meant at all. I'll help with other things but I'm not a writer; believe me, I don't have an artistic bone in my body. I rely on facts, logic and what I can see and touch. Music is artistic, creative, isn't it?'

'Actually, no, it's quite mathematical, actually. But, like you say, we *need* something by Monday. I'll have a go . . . but I'm not promising miracles.'

'I'll see if I can round up some more parent helpers and I'll help where I can. Why don't I give you my mobile number? You can call me if there's a problem. I am a governor, so –' he gave a self-deprecating laugh '– I have some clout, apparently.'

We swapped numbers, in a grown-up, businesslike fashion. I didn't think I'd be swapping any flirty texts with him any time soon. The little tentative butterfly wing quivers of excitement that had fluttered earlier in my stomach had been well and truly swatted by his businesslike attitude.

'One thing we do need to do, and quickly, is to let the parents know what they need to provide, costume-wise, as soon as possible. Everyone is very busy at this time of year and, as Grace mentioned, it really is a faff for parents to have to go out hunting for things. Elaine, my wife, was extremely stressed last year at having to find the right colour leggings and T-shirt.' He winced. 'You've seen the cast list.'

I had indeed, although my mind was otherwise distracted. At last the wife had a name. Elaine sounded like a cool blonde.

'Grace is a crocodile; I'm guessing that's green leggings and T-shirt,' said Nate with a frown. He looked at his watch, again with a little shake of his head. 'I, for one, certainly won't have time to go and buy that sort of thing, and neither will her mother. Work is full-on at the moment.'

I looked at his smart suit and the expensive watch on his wrist, the one that he'd looked at for a third time. Wife. Nanny. Suddenly I felt a little bit sorry for Grace.

'And I guess that is very important,' I said with sudden bite. 'What is it you do?'

If he said brain-surgeon I'd give him a pass.

'I'm a lawyer.'

Of all the jobs he could have said.

Paul was a lawyer and I still had the sour taste of the cold, precise way he'd drawn up lists of our possessions, allocating ownership where it was due before dismantling our relationship once and for all. He gave me a six-page document . . . right before he dumped me.

Chapter 6

I threw another piece of crumpled paper across the room. This was impossible. I wasn't a scriptwriter. How the hell was I supposed to shoehorn the Noah's ark of animals into the story of Jesus' birth?

Bella walked into her kitchen clutching a large glass of white wine and topped my glass up. 'Not made any progress?' she asked with a smirk.

'No, I bloody have not.'

She sniggered, much like she'd been doing ever since I arrived for our usual Sunday evening get-together. For once she'd left me to it while she bathed the girls.

I came most weeks to escape the silence of my flat and the heavy quiet of solo living, which I still hadn't quite got used to. On good days when I'd been busy and out working, I told myself that I was embracing the silence and the independence of single life. The paint colours on the walls were all mine, the chocolate and crisps stayed put unless I'd eaten them and no one hammered on the door when I took an hour-long bath.

But on Sundays the quiet was overpowering, almost

suffocating, especially when everyone else seemed to embrace that night before school need to stay home.

'It really isn't funny,' I said, sitting back and looking at the cast list and the only existing page of script.

'I think "to affinity and Bethlehem" is inspired,' she snorted again.

'You would; you don't have to finish the rest of the story. I mean, seriously, how do I get a unicorn and a narwhal into the story? I'm pretty sure there's not much sea between Nazareth and Bethlehem.'

Bella had all but spat her wine all over the pristine white surfaces in her kitchen when I'd arrived and first told her about the rocking crocodiles, hissing snakes and the armadillos and flamingos. Like Nate, she had grave reservations about the costumes.

'I'm going into school tomorrow; I've got to have something,' I said, despair starting to grip. 'I can't think of any dolphin songs or yak songs or unicorn songs for that matter. I've been racking my brains all weekend for anything suitable.'

'I might be a tad old-fashioned but what's wrong with Christmas carols?' asked Bella.

She had a good point.

'Why don't you take a break?' she suggested. 'While I shove the pizzas in the oven and knock up a quick salad. You could go and read the girls a story.' The latter was added with a sly smile.

I threw my pen down. 'I think I will. Where are they? In the lounge?'

'I said they could watch ten minutes of *Blue Planet*.'

Ella and Rosa were rosy-cheeked and smelled of lavender when I sat down between them on the sofa. I felt a tug at my heart at the sight of them in their matching dressing gowns and little fluffy slippers.

'Who wants a bedtime story?'

'*Jesus's Christmas Party*,' said Rosa, suddenly producing it from underneath a cushion.

'I read that last time.'

'Read it again,' piped up Ella. 'It's our favourite.'

Picking up the book, I read it, the three of us joining in with great gusto at the innkeeper's roared refrain, advising his never-ending stream of visitors to go to the stable.

Halfway through the story, it hit me. As soon as I reached the words 'The End' I bundled the two girls upstairs, calling to Bella to put them to bed, and dashed into the kitchen to pick up my pencil.

By the time Bella came back downstairs, I'd completed a very rough script.

For some reason, even though not one of them was over five foot tall, a surge of fear shot through me and my tongue glued itself to the roof of my mouth. They were all looking up at me with wide-eyed interest as I stood at the front of the large hall.

There was absolutely no sign of Nate Williams, even though when he'd texted back last night he'd said he planned to be here. We'd had a brief text exchange and when I'd told him of my executive decision, he'd agreed that it was for the best and that he would back me a hundred per cent.

'Oak and Apple class, say good morning to Miss Smith,' said

the teaching assistant in a high-pitched, here kitty, kitty sort of voice. She'd been allocated to help me, for which I was very grateful, otherwise I'd have been completely on my own.

'Good. Morning. Miss Smith,' intoned the class in a deadened robotic rhythm that threatened to suck all of the life out of me. Honestly, it was like facing a crowd of Dementors. I had no idea how they were going to respond to the news that Noah's Christmas Ark was no more. The children, all in their green and grey uniforms, were sitting cross-legged in front of me on the polished parquet floor, which had probably had thousands of children's feet pass across its surface over its lifetime.

I took in a breath and said in a voice designed to counteract their joyless greeting, 'Good morning, Oak class. Good morning, Apple class.' I beamed at them like Mary Poppins on acid. 'Shall we try that again? Good morning, Oak class,' I bellowed in a loud voice. 'Good morning, Apple class.'

'Good morning, Miss Smith,' they bellowed back with a lot more energy.

Energy was good. I could work with that. I checked my watch. Where was Nate?

'That's better. I'm looking for people with good loud voices. Do I have any here?'

A sea of hands shot up, waving like little sea anemones. Better and better. Things were looking up. I could do this.

I was on the hoof, making things up as I went along. Actually, that wasn't true at all. I'd planned today with meticulous attention to detail, dividing up the duties between myself and Nate. It was vital we made a good impression as we had to sell them a complete change of plan. I'd decided it was best to be honest and explain that Mrs Davies was too poorly to finish the script, so we were going to start afresh with a new lot of auditions. I'd hoped to palm that job off on Nate but as he still wasn't here and I couldn't stand in front of the children looking like a complete lemon, I got on with it.

Despite a few minor groans most of the children looked interested when I explained that we were going to have new parts and that there'd be fresh auditions today.

'But I still want to be an armadillo,' said Jack, a touch of belligerence in his square plump face.

'There isn't an armadillo in this story.'

'I want to be an armadillo,' he repeated, folding his arms, giving me an implacable stare.

'There'll be other parts. New ones.' I smiled gamely at him as he continued to stare at me.

'I'm not happy. I'm not happy.' He shook his head and I was pretty sure that he was parroting someone else's words.

I gave him a vague smile and moved on. Today I had to get my cast together and teach them the new songs I'd chosen. I needed a loud confident boy to play the innkeeper. A bossy know-it-all to play his wife. A serene Mary. A careful, thoughtful Joseph. Three bouncy kings. As many rustic shepherds as I could get away with. A herd of cows, a flock of sheep, oh, and an angel.

If I could hand all that over to Nate, I could get on and start teaching the children the Christmas carols.

I looked at the door again. Where was he? I looked back at the children, watching me with expectant interest. I was on my own.

'Does anyone know any Christmas carols?' I'd already decided on most of them but I was hoping this little bit of democracy would make the children feel more involved and hopefully forget about marmosets, narwhals and flipping unicorns.

Again the hands shot up, several with that me-me-me fervour you only find in little children. Right under my nose, one little boy waved his hand madly, almost bouncing up and down on the spot trying to get my attention. It would have taken someone with a heart of cold, hard stone to ignore him.

'You there, young man?'

'Do you like football, miss?'

His mate next to him nudged him and giggled.

'George,' the teaching assistant shadowing me cut in, 'if you can't be sensible, you'll have to go and sit in Mrs Roberts' office.'

George looked as if he might have spent a fair bit of time there before because he gave an irrepressible grin and carried on staring at me.

'Anyone else?' The forest of hands shot up again and this time I picked another child, a demure-looking girl with plaits and a green headband which matched her regulation green sweatshirt with the logo of a brown and green tree on the right breast.

'*Away in a Manger*,' she said in a proud little voice.

'Excellent,' I said in the sort of voice that suggested she'd just discovered how to sequence the genome. Actually it was perfect and, unbeknownst to her, already on my list. I turned and wrote it on the whiteboard behind me. I'd already decided I needed five carols to break up the action and to extend the performance.

I picked another waving hand and then realised it was Grace, Nate's daughter.

'You're Daddy's friend,' she said in an accusing voice. The teaching assistant coughed and put her hand over her face. And for some ridiculous reason I blushed bright red, which probably confirmed her assumption.

'I've met your daddy,' I agreed evenly, with a carefully blank face, 'when we talked about the nativity. Do you have a carol for me?'

She shook her head. 'My daddy's very handsome. Don't you want to be his friend?'

'I'm afraid I don't really know him. I only met him that day.'

And there, as if by magic, he was standing at the back of the hall, a look of unholy amusement on his 'very handsome' face.

'He's very nice,' pressed Grace

Aware of the pinkness of my cheeks, I gave her a perfunctory, 'I'm sure he is.' I could see his shoulders shaking even from this distance, the dratted man. I ignored him and turned to the teaching assistant, who had managed to recover from her fit of coughing and thankfully intervened. 'Perhaps we can stick to the Christmas carols, thank you, Grace?'

Grace huffed, folded her arms and pinched her mouth together in an expression of too-adult disgust which had me trying not to laugh as she watched me with continued suspicion.

'Anyone else?' God, how did teachers do it – keep up this bright, sparkly, I'm so excited voice? I pointed to another boy whose hand had shot up dead straight like an arrow in flight.

'*Hark the Harold Angels.*'

I bit back a smile. 'Perfect. Because we're going to need an angel.'

Several eager little girls looked excitedly at each other and started whispering. I looked towards the back of the hall, waiting for Nate to join me, but he was finishing a conversation with Mrs Roberts. Hopefully, he was explaining to her why we'd decided to rewrite the script. I'd emailed it to him the previous evening and he'd agreed to speak to her to let her know we'd decided to take a new direction. He'd also agreed he'd be here to help me this morning.

When I looked up a second later Mrs Roberts had disappeared. I gave Nate an expectant look, waiting for him to cross the hall floor and join me. Instead he waved his phone, mouthed, 'Text you,' and bloody disappeared!

I glared at the empty doorway. This was not what I'd signed up for.

Resigned but with low simmering anger, I turned back to the task at hand. It took some time but eventually I had five carols, all of which would fit perfectly within the story and included *O Little Town of Bethlehem*, *We Three Kings* and *Silent Night*. I was starting to feel a slight sense of euphoria.

'OK, now I need some characters for the nativity. Some really good actors. Could you put your hand up if you would like to say a few lines?'

Jack's hand shot up. 'I want to be the armadillo.'

I gave him another smile – there was no way I was putting an armadillo into my nice traditional script – and turned to some of the other children. I could have predicted that George would be one of them, although I could already see quite a few children sinking back into their little bodies, trying to make themselves invisible and as unobtrusive as possible. 'No one has to say lines if they don't want to,' I added more gently, smiling at some of the anxious faces. 'You can sing the carols with everyone else.'

I had a good thirty children keen to show their stuff. I gave the doorway one last look. It really did look like I was on my own. Thankfully, the teaching assistant, who was pretty capable, agreed to take half the children over to the other side of the hall and she started practising the words to *Away in a Manger* with them, while I tried to get the measure of the children who wanted parts. I looked enviously at the piano. Teaching carols was much more in my comfort zone.

Come on, Viola, you've just got to get on with it. At least I had a script that made some sense now.

I'd shamelessly stolen the story of *Jesus's Christmas Party*, writing the script with a fair bit of padding of my own, while taking complete advantage of Bella's hospitality as she'd put the girls to bed and cooked pizza. During that time I'd created what I hoped was a half hour play and then used her printer to print out the lines for the innkeeper and his wife and other key parts for audition.

When the break bell rang the children all scattered like marbles, racing off at varying speeds towards the long corridor down to their classrooms.

'Well handled,' said the teaching assistant. 'They can be a tricky bunch.'

She didn't know how close I'd come to giving one of the boys a Chinese burn, but I don't think you're allowed to do that.

'I'm more worried about whether Mrs Roberts will approve. This isn't quite as flamboyant . . . and I've heard the previous productions have been . . .' I waved my hands to illustrate all-singing, all-dancing.

She snorted. 'Yes. They have.' She lowered her voice. 'Load of crap. It's all Emperor's New Clothes. *Crocodile Rock!* For Pete's sake, what's that about? Whatever happened to good old Christmas carols?'

'Yeah, but . . .'

'Don't you fret, pet. The parents are going to love it. I've read the script. It's funny, although you're going to have to put an armadillo in it.'

'There isn't going to be an armadillo,' I said firmly with a grin, but her face was deadly serious.

'You don't know Jack.'

'You look like you need a large slice of cake,' said Sally, when I marched with quick, jerky strides into the Daily Grind at eleven o'clock, my coat flapping behind me. I'd just picked up Nate's text.

Meet you later. Coffee. Couldn't make rehearsal. Had a call I had to deal with.

'And the rest,' I snapped, feeling the tension riding in my jaw. 'I don't suppose you do gin at this time of the day?' I glanced around the room, a frown on my face. Where was he?

The morning mums crowd were long gone and there were only a few people dotted about at tables, most hiding behind laptop screens, absorbed in what they were doing.

'Bad morning?'

I heaved out a juddering sigh, feeling my furious pulse finally starting to slow. 'It started well but I was let down.'

'Ah, one of those,' sympathised Sally, snatching up a white china cup and saucer. 'Cappuccino?'

'Oh, God, yes, please. And cake.'

'Coffee and walnut?'

'Perfect.'

'And where would you like it?' she asked, her eyes sliding over my shoulder with definite meaning.

I looked over at the same time that Nate Williams lifted his head from his laptop. I glared at him.

As I approached his table, he pushed his laptop to one side. 'Morning, you got my text then.'

'About two minutes ago,' I snapped.

'Ah, sorry.' At least he had the decency to look a little sheepish.

'It's fine . . . What could be better than managing sixty children on your own?'

He winced. 'How did it go? I . . . I'm sorry I didn't make it. I've had a couple of . . .' he rubbed at one of his eyes '. . . things to sort out this morning.' Studying him properly, I realised he looked tired. One eye was quite bloodshot and there was a grim set to his mouth. 'How was this morning? You did a great job on the new script . . . for someone who's not very artistic. I love that you're telling the story from the innkeeper's point of view.'

'Thank you . . . not my idea, though. I pinched it from a book. *Jesus's Christmas Party.*'

'Well pinched, though. So how did it go down with the children?'

'Good.' I softened. He did look a bit crap. 'And I got through quite a bit this morning. Recast everyone. Your daughter is now the very bossy innkeeper's wife.'

He laughed. 'Typecasting. She can be quite bossy.' Then he sobered, his expression pensive. 'Some of the time.'

'And I've found the most perfect innkeeper.'

'That's great. Sounds like you've made good progress.'

'I'd make more with some help,' I said pointedly.

He winced. 'That might be problematic, this week. Svetlana, she's our nanny, her mum's very ill. She had to catch a train home this morning.'

'A train?' I'd assumed, with her name and accent, home would be a flight away.

Nate let out a mirthless laugh. 'She comes from Wigan. Been here since she was seven. But I'm really stuck without any childcare. I can work from home . . . while Grace is at school but it's almost impossible when she gets home. I'm going to have to maximise those hours when she's at school to get stuff done.'

'Great,' I groaned.

'It's not exactly a picnic for me, trying to juggle everything, but Svetlana says she'll be back in a couple of days.' He glanced back at his computer screen.

'Sorry I interrupted you. You're working.'

He let out a short laugh and turned the screen around to reveal a webpage with the heading, *Simple Gingerbread House Recipe – BBC Good Food.*

'Interesting; I didn't have you down as a baker.'

'I'm not.' He lifted his hands and rubbed his eyes. 'Nothing like. I'm realising just how far from it I am. I was just trying to get ahead of myself. Elaine was a total perfectionist. Christmas in our house has always been the magazine perfect Christmas. I don't want to let Grace down but . . . there's so much to do. She's had a lot of change in her life and she's desperate for Christmas to be just like it was before. She's already fretting about this.' He nodded towards the screen. 'Elaine made one every year and it's Grace's abiding memory of Christmas. But it won't be the same if we don't make it.' His mouth twisted and his eyes clouded, lost in memories.

Oh, God, I hadn't considered that he might be a widower and the shock of the idea made me ask, without proper preparation or tact, 'Is your wife . . . erm . . . dead?'

Nate looked up sharply. 'No. Not dead. Just er . . . she's erm . . . taking some time out from family life.'

My rubbish poker face semaphored startled surprise. What the hell did that mean?

'That must be tough,' I said, trying not to sound the least bit judgmental, but who takes time out from family life when they have a seven-year old?

'Yeah, it is, especially on Grace.' And on him. Now I could see it. Those deep groves on either side of his mouth, not so much chiselled features but worn down, weary features. A weariness around the eyes.

He rubbed at his cheek. 'But we just have to get on with it.' Like a veil had been lifted from my eyes, I saw Nate in a different light. What came across as upright and confident hid a brittleness about him. A stiffness, like someone holding themselves back, retreating from human touch, for fear of a bruise being inadvertently touched again. He held himself aloof. Shutting down quickly when emotion escaped him. Hence the mixed messages that first day I'd met him.

I wanted to ask more questions about his wife but it seemed far too intrusive.

'Maybe Svetlana could make the gingerbread house,' I suggested. 'When she gets back.'

Nate laughed. 'Svetlana is great at many things, but she's no baker. I think asking her to make this –' he looked at the picture on the screen '– would be an ask too much. But Grace is desperate to make one; apparently Cassie De Marco has one every year. I feel like I'm failing her.'

He looked so disconsolate I wanted to help.

'I've had quite a bit of experience with gingerbread houses,' I suddenly blurted out.

'That's not something you hear every day.' There was cool appraisal in his face and I could almost see the barriers going up.

'I have two cousins and between them they have five daughters. I'm dragged in on a regular basis to adjudicate as to who is winning in the best mummy stakes . . . and to help. I blame Martha Stewart or Aldi. I don't remember gingerbread houses being a thing when I was a child. Do you?'

He relaxed slightly. 'You're right. They weren't. Why Aldi?'

'Because they started doing those kits one year, but of course no self-respecting domestic goddess would use a kit. They have to make their own from scratch. And my cousins are experts.' I rolled my eyes. 'Forget houses, think palaces, and I'm already signed up to help one of my cousins after school this week. And I've already stirred two Christmas cakes.'

He looked confused, so I quickly explained the situation, finishing with, 'Basically I'm like the family fairy godmother, parachuted in to help whenever they *need* me.'

'I wish I had one of those. My parents live in Portugal and . . . Elaine's mother, Friend of the Opera House, is not the doting granny type.'

Before I knew it, I'd opened my mouth. 'I could help you.'

To my slight chagrin, Nate didn't immediately accept my offer. Instead he sat there, toying with his coffee cup, weighing up the off-the-cuff offer.

'That's very kind of you . . .'

Turning pink, I batted the air with my hands. 'Don't worry. That was probably a bit forward. I'm sure you've got it covered.'

'No . . . it's not that.' He gave me a pained smile. 'I'm . . . I'm a bit wary, I guess. I don't like making promises to Grace and then having to let her down. Elaine used to do that a lot. Say she'd do something and then she'd have an important meeting or something would crop up and she'd have to take a conference call in the study for an hour. Grace got used to being disappointed. I don't want that to happen to her again. I've worked hard this year to avoid it.' His smile was sad. 'That's why I said I'd help with the nativity originally and now I can't even do that. I feel like she's always being let down.'

'I can understand that,' I said, feeling for Grace. My parents' jobs had always taken priority when I was a child. There were plenty of times when I'd felt as if I was an inconvenience. I came into my own when I was old enough to manage things by myself.

'And . . . well, you've got a high-powered job too.'

I laughed. 'I don't think of it as high-powered. But my hours are set in stone. I know pretty much from month to month what they'll be,' I said, but I wasn't about to beg him for the job.

'If you want some help, I don't work on Sundays. And, apart from performances on Saturday evenings and the odd matinee, I'm free most Saturdays during the day.'

'Sorry. You're offering to help and I'm being pretty churlish. Grace would love it if you could come and teach us how to make a gingerbread house. Could you come over this Saturday morning?'

'We'll need supplies,' I said.

'What sort of supplies?' he asked, getting out his phone to open up the notes app.

'Sweets, boiled for the windows, chocolate buttons, chocolate fingers, icing sugar decorating tube, icing sugar.'

His face dropped with dismay.

'Would you like me to bring the supplies? I can probably raid one of my cousins' cupboards.'

'Would you? I'll pay you for any expenses.'

'It's probably easier that way. OK, text me your address and I'll see you on Saturday at about nine-thirty . . . or is that too early?'

'I have a seven-year-old. It's quite usual for me to have a six o'clock wake-up call complete with cold feet on a Saturday morning.'

Chapter 7

The house lights went up and I blinked as the faces in the audience came into focus. Without exception, I feel the same magical thrill at the end of every performance, as the last notes die out and there's that brief pin-drop silence before the tumultuous applause begins. Every time, it makes my heart beat faster and my spirits soar right up to the gilt-painted ceiling.

I'm so incredibly lucky to work in this amazing building. The London Metropolitan Opera House has been in residence here since 1956 but the theatre was built in 1822 and, while not quite as posh or as big (but only 256 seats less) as the Royal Opera House, it can give it a good run for its money.

As always, I stood for a moment in the black painted pit, the lights glowing over the music stands, and listened to the hum of a well and truly satisfied audience as they filed out of the plush red velvet seats. There was no better feeling but now I had a whole two days off and, much as I loved my job, I was ready for some 'me' time. A little frisson ran through me at the thought that that included seeing Nate on Saturday and I pushed away the other busy Christmas preparation agenda I'd been co-opted into. Sunday was cake decorating at my eldest cousin Tina's.

I gathered up my viola and packed it away quickly. None of us hung around on a Friday night, especially not at this time of year. We had a packed schedule; there were four more performances of *Tales of Hoffmann*, a quirky operatic piece by Offenbach that was actually one of my favourites, before *The Nutcracker* opened.

Grabbing my bag from my locker, I headed for the stage door, grateful for the protection in numbers in the busy streets of Covent Garden at this late hour. I switched on my mobile and was surprised to see that I'd missed six calls from my mother in the last fifteen minutes.

'Mum – are you OK?'

'Viola, at last. I've been calling and calling. Your phone was switched off.' Her peevish voice filled my ear.

'Mum, I was at work.'

'This late?' she snapped, so I refrained from making the obvious comment. While Mum did know what I did for a living, she never seemed to be able to equate it with real work. When it was more convenient to her, she liked to assume it was part-time and I just popped in and out of the theatre when I felt like it and had plenty of time on my hands, which needed filling. Actually, most of my family were of a similar view.

'Yes, Mum. Are you all right?' But she wasn't listening.

'You should keep your phone with you for emergencies. Honestly, why would you switch it off?'

Yeah, right, Mum. While I'm playing a complex piece in front of an audience of two thousand people, I'll just down my bow and take your call. I could just imagine the conductor's reaction to that.

'Our phones have to stay in our lockers.' I was sure I'd told her this before.

'Hmph,' she said, her disdainful tone loud and clear down the line. 'Luckily, Ursula next door answered her phone. She wasn't too busy to come and help me.' There was a distinct ring of triumph in her words and of course the guilt kicked in.

'Oh, Mum – what's happened? Are you all right?'

'She had to call an ambulance.'

Despite being nearly midnight, St Mary's Hospital buzzed with purpose and activity as I half-walked and half-ran to find the entrance to Accident and Emergency. I'd spent the cab ride fiddling with my phone but not actually contacting anyone. It was too late to call either of my cousins and Dad was five hours behind us, so probably still holding court to a packed lecture theatre; besides, until I'd seen Mum, there was no point worrying him.

I sighed, following the signs to A&E, some of which were hung with hopeful strings of tinsel and plastic holly, going over the sketchy information she'd told me on the phone. Apparently she'd fallen in the library; in most homes it would be called the study but this book-lined room in my parents' apartment was most definitely the library. She'd avoided saying how but I could bet it was from falling off the ladder while stretching up to reach a book. She'd hurt her leg so badly she couldn't get up off the floor. Thankfully, she'd been able to crawl to reach her mobile from the table on the other side of the room.

At the busy reception desk, manned by two dancing penguins, a bear dressed as Santa and an elf, I had to wait a while to get anyone's attention, anxiously scanning the packed waiting room for Mum. The soft toys on the desk weren't the only homage to the festive season. Even though it was a few minutes into the fourth of December, it seemed as if the local Christmas elves had been determined to cheer everyone up, no matter how poorly they were feeling, with a wealth of Christmas bling. Silver foil decorations and paper chains obscured the grey ceiling tiles and there were not one but two Christmas trees, one of which was a fibre optic tree which eased its way through a rainbow of colours in a surprisingly soothing way. It was so over the top that you couldn't help but smile.

I couldn't see Mum anywhere, which hopefully meant that she was being seen. When I'd spoken to her, forty minutes ago, she'd already been here for an hour.

At last a harried-looking nurse at the desk gave me a tired smile.

'I'm looking for my mother, Dr . . . Mrs Smith – she came in an ambulance.'

'Ah, yes, Dr Smith.' She gave me a quick measuring glance, the sort that made me wonder if she'd already had some sort of run-in with Mum and she was trying to decide whether she needed to take cover. I responded with a reassuring friendly smile. I am nothing like my mother.

There were a few muttered conversations before another nurse appeared at my side. 'Your mother's in triage. Would you like to follow me?'

She led me back through a set of double doors at the very

end of the waiting room, through which many of the waiting patients looked hopefully. This was obviously the medical equivalent of Nirvana in A&E.

'Here you go.' The nurse opened the curtain around the cubicle and then beat a hasty retreat.

'Mum . . .' I darted forward through the curtain and then stopped, not sure what to do. She's not big on physical displays of affection.

'Well, you took your time – I've been here for hours.'

I studied her for a moment; no doubt she'd been giving the nurses hell already. Judging from the nurse at the reception, she'd already made an impression. Mum's a striking-looking woman, tall and broad, who likes to make her thoughts known. No one would accuse her of being a delicate wallflower and she doesn't know the meaning of the word humility. I do, and I seem to have spent an awful lot of time being embarrassed on her behalf over the years. She has a head of curly hair that as a child I desperately envied, which was once a rich auburn colour but is now in the throes of turning grey.

She was sitting in a wheelchair with her leg propped out in front of her, dressed in her work clothes, a cream shirt, one of her usual tweedy skirts and the perennial American tan tights, the left leg of which was laddered below the knee. She had no shoes on. I stared at her feet. It made her look uncharacteristically unfinished. Where were her sensible brown courts, the Russell & Bromley pair she'd had for at least six years? The sight of her unshod feet unsettled me.

'Have you been seen yet? What's happening?'

'I've been triaged,' said Mum with disdain, 'which translates as being seen by a nurse and offered some painkillers. And that's all. The place is a shambles. No one seems to know what's going on. The place is full of drunken idiots. I'd throw them all out on their ear.'

I crossed the room and took one of her hands. My mother is normally indefatigable. Dad and I call her Boudicca, which she pretends to be irritated by but secretly she's rather pleased about it. She's a professor of history, so I guess that makes sense. Boudicca is one of her heroines.

'Are you all right?' I squeezed her hand, my heart aching a little when I saw the brief sheen of tears in her eyes.

'I wish your dad was here,' she whispered, squeezing my hand back as I crouched down next to her. She leaned back into the wheelchair and closed her eyes as if her get up and go had got up and gone. Up close I could see the lines in her cheeks. She was seventy-one, not much younger than some of my friends' grandparents. As a child I'd always been conscious of having older parents but that was because they were slightly stuffy and set in their ways rather than lacking in energy or drive. They'd have been the same if they'd become parents in their twenties rather than their forties. Today, for the first time, I realised that my mum was getting old. There was a vulnerability about her I'd not seen before.

'Do you want me to call him?' I asked gently, pulling over a chair so that I could sit next to her and hold her hand.

'No, he'll only worry and there's nothing he can do.' She opened her eyes and gave me a determined smile, which suggested logic had just bested emotion.

'He could book a flight back.'

'That would be ridiculous.' She lifted her head and with her haughty tone I saw some of her usual indomitable force reassert itself. 'I've probably just twisted my ankle or something. Let's see what the doctor says. To be honest, I wouldn't have called an ambulance; it was just Ursula fussing.'

'Can I get you anything?'

'I don't think I'm allowed anything until I've been seen by a doctor. All a load of nonsense. You could pass me my bag. I've got a couple of essays I could be marking. This lot of undergrads are actually quite intelligent for a change.'

'Blimey, Mum. That's high praise.' I stood up to collect her leather laptop bag from the end of the bed.

'I said *quite*.' She raised an imperious eyebrow as I handed it to her. 'Although a couple of them do seem to have genuinely enquiring minds.'

I laughed at her. 'By the middle of next term you'll have knocked them into shape.'

'Well, of course.' Although Mum put the fear of God into her students in their first term, by the end of the year they all respected and admired her and she always got the top marks when students graded the faculty teachers.

She fiddled with the zip of the case for a minute and then pushed it away. 'Actually, I think I might just rest my eyes for a little while. My leg . . . it's starting to ache a bit.' Then, with a quiet sigh, she added, 'I'm glad you're here.'

Outside, beyond the curtain, as Mum dozed, I became aware of the groans of another patient a few cubicles down, a crying baby and a slurring drunk refusing to take off his trousers. I'd exhausted the entertainment offered by my phone; I didn't think the current scenery would make a particularly fetching Instagram story.

At last, as I was starting to doze off, a doctor appeared, a young tired-looking woman with a clipboard and a stethoscope around her neck. She introduced herself and asked lots of questions before even looking at Mum's leg.

'We'll have to send you to X-ray. There's a bit of a backlog, I'm afraid. It could be a while.'

Chapter 8

What had happened to my alarm? I woke up knowing it was later than I wanted it to be, sitting bolt upright and fumbling for my phone. The screen was blank. Instead I grabbed my watch from the bedside table.

'Holy shit!' It was ten o'clock.

I shook my phone as if that might help. Ridiculous, it was completely dead. Damn, I was so tired last night . . . no, this morning, by the time I'd got home from the hospital at five o'clock I'd completely forgotten to plug it in to charge.

And where was the charger? Oh, no, I'd left it at work. In my locker. I normally had two but one had broken last week.

What an idiot! And I was expected at Nate's half an hour ago. Damn, after his specific warning about not letting Grace down. I looked at my watch again. At least I knew Mum had an appointment in the fracture clinic at twelve and wasn't expecting me before then. I jumped out of bed. Was I too late to salvage this, if I got dressed now and went straight round to Nate's? I'd still be an hour and a bit late but I would be there.

Outside, the sky had an ominous heavy grey cast to it,

plump fat clouds billowing over the skyline. Snow was forecast for further north but I wondered if we might get a light dusting and, with that in mind, put my heavy boots on, just in case. It only took three snowflakes to fall in London and the whole place ground to a halt.

Making a snap decision, I dived into the shower and dressed at lightning speed. Still damp, I grabbed my coat, shoving my phone in the pocket, hoping I could borrow a charger at Nate's house, pushing my arms through the sleeves even as I was opening the front door and charging up the steps to street level. Running headlong into icy cold air, I quickly remembered I'd forgotten both hat and gloves but I didn't want to waste time going back for them; instead I strode at a fast pace down the street, not even pausing to do my coat up. Just as well that, when Nate had invited me to his house, I'd checked out the route and I could mentally picture the roads I needed to take to get there. It wasn't a street I was familiar with.

Despite the icy temperature and the cars which were covered in heavy frost, I cut through Denbigh Terrace, admiring the colours of the houses, which brightened up the dull day, especially those with festive window baskets of bright red poinsettia and white cyclamen. I dodged a few hardy tourists taking pictures and hit Portobello Road in full Saturday morning throng. Weaving my way through the crowded pavements, I whizzed past the famous landmark of Alice's, its bright red shop front already teeming with shoppers who were keen to peruse the eclectic selection of vintage and antique goodies or just take a snap to remind them of the *Paddington* films. There were families wandering along, their children like small padded Michelin men bundled up in buggies, and lots of trendy hipster couples wandering hand in hand wearing bobble hats and pea coats. Most of the shops and market stalls had already got their Christmas decorations up and it reminded me that I was co-opted for tree decoration at Bella's and Tina's in the next two weeks. Bella liked hers to go up in the second week of December, so she could maximise its value, and Tina's went up anywhere between, depending on when there was time between the children's ballet lessons, taekwondo, English tuition, football practice and French classes – and when I could make it as well.

Two streets and my pace began to slow.

Blimey, this street was posh. No coloured houses here; everything was staid white and Regency rather than Victorian and protected by grand steps up to the houses and bounded by wrought iron railings. There were lots of extremely expensive cars parked in the permit-only bays. The houses were all proper houses, not broken down into flats like in my road. My flat was one of five in what had once been a house.

And look at that glossy, shiny front door with its lion's head brass knocker and the perfectly manicured bay trees on either side. I stopped at the bottom of the imposing set of steps leading up to the door, my fingers crossing in my pockets. This was a proper grown-up, married person's house.

I lifted the heavy knocker and let it drop, hearing the sound echo in the hall beyond. I could feel the beat of my heart thudding a little harder and faster than normal. *Breathe*, I told myself.

The door opened and Grace stood there looking very small

next to its solid glossiness. She was dressed in a cute pink sweatshirt with a sparkly love heart, in which was written *Loves to dance, lives to dance* and a pair of slightly darker pink leggings. The co-ordinated look was completed by matching little pink sheepskin moccasin slippers. With her hair bundled up in a pineapple-style ponytail, she looked cute and savvy in a slightly terrifying way.

'You're late,' she said.

'Yes, I'm sorry.'

'Who is it, Grace?' Nate came hurrying into view looking a little harassed and then his mouth drew in a taut, displeased line. 'Oh, it's you.'

'Hi, sorry I'm late. My phone died. I couldn't call because I left my charger at work.' I pulled it out of my pocket and waved it in the air for want of something to do in the face of his gimlet stare.

'I see,' he said with a terse nod. Hard-face Nate was definitely intimidating; he did it rather well. Unfortunately for him, all I could think was that it added to his overall sexiness. At last he said, his mouth turning down in displeasure, 'Grace, do you want to pop into the kitchen?' It was said with calm nonchalance but I could see the anger bubbling beneath the surface.

'No, Daddy,' she said, looking up at him with an innocent expression.

I almost laughed but a quick glance at Nate's stern expression made me pinch my lips together to suppress the quick burst of misplaced amusement. I could tell from the annoyed glint in his eye I was not helping my case.

'I'd like you to go into the kitchen while I talk to Miss Smith.'

'Are you going to tell her off? For being late. You could take a house point away.'

'Grace, would you do as you're told?' Nate's tone had changed and her mouth squashed into a mutinous line, making her look like a smaller, crosser version of her father.

'OK,' she said and then looked up at me. 'Daddy's very cross with you.' Then she whispered to me, 'But it's OK if you admit you made a mistake and you tell the truth about it and then you apologise properly and say you're sorry.'

'That's good advice, thank you,' I said as gravely as I could manage.

'Grace.' Nate's warning tone had her turning away but she gave me one last almost reassuring look over her shoulder, as if to say, *Don't worry you'll be fine*, before she disappeared through a door at the very end of the rather large entrance hall.

Nate came to stand in the doorway, keeping it half closed. A guard at the gate and I wasn't getting through. I could see that I wasn't about to be invited in, no matter how cold it was.

'I'm sorry I'm so late but—'

'I thought I'd made it quite clear. I'm not in a place where I can let Grace be messed around.' He raised a single eyebrow that spoke volumes.

'I know. You did. But I couldn't phone because my phone's dead and my charger is at work. And that's why I had to come. To explain. I feel really bad about it.' Although, of the two of them, Grace seemed the more forgiving. 'I've come to apologise and explain.'

'Well, thank you for coming and don't worry, I don't need your excuses. If it was important enough for you to come, you'd have been here. Clearly you're a very busy person. Unlike you, I have responsibilities.'

'My mother had an accident,' I blurted out. 'She's in St Mary's. I was there till five o'clock this morning. I slept through my alarm this morning.'

'Oh,' said Nate and I felt a flash of satisfaction at seeing the uptight, snotty front deflate almost immediately. 'My goodness, is she OK? What happened? Has she been in an accident?'

'She had a fall. She's OK but it was a long night. Hence me oversleeping, for which I'm genuinely very sorry. Despite going to bed at five, I wasn't going to let you down. I had every intention of coming but my phone died and I didn't wake up until –' I looked down at my watch '– thirty-five minutes ago.'

'It should be me apologising for being such a dick. I'm sorry, you've had a rough night and you still came here. Have you had breakfast?' he asked suddenly, his eyes running down my body.

'I came straight here.'

'Now you mention it, I can tell,' he said with a twitch of his lips, looking at my coat and stepping back to open the door. 'Come in. You look cold.'

'Forgot my hat and my scarf. And my gloves. I was in a bit of a hurry.'

As soon as I stepped inside, I saw myself in the big gilt

mirror. My coat was inside out and my hair was sticking up on one side where I hadn't brushed it. I looked an absolute sight with my bed head hair, flushed cheeks and scarecrow wardrobe.

'Oh, God, I look a sight.'

'It's an interesting look,' he said. 'Tell me what happened to your mother.'

I rolled my eyes. 'She fell off a ladder.'

He raised an eyebrow.

'She's seventy-one.'

'I'm surprised she's climbing ladders at that age. What was she doing?'

'You don't know my mother. She's an academic; my parents have a lot of books . . . a lot of bookshelves. Some you need a ladder to reach. And apparently some books you just have to have when there's no one else around to help you.'

'Ah, stubborn?'

'You do know my mother.'

He smiled at me, his eyes kinder now and running over my face. 'You look tired. Come on, I'll make you some breakfast. You look like you could do with a nice fry-up.'

'That sounds bliss, thank you. I didn't get much sleep last night but –' I looked at my watch '– I'm sorry I can't stay too long. I've got to go back to the hospital to pick her up.'

'Will you stop apologising?'

'But I'm letting you down. The gingerbread house.'

'The gingerbread house can wait. What time do you need to be at the hospital?'

'She's got an appointment at the fracture clinic at twelve

and, dependent on how that goes, we'll get a taxi back to her place.' I frowned. 'And then I'm not sure what. My dad's away in the States at the moment, although I'm hoping he's going to get a flight home later today.'

'That is bad luck, especially when your dad's not there.'

'Yes, and of course I was at work, so uncontactable. Mum was not best pleased when I finally rocked up at the hospital at midnight.'

Nate led me through the corridor, down some steps to a big square basement kitchen as I surreptitiously took in the beautiful house. I thought Bella's house was all *World of Interiors*; this was even grander. 'Shades of Pemberley,' I murmured to myself. This house was gorgeous. The hall had an octagonal wooden table with an enormous glass vase, which I suspected when his wife was in residence would have always had a large arrangement of tall-stemmed, lush flowers. A rather grand staircase curled away from the hall with a rich chestnut banister that curved elegantly around to the next floor. Its white treads were punctuated by a striped carpet runner in shades of teal and beige which was held in place by shiny brass stair rods.

Off to the left, double glass doors opened into an elegant lounge with deep velvet sofas in pale eau de nil and white-painted furniture including another big mirror over the white plasterworked fireplace. Stylish lamps with overblown shades in pastel colours and big clear glass bases were arranged around the room. It looked light and bright and almost too neat and tidy to venture into. I'd have banned anyone from taking red wine in there.

The kitchen, while echoing those designer statements, felt a lot more homely and it looked as if this was where Grace and Nate spent most of their time. It opened out into an L-shape; to the right a long glass-roofed dining area and to the left a small cosy seating area with a two-seater sofa, an armchair, a television, a DVD player and a stack of Disney DVDs. Grace was sitting at a bar stool at the long wooden breakfast bar that ran the whole length of the kitchen area, surrounded by colouring pencils and bits of paper.

'Tea, coffee?' asked Nate. 'Take a seat.' He waved to the bar stool next to Grace. 'Sorry, I should have taken your coat.'

He seemed a little bit flustered, as if me turning up at the wrong time had thrown the script. I got the impression that if I'd been on time he would have had a script.

'Have you said sorry?' asked Grace, not looking up from the drawing she was colouring in with fierce concentration as I took the stool next to her.

'Yes, and I'd like to say sorry to you too.'

She shrugged and carried on carefully nudging at the lines of the unicorn on the paper with her pink pencil. 'It's OK.'

Her indifference tugged at my heart and I glanced over at Nate and saw his mouth tighten.

'No, Grace, it's not OK. I said I was coming and I really was, but my mum had an accident last night. So she had to go to hospital.'

Grace's mouth pressed in a firm line. But she didn't say anything.

'She broke her leg and she had to stay the night.'

At that the little girl did look up. 'Has she got crutches?'

'I don't know yet. I'm going to see her later, when they put the cast on her leg.'

'Maddie at school got a broken arm. She had a blue cast. I'd have a purple one.'

'Can you choose?'

'Oh, yes, because Edward Palmer had a red one. Because of football. Do you like football?'

'Not especially.'

'Me neither. I do gymnastics and dancing.'

'What sort of dancing do you do?'

'Ballet, jazz and tap. I like the tap dancing. But ballet –' she pulled a face '– it's boring but Mummy likes me to do it.' She sighed. 'When I'm grown up I'm never doing anything boring.'

'That's a good plan,' I said.

Nate rolled his eyes as he poured two cups of coffee and handed one my way. 'I'd offer you a biscuit . . . but the biscuit burglar has been to visit this week and all the chocolate ones have gone.'

Grace was suddenly very studious with her drawing, nodding in agreement.

'I hate it when that happens,' I said. 'And why do they always steal the good biscuits and leave the custard creams behind?'

Nate laughed. 'You have the same burglar.'

'Only when I remember to buy biscuits.' My shopping habits were erratic to say the least.

'We do have custard creams,' said Nate, 'although they're a bit broken and some of them look a bit nibbled around the edges.'

88

Grace tucked her head in a little like a turtle trying to take cover and over her blonde curls Nate shot me a quick conspiratorial smile.

'But if you can bear to wait, I can knock up bacon and eggs. I'll just get them going.'

'That would be lovely, thank you.'

He crossed to the big American-style fridge, shooting me another wide and warm smile. It was the first time since we'd first met that I felt a touch of that original spark. I got the impression that the guards around his emotions had been reinforced and that he'd deliberately put up the barriers.

I turned back to Grace. 'I'm sorry there won't be any gingerbread today. I wondered if you might be free tomorrow.'

Grace's head bobbed up and she looked at her dad with pleading eyes.

His face was sombre. 'I'm not sure; maybe we should leave it for this weekend.'

I'd been afraid he was going to say that.

'Please, Daddy,' said Grace as Nate tossed rashers of bacon in a frying pan, having just cut a large sourdough loaf into slices.

Concern lined his face and I could see his dilemma. Was he prepared to give me a second chance? I could understand his reservations.

'I have no plans for tomorrow.' But I was scared of overpromising and letting him down again. 'And Dad *should* be back tomorrow morning.' Behind my back I crossed my fingers. 'Although I might have to pick him up from the airport, but that won't take all day. What if we said tomorrow afternoon?'

He still had that not-sure look on his face. I watched as Grace carefully schooled hers, the brief flare of hope replaced with a bland impassive expression that was far too grown-up for a seven-year old. She picked up a pencil and went back to her determined colouring. I watched as guilt, sadness, regret and worry warred with each other across Nate's face.

He looked down at his daughter, his mouth crimping at one corner, and then he looked my way, studying me as if trying to measure my trustworthiness. I looked back at him. There was no point saying any more; the decision had to come from him.

'OK,' he said eventually, making it sound like a business meeting, before turning back to the frying pan. 'Tomorrow afternoon. Two?'

Grace didn't look up but her busy pencil paused for a minute, held above one of the lines. I looked down at her bent head, filled with the urge to wrap my arms around her and give her a big hug. When I looked up at Nate he was watching me, wariness in his eyes.

'Two's perfect. That'll give me time to do some shopping.' I copied his businesslike attitude. This was a transaction; I was going to have to start over to earn his trust. 'Can I assume you have the basics, like flour, sugar, butter or should I just bring everything?'

'I think we'd better have a quick look now.' Nate's mouth twisted in a quick lopsided smile and I relaxed a bit. 'I don't think you can assume anything. Baking is not exactly my thing.'

'You do very good cheese on toast, Daddy.'

Nate moved to her side and ruffled her hair. 'I do.'

'That's because you've had lots of practice. And what does practice make?'

'Perfect,' said Nate with a rueful laugh, catching my eye. 'I'm not much of a cook, apart from breakfast.'

'And you were going to attempt a gingerbread house?'

He lifted his shoulders in a brief shrug.

While he cooked breakfast I borrowed a charger and called Mum but her phone was switched off after all that, so I phoned the hospital to find out how she was. I was put through to the ward and apparently she'd had a good night and was due to go down to the fracture clinic some time soon. I looked at my watch. I'd better make breakfast a quick one. I sent Mum a text to let her know I'd see her in the clinic as soon as possible.

'Here you go, William's finest breakfast,' said Nate, pushing a plate towards me.

We'd moved to sit at the dining table in the long end of the L-shaped extension off the kitchen.

'Mmm,' I said, realising I was hungry, which was probably just as well.

'You don't need to be polite,' said Grace. 'Daddy's a terrible cook.' She poked at the white of the fried egg on her plate; it had a bubbly, plasticky consistency and the pale yellow yolk looked extremely dry.

Nate sighed. 'She's right ... I can never seem to get the timing right.'

'When someone else has cooked for me, I'm not complaining. And the bacon looks delicious.'

'That's cos Daddy threw the first lot away.'

There were little burnt bits all over the second batch of bacon.

'Can I make a suggestion?'

Nate looked suspicious but nodded.

'You might find it easier if there was less multitasking.'

He wrinkled his nose. 'You got me. I was checking work emails. Bad habit. I really ought to switch my phone off at the weekends.'

'You should, Daddy. It's boring.' She sounded very grown-up.

He grinned and ruffled her hair. 'Point taken, pumpkin.'

Despite the food not being Cordon Bleu standard, it wasn't that bad and there were three clean plates.

When I rose to help clear up, Nate shook his head. 'No, you stay there. You're the guest.'

'Are you sure?'

'It's all going in the dish—' He was interrupted by his phone and he glanced down at the screen.

'Daddy . . .' Grace's warning tone made me smile.

He tilted an eyebrow. 'What if it's one of your friend's mummies?'

'You can answer it.' Her regal nod made me duck my head to hide my amusement.

'Hi. Yes, we're fine. I'm not sure. Let me check with her.' He broke off the conversation and spoke to Grace. 'It's Sophie's mummy. Do you want to go round there for lunch and to play?'

Grace jumped off her chair. 'Yes, please. Can I take my LOL

dolls? Sophie has the house.' Grace turned to me with shining eyes. 'The real house. It's awesome.' Her eyes widened. 'Awesome sauce.'

'Really?' I widened my eyes to match. Thanks to my cousins' daughters, I knew what LOL dolls were and had bought a fair few over the last couple of years for birthdays and Christmases, which reminded me, I needed to make a start on my shopping. Christmas was creeping up and I'd done nothing yet.

Nate finished making the arrangements while Grace darted off to round up her dolls.

I sat back in my seat, tiredness catching up with me, and couldn't hold back a yawn.

'More coffee?' asked Nate, bringing the cafetière to the table.

'I think I'm going to need it.'

'Would you like me to take you to the hospital? You look knackered.'

I laughed at him. 'Luckily, you prefaced that well; otherwise I might be insulted.'

'Sorry, what I meant was, You look a little tired – would it help if I gave you a lift to the hospital?'

'That's really kind of you.' I hesitated for a moment out of some misplaced politeness. 'I'd be really grateful.'

'If you like, I could wait and take your mum home, save you getting a taxi.'

'Now that really is above and beyond. I don't think I could ask you to do that. You know what hospitals are like; there's probably going to be a lot of hanging around.'

He shrugged his shoulders. 'No problem. Grace will be at Sophie's. I can take my laptop, catch up on those pesky emails and look up how to fry eggs and google the optimum length of time it takes bacon to cook. And if it's taking too long I can always leave.'

'Still feels like a terrible imposition.'

'Viola, would you like a nice, peaceful lift in a car to the hospital or do battle on the underground?'

'When you put it like that, I'd love a nice, peaceful car journey.'

Chapter 9

I made my way through a warren of corridors to the fracture clinic, my journey accompanied by querulous texts from Mum, asking where I was and directing me to where she was. Nate had dropped me at the door and then gone to find a space in the very busy car park.

'Ah, there you are, Viola,' said Bella as I walked into a crowded waiting room full of very upright grey-green chairs. Mum was sitting in a wheelchair with a bright purple cast on her leg, surrounded by my Aunt Gabbi and my cousins, Bella and Tina.

'Hello,' I said, pausing very briefly before adding, 'everyone.' What were they all doing here?

'Well, you've taken your time,' said Mum. 'I've got the cast on now. They brought me down early. So I had to phone poor Gabbi. You weren't answering your phone.'

'It was out of charge but I said I'd be here at twelve-thirty,' I replied sharply, wondering how she thought I could have assisted even if I'd arrived earlier. Orthopaedics had never been a specialist hobby of mine.

It was actually only twelve-fifteen. The journey in Nate's

lovely comfortable Land Rover Discovery had taken less time than I'd thought it would. Shame because it had been restful and I'd even dozed off for twenty minutes.

'Hmph,' said Mum. 'Good job your cousins weren't too busy to come when I needed them.'

Aunt Gabbi preened slightly. Mum had always played my cousins and me off against each other. Over the years being compared to them had eventually worn thin. They were both Wonder Women, married with children, perfect husbands and nice houses. Thank goodness they were lovely, otherwise I might well have emigrated and gone to live the other side of the world.

'I didn't get to bed until five o'clock this morning,' I pointed out.

'Well, you're used to working unsociable hours,' said Mum, as if that answered everything.

'Have you heard from Dad?' I asked.

'Yes,' said Mum. 'He called this morning, although it's the middle of the night there.'

'And when's he getting back? Do I need to pick him up from the airport?'

'No, I told him not to bother. There's nothing he can do. So he might as well stay for the rest of the trip. It's only five more nights.'

'But . . . how are you going to manage –' I looked at the purple cast on her leg, sticking out from the wheelchair, and the pair of crutches propped up against it '– in the apartment on your own?'

Everyone looked at me.

'It's all been sorted out,' said Mum with a wave towards my cousins and aunt.

Ah, hence the family gathering.

'You're going to stay with Aunt Gabbi?' I asked, relieved that she'd have someone with her. Personally, I thought Dad would have been better coming home and then she could stay in her own home but, from a practical point of view, Gabbi's ground floor apartment in Bayswater would be perfect; there were no stairs and she had plenty of space, with two spare bedrooms.

Mum shook her head. 'Don't be silly. Gabbi's far too busy; I couldn't possibly stay with her.'

Both Bella and Tina looked mildly surprised by Mum's outrageous declaration. Gabbi was famously always busy, but no one had any idea what it was she did. She hadn't worked since she'd got married, managed to complete *The Times* cryptic crossword every day and her husband cooked dinner every night after a day in the City but, since the year dot, especially since the births of her five grandchildren, she'd always been too busy to babysit for any of them, too busy to help her daughters with birthday parties, to go to sports days, summer fetes or school plays. Our Gabbi was apparently a very busy woman.

I looked around at my cousins, noticing that Nate had appeared behind them. Suddenly both of them seemed to be fiddling with handbags or phones.

'You can come and stay with me,' announced my mother, lifting her head imperiously.

'Me?' I actually did that pointing to my own chest thing because I was so flabbergasted.

Over everyone's heads Nate's eyes narrowed and I felt the unspoken support in the look of surprised disapproval he directed towards my mother.

'Yes,' she replied as if I was being obtuse. 'It's obvious I can't stay at home on my own. And I can't come to you, not in that basement flat. So we decided that the best option was for you to move in with me for a few days until your father comes home.'

No wonder everyone was looking sheepish; it had been decided before I'd arrived.

'What a good job it's so close to the end of term,' my mother added before I could say a word. 'All the lectures are over. So I don't have to go in. You can pop to my office and collect the rest of the essays I've got to mark. Oh, and you could go to the library to collect the research papers I've requested. And I'll need you to take some things over to Professor Appleby before he heads back to the States for Christmas. I think he goes on Wednesday. So that'll have to be Tuesday.' She rubbed at her forehead. 'Gosh, there's so much to think about.'

'But I'm working this week,' I protested. 'It's one of our busiest times of the year.'

'Yes, but it's only a couple of hours in the evening, isn't it?' replied Mum with the blithe air of someone who knew best. 'And you'll need to be around so that I can brief you on Christmas. You're going to have to take over as I'm going to be out of action for the next few weeks. I can't possibly manage Christmas without you.'

Neither of my cousins would look me in the eye.

Gabbi beamed at me. 'It's the best solution, Viola. And surely you can take a few days off work.'

Bella sucked in a sharp breath. Of all the family, she did actually understand that my job required me physically being in situ at the necessary times.

'Mum,' I said firmly, mortified that Nate was witness to this, 'I'm going to be at the theatre most nights and I'm rehearsing quite often in the afternoons and I've got this nativity to sort out, so I'll be at the school for a couple of hours every morning.' Not to mention the practise I needed to get in for a forthcoming production in January, in my own time. That wouldn't go down well with Mum's neighbours. Not the ones upstairs anyway, who complained at everything; the immediate neighbour, Ursula, was in the minority, she loved music.

'It's not a lot to ask, Viola. She's your own mother.' Gabbi tutted and looked fondly at her daughters as if they would both leap into action if she became infirm in any way.

'I'm not saying I won't do it,' I explained, giving her a level look when I wanted to shake her. What was she doing that was so much more important? 'It's just that I'm not going to be around that much.'

'Well, if it's too much trouble,' said Mum, 'I'll have to stay in hospital.'

Nate gave the ghost of a smile and amusement shone in his eyes as they caught mine. He was still a few paces behind my cousins.

'I'm sure someone could come and look after you while I'm at work,' I said, giving everyone a matter-of-fact smile. Once again, everyone's heads ducked down. Seriously?

'Well, of course we'll visit. But Viola, someone needs to

stay with your mother. What if there's an emergency in the night?' Gabbi shot me another of her small, tight, smiles.

Nate stepped forward and all eyes swung his way.

'Everyone, this is Nate Williams . . . We're . . .'

'Hello,' said Nate smoothly, not bothering to qualify things further as he turned to my mother, earning my undying admiration. 'Viola mentioned your accident, so I offered to give her a lift because she didn't get home until five this morning and I was worried about her travelling on her own on the tube.'

I could have kissed him. What a hero! Sincerity rang in his words and all the women in my family turned to look at him.

'That was very good of you,' said my mother. 'It was rather late.' She gave me a sharp, assessing look.

'Mrs Smith,' called a nurse.

'Dr Smith,' said my mother with her usual iron maiden frosty tones.

'Oh, I'm sorry, madam. It says Mrs on your notes; I'll have them amended. Would you like to come through?'

'Want me to come with you?' I asked.

My mother gave me a withering look. 'No, I'm incapacitated, not senile. I'm perfectly capable of seeing a doctor on my own.'

'I meant to push the chair.'

'Oh.' My mother sniffed and allowed me to wheel her as far as the threshold of the doctor's office.

As soon as the door closed, the rest of the family turned to study Nate with forthright interest.

'Nate, this is my Aunt Gabbi and my cousins, Bella and Tina.'

Bella shot me an enquiring look, not bothering to hide it

as she stepped forward to take Nate's hand. 'Nice to meet you. How did you say you met?'

'We're just friends, Bella,' I said in a fierce undertone as Tina and Gabbi looked on with obvious interest. 'You know I'm doing the nativity at the school – Nate is helping and we've been . . . working on the script together.'

Bella raised her eyebrows.

'Well, I think you should consider your mother's needs over some school nativity.' Gabbi sniffed, shaking her head sorrowfully. 'Poor Phyllis. This has knocked her for six. I think it's going to take her a long time to recover. Not good at her age. Broken bones. Falls. It's just the start.'

'It's being so cheerful keeps you going,' said Bella, who had the least patience with her mother.

'I'm just observing,' retorted Gabbi, 'and I think you'll find I'm factually correct. People who've had one fall are more likely to have another.'

'Phyllis is very fit and active for her age,' said Tina. 'She'll be fine. And I'm sure Viola won't need to nursemaid her all the time.'

Nate frowned and turned to me, already urging me towards one of the upright chairs. 'Do you want to sit down? You look tired.'

Before I could nod, I found myself sitting down. 'Would you like me to get you a coffee or anything? You must be shattered. You've hardly had any sleep.'

'No, I'm OK, thanks.' I shot him a look of gratitude.

He gave me a grave nod and sat down in the chair next to me, pulling out his phone. 'I'll just catch up with some emails,' he said with a surreptitious wink that none of my family could see.

Bella came and sat down next to me. 'You OK?'

'Yes,' I said. 'Just tired and a bit worried. I can't stay with Mum all the time. I do have to go to work.' Then I remembered. 'Oh, no –' I turned to Nate '– the gingerbread house. Sorry, Nate, I'm going to have to . . .' I pulled an apologetic face but, before I could finish, he touched my shoulder.

'Gingerbread house?' Bella's eyes brightened.

'Yes, I was going to help Nate's daughter make one.'

'And . . . you still can,' she said cheerfully. 'Just do it at your mum's.' She turned to Nate. 'Her kitchen is huge.' Her face lit up. 'I could bring Ella and Rosa over. I've got all the stuff, so I could bring that with me.' She clapped her hands together. 'Perfect solution. That way, no one is disappointed.'

I narrowed my eyes at her. Cheeky minx. I could see Nate biting back a smile.

'I've got all the sweets and all the icing tubes,' continued Bella with blithe confidence. 'And the boiled sweets. You don't want to have to buy things like golden syrup and cinnamon that are going to live in your cupboard for the next ten years. What time shall I come round?'

It seemed to take forever to sort out the discharge paperwork, involving an endless wait at the hospital pharmacy before Mum was finally released. The rest of the family were long gone but Nate insisted on waiting with us.

'You really don't have to,' I'd whispered a couple of times

but he'd simply shrugged and carried on working on his laptop while Mum complained querulously about the wait, the hospital coffee, the colour of her cast and the inefficiency of the NHS. I felt slightly embarrassed by her constant tirade, which wasn't like her at all.

'I'm sorry about Mum,' I said while she was seeing the consultant which, hopefully, was the last hurdle.

'Don't worry.' Nate's voice held gentle reassurance. 'She's in pain and clearly frustrated about being incapacitated.' He gave me a quick grin. 'I get the impression she's quite independent and this has . . . unbalanced her.'

I laughed. 'You're not kidding. She's an indomitable old stick. Hates being told what to do and hates inactivity. This is going to drive her round the twist.'

At last, armed with painkillers, we were able to wheel Mum across the car park to Nate's car and he helped her up into the car.

'Thank you, dear,' she said rather regally as she handed him her crutches. 'This is a very nice car.'

'Thank you,' said Nate, closing the door on her and winking at me.

'The address is . . .' Mum reeled it off as Nate got into the driving seat, as if he were her own private chauffeur. 'Do you think you can find it?'

Nate nodded. 'I think so.'

'I don't trust those satellite navigation systems. I can direct you far better. They always take you on the most roundabout route.'

'I live on Lansdowne Road,' he said. 'I know the way.'

'Do you?' Mum looked impressed as she arranged herself in the front seat, sitting with her handbag on her lap, looking all around her with some satisfaction.

'Yes,' said Nate, starting up the car.

'So what is it you do?' asked Mum, eyeing the posh dashboard which in comparison to her trusty Fiesta probably looked like the bridge of the *Starship Enterprise*.

'I'm a lawyer.'

'You're a lawyer?' asked Mum, looking over her shoulder at me with a decided smirk before asking,' Where did you do your degree?'

'I went to Warwick.'

'Very good university. Well done.'

He might have got the golden ticket of approval from Mum, but I winced. Another bloody solicitor. What was it about me that brought them out of the woodwork?

Nate caught me frowning in the rear-view mirror and looked a little nonplussed.

'Viola has a problem with lawyers. Her last boyfriend was a lawyer as well,' explained Mum helpfully.

'Some of us are OK,' said Nate, equally helpfully.

'He's not my boyfriend,' I growled to Mum, sending her a warning look which of course she chose to ignore and she gave me another one of her blithe, have-I-done-something-wrong looks, when she knew full well the boyfriend comment had been pushy.

Mum turned around and gave me an appraising stare, followed by a very unsubtle nod of approval.

Thankfully she didn't make any more observations

before Nate pulled up outside the front doors. I hopped out and he came round the car to open Mum's door.

'Is it OK if I drop you here? I need to get back to pick Grace up,' he said, looking at his watch.

'Oh, God, yes. I'm so grateful that you've brought us home.'

'I meant will you be all right getting upstairs?'

'Yes, there's a lift and you've done more than enough today. I'm really grateful.'

'It's OK. I got some work done. And I'm glad I was able to help.' His eyes met mine and there was sympathy in them. 'Your mum's quite a character.'

'They all are.' I sighed. 'And just a bit . . . bossy.'

He raised a sceptical eyebrow before asking, 'Are you sure it's OK for Grace and me to come tomorrow? You're going to have enough on your plate looking after your mum. We can take a rain check.'

'I don't want to disappoint Grace.'

'I think, under the circumstances, she'll understand. I'll explain to her and we can rearrange it for another day.'

I laid a hand on his forearm. 'No. Don't. It will be fine. Mum will shut herself in her study. I promise you she'll be oblivious and Bella's bringing her kids over, so I'm going to be making a gingerbread house anyway.'

'You could put her off.'

I shook my head. 'No. Honestly. It will give me something to do.'

Mum rapped on the window and I opened the door.

'I was beginning to think you'd forgotten about me.' She handed me her handbag and held out her arm to Nate.

He winked at me and helped her down from the car.

'Thank you very much young man for bringing me home. Much more pleasant than some unsavoury taxi. And you're easier on the eye than most of the drivers.' She turned to me. 'Viola, I'm thinking roast chicken for dinner tomorrow. Would your young man and his daughter like to stay for dinner?' She turned back to Nate. 'Viola does make wonderful Yorkshire puddings and a very nice gravy.'

Nate's lips twitched as he said gravely. 'I am rather partial to Yorkshire puddings and gravy. That sounds lovely. I'm not one to turn down a decent meal and I haven't had a nice roast for a long time.' We shared a look and I wondered if he too was remembering this morning's eggs and bacon.

Mum's less than subtle attempt at matchmaking was positively medieval but then that was her specialist subject.

'Phyllis, you're home!' Ursula's door flew open. 'Oh, my goodness, look at you. You poor thing. It was broken – I told John it was. I didn't like the look of it. You're so brave, Phyllis. I knew it was bad. I knew it.' Ursula flapped her hands and tweeted like a small agitated sparrow from the doorway of the apartment across the hall, standing in her pale blue fluffy mules.

'Yes. Broken,' agreed Mum brusquely. 'But I've got a cast. Off in six weeks.'

'Well, if there's anything I can do, you just let me know. I was saying to John, because I just knew it was broken, that we should think about setting up some sort of bell system, that you could ring if you need anything. And for emergencies in the future. I mean, none of us are getting any younger.'

'I believe we have mobile phones,' said my mother, swinging her way to the front door with a sudden burst of speed. 'Viola?'

I sprang forward with the front door key.

'Well, you know where I am. You've got my number. Perhaps you'd like to come over for dinner. Cooking with those things . . . it's going to be mighty difficult.' Ursula let out a small twittering noise and I saw Mum wince.

I settled Mum in an armchair by the window and spent the next hour rearranging the furniture to her satisfaction. On her right hand side she was now within easy reach of a high-legged plant stand, which was the perfect height for her cup of tea, mobile phone and bottle of water. To her left was the desk that she'd insisted that I brought through from the study, so that she had complete access to her pens, pencils, paperclips, diary and various folders of research notes. She was currently writing a paper on Margaret of Anjou and a broken leg certainly wasn't going to slow her down; she was already busy tapping away at her laptop as I huffed and puffed, moving furniture.

'Do you want anything to eat?' I asked.

It took her a full minute to look up from her laptop, before she peered over her half-moon glasses at me. She really did look like the quintessential academic.

'No, dear. But you'd better pop down to Waitrose to get a chicken for tomorrow.' Her eyes suddenly twinkled at me before she added, 'He's a very handsome young man. Intelligent too.'

I laughed. Mum would say that.

Chapter 10

The bell on the intercom rang at exactly two o'clock and I buzzed Nate up. When the lift doors opened I saw Grace clinging to her dad's hand, hopping up and down.

It hit again, like seeing him for the first time, as he took the first stride out of the lift, that flutter of interest just beneath my breastbone, along with a little hitch in my breath. There was something about him that ticked all my boxes, although, being logical, how could you fancy someone just because of their jawline and the way they walk?

''lo, Viola,' called Grace, letting go of her dad's hand as she rushed forward, waving with a bunch of flowers in her hand. 'These are for you because you're the host and you're making Yorkshire puddings and chicken. Will there be pudding? I like ice cream.'

'Ooh, I'm not sure.' I hadn't even thought about dessert. 'Perhaps after you've made the gingerbread, you might not want pudding.'

'Are we really going to make a house? A proper one with icing and a roof. Mummy always made ours. I wasn't allowed to help because I'd get in the way. It probably won't look very good if I make it.' She scrunched her little face into a frown. 'And will it have sweeties on it?'

I smiled at her. It made my mad dash over to Bella's first thing this morning to collect gingerbread essentials worthwhile. Of course when I was relying on her to make this easier, she'd gone and cancelled on me.

Without thinking, I crouched down in front of Grace, wanting to rub away the deep groove between her fine eyebrows. 'It doesn't matter what it looks like, it's what it tastes like and we've got lots of lovely things to stick on, so it's going to taste delicious.' I stood up and took her hand and waited for Nate to catch up.

There was sadness in his eyes as they dwelled on Grace for a second. When he looked up at me I gave him a gentle smile and our gazes held for a wordless moment although plenty was said.

'Hi, Viola, I brought wine as well.' He held out a bottle.

'Thank you, that's nice of you. Come on in.'

After taking their damp coats, hats and scarves and hanging them up, I took them through to the lounge where Mum was already buried in her work and we literally had to stand and wait for her to refocus on real life again.

'Mum, this is Grace.'

She looked up over her glasses. 'Ah, the gingerbread crew. Welcome, Grace. Sorry if I don't get up. Viola probably told you I had a bit of an accident.'

'I like the purple,' said Grace almost reverentially, reaching out to touch Mum's cast.

'Yes. It's very regal. That's why I chose it. Do you know what regal means?'

Grace shook her head.

'It's like royal. Fit for a princess or a prince or a king or a queen.'

'I thought pink was a princess colour.' I hid a grin. Once again Grace was dressed from head to foot in pink: pink jeans, pink hairband and a pink sweatshirt with a big white bear on the front.

Mum tilted her head to one side, considering the implications of Grace's statement for a moment. 'Well, it can be but purple came first. It was associated with the imperial classes of Rome, Egypt and Persia because only the very wealthy could afford the dye, Tyrian purple, which was traded by the Phoenicians. It came from a sea snail, Bolinus brandaris, which was so rare that it was worth its weight in gold. In fact one . . .'

Grace's mouth dropped open. I think she was too bamboozled to make one of her usual incisive little comments.

'That's fascinating, Mrs Smith. Are you a historian, by any chance?' Nate's eyes slid to the bookshelves which filled the entire wall.

'It's Dr Smith but yes, I am. Are you interested in history?' You could see Mum straightening and taking proper notice now at the prospect of a willing victim.

'Yes,' said Nate. 'I did a degree in history before I did my law conversion course.'

'I'm going to get our guests a drink,' I interrupted. 'Would you like anything?'

'Not just at the moment. Nice to meet you, young lady,

and you again, sir.' Mum nodded in quick dismissal and went back to her laptop screen.

A dimple appeared in Nate's cheek and there was a distinct twinkle in his eyes as he turned to me.

I led the way through the apartment, which had been built in the thirties when rooms were spacious and the layout spread out. Now a property developer would have divided up the same space into three flats. Crossing the large hallway, we went into a big square kitchen. It had been modernised a couple of years ago and now boasted a large central island which was absolutely perfect for communal baking.

'I thought I'd get a head start and I made the walls and roof of the house this morning,' I said to Grace. Her brow puckered.

'But I saved you a little bit of dough so you could make some gingerbread decorations to hang on the tree.' I showed the cutters that I'd borrowed from Bella. 'I'm afraid my cousin and her two daughters were supposed to come over but they . . . were invited to the cinema.'

Or rather the girls were and Bella had accepted so that she could have an afternoon to herself to do some Christmas shopping.

'Are they going to see *Frozen II*? I've seen it three times now.' A calculating look crossed her face. 'Have you seen it?'

I shook my head.

'You could come with me,' she offered. 'Couldn't she, Daddy?'

Nate did a very bad job of hiding his laughter. 'But haven't you've seen it . . . three times already?'

Lifting her chin, she regarded me with, from a seven-year-old, terrifying lofty superiority. 'You can never see *Frozen* too many times.'

'I'll check my diary,' I said.

'Can we make Olaf and Sven decorations?' she asked.

Luckily I was clued up on the original *Frozen*. 'Yes, we've got a snowman and a reindeer cutter.'

'And we can hang them on the tree?' Grace's face lit up with wonder as she turned to her dad.

'You have to put a little bit of ribbon through, but yes,' I said, surprised by her wide-eyed disbelief.

'Can I, Daddy?' she asked. 'Really?'

'Yes, you can.' He nodded and the words sounded like a declaration or a promise. There clearly was something in the exchange that I was missing.

'I think we'd better put an apron on; we don't want your lovely bear to get all messed up, do we?'

Grace giggled and shook her head as I put on the tiny apron, borrowed from Bella.

'Here are the walls and roof pieces for our house,' I said as I helped Grace hop up onto one of the stools at the island so that she could see properly. 'I had to make them this morning because they needed to cool before you can start doing the fun stuff.' I paused and pointed to the tray full of coloured icing tubes, Smarties, chocolate buttons, a bowl of royal icing and a packet of chocolate fingers. 'The decorating.'

Grace stretched out a tentative finger to touch one of the walls on the cooling trays. 'And I can help?' she asked in a high-pitched hopeful voice.

'Well, I hope you will. This is your house.'

'And I can stick things on?'

'Absolutely. It's your house – you can do whatever you like. I've got some suggestions but you decide.'

She heaved a heavy sigh and sat with her hands clasped together over her heart, her eyes scanning the counter top.

'OK, first up is the roof. I thought the chocolate buttons would make good roof tiles. What do you think?'

Grace nodded. I dribbled three careful tramlines of royal icing along the surface of the gingerbread and then showed Grace how to stick on the chocolate buttons in small neat rows.

'You have to help, Daddy, so that you know how to do it next time,' said Grace.

Nate moved to stand next to her, pulling off his black cashmere sweater to reveal a black T-shirt with some minimalist design of grey and white on it which didn't distract the eye from the way it clung rather nicely to his body.

'Do you want an apron?' I asked, rather conscious of his broad chest, hastily lifting my gaze to his eyes. 'It's going to be a bit of an icing sugar fest. You don't want to get icing all over.' I nodded my head downwards, resolutely keeping my eyes fixed above his collarbone.

His mouth twitched but he kept his gaze on mine.

Busted. I could feel my cheeks heating. But, with a body like that, he was probably used to it. Until now, I hadn't quite appreciated his build: big, broad-shouldered, masculine. Very masculine. That was the dead of winter for you – everyone was always bundled up.

I wondered for a minute whether he'd see me in a different light today, minus Mafia accessories. I'd tried to make some effort today, without it looking as if I'd made any at all. That barely-there make-up, that actually takes ages to achieve, and my favourite jeans that fit really well and a floaty red blouse that hints at cleavage without being too obvious.

'I'll be OK,' said Nate with another one of those amused smiles as he leaned forward to help Grace select a few chocolate buttons. I'd forgotten the flipping question. Apron. That was it.

I stepped back to watch the two of them, one dark and one blonde head bent together as they carefully applied the sweets. The tip of Grace's tongue poked out as she concentrated hard.

'While you two are doing that I'll open the chocolate fingers. They're going to be the logs on the back and side walls of the house, because this is a log cabin style.

'I like chocolate fingers,' said Grace, her small fingers slipping a chocolate button in her mouth with the quickness of a lively squirrel.

'And chocolate buttons, I think,' I said with a smile.

Her eyes darted away with guilt.

'It's all right; it's very important that you check the quality of the ingredients.' I took a chocolate button and popped it into my mouth. 'Mmm, my favourites.'

Nate took one as well. 'These are good ones.'

Grace's shoulders relaxed as she picked up another button and popped it into her mouth with a little, 'Mmm.'

Grace and I left Nate to do the rest of the roof panels while we started sticking the chocolate fingers to the walls. It was actually quite repetitive and laborious, but Grace was very diligent and precise, almost a little too determined for everything to be perfect, but the overall effect was evident very quickly.

'We could put a bit of snow on the roof,' I said, handing Grace one of the small icing tubes.

'What, me?' she asked, shaking her head and refusing to touch the small tube. 'I might make a mess.'

'It doesn't matter,' I said. 'It's your house, and I always think it looks a bit better if it's not perfect. Anyone can make a perfect cake or a perfect gingerbread house, but that's boring; how will anyone know that this is the house that Grace built, unless it has a personal touch?

'OK,' said Grace, radiating suspicion as she took the tube from me, looking a little fearful. 'But what if I do make a bad mess?'

'Well, if you're really not happy we can scrape the icing off with a knife and start again.' I paused and winked at her, my heart pinching a little at the worried expression on her upturned face. 'Or we can blame Daddy.'

Grace let out a delighted laugh. 'OK.' With her tongue poking out between her lips, she squeezed the tube and with painful slowness put tiny smears of white icing on the small brown discs.

'Thank you,' mouthed Nate over her head, with heartfelt gratitude.

For a moment I felt like he'd handed me some big prize as I smiled back at him.

I'd deliberately kept the design simple because I'd discovered over the years of Bella and Tina's overweening ambition that when it comes to decoration, less is most definitely more. The fancy little white lines of piping around the doors and windows in all the pictures look fabulous but, unless you have serious *Bake Off* skills, they are almost impossible to achieve. I always found that the little lines of icing from the tubes tended to curl up away from the gingerbread like caterpillars with a life of their own. My strategy of sticking things on seemed to work best and created the best effect and was by far the easiest way to make the outside of the house look good.

'And now if we attach Smarties around the door they'll look like coloured fairy lights.' I put blobs of icing round the doorway in readiness for Grace to stick the Smarties on. I'd already pre-selected the green and red ones in advance, to give the correct festive feel and also to make it seem less prescriptive. Despite trying to reassure her, I could see that it was really important to Grace that this house looked good. If it turned out too wonky, too messy or too untidy, I knew it would be a disappointment to her, although she'd probably never breathe a word.

'Almost there,' I said as she applied the last of the Smarties to the doorway. 'This is going to look ace.'

'When can we stick it together?' asked Grace.

'Well, it's best to let the icing set so that nothing falls off. I usually leave it overnight in an airtight container. I'll give you some icing to take home and maybe you and Svetlana . . .' I looked at Nate; I didn't know if she was due back or not this weekend '. . . or Daddy can glue it together tomorrow after school.'

'Svetlana's due back tomorrow morning,' said Nate, adding with a naughty grin, 'I'm sure she'll be able to help.'

'Chicken,' I teased.

Grace looked up at her dad, an anxious line appearing above her wrinkled nose again, and he pulled a worried face. 'What if it breaks?'

'It shouldn't if you're very careful. With all the icing and decoration it will be quite strong. And if it does the icing is just like glue, you can stick it back together.' I was deliberately upbeat and enthusiastic and then felt guilty because it could go horribly wrong and I couldn't bear the thought of Grace being so disappointed.

Her mouth folded into a mutinous line. 'Can't you come?'

'I'm working tomorrow night in the theatre . . .' the sight of her immediate quiet resignation tweaked my heart and I felt a little ache for her '. . . but I could pop round after school, if it's all right with Daddy.'

He shot me a grateful smile. 'That would be great. You seem to be an expert. And I'd hate all this hard work to be ruined by my inadequacy.'

'Yes, Daddy, you're not very good in the kitchen.' Grace put a hand to her mouth and whispered, 'He burns lots of things, not just bacon.'

'Oh, dear,' I said.

'Thanks, Grace, you're doing a great PR job for me.'

'I don't know what that means,' she said, surreptitiously palming a chocolate finger under the table onto her lap.

'It means that you're telling Viola all my bad habits instead of my good ones.'

She scrunched up her face. 'He's very good at kissing.'

'I-is he?' I asked. Nate and I immediately looked at each other. It should have been funny, but somehow neither of us seemed to be able to laugh it off. Instead there was an awkward pause like a bump in the road.

'And cuddles. When I'm feeling sad, he kisses my nose.'

God, this child was going to finish me off.

Nate came over to Grace, touched the tip of her nose before bending to kiss it and then took the chocolate finger she'd secreted on her lap and offered it to her.

She bit at it, giving him an adoring grin. 'I love you, Daddy.'

Mascara warning. I blinked my eyes.

'And I love you too, sweetie.'

'Who loves you?' asked Grace, turning to me, waving half her chocolate finger at me, her own fingers smeared with chocolate and icing sugar.

'Lots of people,' I said with a big smile, feeling stupidly envious. The love Nate had for his daughter filled the room, the pure emotion almost tangible. I wanted that. Mum and Dad loved me, of course they did, they just weren't into displays of affection like this. They were practical, sensible people. They didn't need to say it for me to know ... but I guess everyone likes to hear the words sometimes.

Nate caught my eye again and he gave me a piercing stare. God, was he some kind of mind-reader or something? He had a real talent for reading me.

And I was getting melancholy and silly, which wasn't me at all.

'Right, I think we're nearly done. We'll tidy up and then you can help me lay the table. That chicken is starting to smell delicious and I need to make gravy and put the Yorkshires in.'

'Can I do anything?' asked Nate.

'You could just check and see if Mum needs anything, if you don't mind. And you could open the wine. She'll probably love a glass. You brought a good one. She's rather partial to a Chablis.' For some reason I felt a little teary, which was ridiculous and silly and stupid. I turned my back on the pair of them under the pretext of filling up the washing-up bowl.

'And what are you partial to?' asked Nate. 'The wine is for you.'

'That's a lovely one.'

'Yes, but what's your favourite?'

'I like a red, a fruity Cabernet Sauvignon.'

'I'll remember that.' His soft voice sent a little tremor through me. For next time?

With a swallow, I managed to get my stupid runaway emotions back under control and turned around with a bright smile. 'How are you at washing up, young Grace?'

Kitted out with a pair of far too large rubber gloves, Grace stood on a chair at the sink, happily playing with the bubbles and swishing the utensils we'd used around in the water. I'd probably have to wash them again but it kept her occupied while I wiped down all the surfaces, tidied up and put the pudding tins in the second oven with the fat to heat up.

With the Yorkshire puds in, I took Grace into the dining room and she helped me lay the table, with that careful grown-up concentration she applied to everything.

Nate had returned to pour a glass of wine for Mum but hadn't come back after that, to my surprise. Was Mum grilling him on his history knowledge or his intentions towards me? Paul was the only man I'd ever brought to meet them.

With everything almost ready to go and Grace occupied drawing on a notepad, I popped into the lounge to find Mum and Nate deep in conversation about *Game of Thrones*.

'I never fancied it,' said Mum. 'But you've intrigued me. Ah, Viola, Nate's been telling me that *Game of Thrones* has lots of parallels with The Wars of the Roses and that one of the main characters . . . what was her name again? I must write it down . . .'

'Cersei Lannister,' said Nate.

'Yes, well, she has parallels with Margaret of Anjou. Fancy that. I think I'm going to have to take a look.'

With that surprising declaration, she lifted her glass in toast to Nate.

'Would you like to come and sit down for supper?'

There were empty plates all round. Conversation had bowled along quite merrily; Nate fed Mum's desire to dominate the conversation, bringing most things back to history, for which I was grateful, while Grace and I talked about school and her school friends.

'That was yummy, Viola,' said Grace, neatly placing her knife and fork together and picking up her napkin and wiping her mouth. She had impeccable manners.

'It was,' said Nate. 'Especially the Yorkshires.'

'Good hot oven,' said Mum. 'Nothing to it really. As long

as you get the fat nice and hot before you put the batter in. Shame about the vegetables, though.' She poked at the solitary carrot lying in the bowl in the middle of the table.

'Thanks, Mum,' I said, heavy on the irony. There was no pleasing some. 'But these are better for you.'

I'd planned to bake the carrots with butter and black pepper, just the way she liked them, but had forgotten to prepare them in time, along with the parsnips, which hadn't been roasted in honey and mustard as per her preference. Instead we'd had steamed carrots and hastily boiled frozen peas. I hadn't even got as far as peeling the parsnips.

'I thought it was all delicious and I'm very grateful. It's been a while since we had a home-cooked roast dinner.'

'I miss roast chicken, Daddy. Do you think you could learn not to burn things? Maybe Viola could teach you?' There was no mistaking the hopeful tilt of her head as she put her chin in her hand and leaned on the table, or the slightly thoughtful expression.

This time the pause was painful. Nate's eyes were shuttered and he took his time folding his napkin.

Luckily, before I could answer, Mum chipped in. 'You'll need to be better organised when you do Christmas lunch.'

I turned my head quickly to face her.

'Well, who do you think is going to do it?' Mum pointed downwards at her leg. 'Your father?' Actually, Dad was quite a good cook but she never seemed to be able to give him the credit for it.

'I'm going to need you to do it this year. In fact you're going to have to take over everything.'

'But . . .'

'Seriously, Viola, I'm not going anywhere with this leg. It'll give me time to really get on with my work; I might even get a first draft done by the New Year – that would make breaking a leg almost worth it.

'Besides, there's not that much to do; I'll give you lists. It's the thinking about everything that's the hard part. All you'll have to do is buy the food, sort the turkey out. You'll need to go to Lidgates – they have the best Kelly Bronzes. Oh, and you'll have to get the tree. Put it up. I can wrap presents but you'll have to buy them for me . . . Don't look so worried; I'll tell you what to buy for everyone.'

I opened my mouth. Oh, God, I could see this being the worst Christmas ever.

'Or you could get a lot of things online,' suggested Nate without glancing my way.

'Online?' Mum levelled one of her famous history professor stares at him over her glasses.

Impressively, he didn't so much as quail; he could teach those poor undergrads on Mum's course a thing or two. 'I find you often save a lot of money doing it that way.'

'Oh.' She stroked her chin in her classic considering pose. Mum had a lot of studied gestures, as befitting her position. 'Maybe you could be right.' This was one *massive* concession. Other people were rarely, if ever, right.

'And you often find you have a lot more choice as well. It's easier to compare prices and . . .' Nate's voice lifted; he was really selling this '. . . you often have customer reviews of the products.'

Thank you, thank you, Nate. If he saved me from this one thing, it would make a huge difference; I had plenty of shopping of my own to do. Although, thanks to Tilly, I'd already decided on posh make-up for my cousins and their elder children, which would be one trip to John Lewis on Oxford Street, which I was already dreading. And, on top of everything, I still had the flipping nativity to sort out.

He still didn't look at me and I felt a tiny sense of foreboding.

Nate helped me clear up, taking everything from the dining room through to the kitchen.

As I began to stack the dishwasher, he brought the last of the plates through.

'Thanks for today. Grace has had a wonderful time.'

'Bless her, she's a real sweetie.' I wondered whether to say anything about her obvious anxieties; I wouldn't be telling Nate anything he didn't already know. 'I hope she enjoyed herself. I think the house is going to look wonderful, not too perfect.'

He sighed. 'You noticed.'

'Yes.'

'Everything has to be perfect because that's the way Elaine likes things. Grace . . . misses her mum. It's . . . it's not easy for her. Elaine's a very talented lawyer, very driven and ambitious. It takes its toll on family life. Grace was disappointed a lot.' He pulled a face. 'And now Elaine's in New York.'

The grim expression on his face put me off asking if that meant a permanent end to their marriage. Were they divorced or separated?

'Grace likes you,' he suddenly said, although, from the way he said it, I knew it wasn't necessarily a good thing.

He sighed. I almost wanted to hold up a hand and stop him there because I could already see what was coming. The talk.

'And I like you . . .' He pushed his hair back from his forehead. Yup, definitely the talk. 'I'm sorry if I might have given you the wrong impression. The thing is, I can't afford to . . . well, I'm not in the right place for a relationship at the moment.'

I reached out and placed a hand on his forearm, anxious to reassure him and ease away the strain around his mouth. 'Don't worry. It's fine.'

'Grace likes you but she's really vulnerable right now. Desperate for love but wary at the same time. Today might have been a mistake. I feel like I've dangled a carrot in front of her which I shouldn't have done.'

Ouch. I managed not to flinch.

'Sorry, that's not fair. You're good with her, not overpromising or fussing. Down-to-earth and honest. I really like that about you.' His eyes met mine with candid approval and, despite his words, my stomach still did that stupid hopeful flip. 'It wasn't a mistake . . . but I don't want her to get her hopes up. You have a demanding job, lots of family obligations. You're not the right person for me right now.'

Ouch again. That told me.

'I understand,' I said with a smile, my heart contracting with sadness. Not just because there was no future for us but also that his world was so fragile. Grace was desperate for love and affection but scared to trust. Part of me wanted to say, *Take a chance on me, let me prove that I could be steadfast and true,* but another recognised that, in his own way, he was as damaged as Grace, although I wasn't so sure he knew it.

Chapter 11

I handed George's script to him and gave him a big smile. 'Ready?'

Then I noticed that his usual ebullience was missing.

'What's wrong?' I asked in a gentle voice, horrified to see his lower lip start to tremble. 'George, this isn't like you. You've got this.' I put out a hand to fist bump against his but his mouth crumpled. 'Hey, buddy, what's the matter?'

With an audible gulp, he wiped a muddy hand across his eyes. It was then I noticed that his uniform was quite grubby, the white shirt more grey than white and a greasy stain on his sweatshirt.

'Haven't been practising.' He waved a hand at the boys standing nearby. 'Patrick's mum helped him and Jack's. They practised all over the weekend.'

My heart sank; I couldn't win. To save paper and photocopying time as the ladies in the office always seemed so busy, I'd sent lines home with the children who had them, rather than whole scripts, so that they could start learning their lines. We'd made a good start the previous week and I'd managed to get into the school to rehearse on the Tuesday and Thursday, although with no backup.

Apparently a couple of parents had complained, wanting to see the full script, although the lady in the office had dismissed the complaints with a wave of her hand. 'Competitive parenting. They just want to see how many lines their child has compared to another and then they really will complain.'

'That's OK, George. You're doing great.' But now I had him one-to-one, I might as well give him a bit of extra guidance. 'Have you got any brothers or sisters?'

'Three brothers.'

'OK. Imagine how cross you'd be if one of your brothers woke you up. Came and jumped on your head. And then they wanted something and you wanted to go back to sleep.'

George scrunched his face up. 'I'd be mad.'

'Yes, like the innkeeper was. He didn't like being woken up. So just go out and read the lines. You don't need to know them off by heart yet.' I stopped. He was only seven and kids learned at different ages. 'You can read, can't you?'

He looked scornfully at me, his usual cocky attitude reasserting itself. 'I'm not thick.'

'You're going to make a really good innkeeper.' I held out my fist again. This time he brought his hand up to touch mine. 'You've got this.'

With a quick shy grin, he nodded.

George lumbered onto the stage, already in character. He rubbed his eyes and yawned as if he'd just got out of bed. He was a natural.

He squinted down at the audience. 'Do you know what

time it is?' he asked angrily, with his hands on his hips. 'This is the fourth time I've been woken up today. First it was shepherds who were lost. Then three kings on their way to a birthday party. Then an angel, looking for the son of God.' He showed his exasperation beautifully. 'What do you want?'

A very timid shepherd, one of nine I'd allocated parts to, whispered her lines back at him.

'There's no room. We're full.' George mimed closing the door and stomping back up the stairs, even pretending to climb back into bed and throwing a blanket over him. I grinned. George had nailed it.

There was a quick solitary round of applause from behind me which came nearer and I turned, surprised to see Nate walking across the hall towards me. I'd suspected after yesterday he'd avoid me and keep his distance.

As he clapped his sleeve rode up and white shirt peeped out, the cuff revealing the dark hair covered wrists which I seemed to have developed some kind of obsession with. The brief glimpse of bare skin made me wonder what the rest of his body was like and stirred a low ache of longing. My body, it seemed, refused to accept that Nate Williams was out of bounds. I focused on the slim white-faced watch with a black strap, as if my life depended on me committing its exact details to memory. The watch summed him up, elegant, smart and understated and, darn it, those bloody dark hairs reminded me of his masculinity and yesterday's taut T-shirt stretched over his chest.

Clearly I had issues with my hormones. It had been a while since I'd had sex and I was fidgety just looking at a flaming wrist. Maybe I'd take a look at Tinder again.

So much for my resolution yesterday that I'd avoid him wherever possible in the future. I'd got it all worked out for today. I was going to drop in at his house after school and put the finishing touches to the gingerbread house with Grace and Svetlana before he got home from work, so as to make it quite clear that I had no designs on him.

Ignoring Nate's presence, I cued Grace, who was next on stage. She bounced on and marched over to the sleeping George, hands on hips, snippiness in her stride.

'Mr Innkeeper!' she bellowed.

George let out a snore, followed by a snuffle and then a snort.

Interestingly, among her friends, Grace was a very different child, a lot less anxious and in need of approval and a lot more bossy, especially with the boys on the row in front of her. It was as if her natural character asserted itself at school, which made me feel sad for her all over again.

'Mr Innkeeper!' she shouted even more loudly. A couple of the children giggled. Grace glared.

George sat up, rubbing his eyes. 'What is it now? I'm trying to sleep.'

'Why is there a flock of sheep in my front garden, eating my prize roses?'

George groaned, threw back his imaginary covers and marched off stage to sort things out, muttering under his breath, 'Pesky shepherds.'

Grace shook her head, hands still on hips. 'Pesky husbands.' And she followed him off stage.

I clapped. 'Very good, guys. Can we have all the sheep on

stage now? And remember that when Grace says "Pesky husbands" and comes off the stage on that side, it's your cue to come on stage on the other side.'

I hastily scribbled a note to myself, making a list of all the different cues for the children to come onto stage. I'd quickly realised that was the main area they needed help on.

'It's shaping up already,' said Nate, standing a lot closer than I wanted him to. 'You're doing a great job.'

'Thank you.'

God, it all sounded so formal.

The sheep milled about on stage, pretending to eat the roses, until I waved the nine shepherds on stage.

'I just popped in; I can't stay. I'm sorry to . . .' I looked at him and realised his face looked taut and tense, nothing like the easy relaxed man of yesterday talking *Game of Thrones* and stealing chocolate buttons.

'What's wrong?' I glanced at the stage. A couple of children were chasing each other in circles and I could see that bedlam was about to ensue.

'Shepherds, round your sheep up and lead them to the stable.' Twice round the stage like we practised last time.

'Nate?'

He let out a long low sigh. 'Svetlana came back late last night. Her mother's taken a turn for the worse and she wants to be with her. She's going home today but she's decided she's not coming back.'

'Oh, heck.'

'Yes, Grace doesn't know yet. I didn't want to tell her this morning before school. Svetlana decided it would be too upsetting to say goodbye; she's already upset about her mother. I'm not sure I agree but . . .' he spread his hands out and shrugged '. . . Svetlana doesn't work on Monday mornings, so Grace didn't question it this morning.' He winced. 'Svetlana's been a constant in Grace's life since Elaine went. I'll need to break it to her gently after school. I've just been to see the head to explain and I had to pop in to tell you. I'm sorry but there's no way I can come in and help for the rest of the week.'

I waved encouragingly at the shepherds as they rounded the sheep up and led them round the stage, towards what would be the stable.

'Don't worry about it,' I said, wanting to ease the strain tugging at his eyes. 'Things are already well on track.' I waved blithely towards the stage, ignoring the small jump of panic in my stomach. 'I can manage.' Only this morning, on my way in, the school secretary had grabbed me, asking when the letter about the costumes would be going out, who was in charge of props and painting the backdrop and what did I want to do about the programmes?

'I've got to go. I've got a lunchtime meeting and I need to be back to pick up Grace.' He rubbed a hand through his hair. 'Brief one of my colleagues about a case. Switch all my meetings to midday. See if I can find a temporary nanny for the next couple of weeks.' He'd already retreated and I could see he was mentally running through a list of what he needed to do.

There was an outraged scream from the stage. I gave Nate a quick reassuring smile and went to sort out the small altercation between shepherd one and shepherd three.

I didn't even see Nate leave. By the time I'd calmed things down and organised shepherds and sheep into a loose choir arrangement, he was long gone.

I allowed myself a small sigh and then turned to the children. 'OK, and this is where you sing *Silent Night*. You're outside the stable. Everyone has arrived and Stan –' I pointed to a very tall, lanky boy '– you say your line.'

He gave me an irrepressible grin, which seemed his default expression. I smiled back at him. 'And try and look very serious. This is a big deal; baby Jesus is just about to be born.'

'Yes, miss,' he said, his grin widening even more.

He delivered the line as I walked to the piano.

Poor Nate. He'd looked so troubled and I got the impression the thing that worried him the most was breaking the news to Grace. Being a single parent was such a responsibility. I knew from helping Bella out so often, and she did have a husband, even though he was frequently absent.

'Miss,' prompted a voice.

Oh, God, I needed to focus on the children. Being in sole charge of sixty of them was a responsibility.

'OK. One, two, three.' I began to play, forcing Nate to the back of my mind. There was nothing I could do and I had enough on my plate. I really was on my own with the nativity now. Thank God for the music teacher who came in in the afternoons; she'd been helping to teach the children the carols and she'd taught them well. I lifted my head and watched the children on stage. Already they were singing beautifully, nice and loud and with that clear piping quality that children had.

I singled out a couple of the girls and one particular boy; each of them had beautiful voices. I listened hard, tipping my head to one side. Yes, the three of them would harmonise perfectly.

I stopped playing, feeling confident that at least with the musical side of things I knew what I was doing. 'OK, I'm going to make a couple of changes.'

By the time I'd finished my practise, having nipped home and changed into one of my performance black dresses, I was running late.

'What time do you call this?' Mum called as I let myself into the apartment.

'Quarter to two,' I said, standing in the doorway of her study where she was ensconced in the chair with her laptop. I held up a Gail's paper bag. 'But you have warm fresh bread.'

'Hmph,' she said, pushing her glasses up onto the top of her head. 'Late lunch, then.'

'Better than no lunch at all,' I called over my shoulder as I headed into the kitchen, dumping the stack of scripts I'd been asked to mark up for the children for the next rehearsal tomorrow morning. After two hours' practise, the anxious restlessness that had dogged me since I'd woken up in Mum's spare bedroom this morning had calmed. I didn't like being away from my flat and my usual practise routine; it made me feel unbalanced.

Quickly pulling out the breadboard, I sliced the bread and heated up the soup, singing *Silent Night* softly to myself, working out the harmonies I was going to teach those three children.

Funnily enough, when I served lunch at the kitchen table Mum was able to hobble quite happily from her study to come and sit down to eat. I felt as if I'd been chasing my tail all day and it was only halfway through. I still had to come back and cook something for dinner before I headed into the theatre. Thank goodness I'd taken the precaution of changing into one of my many black performance dresses already.

It was only when I washed up the soup plates I noticed the pile of Tupperware boxes of gingerbread house parts. Now Svetlana wasn't coming back Nate would have to do it on his own with Grace. I'd drop them in to the house after I'd taken the scripts back to school. It wasn't difficult as long as you had two people on hand. Grace was sensible enough to help him.

That would still give me time to get back here to cook dinner for Mum. Suddenly I was very glad that I'd bought up half of Waitrose's ready meal selection. I would shove the chicken and leek pie in the oven along with the pack of pre-prepared rosemary potatoes and put on some frozen peas. Sorted.

Feeling at last that I was on top of things, I sat down at the kitchen table with the pile of scripts and steadily worked my way through them, only interrupted a couple of times by Mum wanting more coffee and the television switching on. Of course I lost track of time and suddenly it was three-thirty.

I was out of breath when I rushed into the school reception and as it was ten minutes after the end of the school day I was relieved to see that the office was still a hive of activity.

'Phew, I thought I might have missed you,' I said, still panting from the undignified dash down the street clutching the Tupperware boxes.

'No, you're all right. We still have a few strays waiting to be picked up.'

I looked over her shoulder and recognised the sad little person sitting in a big office chair, her legs dangling over the edge, looking small and rather lost. She was playing with a small stuffed toy on her lap, talking to it and then snuggling it into her neck.

'Hello, Grace.'

'Hello.' She looked the picture of indifferent boredom and I could have been anyone. I recognised in it a defence mechanism.

'What's happened to you?'

She shrugged. 'Daddy's late.'

'Oh, dear. That's a shame.' I frowned and looked at my watch. I was on a tight time schedule. Maybe I could leave the gingerbread pieces for Nate to take back.

The other woman at the desk called over to Alison, the secretary, 'I can't get hold of Mr Williams. His phone keeps going to voicemail.'

'Keep trying.'

'Grace, did Daddy definitely say he was picking you up today? What about the lady who normally picks you up? Are you sure it's not her picking you up? Shall I call her?'

'Daddy said he was coming today,' said Grace with stubborn insistence.

I knew from my conversation with him this morning she was correct.

'I did speak to him this morning and he did say he was picking her up,' I interjected.

Both of them looked disapproving and looked back at the big clock just above Grace's head.

I stood there wondering whether I dared ask if I could leave the Tupperware box with Grace and explain to her that I'd go over tomorrow instead of today but, looking at her impassive little face, I couldn't do it. I looked at my watch again, mentally recalculating my plans.

'I'll try again,' said the secretary. I watched as she made the call. She shook her head and spoke in the sort of voice that meant she was talking to voicemail. 'Mr Williams, it's Grove Leys School. I'm afraid no one has come to pick up Grace. Please can you call the school urgently.' Her loud voice carried, full of accusation, and I felt the injustice of it. It wasn't poor Grace's fault.

The secretary's mouth tightened and she looked at the clock. 'I need to go soon,' she said to her colleague.

Just then the phone rang and she grabbed it.

'Mr Williams . . . Oh . . . The office closes in five minutes.' She shook her head and her mouth tightened. 'Is there anyone else that could pick Grace up?'

I couldn't hear his response but I could tell she wasn't impressed with his answer.

'Excuse me.' I leaned forward. 'Do you think I could speak to Mr Williams?'

Her beady eyes homed in on me, sharp and inquisitive, scenting a possible resolution. 'Just a moment, Mr Williams.' She covered the mouthpiece of the phone. 'Could you take Grace?'

'Let me speak to him.'

Grudgingly, she handed the phone over to me.

'Nate, it's Viola. I just happened to be in the office. Look, I could take Grace home for an hour or two.'

'Viola?'

'Yes. I'm at the office now. Do you want me to take her until you can get home?'

'Could you? Oh, God, that would be amazing. I've been stuck on a train outside Waterloo without a phone signal. There's been a fatality on the line but we've just started moving and I've only just got a phone signal. I should be home in the next hour. Grace has an emergency key in her school bag. If you could take her home, that would be . . . really, really helpful.'

'As long as you're back by six-thirty. I can look after Grace until then, but after that I absolutely have to leave. I have to get to work.'

'Yes, of course. And thanks, Viola. I'm really grateful. This has never happened before.' There was a pause before he asked, worry softening his voice, 'Is Grace OK?'

I looked at her; she was watching my face with furtive hope.

'She's fine,' I said, lying because I could tell from her straight, tense posture that she wasn't at all, but I figured Nate probably knew that and didn't need it rubbed in.

'OK, I'll see you at the house. And thanks again, Viola. It's really kind of you. I'm on my way.'

The secretary was making signalling gestures. 'I think the office wants to speak to you again.'

'OK, see you soon.'

I handed the phone back.

'I gather, Mr Williams, that Miss Smith is going to take Grace home,' she said. 'Can you confirm that you're giving permission?' She nodded. 'Thank you, Mr Williams.'

She put down the phone and, with a complete about-turn of attitude, gave me a grateful smile. 'Thank you, Miss Smith, it's very kind of you. Don't get me wrong, I sympathise with Mr Williams, he's always been so reliable, but it's a difficult one. We have to be strict.' She lowered her voice. 'Otherwise we'd end up running a crèche in here and I need to go and pick up my own kids from after-school club. I get fined if I'm late.'

'I understand. It must be difficult.'

'Grace, do you want to put your coat on? You're going home with Miss Smith.'

I smiled encouragingly at Grace, who hopped off the chair and carefully put the toy down with a quick kiss to its head before gathering up her bag and her coat. The bossy, chatty, leader of the pack little girl of this morning had disappeared.

I waited for her at the glass doors and she was buzzed through and I felt the weight of responsibility as she was released into my care.

Chapter 12

It felt a little weird letting myself into Nate's house and, with Grace leading the way, I was the child and she was the adult.

I put the box of gingerbread on the table, thinking it looked messy and out of place, as I took my coat off. Elaine probably wouldn't approve; it wasn't your usual hall dumping table where you left car keys, the post, sunglasses and shopping bags.

Grace headed towards the beautiful staircase. 'I'll just go and see Svetlana. She came back last night. I heard her after I was in bed.'

'Why don't you leave it?' I said. 'Shall we get a drink? Do you have juice and a biscuit when you come home?'

Grace's eyes lit up. 'Daddy went shopping on Saturday when I was at Sophie's. We have cookies. Proper ones.'

'Come on then, lead the way to the cookies.' I grabbed the Tupperware box to follow her down the stairs to the basement kitchen.

I put the kettle on. 'So where are these cookies then?' I glanced at my watch, calculating the best time to phone

Bella to see if she would call in on Mum for me as I wasn't sure how long Nate would be.

'Here,' said Grace, dragging one of the stools to the kitchen counter and scrambling up. Then she stood on the counter, opened a cupboard and stood on tiptoe to pull an old Walkers shortbread tin from the top shelf.

'Are you supposed to be up there?' I asked, amused at her careful machinations. She was a young lady on a mission.

She scrambled back down, offering me the tin, and peeped up at me through her eyelashes. 'It's OK, you're a guest.'

I bit back a smile. 'OK. What do you normally do when you come home from school?'

'Watch *Frozen* while Svetlana is on her phone. She has a boyfriend. Then she makes tea. Sometimes I do some drawing.'

'How would you like to do some drawing for me?' I could get Grace to design the front of the programme for me.

Leaving her to her coloured pencils, I sat down at the breakfast bar next to her with an A4 sheet of paper and started work drawing up the cast list for the back of the programme, trying to remember all the children's names so that I could type it up when I had a spare minute.

'Can I put the telly on?' she asked and absently I nodded as I tried to remember the names of the shepherds in alphabetical order.

I was so absorbed I didn't realise that Grace had slipped away. When I looked up, she wasn't in the kitchen any more. I listened hard but I couldn't hear anything. Presumably she was safe in the house . . . but unease gnawed at me. I had no idea where she was and what she was doing. Padding up the stairs, I reached the ground floor, stopped and listened. I peered into the elegantly appointed lounge on one side of the hallway. No sign of Grace.

I started up the stairs, fighting a combination of curiosity and awkwardness. I wanted to know what the rooms looked like but was conscious of not taking advantage of Nate's absence to indulge in nosiness. On the first floor I could see open doors, one to a bedroom with a definite pink glow, and I could just see the white cast iron headboard and a string of white heart fairy lights, a bathroom with white tiles and navy walls and the tasteful beige walls, painted in what was probably Farrow & Ball's Elephant's Breath, of the hallway.

I carried on up to the attic with a mounting sense of foreboding.

The door opened into a suite of rooms, a pretty little living room with nice simple furnishings and a few pictures on the wall. Beyond it was a small kitchen.

To my left, movement caught my eye. Grace was just taking a few steps into the small bedroom there.

The first thing I noticed when I followed her in were the Blu Tack blobs on the empty walls and the open wardrobe doors, where a few solitary items hung on the hangers.

Grace turned and lifted her chin. Neither of us said anything. She swallowed, her delicate face stoic while her narrow little shoulders hunched. She took a step towards the chest of drawers. At the sight of her scrawny wrist as she poked one small hand into the empty, half pulled out drawer, my heart almost cracked. I felt the crushing weight of the rejection.

With a stilted walk, she went towards the wardrobe and with her back to me stood in front of it, her fingers touching the edge of the open door. Then she turned around and looked at me.

'She's gone. Svetlana's gone. She's not coming back.'

At the stricken expression in her solemn brown eyes, I scooped her up and hugged the tiny bones to me.

'Oh, honey,' I breathed into the soft blonde hair as she nestled into me, her arms clinging to my neck. The first sob racked her body and I felt so helpless and useless. Sitting down on the bed, all I could do was stroke her back, hold her tight and murmur to her as she cried.

'Bella, it's Viola.'

'Viola, how's your mum?' She'd completely missed the urgency in my tone. 'I can't believe she's broken her leg and when your dad's away—'

'Bella, sorry, I need a favour. I'm . . . I can't get to Mum's before I have to go to work. Is there any chance you could pop in and give her some dinner? I've stocked up the fridge and there are some ready meals ready to go. It's just I'm . . .' I gave Grace a reassuring look. 'It would really help me.'

'What, now?' asked Bella. 'I've got to give the girls tea and I'm not long in.' Which translated as she'd just opened a bottle of wine. I knew her routine. 'I can't really leave the girls.'

'Couldn't Laura look after them for an hour?' She was sixteen.

'Oh, no, it's not fair to ask her. Perhaps Tina is free? I wish I could help, I really do.'

144

'Fine,' I said. 'Don't worry.' I didn't have time to waste grovelling.

'See you on Saturday.'

'Saturday?'

'We're getting the tree. Didn't I mention it? I need you to come and help decorate with me. Ella and Rosa are so excited. And you're so much better at putting the lights on than I am.'

'I'll see,' I said, hurrying to end the call so that I could phone Tina.

Although Grace was sitting watching a DVD with a biscuit and a glass of milk, I could tell that she was listening in.

When I asked Tina, explaining as delicately as I could that I was tied up elsewhere, her exasperated response was, 'Viola, do you know what time it is? It's bedlam here. The girls have just come in from ballet and I'm exhausted. We've just had a marathon PTA meeting about the Christmas fete – you are coming, by the way, aren't you? It's on the second last Saturday before Christmas. Actually, I was going to ask you if you might play for us. A couple of carols. It would be so lovely. Just in the hall, a little bit of accompaniment for people with their mulled wine and mince pies.'

'I'll have to check my diary,' I said, short for once, which I could tell surprised Tina.

'Look, I'm sorry I'm busy. Can't you ask Bella? She is only round the corner from your mum.'

'She's busy too,' I said and I hung up.

With a sigh, I called Ursula.

'I'm really sorry to ask, Ursula, but do you think you could pop in and see Mum—?'

'Oh, darling, of course I will. You know you only have to ask. I know how busy you are and with such a big job. Your parents must be so proud of you. I so enjoyed the ballet that you got me tickets for.'

I'd forgotten how much she'd appreciated the tickets I'd got her to the General, which is our dress rehearsal but you'd never know; by then everything is polished so that Friends of the theatre, patrons and friends and family are invited.

'You're an absolute saint, looking after your mother. I don't mind at all. In fact, she's got those crutches; she could come here for dinner. I'm sure she'd be glad of the company.'

'Thank you, that's really kind of you.' Bless Ursula. I didn't even have to ask if she'd sort dinner out.

'Don't be silly; it's absolutely no trouble at all. I'll nip out to Tesco Metro and buy some more chicken and some extra vegetables. It will be lovely to see her. And if she doesn't want to stay for the evening, I won't be the least bit offended. Or I can just take some dinner over to her, whichever she prefers.'

'Thank you, Ursula, I really am grateful.'

'You're a good girl, Viola. I'm glad I can help you. It's my pleasure.'

I almost sagged with relief when I put the phone down. Mum might not be pleased but on this occasion it was tough.

I clapped my hands together. 'All sorted. Shall we make this house? Or do you want some tea? What do you usually do after school?'

Grace came into the kitchen and climbed up onto the stool next to me.

'Svetlana makes me tea. And then I watch television until Daddy comes home.'

'OK, well, why don't I make the tea and we'll make the gingerbread house as well.

I looked in the fridge but there were fairly slim pickings on the shelves. The freezer offered plenty – fish fingers, fish fillets, pies, pizza and lasagne. Children's food and adult food. My parents hadn't been terribly child-focused but we'd always eaten together. The joy of fish finger sandwiches had come late in life to me. A university hangover treat.

Tonight Grace needed company and normality. She needed to be with her dad when he came home.

I wrestled the solitary pack of mince from the bottom of one of the freezer drawers. 'Do you like Spaghetti Bolognese?'

I could kill my subconscious. Only when I heard the front door upstairs slam, with the Bolognese sauce bubbling on the gas hob and Grace and I putting the finishing touches to the house together, did it occur to me what I'd done.

'Daddy, Daddy!' Grace jumped up and ran to the bottom of the stairs. 'Come see what we've done.'

As Nate appeared on the bottom step I saw his eyes sweep the room, taking in the inviting glow of the lights, the table laid ready for dinner and the seating area with cushions plumped. Quite unintentionally, I'd managed to create a scene of perfect domesticity.

His eyes came to rest on me, in a Cath Kidston pinny that Grace had rummaged through several drawers to find. It was practical, I could hardly perform in an icing sugar dusted dress, but it probably did look rather clichéd.

'Hi,' I said, feeling like a usurper, as if I'd made myself a little too much at home. I hadn't meant to but I'd been determined to normalise the evening for the sake of Grace, so that she didn't feel an inconvenience or a burden.

'Hi.' He smiled, looking a little dazed and, from the state of his hair, extremely rumpled. 'Something smells good. And that looks amazing.'

He came over and kissed Grace on the head, who turned and scrambled into his arms.

'Daddy, Svetlana's gone.'

He pulled a face, an amazing combination of reassurance and we'll-get-through-this exasperation. 'I know. She told me. I was going to tell you this evening. Sorry, pumpkin, I got stuck on the train, otherwise I'd have been at school to collect you. I'm really sorry.'

'Is she coming back?'

He shook his head. 'No, her mum's not well so she's decided to stay at home to look after her.'

'Viola's mummy's not well but she stayed with me. And she's made s'ghetti for our tea.' Grace's stout-hearted words made me swallow.

Nate hoisted her up a little higher and flashed me a smile of gratitude. 'Viola is very kind.'

'And look at our house. Do you like it? Look how good it is.'

Even I had to admit, it looked pretty good. Less is more worked every time. The gingerbread biscuits to hang on the tree, in contrast, were a complete dog's dinner, but Grace had had proper little girl fun with icing tubes, the sprinkles and the glittery sugar dust. They were probably instant tooth decay in one bite.

'Can you take a picture and put it on your Facebook page and tell everybody that we made it? Then Mummy can see it in New York. And she can see how good it is.'

Nate put her down on the stool and tilted his head, examining the finished house. He walked around the island to the other side and again tipped his head before pronouncing, 'That is the best gingerbread house I've ever seen.' He held up his hand and Grace high-fived him with a squeal.

'It is! It is, isn't it? And we made biscuits for the tree. To hang on the tree.' She slithered down and danced around the room, waving her arms in the air and singing. It was the first time since we'd come in that she'd let herself go and be happy.

Nate took several pictures with his phone, while I measured out some spaghetti and Grace jumped all over the sofa before settling down to watch *Frozen*.

'When do you eat?' Nate looked over at the two place settings at the table.

'I . . . er . . . I'll grab something on the way to the theatre.'

He frowned. 'That's not very good for you.'

'Hello, Mr Frozen Food. I've been through your fridge and freezer. Sorry, that makes me sound like some kind of stalker. I was looking for something to feed Grace.'

'Yeah, I keep meaning to be more organised. Better. Svetlana wasn't much of a cook and she wouldn't have cooked for me anyway. Her job was looking after Grace, not me.'

He looked at the trendy old-fashioned large clock face on the wall. 'If you eat and run you've got time; you said you had to be at the theatre for seven. Even if you leave at quarter past six you'll get there.'

I grimaced and wavered; his house was closer to the tube station than mine.

'I can run you to the station in the car.'

'OK.'

Grace disappeared upstairs while I was cooking the pasta.

'Was she OK?' asked Nate.

I shook my head; it was almost too hard to speak. I swallowed down a lump and managed to stutter out, 'N-not really . . . no.' A tear escaped. 'God, I'm sorry. She sobbed.' I covered my face with a hand.

'Hey, Viola.' He put an arm around me and pulled me into his warm, hard body. I stiffened, not wanting his comfort.

'She was s-so sad but . . . so dignified and grown-up at first.' Then my tears came thick and fast. 'But it's not really about Svetlana, is it?'

Nate sighed and squeezed me. 'No. I'm not sure how much Grace misses Elaine – the job always came first – but I think she feels the rejection.'

Maybe that was why I was so upset; I could relate to how Grace felt. I'd been trying to catch up ever since.

I lifted my head to meet kind eyes staring down at me. I looked at the damp stains on his shirt. 'Oh, God, I've put make-up all over you. I'm going to look a sight this evening.'

He brushed one thumb under my eye and then the other under my other eye, with that careful concentration I'd seen on Grace's face. 'You'll do.'

His gentle smile sent my heart racing and I sucked in a noisy breath. His eyes narrowed as his eyes roved over my face, his fingers lifting to smooth a strand of hair away. My heart leaped at the sudden jolt of surprise in his eyes and then he studied me again. My lips parted and I held my breath – he was going to kiss me. I could see the intent, the flare of his nostrils, the almost puckering of his lips. And then he closed down and pulled back.

'Thank you for looking after Grace. You're a very kind person.'

'I just happened to be there at the right time.' I gave him an over-bright, perky smile. 'What are you going to do?'

'I haven't got a clue.' He slumped wearily against the counter, picking up the black coffee I'd made him earlier.

'Will you get another nanny?'

'I'll have to.'

'Was Svetlana with you for long?'

'Not that long, although –' his laugh was derisive '– longer than most. I hired her after Elaine left. Elaine was quite tough on nannies.'

'Oh.' Elaine really didn't sound very nice.

I pushed myself upright, lifting my chin to give him a Boudicca look my mother would have been proud of. 'Look, I know you don't want to get involved with me. And I completely get that, so this is nothing to do with that. I'm not trying to worm my way in. You're an attractive guy. I bet you have women throwing themselves at you all the time. But this is not about you; it's for Grace.' I linked my fingers, almost regretting even starting this conversation. 'I'm sure I can resist you.' He looked a little taken aback. 'But, if it helps, I could pick her up after school for the rest of this week. Just while you make other arrangements.'

Nate stared at me. 'That's a very generous offer.'

'I know. I'm mad,' I said. 'I've got enough on my plate with my mother. But, like I said, it's not for you.' I paused, my breath hitching into a near sob. 'Grace needs someone on her side.'

Chapter 13

'Viola, Viola!' Grace waved, her hands a blur in red gloves as she stood next to the teacher in the doorway. When I went over she gave me a huge beam. 'You came.'

'Of course I came. I said I would.'

Grace gave a quiet little nod of satisfaction as if we had a pact and I'd fulfilled my end of the deal. For some reason it filled my heart with a burst of warmth. I'd done good.

She turned to another little girl, who I recognised, saying to her, 'See, I told you Miss Smith was picking me up today.'

The little girl's glamorous, immaculately made-up mother, wearing a Cossack hat and a full-length down coat, raised her eyebrows in a sceptical way and caught my eye.

The little girl, who I now remembered was called Cassie, tugged her mother's hand. 'This is Miss Smith. The nativity lady.'

The woman turned to me with a winning smile which didn't touch her eyes. 'Hello, I'm Cassie's mummy. She's the angel. I ought to tell you Cassie has a beautiful voice; you might not have realised it, being new to the school.'

'No, I . . . er . . . I'm still getting to know all the children.'

'She's picking Grace up today,' interjected Cassie helpfully.

'Is she?' The woman managed to include a wealth of amused disdain in her words. 'Nannying as well. You're a woman of many talents.'

'I'm just helping out,' I responded, grateful when another woman claimed her attention with a shrill cry.

'Zoe, darling, I just adore your hat. Where did you get it?'

The teacher, who had been involved in a conversation with another mum, looked up and said to me cheerfully, 'Hello, I'm Grace's teacher. You must be her new nanny . . . oh, but didn't I see you in the staffroom earlier?'

'Yes, I'm doing the nativity this year but I'm also picking Grace up after school this week.'

'Oh.' She looked a little puzzled. 'How does that work? Are you a friend of Mr Williams as well?' I heard the woman in the Cossack hat give a small snort which, thankfully, the teacher ignored. 'He sent a note saying someone *new* would be picking up. Is this a permanent arrangement?'

'Erm . . .' I blushed as I realised Cassie's mum was listening avidly. I knew exactly what she was getting at.

Grace's hand slipped into mine and she squeezed it, a little signal of solidarity. I glanced down at her and she grinned at me.

'I'm Grace's friend. I'm just helping out for the time being.'

'Oh,' said the teacher, clearly a little put out that she was being denied any confirmation of the gossip she was so clearly keen to capitalise on. 'Right, well, there's some homework in the book bag and you should be getting an email about costumes tonight.' She broke off and, with a stilted laugh, added, 'But you probably know all about that.'

'Yes,' I said, ready to leave. It was getting chilly and the playground had emptied, although that was no bad thing. Cassie's mum had melted away.

'And how is the nativity coming along? We're all very excited to see what you do. You've got a tough act to follow after last year but then –' she shrugged '– I guess you're a professional; this is all second nature to you. I'm sure you've got something amazing up your sleeve.'

Oh, dear God, if only she knew. After that little encounter with the rabidly curious mum I was feeling even more out of my depth.

'I was good today. I got a house point.'

'Did you? What was that for?'

'Eating all my lunch.'

'Well done.'

'It wasn't as nice as your s'ghetti. That's the best meal I've ever had.'

I laughed. 'Wow. You need to get out more.'

'Can we have it again?'

'Not tonight. I thought I'd make you some special chicken.' It was a favourite with Bella's kids when I looked after them. Chicken and broccoli stir fry with a few secret ingredients of my own.

'We'll pop to the shop on the way home. You can help me cook it if you like.'

'Really?' Her eyes shone. 'Will you make it for Daddy too?'

'Yes. It's silly not to. And it's always nicer eating with someone else instead of by yourself, isn't it?'

'Yes,' she said with delightful round-eyed childish enthusiasm, before adding with a considering expression, 'And will you have some, like you did last night?'

'I . . . I don't think so. I need to go to work.'

'But you have to eat,' she said, sounding remarkably like her father had done the night before.

'Come on, I'm getting cold. I think it might snow this week.' They were forecasting heavy snowfall in the north and midlands of England; there was some talk of it working its way further south.

'Did you know . . .' Grace began.

I looked down at her; she was clearly after my full attention.

'That the Egyptians took their cats with them when they were dead? In bandages in case they got poorly in the afterlife.'

'Did they?'

'Yes, and they called them mummies, even though they were catties. And . . .' she paused '. . . there weren't any daddies.'

I laughed. 'That's a good thought. I wonder why not.'

'And Tutankhamun wore a big necklace. Blue and gold and he had a gold face when Howard Carter found him.'

As we walked home, diverting briefly to the Tesco Metro, Grace skipped alongside me, telling me in minute detail everything she'd done that day.

'I'm worn out just listening to what a busy day you've had,' I said as we climbed the steps to the front door of the house.

'Me too,' she said. 'Do you think it will snow?' she asked, looking up at the dull grey sky.

'Who knows? We'll have to watch the weatherman and see what he says.'

'Do you want to come and see my bedroom?' asked Grace, her eyes bright with anticipation, unzipping her coat and letting her scarf drop to the floor. 'I've got fairy lights and a special princess bed.' She darted towards the stairs, glancing back at me over her shoulder, waiting impatiently for me to follow.

'Shouldn't you take your shoes off first?' I eyed the expensive-looking stair carpet and the white boards, sure that there was a no-shoes rule in this immaculate showroom house.

Grace's face fell, her expression suddenly shuttered. Obediently, she ducked to her knees where she stood, took her shoes off and padded in her grey tights to the white panelled wall under the stairs. When she pushed, it sprang open to reveal a concealed cupboard ruthlessly organised with shoe racks, shelves and coat hooks. There was a place for everything and everything was in its place. Without looking at me, Grace paired up her shoes and neatly placed them on one of the racks before taking off her coat and asking in a small, polite voice, 'Please could you hang this up for me? I can't reach.'

I felt as if I'd kicked a puppy as I hung it next to an elegant pale blue wool coat. Elaine's, I guessed. It was the sort of thing the cool blonde I'd imagined with Nate that very first day I'd met him would wear. For some reason it was disappointing that I'd got it right.

On the shoe rack there were a pair of beige high heeled

court shoes, some pale green snow boots that didn't look as if they'd ever been on a ski trip, some Nike trainers and flowery ankle wellies that looked hopelessly impractical for anything.

There were more of Elaine's things on the shelves – a couple of handbags, some scarves and gloves and a leather laptop bag, which could have been hers or Nate's. It was strangely disconcerting, as if her absence was temporary and she'd marked her territory.

'Gosh, this is all very neat and tidy,' I said. 'My house is a bit messy. I don't have a cupboard like this.'

'Don't you?'

I shook my head and ducked down to whisper in her ear, 'And this cupboard is bigger than my whole wardrobe. It's nearly as big as my bathroom.' I poked my head around the corner. 'Is there a bath in here?'

Grace giggled. 'No, silly. It's upstairs.'

'Phew. Now, are you going to show me your super-duper bedroom?'

The dark evening was starting to close in as we went up the stairs.

'Look,' Grace said as she darted into her dark bedroom, 'I have fairy lights.' She switched them on and they cast a warm glow around her bed. It took me a minute for my eyes to adjust. It was only when she switched on the main light that I could see the pale pink walls and the white cast iron day bed with its white net canopy over the top. Her bedroom was everything a little girl's princess palace should be.

'This is very pretty. Shall we close the curtains?'

I pulled the pink curtains closed, shutting out the night. They were covered in fairies and flower blossoms. I smiled, remembering Grace's bossy innkeeper's wife performance. She wasn't a fairy and blossoms character.

Over on the right, taking up most of the wall, was a lovely wooden book shelf and I bent to study the books. There were complete box sets of Enid Blyton, *Harry Potter*, endless *Rainbow Fairy* books and at the very end a solitary, slightly dog-eared *Beast Quest* book. I recognised it because Rosa, Bella's middle child, was obsessed with them. It was the only book that looked as if it had been read.

The whole room looked showroom perfect, almost as if Grace never set foot in here. There wasn't a toy out of place, every book was in series order and not a stray sock or pair of pants on the floor.

'You've got lots of books. I love *Harry Potter*. Have you read any of them?' I asked.

She shrugged and turned her back on me.

'What do you like reading? *Rainbow Fairies?*'

She shrugged again.

'This?' I pulled the *Beast Quest* book out.

She peeped up at me from under her lashes and nodded.

'My niece, Rosa, has lots of them. Would you like me to see if I can borrow a few?'

Her eyes lit up. 'Yes, please. There are some in the school library. I borrow those but I always take them back. You can tell her that I'd give them back.'

'Want to read this one to me?'

'Can I?'

'Yes, but let's go downstairs to the kitchen. It's a bit . . . warmer down there.' And far more homely. I wanted to mess this room up, pull a few books from the shelves, rumple the bed and scatter colouring pencils on the floor.

'Do you want to see Daddy's room?'

Before I could say no, she'd opened the door and switched on the light. To my surprise, it was far more subdued than I was expecting. No sign of Elaine's signature showroom design in here. Everything was plain and simple and even a touch untidy. An open book by the bedside table along with a handful of receipts and business cards and a shirt tossed on the armchair by the window.

'Very nice,' I said, stepping back quickly. The last thing I wanted to imagine was Nate Williams sleeping in that big oak bed or hanging his smart suits and crisp cotton shirts in the matching wardrobe and I certainly didn't want to picture him in nothing but a towel emerging from the en suite bathroom.

Chapter 14

'Shall we have some music on?' I asked as I piled the ingredients on the chopping board, my heart still a little sore. This big house was far too quiet and staid for a little girl. As one of my friends would say, it needed a bit of a tickle. Actually, she said that about miserable people but I felt in this case it was applicable to this home: very beautiful but stark and cold. I looked around for a radio and spotted a leaf-green Roberts radio high up on a shelf, the colour co-ordinating perfectly with the kitchen.

Standing on a chair, I pulled it down and wiped off a layer of dust and patted it. Poor neglected thing. Had anyone ever realised it had a practical use?

Soon we were dancing away to Radio 2 while we chopped broccoli and dusted the chicken in Chinese Five-spice and cornflower.

'Is this the right size?' asked Grace, pointing with her knife at a small tree of broccoli, humming along to Mel Smith and Kim Wilde's *Rockin' Around the Christmas Tree*.

'Perfect, but it doesn't really matter, because it all goes in together. If you can make them a similar size to that then it's

161

a bit better because it all cooks at the same time, but no one's going to complain.' I put on a mock stern face. 'Or they can cook their own tea.'

Grace giggled and went back to her careful chopping. Despite my words, she still measured each piece against each other.

'Can we have that song again?' she asked, still humming the tune.

'The radio doesn't work like that but I can find it on my phone on YouTube,' I said.

'Yes, please.' She watched avidly as I fiddled with my phone and then found the video. As I started it, she began to sway from side to side, while insisting that the radio stayed on as well in case we missed anything that might be good, singing along before she watched it another three times while I chopped the chicken and soaked the rice.

I watched her happily warbling away, her face relaxed.

When we laid the table, I decided to move it. At the moment it was in a dark corner under a pedestal light, which was fine for dinner parties, although there was a very formal dining room upstairs, but it was cheerless, so I pulled all the chairs out and, with Grace's help – well, she thought she was helping – I shunted it across the room, turning it the other way so that it was now parallel to the kitchen area and encompassed by the bright glow of the lights. I also covered the chilly glass top with a wipe-clean tablecloth covered in brightly covered chickens which I'd found at the bottom of the drawer, the same one that the Cath Kidston apron had come from. There were quite a few other unlikely items in there, along with some matching napkins and some quite ugly table mats. Because I felt sorry for them and had a sneaking suspicion this was Elaine's drawer of unwanted Christmas gifts, I put them out.

Today I didn't care what Nate would think. I wasn't nesting or trying to impress him with my domestic skills; I was trying to create a more homely environment for Grace.

Ugly table mats aside, it all looked a lot cosier in here.

'Don't be so grumpy,' Grace scolded, putting her hands on her hips and shaking her head with pretty convincing exasperation. 'These poor people need somewhere to stay.'

'Well, there's no room,' I said in a deep voice, which made her falter for a second and she almost laughed before she was back in character.

With dinner ready to reheat as soon as Nate came home, we'd moved into the little snug just to the left of the kitchen to practice Grace's lines for the play. The sofa was now the wall of the hallway of the innkeepers' house.

'What about the stable?' she demanded, her long-suffering tone underlining the unspoken words, *you silly man*, perfectly.

'The stable?' I said in a passable King Henry VIII sort of voice, pretending to pat a big, round belly. I'd already decided I'd pad George out at the front and make him into a little rotund innkeeper, if he ever returned from flipping Disneyland Paris. He'd been absent for the last two days. 'But it's full of cows and oxen and sheep and dolphins.'

'Mr Innkeeper, we don't have dolphins in the stable.' Her long-suffering rebuke was spot on.

'We don't?'

Grace shook her head and stuck her nose up in the air with a perfectly superior tilt.

'Oh,' I replied in suitably chastened innkeeper tones.

Turning to an imaginary Joseph and Mary, Grace said, 'There's a stable out the back. It's not much but it has a roof and a door and, with the straw, it will be nice and cosy.'

'Well, you two look like you're having fun.'

'Daddy!' yelled Grace, the bossy innkeeper's wife vanishing in a flash as she ran across the room and hurled herself at him. 'We're rehearsling for the play.'

'Rehearsling?' Nate caught my eye and we both bit back our smiles as Grace chattered on.

'And Viola says I'm really good. I need a costume, though. We can use an old sheet and cut a hole in the top and put a belt round. The three kings need old curtains for their cloaks.'

Nate nodded but, before he could say anything, she was off again.

'And we cooked tea. And listened to music – Christmas songs. Do you know Christmas songs, Daddy?'

With a happy twirl, she launched into a loud and almost tuneful rendition of a few lines of *Rockin' Around the Christmas Tree*, which she then repeated three times because they were the only ones she knew.

'I know that one,' he said, laughing. 'Well, I do now.'

'And I watched the video on Viola's phone. They had a Christmas tree. When are we going to get a tree, Daddy?'

'I'm not sure.' Nate looked uncomfortable. 'Isn't it a bit early?'

Grace and I looked at each other with unified horror.

'It's never too early,' I said with exaggerated indignation. The decorations in the local shops were already starting to go up and this weekend, the second in December, would be the start of many of them gearing up for Christmas. There'd been mince pies in Marks for weeks now, although I'd yet to succumb. I preferred to make my own. 'Or for the first mince pie.'

Our eyes met in sudden remembrance.

'Mmm,' said Nate, 'I agree with you there. I do love a mince pie. Warm from the oven.' Was he thinking of the first day we'd met? That flirty frisson between us?

'Talking of food, something smells good.'

'I made it,' said Grace, taking his hand and dragging him over to the hob.

'Really?' Over her head, Nate raised an eyebrow at me.

'I did all the broccoli.'

'Well, it looks delicious and I'm hungry. We'd better eat now so that Viola can get to work on time.' He shot me a quick grin as Grace ran to sit down at the table. 'Can I give you a hand?' Then he looked back at the table, raised an eyebrow but didn't say anything. I lifted my chin. He could always move it back if he didn't like it.

'Could you grab some plates? Bowls preferably, and I'll dish up.'

He loomed over my shoulder and looked at the contents of the wok. 'That does look good and, unless the broccoli fairy does deliveries, you've been shopping. I must give you some money; you can't keep buying food for us.'

'I am eating some of it,' I said as I ladled out a spoonful of rice.

'Not that much and it still doesn't seem right. You looking after my daughter and buying the food.'

'Daddy, shall I get a candle from upstairs? Make it look like proper dinner.' Grace had already bounced up from her seat and was halfway across the basement room.

'Yes, if you want.' He watched her go with a smile on his lips. 'She's full of beans tonight. Thank you. And I do need to give you some money.'

'It's fine. We can sort it out later. If I was doing it for any longer, I'd suggest an online shop.'

As I carried on serving, I realised that Nate had gone quite still, his face guarded. He slid a quick look towards the doorway leading upstairs. Poor Grace; she'd been dealt a rubbish hand. I felt for her.

'Actually, if it helps I could . . . I could pick Grace up next week as well.' I said it in a hurry, blurting it out suddenly before I had time to think that perhaps I was being a bit presumptuous in assuming that I could take care of Grace and see to her needs better than someone else. But it wouldn't be a hardship. I enjoyed her company and I knew a little too well what it was like for her.

Nate was silent for a minute, staring at me.

'That's . . . very generous of you. I . . . I feel I ought to say no, it feels like I'm exploiting you but . . . she likes you and you have a rapport with her.' He sighed. 'I've been racking my brains, trying to think what's the best thing to do. I've been onto every nanny agency and I'm struggling to find anyone this close to Christmas. The following week I can probably work from home a couple of days but at the moment it's manic, everyone wanting everything done before the holidays.'

I lifted my shoulders in a quick shrug. 'It wouldn't be any trouble. I know my schedule.

I've got one afternoon rehearsal next week, so I can't help that day but I'm pretty clear after that. And I've got Thursday and Friday off this week and then *The Nutcracker* opens on Saturday, so you don't need to worry about rushing home.' I sighed with pleasure at the very thought. I might love my job but I didn't enjoy schlepping home late at night. Coming back at that time seemed to emphasise the emptiness of a home.

'That would be . . . well, amazing doesn't begin to cover it. It's been a struggle and I hate asking for help.' He looked at me, his warm brown eyes resting on my face. 'If I'm totally honest it would be a real relief to know that you're here, but I can't help feeling I'm taking advantage.' He closed his eyes and then opened them, looking up at the ceiling, his face creasing in sudden misery. 'I feel so guilty.'

I didn't answer. I got the impression he needed to talk.

'I feel guilty about everything. Even considering asking you to help, but then . . . Grace seems to have taken to you. I spend as much time as I can with her. But I still don't feel as if I'm doing enough.'

Sadness washed over his face. 'The thing I feel the most guilty about . . .' he swallowed hard; I watched him punishing his Adam's apple as he still looked up at the ceiling '. . . is not persuading Elaine to stay. For failing at our marriage.' He rubbed a finger back and forth across his forehead. 'A little girl needs her mother.'

A sudden flare of anger pinched tight at my heart. The power of it shocked me. 'No,' I said firmly, gripping the handle of the wok, 'she just needs love and attention.' I ground the words out through clenched teeth. 'You can give her those things.'

'Thanks.' He looked up at me and smiled gratefully as if I'd handed him a convenient platitude.

'I'm serious,' I said, my voice fierce as I checked the doorway to make sure Grace wasn't back to hear. 'Grace just needs to be loved and shown that she's loved in her own right. Loved for who she is.' I pursed my lips and gave him a stern look, wondering how far I dare go. 'You can do that. You're already doing that.'

His brow creased as if he was trying to understand what I was saying, but I could tell he didn't get it. It wasn't my place to criticise his wife.

'Thank you. I appreciate you saying it. I do my best . . . and I probably need to start with the cooking. This sort of freshly cooked food is so much healthier and better.'

I nodded, still a little surprised by my internal anger.

Oblivious, he looked a touch sheepish. 'I feel like I'm taking advantage, but I'm not in a position to argue.'

'Don't be ridiculous,' I said a little too sharply. 'I offered . . . because I can help. For Grace's sake more than anything else.' I paused and then said more pragmatically, 'In which case, you need to do an online shop. I can give you a list. Have you got an account with anyone?' I asked as Grace staggered back into the room, clutching a glass hurricane lamp nearly as big as she was.

'Grace!' Nate dashed over to relieve her of her burden and her triumphant smile waned.

'I wasn't going to drop it, Daddy. Honest.' She pouted but I saw her lip tremble.

'No, sweetheart –' I jumped in as Nate lifted the lamp out of her hands '– Daddy was just worried you might hurt yourself.'

'Oh.' Her face brightened. 'It was very heavy. But I thought it looked the nicest to go in here.'

'It's perfect,' I said. 'Where do you want to put it?'

'On the table,' said Grace with an indignant isn't-it-obvious lift of her eyebrows that had both Nate and I smiling. 'And you can light it, Daddy,' she added, as if conferring a great honour on him.

The glow of the candle on the table softened the lighting and Nate turned off the overhead kitchen lights, leaving the gentler under-cabinet lights on. The scene was far too cosy and I had to stop myself being seduced into feeling ridiculously at home. Nate was easy company and Grace was smart, cute and in need of a permanent solution. This was temporary and I shouldn't get too close.

But when I sneaked a glance at Nate, he looked up at the same moment, our eyes meeting and holding for a second too long. Was it the flicker of the candlelight or did I see something in them that warranted the sudden, ridiculous lamblike skip of my heart? There was an unexpected warmth in those chocolate-brown eyes and then he gave me the gentlest of smiles that hit me straight in the chest, making my throat constrict and my skin flush with heat. Thankfully, before I made an idiot of myself, Grace put down her fork and turned to Nate, saying conversationally, 'So when are we going to get the tree?'

She sounded so adult and so very much like a wife I very nearly choked.

'Er . . .'

'And who's going to decorate it?'

'Er . . .'

I looked from Grace to Nate.

Nate grimaced. 'Elaine always did it. She liked to . . . to do it her way.'

'That's good,' I said. 'It means this year you and Grace can do it together, and do it your way.'

'I'm not completely sure I know where all the decorations are.' He grimaced. Grace's worried face watched this exchange as if she were an umpire at a tennis match. 'I guess they're up in the attic storeroom somewhere.'

'Men!' I said, winking at her. 'Why don't Grace and I have a look for them tomorrow after school? And might we find an old sheet up there?'

'That would be good, thank you,' he mumbled. 'Not sure about the sheet.'

'I'll have a look and if not you can always buy a cheap one when you do the online shop.'

'That would be great.' Nate pulled a face. 'I don't suppose you know where's the best place to get a tree? I don't even know what sort of tree to get. It was always Elaine's department.'

'Grace, your dad is officially rubbish,' I declared before

turning to him. 'Do you ever actually walk around Notting Hill?'

'Sometimes,' he said with that cautious air of someone who knows they're about to be caught out.

'Pines and Needles. At St John's Church, Lansdowne Crescent, just around the corner. They do the best trees. You can get Nordmann Fir or a Norway Spruce, depending on whether you want a non-drop tree or you want that lovely piney smell.'

'I've no idea. I don't even know what size to get.'

I shook my head and turned to Grace, grinning as I rolled my eyes at his uselessness, relieved by his self-deprecating, teasing tone.

'I saw that,' he said. 'Tell you what, why don't you come with us? You sound as if you're an expert . . .' He flashed me a sudden grin. 'I could treat you to lunch as a thank you for being chief Christmas tree consultant, if it's not too much of an imposition.'

'It's no problem. I love Christmas tree shopping.' I winked at Grace 'And I wouldn't want you ending up with a wonky one because you had a complete amateur on the case. We could go this Saturday, if you're free.'

'Please, Daddy. Please.'

I winced a sort of apology at Nate, realising I'd put him on the spot, which I hadn't intended to do.

'OK, it's a d . . .' Now it was Nate's turn to wince. 'It's a yes from me,' amended Nate with an admirable save.

Chapter 15

Thankfully, Dad arrived home on Thursday on the red-eye from New York, just beating the forecast snow and walking in as I was having breakfast.

'Good morning, Viola,' he said as I was standing at the kitchen window watching the street below, eating my Weetabix. I was absolutely bushed, thanks to Mum's obsession with *Game of Thrones*. She was already on season two; yet again last night she'd kept me up until gone two. I couldn't wait to get back to my own little flat and Dad's arrival was my signal to pack my bag. I'd drop it off on my way to the school.

'Hi Dad, how was your trip?'

'Good, very good. How's your mother? Is she feeling better?'

'She's fine, apart from developing a very unhealthy obsession with dragon princesses and an alternative medieval world which mirrors her *Mastermind* subject of the Wars of the Roses.'

'Jolly good,' he responded in his usual vague way, patting me on the shoulder. 'Is she still in bed?'

'Yes, sleeping off the aftermath of genocide, incest and world domination.'

'Sounds like your mother.' His eyes twinkled. 'And what have you been up to?'

'Organising a nativity as part of an outreach programme. Actually, it isn't that different. The parents are up in arms because they don't like that they've been asked to organise costumes with no notice, my leading man has gone AWOL and the angel's mother is threatening rebellion.'

'A lot of fun, then,' observed Dad, pulling open a cupboard and shaking a jar of instant coffee. 'I'm sure it will be wonderful. I don't remember any of your nativity plays at school. Weren't you Mary one year?'

'Yes, I was.' I turned my back and spooned in another mouthful of Weetabix.

'Did we come to that?' he asked, switching on the kettle. I could hear the chink, chink of him sorting through the china mugs with Goldilocks's thoroughness before he found one he liked the look of.

'No.' I stared out of the window, stiffening, and deliberately kept my back to him.

I'm not sure Dad even noticed as he carried on pottering. The clatter of the spoon in the mug. The click of the kettle reaching its boil. The swoosh of water poured. 'Didn't we? Oh, that's a shame. Well, I'm sure you were wonderful.'

I didn't say anything.

The snow started at one p.m. The radio forecast said that a heavy band of snow moving in from the east would skirt London.

The forecast lied. By half past one as I packed away my viola, after practising for a good few hours at home with the heating cranked right up, great fluffy flakes were parachuting out of the sky in a never-ending swirling flurry sweeping past the window. I pressed my nose to the window, fascinated, watching as the snow whirled and skimmed in the air like swallows in summer. It was settling surprisingly quickly.

I nipped outside, crunching up my basement stairs to street level, my feet leaving squeaky snow-crunched virgin footprints on the steps. There was a proper layer of snow blanketing the pavements. Wrapping myself up warm, I unearthed my festival wellies from the very back of my wardrobe and sent a hasty text to Nate.

Snow coming down quite heavily here. Would you mind if I popped into the house to grab a pair of wellies for Grace?

Not at all. Good thinking Batman. Thank you. He'd added a smiley face, a snowman and a snowflake emoji to his text.

Two seconds later I received another text.

School closing at half past two, are you able to pick Grace up then?

It felt odd letting myself into the house, knocking the snow off my wellies at the front door before I stepped inside. My feet were absolutely freezing even though I'd put two pairs of socks on. I'd better grab spare pairs for Grace.

However, as soon as I toed the first boot off, I realised why one of my feet was so cold. My left foot welly sock was absolutely sodden and when I picked up my welly I could see why. The plastic had split along the seam between the boot and the sole and the same thing was imminent with the other

175

boot. They hadn't been expensive and I hadn't been to a festival in two years. Clearly, they'd perished through neglect at the back of my wardrobe.

'Damn.' The best option would be to wear them but protect my feet from the wet with some plastic carrier bags, but I'd need some warm, thick socks. Surely Nate wouldn't mind me pinching a pair or two of his. I wasn't going to fit into any of Grace's, that was for sure.

I sent him another quick text.

Emergency. Please can I borrow a pair of socks? My wellies have holes in them.

Stripping off my soggy socks, I left them on the mat and padded to the cupboard. Sure enough, there on one of the shelves was a pair of Grace-sized Joules wellies with little dogs all over them. Perfect. My eyes slid to the snow boots I'd seen the previous day. Elaine's boots. I bet they'd be warm.

I picked them up and then put them back down. I couldn't. Instead I grabbed Grace's wellies and then padded upstairs to her bedroom to find some nice thick socks for her. Of course, nestled in her drawer, were a pair of proper Joules branded welly socks, pink with little horses' faces on them. Shame they wouldn't fit me.

I checked my phone. No response from Nate. But surely he wouldn't mind. I'd asked. He could hardly say no, could he?

Deciding that I didn't have time to wait, I needed to get to school to pick Grace up, I pushed open the door into Nate's room and approached the oak chest of drawers. Solid and squat, it reminded me of a sentry on duty and, given I shouldn't really be in here, it was more than a little off-putting. But you're not snooping, I told myself. And I'd asked permission.

Telling myself to stop being so silly, I yanked open the first drawer, relieved to find that I'd hit the jackpot first time round. Pants and socks. Not as neat as Grace's drawers, but I guessed that was probably Svetlana's doing. Without having to rummage too much, I found myself a pair of hiking socks and a thin pair of fine wool ones. Perfect. My feet were so cold I hurried to sit on the end of the bed. The fine wool socks slid on like silk, they were a bit too big but deliciously soft. Probably contained cashmere. Had Elaine bought them for Nate? She seemed to have an abundance of taste and liked luxury.

Almost as if I'd conjured her up, I looked over to an archway recessed into the wall. It had a couple of shelves which held ornamental, antique-style pill boxes and a framed wedding photo.

Nate and Elaine were flanked in the picture by what looked like almost a dozen adorable little bridesmaids ranging in age from five to nine. The cutest age, I thought cynically. Elaine's dress swirled around her, the heavy fabric pooled in folds at her feet and a fine full-length train drifted down behind her from an ornate fairy tiara on top of blonde, artfully arranged hair. Stray ringlets framed her classically beautiful face, with its cream and rose complexion, clear blue eyes and delicate features. She was beautiful, there was no other word for it. Absolutely flipping gorgeous and I could see where Grace got her fine features – she had the same bone structure, with high cheekbones, elegant browbones and slightly aquiline nose.

Everything about the picture spoke class and elegance. It was obvious that this was a wedding where no expense had been spared. You could tell Elaine was a perfectionist, which was probably why she had such a successful career and had been headhunted by some swanky acquisitions and mergers firm in New York, which I'd now picked up from various comments by Nate.

Now that my toes were thankfully starting to warm up, I left the room and ran lightly down the stairs, once again admiring how light and airy the hallway was. Even the snow-filled sky didn't dim its brightness, although I still put a light on.

See text from school about dropping wellies in at reception desk.

Nate had forwarded a text from the school with instructions followed by,

Help yourself to anything you need.

Nate's message swung it and I took him at his word. My wellies were well and truly knackered. There was a perfectly good pair of snow boots sitting there and my feet had only just warmed up.

I grabbed Elaine's snow boots and sat on the stairs to pull them on. They were a half size bigger than I was but with two pairs of Nate's socks fitted perfectly.

It was far easier walking along in the heavy-soled boots and as I strode along listening to the creaking, crunching underfoot I was aware of the unearthly quiet, the snow deadening the sound, and the eerie silence in the streets. The heavy flakes blurred the Christmas lights decorating hedges and shrubs along the route, turning the gardens into enchanted fairy lands. The busy traffic had slowed to a trickle and the usual noise and fumes had been replaced by the occasional hiss of a car crawling along at snail's pace, the snow slushing under the wheels. It seemed as if no one wanted to venture out.

I hurried along, the only person in the street. There was a flat grey light to the sky and the snow was now so thick it was getting harder and harder to see beyond the end of the street. Lights were on in the houses even though it was early afternoon, creating cheery snapshots of people's homes with their Christmas trees, strings of cards and festive decorations. Streams of tinsel here, baubles suspended on ribbons there and rows of candle holders on window sills. Christmas Day was just over two weeks away and creeping up. I needed to start getting organised. I was too late to book an online shopping slot and I had a horrible feeling I'd missed the deadline to order the turkey. The eighth of December was ringing bells – the deadline was yesterday.

Even though the icy flakes bit into my skin, I lifted my face. It felt as if I was in my very own snow globe, with the backdrop of all the pretty houses and their festive windows. There was something magical about snow so close to Christmas. Still in a daydream, imagining carol singers at doors, the smell of mince pieces and families gathered around fireplaces hung with stockings, I turned the corner and started when I realised that there was someone right behind me.

They were walking in the same direction but I hadn't heard them at all. With their head bowed under a heavy dark hood, I couldn't see their face. The realisation that someone had been there, and that the sound of their footsteps had been absorbed by the snow, creeped me out. I loitered in a gateway for a moment, studying the holly wreath on the nearest front door, waiting for them to pass, feeling a little nervous when they drew alongside. They passed without a word, head down, probably like me, headed somewhere and trying to keep the snow out of their face. I let them draw ahead, waiting for the uncomfortable thud of my pulse to settle.

There was even a rare silence in the school playground when I arrived, with solitary figures of parents dotted about instead of in their usual gangs, as if they were too muffled up and snug inside hats and scarves to try and identify each other. Snow clung to the wool of my scarf, wrapped across my face. I'd dropped Grace's wellies off at reception, where the poor office staff were running relays of boots and coats down to the classrooms.

At last the first of the classroom doors opened and with that the air was filled with the joyous shrieks of children hurling themselves through the doorways into the first snow-fall of the year.

'Snow!' The high-pitched delight was squealed over and over as the children tumbled out in a colourful moving mass of hats and scarves, coloured wellies and ski jackets.

'It's snowing!'

'Let's build a snowman.'

'Snowball fight.'

Several children charged off to the field, their feet kicking up through the heavy blanket already covering the playground. I spotted Grace straight away in her pink caterpillar coat and her blue wellies as she limped towards me, doing a passable impression of John Wayne.

'Sweetie, what's the matter?'

Her big eyes brimming with tears, she looked up at me. 'My wellies are too small.'

'Oh, sweet pea, I'm so sorry. I just took them from the cupboard.'

How stupid. Little girls' feet grew quickly. The boots had probably been there for at least a year.

'Are they really tight? What about if we took your thick socks off?'

She blinked and nodded.

'Come here.' I picked her up and waded through the snow back to the classroom. She was too heavy to carry all the way home.

Her teacher looked up.

'Sorry, can we just do a bit of jiggery-pokery here? Grace's wellies are too tight.'

'I did wonder when she staggered off, but I was too late to catch her. Grace, you should have said something.'

Grace lifted her shoulders in resignation.

'It's all right, I think they'll be OK if we do some sock swapping.'

It took some tugging to get her wellies off. Then I took mine off.

'What are you doing?' asked Grace as I pushed up her grey trousers.

'You have to wear some socks, otherwise your feet will get very cold. Lucky for us, I've got two pairs on.'

I quickly whipped off Nate's nice thin wool socks, which were still warm, and put them on Grace's narrow feet and slipped her socks into my pocket.

When she put her wellies back on, she managed to get her foot all the way in.

'How's that?' I asked, looking at her dubious face.

'My toes are at the very, very end.' She stood up and took a few exploratory steps. 'They're a bit scrunched but I can walk.'

'Are you sure?'

With a determined nod, she picked up her school bag.

I quickly shoved my feet back into Elaine's super toasty snow boots and decided that we'd walk back as quickly as possible. In those thin socks, cashmere or not, her feet would soon get cold.

At first Grace was diverted by the falling snow on the way home, sticking her tongue out and catching snowflakes in her outstretched hands, but before long I could tell by her pinched face that she was getting cold. It was a good twenty-minute walk home and we still had another fifteen minutes. When we passed one of the many charity shops in the area, I pulled on her hand, doubling back, and stopped outside.

'Let's have a quick look in here.' At the worst it would be a brief reprieve for her cold feet and we might just find a second-hand pair of boots.

Grace followed me in, her nose wrinkling slightly at the usual charity shop mothball and stale smell.

There was a large selection of children's shoes and, to my delight, there were several pairs of snow boots. You do get a better quality of charity shop in Notting Hill. I picked up a pair of boots that looked approximately the right size, given I was no expert.

'I don't suppose you know what size feet you have?'

'Thirteen.'

'That's brilliant.'

The size on the bottom was a European size. Thirty-four. I had no idea how that would translate. I was a size six, which was a thirty-nine.

'Svetlana took me to get new shoes in September. And in her country that's thirty-two.'

I grinned at Grace and held up my hand for a high five. Good old Svetlana.

'These are probably going to be a little bit big . . . but with your welly socks they might be just right.'

Grace eyed them dubiously. They weren't in the first flush of youth. They were navy with criss-cross laces up the front, holding in slightly scrappy sheepskin.

'Try them on,' I encouraged. 'They'll be lovely and toasty.'

With a small crimp to her mouth she sat down on the floor and I tugged off the too tight wellies, Nate's outsize socks peeling off with them to reveal her narrow pink-white piebald feet, the ends of her big toes glowing red. Despite the angry colour, when I touched them they were like ice. Taking them in my hands, I gave them a quick rub.

'Oh, sweetheart. Quick, put these on.' I pulled the welly socks from my pocket and we each put one on.

Her face was still unsure when she slid her feet into the boots. But then she clomped a few steps in them, stamping her feet a little.

'How do those feel?'

She hesitated.

'Are they OK?'

She frowned and looked down at them.

'I know they're not very pretty but they'll keep your feet nice and toasty.'

'They're not too tight,' she conceded.

'Great.'

I picked up her smart but redundant Joules wellies and went to the cash desk with her trailing disconsolately behind me like Eeyore.

'We'll take these,' I said, pointing to Grace's feet and handing over the price tag I'd peeled from one of the soles.

'Perfect for today,' said the older woman. 'Would you like a bag for your welly boots?'

'That would be great, thank you.'

'Aren't you lucky? Mummy buying you new boots,' she said to Grace, who scowled and didn't respond but as we left the shop I heard her mutter.

'They're not new.'

I kept quiet, still unsettled by how I'd felt when the shopkeeper had called me Mummy, disconcerted by that sudden squeeze to my heart and the odd tears that pricked my eyes.

Five minutes later, as we walked down the street, I could tell Grace was feeling much more cheerful; her hand was swinging in mine and she was back to trying to eat the snowflakes and laughing when they landed on her eyelashes. I, on the other hand, was still feeling a little disorientated.

'I think we need hot chocolate with marshmallows,' I said as we shook the snow from our clothes before stepping inside the house, waving the carrier bag with the wellies and the recently purchased supplies from Tesco Metro. And I really needed to get on and do that online shop. Nate had left me a credit card to set up an account and do a food shop.

'Can we?' Grace bobbed up and down as she wriggled her way out of her coat and kicked off her boots. There were small puddles of water already forming on the beautiful bleach wood floor, which immediately sent me rushing to the kitchen to get a couple of cloths.

We took all the wet things downstairs to hang in the utility room just off the kitchen. It was always toasty in there with its Bosch washing machine, dryer, big steam generator iron, trouser press, steam cleaner and every other domestic appliance you could possibly imagine.

Once I'd made the hot chocolate with squirty cream and marshmallows, and bunged some potatoes in the oven, I managed to light the small squat wood-burner that sat in the corner of the snug. We sat there sipping hot chocolate, toasting our toes in front of the open door of the wood-burner, watching the snow billowing down like feathers set loose in a pillow fight. Grace had nestled into me on the sofa, making little purring noises.

'You've got cream on your nose,' I said, laughing and dabbing at it. 'Enjoying that?'

'It's awesome,' said Grace, picking a marshmallow out with her fingers and popping it into her mouth. 'Yummy, yummy, yummy. When I'm big I'm going to have this every day.'

'I think you'd soon get sick of it,' I teased.

She shook her head violently, her hair whipping through the cream.

'Watch it,' I said. 'Hang on.' I wiped the strands quickly with my fingers, looked at my sticky hands and then, with Grace's wide-eyed gaze on me, shrugged and wiped them on my jeans.

Her mouth dropped open.

'Shh, don't tell anyone,' I whispered. 'It's all right, I do the washing.'

With a smile, she took another sip and wriggled closer to me.

Unable to help myself, I lifted my arm and put it around her and she snuggled in, her small warm body a barely-there weight against me.

Together we sat in silence, the flames in the wood-burner snap, crackle and popping, casting a warm golden glow across our outstretched legs. Outside, the white of the snow contrasted sharply with the shadows of the patio, a thick quilt pillowed on top of the bistro table and the three chairs.

'We could build a snowman,' I said, burying my nose in the soft, sweet smell of Grace's hair and then moving sharply when she sat up straighter. 'Just a small one.' There wasn't that much room in the tiny patio garden; it would be tight. 'Maybe a snowdog or a snowcat.'

'Can we? Really? An Olaf.'

'Yes, but I've only just thawed out. Let's wait until after tea. I don't have to go to work tonight, so I don't have to rush off anywhere.'

She snuggled back into me. 'This is nice. I like hot chocolate. I like the snow. And I like you.'

I dropped a kiss on top of her head. 'And I like you.'

We lapsed into silence and it was so warm and cosy that I could feel Grace's head start to droop. I rescued her drink and let her doze against me, thinking it was so lovely and warm I'd just close my eyes for a moment too.

Chapter 16

Something woke me, a log collapsing in the grate, and I realised that Nate was home and sitting opposite in the armchair, toasting his toes, watching Grace sleeping against me.

'Evening,' he said softly.

'Oh, God,' I whispered. 'What time is it?'

'It's only five. I left the office early. Didn't fancy my chances on public transport if I left it any longer.'

Beyond him, it was dark outside now and the snow fell thickly, just as fast as ever.

'Sorry, I only meant to shut my eyes for a minute but it was so cosy. Poor Grace is shattered.'

'Yes, it's been a long term. She's ready for the holidays. It's a struggle to wake her up in the mornings.'

I nodded. I had no knowledge of such things and for a minute I felt like the outsider again. I looked down at Grace's relaxed face, the fine white skin, her eyelashes fluttering against her cheek. Asleep, she looked even more small and defenceless. I probably shouldn't have encouraged her to snuggle in, but it had seemed the right thing to do. Now I felt guilty. I wasn't going to be around for ever and I didn't want Nate thinking the wrong thing.

'Sorry . . .' I indicated the sleeping child with a tilt of my head '. . . this probably isn't appropriate – we were both warm and sleepy.'

'You both looked so peaceful, a pair of Sleeping Beauties. I couldn't bear to wake you, although I'm worried about Grace not sleeping at bedtime.'

'She could have another five minutes. Why don't you take over while I make dinner?'

I wriggled free, not wanting to leave the warm cocoon of the sofa. Grace murmured a gentle sleepy protest but Nate was standing in front of me, ready to take my place. As I laboured to my feet rather inelegantly, he took my arm, hauling me upright, but somehow he'd misjudged the distance and when I rose to my feet my chest came to rest against his and we stood there, our noses almost touching, warily gazing at each other. His eyes widened and I stared at the tiny chocolate flecks in them. My breath caught in my throat as I heard his hitch, a quick, sharp inhalation that made my heart jump. Tiny black bristles like coal dust dotted his chin. Between us there was a flare of awareness. Fast and fleeting, like a firework going up and fizzing into the sky. The pulse in his throat quickened and I felt hollow with sudden longing.

Look away, look away. But it was impossible. It was one of those moments when you're so aware of the other person but it feels as if neither of you can move or do anything in case it's the wrong move. I resisted the terrible urge to step forward, lay my lips on his, give in and kiss him. I could be making a terrible mistake. Misreading the signs. He'd already laid it on the line. This was nothing more than a burst of sexual attraction. He was a good-looking man and I was in very close proximity.

There was almost pain on his face, strain in his eyes as his hands grasped my forearms to hold me up. His eyes narrowed, roving across my face as if checking out all of my features, inventorying them one by one until they rested on my lips.

He lifted a hand and with one finger brushed my lower lip so slowly it was as if he were mapping every tiny line. I pressed a tiny kiss onto his finger, so small it was less of a kiss and more of a press, a whisper of skin against skin. The small, intimate touch lit my nerve endings, as everything in my body went on knife-edge red alert.

'Viola . . .' He whispered my name, the hoarse sound like sandpaper on my heart. His hand dropped to his side. He didn't want this, was fighting it.

Move damn it, move. I was sandwiched between him and the sofa with nowhere to go and still he held my eyes, his haunted with a mixture of longing and guilt. It was almost a relief when he closed his, severing the connection. With a gentle push I pressed at his chest and mercifully he stepped back.

'I'd better get on with dinner,' I said brightly. 'Sausage and mash and baked beans for those that want them.' I glanced down at Grace. 'Special request.'

There was a small silence, punctuated by the hiss of the wood in the log-burner.

'Thanks, Viola, I don't know what we'd do without you at

the moment.' His voice held that same hint of strain I'd seen on his face.

I patted him on the arm, a deliberate matey physical touch, to make it clear that the last few minutes were over and done and forgotten.

'Don't worry about it,' I said. Could he hear the false breeziness? 'I enjoy Grace's company and I like cooking.'

'I'm sorry . . . about . . .'

'Nate, forget it –' brisk, don't-blame-yourself no-nonsense in my voice '– I'd just woken up, I was half asleep. Now, sit down with Grace for a moment while I get on.'

I scooted around him and into the kitchen area, following the smell of baking potatoes. *Scoop out the middles and mix them with a dash of butter and a touch of milk. Think about food, not about what just happened. Put the sausages in the oven, bake them, so I can make gravy with the sticky sweet residue in the baking tray.* Had I just kissed his finger? *Gravy. Yes, make some gravy.* The touch of my lips had been instinctive. Of the moment.

I clattered about in the kitchen, putting the radio on. *Be normal. Get on with things. Just make tea before you head for home.* Home. The thought of trudging back to my empty flat in the snow was suddenly deeply depressing. Normally a night in at home was such a novelty I revelled in it. Lying full length on my sofa reading a book with the television on in the background, a whole evening to myself, with a bottle of wine and a carpet picnic of Marks & Spencer treats, because I'd be too lazy to cook for one. Now it just sounded a little sad.

It wasn't long before the sausages were sizzling and I heard

Grace's voice chirping away telling Nate all about her day and the snow. I laid the table with a smile, listening to her repeating things I'd said verbatim.

'Tea's ready,' I called with a small hum of satisfaction as I heard Grace scrambling to her feet.

'Sausages! Baking beans.' She came running into the kitchen. 'I'm starvacious.'

'Starvacious. That's a very good word,' I said with a grin.

'It means I'm really, really hungry.' She patted her tiny stomach, dancing around my feet as I tried to pour the hot gravy into an equally hot gravy boat.

'Careful, now go sit down,' I said, putting the pan down and waving my oven-gloved hands at her, wanting her out of the way of the hot pans. I probably should have told her to go and wash her hands. It seemed to be one of those peculiar naggy things that adults made a point of telling children to do but never did themselves.

The sleep seemed to have done Grace the power of good and she was like a small all-action dynamo again, playing with her cutlery and chattering away nineteen-to-the-dozen. Her happiness glowed and it made my heart sing. It was wonderful to see her like this rather than the subdued little girl she so often was at home. Maybe being at home reminded her too much of her mum.

'Grace, calm down,' said Nate. 'You're full of beans this evening.'

'Baking beans,' she said gleefully, holding up a forkful and losing a few on the table.

'You're making a mess,' he said with a shake of his head.

'Sorry, Daddy. Can we go out in the snow? Can we build a snowman? Viola can help.'

For a fraction of a second I hesitated and glanced at Nate, wondering if he'd rather I pushed off after the earlier brief awkwardness but, to my relief, he grinned.

'I'm hoping she will. I think it's going to be a big job.'

'OK,' I said doubtfully, looking out of the windows at the tiny patio area, but there was no way I was going to rain on Grace's parade. Surely there wasn't room for all three of us out there. By the time we'd stood on the snow there wouldn't be enough to build a snow hobbit let alone a man.

Grace and Nate shot each other a look that I couldn't interpret and then they both smiled with such smug expressions, looking so alike that I burst out laughing.

'You two look as if you're up to something. The first person who tries to put snow down my neck will not get fed for a week,' I threatened.

'Now, there's a thought,' teased Nate, flashing Grace another conspiratorial grin.

'Daddy, that's not nice. You have to be nice to Viola. Have we got a carrot for a nose?' She looked worried for a second. 'We don't have no coal. But we have scarves.' She bounced in her seat. 'Can I go get one?'

'I think snowman-building might be just the thing,' said Nate. 'It might get rid of some of those extra beans, missy.'

Grace beamed at her dad and jumped up from her seat, running to the stairs, and we heard her pattering up them.

'The joy of snow when you're seven. All I could think when I looked out the office window was that getting home would be a nightmare and everyone would smell of damp dog on the tube.'

'And did they?' I asked.

'Yes, and everyone was miserable. But this makes it better. Makes coming home worthwhile.'

'You enjoy your job, don't you?'

'Yeah, sorry, am I sounding like a miserable old git?'

'No, I guess it must be quite . . .' I looked around at the kitchen '. . . well paid.'

He laughed. 'Viola, you're never being tactful, are you?'

'OK, Mr Shit-hot solicitor, lawyer . . . whatever you are – what is it you do?'

'I specialise in sports law.'

'Sports law?'

'That's surprised you.'

'Yes, I didn't even know there was such a thing. It sounds almost respectable. I mean, not like a human rights lawyer or anything but sort of. What sort of things do you do?'

'We represent sports people, like athletes, footballers, jockeys when they might have fallen foul of anti-doping rules, or if they're in dispute with their governing body. We also represent Sports Governing Bodies when a decision they've made has been legally challenged elsewhere or by an International Sports Body.'

'Wow, that must be interesting.'

'I think so.'

'So do you get to meet lots of famous sports people?'

'Says she who mixes with world-famous singers and dancers all the time.'

'That's different, it's just work and I'm a tiny cog in a big machine. It sounds like you're quite important. I'm not being rude . . . but this is one heck of a house.'

'I got lucky. You ever seen the Tom Cruise and Cuba Gooding Junior film, *Jerry Maguire?*'

I nodded. 'Ages ago.'

'I was working for a small firm with a couple of sports clients and I met a rugby player, who got embroiled in a nasty scandal with quite a famous actress.'

'You mean . . .?' My eyes widened. It had been a very famous case about ten years ago. 'J—'

He put up a hand to stop me. 'Don't say it. Client confidentiality. I can't say any more if you do.'

'And that's why you're the lawyer,' I said.

'Exactly. No one wanted to know him. But I'd met him a couple of times, really liked the guy. He had integrity. I guess it was gut feeling. I didn't think he'd done what he was accused of. So I managed to get a business card to him. Said I'd represent him. The company I was working for didn't want to know. So I went out on a limb. I'd just started dating Elaine at the time . . . she was pretty horrified at first. Anyway. Someone had some rather useful CCTV footage, got him off the hook. The next day he was reinstated to the national side and scored the winning try in the dying seconds of the game, to win a major international game against all odds. Instant hero. As his cachet hit the big time, so did my reputation. Overnight, I had requests for representation and most of them have stuck with me ever since.'

'Wow, so you're one of the good guys.'

'I like to think so. I take it from something your mother said, you're not keen on the legal profession.'

'Ex-boyfriend. Paul. Corporate law. Definitely not one of the good guys. He thought his job was more important than mine.' I winced at the memory. The night he'd kindly explained why he was leaving me and what had forced him into the arms of another woman.

'Ouch. He sounds an . . .'

Grace came running in with a big wide red scarf and a floppy black hat. 'Look what I found.'

'Perfect,' I said. 'Let's see what else we can find for his face.'

'I . . . er . . . I hope you don't mind but I borrowed some of your socks,' I said, coming down the stairs, suddenly feeling a little flushed. I'd just been up to Grace's room to help her find some suitable outdoor clothing and while I'd been gone Nate had changed out of his suit.

The long-sleeved navy Henley T-shirt suited him far too well, emphasising broad shoulders, and the buttons at the front revealed a small vee of skin with a dusting of hair. That little glimpse of skin suggested there was a whole lot more to him than I'd considered before. Unfortunately the bulky ski trousers that hid plenty didn't stop my imagination filling in the gaps. I was already thinking about his long legs and wondering things that were making me feel a little heated.

'Didn't you get my text?' he asked, leaning down and pulling a thick pair of socks onto long narrow feet, almost identical in shape to Grace's.

'Yes, but I also . . . my wellies were letting the wet in. I . . . erm . . . borrowed a pair of Elaine's, I assume they're hers, snow boots.'

'Of course I don't mind.' He straightened up, carelessly pushing his hand through his unruly hair. 'It's not like she's using them at the moment. She's probably bought another pair by now anyway.'

'So . . . she's not coming back?' I asked.

Nate's mouth went flat. 'Doesn't look like it.'

'Sorry.'

'It's . . .' he lifted his shoulders '. . . it's been nearly a year. She left in January. But she'd been working in New York for nine months already by then. Commuting back and forth over the Atlantic. I guess, in hindsight, it shouldn't have been a huge shock. I'd have gone with her if she'd asked.' The sad, quiet admission made me look up at him sharply. He'd spoken earlier of his job and his passion.

'Leave your company?'

He shrugged. 'There would have been a way round. I'd have compromised. She didn't want to.'

'I'm sorry.'

'Don't be. It's worse for Grace. People fall out of love. People get divorced. Although I never thought it would happen to . . . to us. When you get married and have a child, you think it's going to be for ever. It never occurred to me I'd join the failed marriages statistics. But I did. I failed at being married. Failed Elaine somehow. That was no one's fault but ours. But it seems so unfair on Grace. We failed but she's the one most affected. She didn't ask for this. Elaine and I should have been able to fix it for her sake. Shouldn't we?' He gave me an anguished look.

'I don't know. But she's got you and you seem to be a

pretty good dad to me. Some people have both parents and are still . . .' *neglected* seemed too strong a word; it suggested deliberate intent rather than preoccupation with other weightier matters '. . . forgotten.'

'Yeah, I guess. I still worry about her. Elaine barely keeps in touch. The odd Skype call and that's about it. Every now and then she'll send some "darling" outfit that she saw in "Bloomies" and she just couldn't resist, which Grace will insist on wearing even though it's either too small – Elaine seems to have forgotten children grow and that Grace is now seven and not five – or it's totally inappropriate.' He gave a bitter laugh. 'Grace could attend the Oscars and not be out-sparkled.'

'Damn, you couldn't tell her that Grace has had a growth spurt and is now a size ten, could you? I can always use a new party frock.'

Nate laughed. 'Am I sounding bitter and twisted?'

'No, you care about Grace. Which makes you a good dad. You can't compensate for Elaine's behaviour. All you can do is your best and I think it's coming up to scratch.'

'I'm ready,' said Grace, rustling her way through the kitchen to the patio doors in a pair of pink ski trousers and a matching pink and cream ski jacket, carrying the blue snow boots at arm's length.

'You look very smart,' I said, patting the outside of my heavy wool red coat; it wasn't exactly snow-proof and was still quite soggy after the walk home from school.

'Do you want to borrow something?' asked Nate. 'I've got another ski jacket. It will be a bit big for you, but it will keep you warm and dry.'

199

Chapter 17

Getting dressed had been like preparing for an expedition to the Arctic, which was ridiculous considering the postage stamp sized patio garden.

'Close your eyes, Viola,' said Grace when we were finally all kitted out and ready for the off. There'd only been a little bit of grumbling about the blue boots again.

Nate and Grace began whispering as we stepped outside.

'Really?'

'Yes,' she said. 'There's a surprise.'

'OK.'

Nate took one hand and Grace the other.

'Keep them shut tight. No peeping,' she instructed in her bossy little voice.

'There are a couple of steps here, five in total,' said Nate, now cradling my elbow. 'One. Two. Three. Four. Five. A few more steps forward.'

Robbed of my sight, my ears strained. Apart from Grace's little excited pants, the rustle of our breathable, waterproof super fabrics and the crunch of our feet on the snow, there wasn't a sound. It was difficult to believe we were in the middle of a busy city.

'You can look now,' said Grace, tugging at my hand as if trying to open my eyes herself. 'Look.'

I opened my eyes. Stretching out ahead was a pure white blanket edged with the shadows of snow-laden foliage. 'Oh, my goodness. Is this all yours?'

Nate laughed. 'I earn well, but not that well. It's a communal garden.'

Of course it was. Notting Hill was famous for them, although most people thought of the gated and fenced parks as featured in the famous film, but many were tucked away out of sight behind the houses.

'It's beautiful.' I glanced down at Grace. 'And perfect for snowmen – you've got enough snow here for a whole snow family.'

'Shall we start with one?' suggested Nate, looking a little worried. 'It's quite late.'

Nate began to roll a ball of snow and I showed Grace how to get started and between us we began to roll a ball, collecting snow as we went, leaving a green path in our wake.

'You can do the main body,' I said, watching Nate stop to rest for a second.

'Funny, that. Leave the big job to me.'

It was harder work than I remembered and I had to keep steering Grace, otherwise the ball would have been a very funny shape. After a while she started to get bored, so I suggested she find some twigs under the trees for the snow-man's arms, which she much preferred the idea of, running away and laughing as she knocked the snow from the leaves of the low-hanging branches of the small trees lining the garden.

'Gosh, I'm kn- tired out,' said Nate, stopping for another breather just a few feet in front of me, his breath billowing out in plumes of steam. Snow dusted his bare head and he shook it off and wiped a gloved hand across his dark brows, where the odd flake had also collected. 'Do you think it's big enough?'

'Do you worry about that often?' I asked with a mischievous grin at him.

There was a beat before he answered airily, 'No, I'm quite confident in my own attributes. There haven't been any complaints to my knowledge.'

'Good to know,' I said equally airily, trying not to laugh as I gave my outsize ball a push towards him and what was going to be the bottom half of one heck of a big snowman.

'That's one big head,' said Nate, his voice as dry as dust.

I turned away to swallow a giggle and felt a thud on the back of my head along with the explosion of snow and a cascade of ice work its way down between my scarf and my neck.

'Oi!' I yelled, whipping round to find Nate with both arms clamped to his sides like a toy soldier, an expression of unholy innocence on his face.

I narrowed my eyes at him.

'What?' he asked, his eyes ridiculously wide, his mouth already twitching.

'There is no one else here?' I said.

'Grace.'

I burst out laughing at his deadpan expression.

'You're accusing your own daughter. That's low.'

'Merely stating the facts.' There was a quirk to his lips.

I laughed and cautiously turned to where she was foraging in the trees. I wasn't giving him the chance to sneak another snowball in.

Tipping my head to one side, I gave him an appraising stare. 'I don't think her aim is quite that accurate or she has the strength to throw this far.'

'That would be supposition.' Amusement twinkled in his eyes as he took a step forward.

'Really? You're playing that card.' I squared up to him and took a step forward as well.

'Absolutely.' He took another step. I could see the snow crystals glittering on his face and fine drops of water on his eyelashes.

'I'd still say you are the prime suspect.' I had to tilt my head to look up at him as the clouds of steam from our breath merged.

'Mmm –' his voice was silky and a little shiver of awareness fluttered in the base of my belly '– that's a reasonable conclusion. However, I would still contend there is no firm evidence. Innocent until proven guilty.' Our quiet conversation in the snow-brightened, sound-deadened night seemed to resonate with intimacy.

'Or until I catch you in the act,' I said, my voice unaccountably throaty. I didn't mean it to come out like that but instinct had taken over.

'There is that,' he said gravely, quiet amusement still dancing in his dark brown eyes.

I swallowed. There was a thickness in the air. Desire? Longing?

Now we were just looking at each other. We'd both run out of things to say. I saw him swallow, look at my mouth, swallow again.

Just one kiss. One kiss. Would it be so bad? I couldn't help it, I parted my lips. An invitation. Held my breath as he stepped forward again. His eyes slid right, very briefly, over my shoulder.

And he kissed me!

The touch of cold lips startled as much as thrilled me, then the warmth of his breath when he exhaled. A hand on my waist steadied me as I lifted my mouth. We kissed again, a more confident touch this time, his mouth moving over mine, and inside I felt little pockets of happiness unfurl, in my chest, my stomach, my heart, my core, like a series of firecrackers. I needed that hand on my waist.

Nate sighed into my mouth like a surrender and deepened the kiss. My heart clenched as I felt his fingers grip my waist. They dug in with want. Our eyes were still open, looking at each other.

Then he pulled back, rested his forehead against mine for a brief second. 'Oh God, Viola.'

His fingers released my waist and he looked at me. The smoky desire was already fading.

'Sorry, I shouldn't have done that.' His eyes slid right over my shoulder. 'Not in front of Grace.'

Guilt pinched hard at me. I'd completely forgotten her for those few seconds. 'Sorry,' I whispered back.

We both turned to watch her; she was still dancing in the snowy shrubs like a small winter pixie in her bright red hat.

'You have nothing to be sorry about.'

I gave him a candid look. 'I wanted you to kiss me.'

He rubbed a hand through his hair and gave me a rueful smile. 'I've been wanting to kiss you since that first day on the tube.'

I smiled back at him, his words feeding the small glow lodged in my chest.

'I saw you before you got on the train. You looked so alive, bright and in love with life. As if there could be an adventure around the very next corner. Then that woman barged you. I was so angry with her, it shocked me. And then I was worried you were hurt and that shocked me even more.'

'I have a confession to make.'

'You do? You do realise it may be taken down as evidence?'

'When I . . . I . . . er . . . rammed you at the Opera House, I was . . . well, I decided I couldn't let you walk away. I was . . . er . . . sort of running after you.'

'A novel way of showing your interest.'

'Oh –' I shrugged '– I thought that was quite subtle. I usually just club men over the head and drag them back to my cave.'

He laughed, the sound echoing around the houses circling the garden, and Grace looked up and waved.

'I've got some arms,' she called. 'Look.' She came running over, weaving from side to side waving a stick in each hand like crazy antennae. Both Nate and I grinned at her joyous zigzag progress across the virgin snow.

'Perfect,' I said as she reached me, her cheeks pink and her eyes bright with excitement. 'These will be absolutely perfect. Let's help Daddy put the body onto the bottom and then all we need to do is roll a small ball for the head.'

'We're going for the three-tier approach?' said Nate.

'Yes!' I said. 'With this much snow all to ourselves, of course we are.'

'That's what Olaf looks like,' said Grace, ''cept we don't have a carrot.'

'Olaf another time. This can be . . . Mr Snow.'

She clapped her hands in delight as we began to assemble the snowman. Once he was in situ I handed out the lids of the empty spice jars I'd pinched from the utility room while Grace and Nate were changing. With a sharpie I'd found in the pen pot on top of the fridge I'd drawn half circles on the inside of two lids, which made very effective if quite comical eyes. I'd coloured the rest of the lids in to make three buttons and I'd sliced up a Washington Red apple to make a pair of ruby-red lips in the absence of a carrot.

Nate lifted a wriggling and giggling Grace to put the black hat on the top as the final touch and we stepped back to review our handiwork.

'Take a picture of me and Mr Snow,' said Grace, standing next to the snowman and putting her arms around him. 'We can send it to Mummy. It's the best snowman ever. Do you think she'll like it?'

Nate hesitated and I could see the conflict in his eyes, torn between telling Grace what she wanted to hear and not lying to her.

'It is the best snowman I've ever seen,' I said. 'Can you send me the picture?' It would make a lovely Christmas card for Nate and Grace.

He shot me a grateful smile.

'I think we deserve champion snowman-building medals and hot chocolates,' I said.

Nate carried Grace back into the snug looking pink and cosy, bundled up in a grey rabbit onesie. While he'd been upstairs bathing her, I'd made us all hot chocolates and was standing by the wood-burner thawing out my extremities, hoping my damp jeans might warm through a little as I watched the glowing logs flickering black and orange.

'We got a snow day,' she said, bouncing in her dad's arms. 'No school tomorrow.'

'Really?'

'I had a phone call from Mrs Roberts, wanting my opinion on whether to close the school. And then, not long after that, an official text saying the school will be closed for the day. Too many teachers have to drive in; they might not have enough staff.'

'No school! No school! And Daddy's going to work from home. Will you read me a story?' she asked, waving a book as she slithered down out of his arms and skidded over to my side, hopping up on the sofa beside me. I was surprised to see it was one of the *Harry Potter* books.

'Not *Beast Quest*?'

She shook her head. 'No, I've read it lots of times before. I thought I'd try something new,' she said in a prim little voice, sounding very grown-up.

She snuggled in, deliciously warm and smelling of roses. I handed her a small mug of very milky hot chocolate and she wrinkled her nose.

'No marshmallows or cream?' she complained.

'Not this close to bedtime. You'll be too full of sugar and you won't sleep,' I said.

'Hmph,' she said, her mouth crumpling in disgust. 'Daddy's got them.'

'Daddy didn't have half a packet earlier,' I said gently.

'I think Daddy missed out,' said Nate, poking mournfully at his marshmallows as he sat down on the sofa on the other side of Grace, propping his feet up on the coffee table towards the wood-burner. 'I only got three.'

'Never mind. We can go to the shops again tomorrow,' said Grace, patting him on the knee.

'I'm so glad I don't have to go to work tomorrow,' I said, looking out of the window. The snow hadn't let up and while Nate had taken Grace upstairs I'd taken the pile of soggy, wet clothes and snow-encrusted boots into the utility room and hung all the clothes up on the old-fashioned Sheila Maid hanging above the washing machine. I wasn't looking forward to having to walk home in this. My red wool coat was still damp even though it was hanging up next to the boiler.

Almost as if he'd read my mind, Nate said, 'I'm not sure you should walk home in this on your own tonight.'

'It's not far.'

'It might not be but I'd rather you weren't alone. I'd offer to walk you . . . but I can't leave Grace and it would asking for trouble to get the car out in this, even if it is a four-wheel drive. I don't trust the other idiots on the road.'

'God, no. It's fine.'

'The streets will be deserted. If you fall or get into trouble . . . Bad people don't stay indoors because of the snow.'

Thanks, Nate, for reminding me of my earlier unease.

'You could stay here. There's a spare room and there are –' he paused '– things you could borrow.'

Elaine's things.

'You could have a sleepover,' said Grace, her eyes shining.

'I . . .'

The thought of putting my damp coat on and tramping through the dark, deserted streets wasn't terribly appealing and neither was going back to my flat. I was being weak-willed. I shouldn't stay. I was starting to feel far too much at home here and ill-advised butterflies were doing a low-level fly-by in the pit of my stomach.

'Please, Viola. Stay and we can build Mrs Snow in the morning. And buy more marshmallows.'

Nate didn't say a word, he just stared down at his hot chocolate, the ghost of a smile on his face.

'And you can put me to bed,' added Grace, blinking at me with pitiful puppy dog eyes, making me laugh at her and put her in a mock headlock.

'You're such a fraud, Grace Williams.'

'I know,' she said simply, which made me laugh even more.

I sighed and looked at Nate, who now raised his head, an

almost bland expression on his face apart from the tiny tell-tale lift of the left side of his mouth.

'Thank you for the invitation Nate.' I kept my words formal because it felt too normal to be staying. It felt right and it shouldn't. 'If you don't mind I will take you up on your kind offer because I really don't fancy walking home on my own in this weather, and my coat's still quite damp.'

'I think it's for the best,' he said, as if we were talking health and safety or something equally dull. 'I'll just go check the heating is on in the . . . spare bedroom and that there are some towels in the bathroom.'

While he disappeared, I opened Grace's pristine copy of *Harry Potter and the Philosopher's Stone* and began to read her the first chapter.

As good as the story was, even with my best Dursley villain voices, it wasn't long before I felt Grace's body relax next to mine and her head slide down my arm. Nate, sitting opposite in the armchair by the wood-burner, was reading some paperwork but had been looking up and checking how she was doing periodically. I caught his eye and he tilted his head to see her face.

'Her eyes are closed,' he mouthed.

I nodded at him and he rose to his feet and came over to scoop Grace up into his arms. 'Come on pumpkin, bedtime.'

A sudden lump filled my throat as I looked at her little legs and skinny ankles dangling over his arm. She was so small and vulnerable it made my chest hurt.

Her eyes fluttered open and she held out a hand. 'You come too, Viola.'

Unable to swallow for a minute, I stared at her, mute, until she gave me an unaffected sleepy smile. My heart melted right into a puddle and I rose to my feet and squeezed her hand.

I followed Nate up the stairs to her bedroom, where the fairy lights were glowing and a small nightlight guided us in to her bed. He tucked her in and gave her a kiss.

'Love you, pumpkin.'

'Love you, Daddy.' After laying a gentle hand on her forehead, he rose and stepped back and went to the door as if giving Grace and I a moment to ourselves.

'Night, night, sleep tight. Don't let the bed bugs bite,' I whispered, sitting on the edge of the bed. I leaned forward and dropped a kiss on her cheek. 'Sweet dreams, sweet pea.'

'Night, night, Viola.' She sighed and settled into her pillow, her hand on the cheek I'd just kissed, her eyes already closed, and whispered, 'I love you.'

I joined Nate at the door and together we looked at her in the small glow of the lamp before he pulled it to. I guessed this was what parents did.

'She's bushed,' he said quietly. 'Do you want me to show you your room?'

Still too choked to speak, I nodded and followed him to the end of the hallway. He opened a door to a magnificent room with expensive-looking floral wallpaper with lush, exotic blooms in shades of pearl and green and billowing plump curtains in exactly the same shade of green.

'Crikey, is that an Emperor-size bed or something?' I asked, turning and spotting the biggest bed I'd ever seen.

'Or something,' said Nate dryly. 'It took four men to get the sodding mattress up here.'

'This is a beautiful room,' I said, feeling I ought to say something complimentary, even though, despite the size of it, it felt claustrophobic, as if the walls might close in at any second. There was something decidedly creepy about the wallpaper, with its suggestive erotic undertones and dark shadows hinting at hidden voyeurs.

'I hate it, always have done. Never felt comfortable in here. I think I always had a fear that one of those bloody plants would come to life one night and wrap its vines around me and squeeze me to death like a boa constrictor.'

'Thanks,' I said. 'Now I'll be having nightmares.'

'Sorry. Overactive imagination. Not my usual style. I promise you the wallpaper is really quite benign. It was probably the stress of my marriage breaking up.' It was obvious that this had been his and Elaine's room.

'The bathroom's very nice,' he said.

'No serpents in the S-bends or spiders under the toilet seats?'

'No, the bathroom is . . . good. I had a say in . . . I had a say in choosing the shower. I miss it. The best one in the house.'

'Now you sound like an estate agent,' I teased. 'And how many showers do you have?'

'Three,' he said almost apologetically. 'Not including the one in the nanny flat. One in each of the en suites and one in the family bathroom.

'There are fresh towels in here –' he pointed to the door

to the en suite '– and toiletries. And a robe on the back of the door. If there's anything else you need, have a look in the drawers. Help yourself.'

With that he withdrew, leaving me in the overpowering jungle environment. He'd sounded matter-of-fact and practical about me borrowing things but I felt uncomfortable about wearing any items of clothing that belonged to Elaine. The snow boots had been practical emergency and something kept in a cupboard downstairs didn't feel as intimate as something from one of her bedroom drawers. Even though I hadn't met her I had an acute dislike of her but I couldn't gauge how Nate felt about her. Was he heartbroken? Still in love with her? I feared he was resigned to her absence and in some kind of no-man's-land love limbo.

I sank onto the bed, hearing the luxurious rustle of the feather duvet with some mighty tog rating. With a heavy sigh, I surveyed the room; my jeans were damp and heavy and my legs were still cold. A hot shower seemed like heaven but the thought of putting my jeans back on afterwards miserable. Perhaps if I warmed them on the radiator while I was in the shower it might be bearable.

Chapter 18

'Would you like a glass of wine?' Nate looked up as I padded, wearing his socks, back into the kitchen, carrying my jeans and, hidden from view, my hurriedly washed knickers. There was a bottle of red on the kitchen island and one glass already poured with a second waiting.

'That would be lovely, thank you.'

'I'd offer you some cheese but the cupboard is bare.'

'Wine will do, thanks.'

'Nice outfit.' He studied the turn-ups on the oversized sweat pants I was hanging onto with one hand before pouring me a glass and handing it to me.

I glanced down at grey fleecy sweats, which I'd been very grateful to find after my shower.

'Sorry, my legs were so cold I needed to warm up. Would you mind if I shove these in the tumble dryer? I didn't feel right borrowing Elaine's things and these were in one of the drawers. I figured you weren't using them.'

'I'd forgotten I'd got them. They're "designated" gardening or decorating clothes.'

I raised an eyebrow. 'Do you garden or decorate?' The sweatshirt I was wearing felt quite new and soft.

Nate snorted. 'No, it's a euphemism for Elaine didn't like me wearing them and we always got a man in to do any decorating, even though I don't mind doing a bit of painting. She didn't trust me to do it right. Although I'm happy to leave the gardening to the professionals, we pay a fee to cover the garden maintenance. I think it would take me all Saturday to mow that lawn.'

'That communal garden is a lovely thing to have, though,' I said with a touch of envy. The stairs up to pavement level was the only bit of outdoors I had access to. 'Do you all get together in the summer and have barbecues and summer parties out there? I bet it's great for Grace. Completely safe.'

'Today's the first time I've been out there in months.' Nate looked shame-faced. 'And Grace. I don't think Svetlana ever went out there. And we don't really know the other people who use the garden. I've hardly ever seen anyone else out there; people tend to stay close to their own patio areas, I guess.'

'That's such a shame. To have your own private space in London, people would kill for that. Although I guess it means Mr Snow won't get vandalised any time soon.'

'There is always that,' said Nate, lifting his glass in toast. 'To snowmen.'

I took a sip of the meaty red wine. 'This is nice.'

'It's a Cab Sauv I've been saving. As no one has to get up in the morning, it seemed the right occasion to open it.'

I felt a ping. He'd remembered.

'I forgot to tell you, you've created a monster. I think my mother is on series three of *Game of Thrones* already.'

'I take it you're not staying there any more.'

'No, Dad is back. And, thanks to you again, Mum is ploughing through her Christmas shopping. Now, if you could just solve my turkey problem.'

'Turkey problem?'

'Yes, apparently I've left it too late to order the right sort from the butcher. We always use Lidgates on Holland Park Avenue and we always get a Kelly Bronze. The deadline was Monday and with everything going on, I completely forgot.'

With a sigh, I put down my wine glass. 'I wish it would keep snowing and everyone got snowed in.' And I could stay here, warm and snug, without all the problems I still had to solve. And stupidly, out of nowhere, a tear welled up in my eye.

'Hey.' He came around the island and put his arms around me, pulling me into his chest. 'I'm pretty sure Sainsbury's, Marks & Spencer and a whole load of other people do turkeys. Come the day, is anyone going to complain?'

'No, I'm being silly,' I sniffed into his soft lambswool sweater, but he'd done that fatal thing of being nice when he should have given me some tough love and told me to pull myself together. Somehow the combination of softness, the broad chest and sympathy tipped me over the edge and, like an avalanche, all the things I'd been worrying about came flooding down, gathering pace, getting bigger and bigger.

'I . . . I . . .' It was no good, I began to cry. Proper hiccoughy sobs with unladylike sniffs and a runny nose. 'It's the n-nat-tiv-vity as well.' I buried my head in his chest. 'Parents are complaining. George, who's playing the lead, is off school, apparently gone to Disneyland and is probably going to be snowed in in Paris for another week; I haven't got props, the costumes are going to be rubbish and there's no backdrop. It's going to be a disaster. I think this is going to be the worst Christmas ever!' I finished on a wail, drawing in a much needed breath.

Nate rubbed my back as my sobs slowed and between sniffles I gradually managed to get control of myself again.

'Come and sit down,' he said, leading me to and settling me into the sofa. He tossed a new log on the fire and came to sit next to me.

'Sounds like you've got a lot on your plate.'

I took in a snuffly breath and looked at him, feeling as woebegone and pathetic as Grace had been the other day. 'Yes.'

'Viola, you can ask for help, you know.' He said it in such a calm, obvious way, I pushed back all the panicky fear and actually focused on what he'd said instead of the usual quick denial that sprang to my lips.

'It's like that saying, how do you eat an elephant? One bit at a time. You've let everything build up, a bit like a snowball running down a hill, getting bigger and bigger.'

We both looked outside to the snowy backdrop and I gave him a weak, sniffly smile, now a little embarrassed at letting myself go.

'Sorry, I'm not normally such a wimp . . . It just all got on top of me. Mum. The nativity and a piece that I should have been practising every day and I haven't. Normally, I never let anything get in the way of work. I need to practise every day. I've been too busy firefighting to stop and think what I really need to do.'

'You've got family and there's an army of parent volunteers at the school; they can help.'

'Will they? All they've done so far is complain.'

'They're not representative of all the parents, I promise you.'

'Hmph,' I said, not sure he was right there.

'I'm a great believer in lists. Seeing things written down helps. Then you can see each thing on its own and work out a strategy to deal with each one.' He rose and a second later returned with a notepad and pen.

'Right, top of the list. Turkey or nativity?'

'Nativity.'

'OK and what can you do, what you can ask other people to do and what is out of your control.'

'George is out of my control. If he doesn't come back on Monday I'll have to give his part to someone else.'

'See, you've solved that already. What next?'

'Costumes. Particularly the animals. I can see why Mrs Davies got a donkey in. I need masks or something so people know they're cows or sheep or oxen.' Then I sat up straighter. 'Oh my God, I'm so stupid. Tilly and Leonie. And . . . why didn't I think of this before?'

I leaned forward and kissed Nate on the cheek. 'You're brilliant.'

'Not sure what I've done, but I'll always take a "brilliant" and a kiss.'

I put up a hand to my suddenly burning face. 'Oh God, sorry, that was a bit . . .' It had just felt so natural and normal, I hadn't even stopped to think.

He took my hand and gave it a quick squeeze before putting it back in my lap. 'I'm not complaining but . . . I guess we need to talk about . . .' a faint flush stained his cheeks '. . . things.'

I dropped my head. I knew what was coming. The kiss in the garden. Where did that put us now? He'd made things quite clear before. Had we just got a bit carried away outside? The magic of the snow. There was Grace to consider . . . and he was officially still married. And he'd told me on day one that he wasn't in the right place for a relationship at the moment.

'I'm sorry. I shouldn't have kissed you . . .'

'Don't . . . it's fine. The snow. It makes everything . . . well, you know. It was the heat . . .' I tried to lighten things '. . . or rather the cool of the moment.'

He nodded, studying the wine in his glass, saying without looking up, 'Yes . . . but I shouldn't have . . . especially not when Grace could have seen us.'

A flush of shame washed over my face as I remembered that in that moment I'd completely forgotten her.

Worse, now I remembered parting my lips and gazing up at him. I'd pretty much thrown myself at him.

'I shouldn't have . . . It was . . .' he blushed '. . . lovely but . . . I shouldn't have.' With a swallow he looked down at his hands before lifting his eyes, a look of guilt clouding them.

'Let's just put it down to a *Frozen* moment,' I said with a glib smile before adding briskly, 'Give me that pen and I'll start making my lists. You're right, dividing everything up into manageable bits will help. I don't know why I got myself into such a state. Sorry for breaking down on you like that. Stupid really. It's only a school nativity play. Everything will be all right on the night.' I was babbling.

Nate stared at me for a moment, his eyes grave and thoughtful, before he nodded and handed over the pen in a movement that closed off the brief moment between us as effectively as a pair of scissors snipping at a thread.

'Sounds like you're feeling better already,' he said, glancing towards some papers on the coffee table. 'Do you mind if I do a bit of work? With this snow, I think tomorrow might be a write-off.'

'No, no problem.' I nodded towards the pad of paper. 'I've got plenty to think about.'

Despite that brief awkwardness, the rest of the evening passed in companionable silence, which would have been nice if I hadn't been so aware of him sitting quietly next to me, turning the odd page, his brow creased in concentration. Every now and then I sneaked a glance at his handsome profile, almost unable to help myself. And every time I did the annoying insistent memory of that kiss popped back into my head and I could almost feel the soft graze of his lips and the gentle sandpaper brush of bristles on my skin. I was relieved that he seemed completely absorbed and didn't catch my frequent sidelong glances.

This was a friendship of sorts, I told myself, and that was all Nate wanted and I had to remember it, instead of letting my wayward hormones take the lead. And there was Grace to consider. She needed a friend, someone who cared about her wants and needs and not about their own inappropriate fantasies about her too-handsome-for-his-own-good father.

With a small internal sigh I forced myself to focus on my list and all the things I needed to do over the next week, determined not to give in and look at Nate again.

Chapter 19

I woke to a small cold pair of feet poking into my thighs. Groggily, I turned over and opened bleary eyes. It was still dark, although the snow-reflected light crept through the curtains and I could just make out Grace, bright-eyed and extremely bushy-tailed, beaming at me from the pillow next to me.

'Viola! It's still snowing outside. Do you want some breakfast? Do you want some Weetabix?' Her cold feet wriggled against my legs. Seriously? This bed was huge. You could get a coachload of people in here.

'What time is it?' I mumbled, still sleep-befuddled.

'Morning.'

'Mmm.' My eyelids were still too heavy; they refused to stay open. I reached out and patted her arm and she wriggled closer. With a sigh, I put my arm around her. 'It's still early, Grace.'

'Yes, Daddy told me to go back to sleep. But I was bored. Do you want to watch *Frozen* with me?'

Daddy had the right idea.

'Not right now, sweetie,' I said, yawning, not wanting to disappoint her, but my body clock was telling me it was still the middle of the night. 'Your feet are cold.'

'Daddy said that too.'

'I wonder why,' I grumbled. 'You need bed socks or some slippers.'

'Hmph,' she said. 'Do you want to read me some more *Harry Potter*?'

'Not right now. How about later? Tell you what, if you let me sleep a bit longer I'll make pancakes for breakfast.'

'Pancakes! With Nutella!'

'Mmm.' At that moment I think I'd have promised her anything if she'd just let me sleep. Thankfully, with a wriggle and a bounce, she was gone and I fell asleep again, thinking I'd make a terrible mother.

The next time I woke it was to see the light streaming in from the landing and Grace creeping on exaggerated tiptoes with a cup of tea towards the bed.

'Good morning. Are you the tea lady?'

'Daddy made it.' She placed it very carefully on a coaster on the bedside table. 'We didn't know if you liked tea or coffee, but you only have to ask if you'd rather have the coffee.'

I could hear Nate's words in her carefully constructed sentence. Putting on the bedside lamp, I reached for my phone. Ten past eight. That felt a lot more acceptable.

Grace saw my face. 'Sorry I woked you up before. Daddy says five o'clock is far too early.'

'Daddy's right,' I said.

'And he said I mustn't get into your bed unless you say it's all right. Can I?' I suspected Nate's wording might have been a little different to that but I pulled back the cover.

'Hop in. But –' I paused and gave her a mock look of threat '– but you keep your cold feet to yourself, missy.'

She giggled and planted them straight on my stomach. I howled in protest and lunged for her and began tickling her and that was how Nate found us a few minutes later, rolling around the enormous bed, shrieking and laughing.

'I thought someone was being murdered,' he said, standing in the doorway.

Grace took the opportunity of me being diverted to jump on me and start tickling my ribs.

I laughed again. 'You're a monster.' I reared up and tickled her back.

She shrieked again, jumped off the bed and ran to hide behind her dad's legs.

'Yup, you've definitely bred a monster, with the coldest feet on the planet,' I said, pushing my hair out of my face, feeling a little hot and sticky. 'You just wait, Grace.' I pretended to make a move to get out of bed to chase her and she squealed and clung to Nate's legs.

'Save me, Daddy!'

Nate's eyes shone and I was shocked to realise that they were alight with unshed tears.

'I'm not sure. I think I should throw you and your cold feet to the hungry lions. Five o'clock, Grace Williams. Five o'clock and then you went and woke poor Viola.'

Grace hung her head.

'I think lions are too good for her,' I said. 'I think it's death by tickling.'

'I think you're right,' said Nate, bending quickly and

scooping her up to throw her back on the bed and advanced, waggling his fingers. 'Death by tickling.'

'No, no, no!' she squealed in between giggles as I pretended to hold her down.

Nate leaned over and managed to avoid her flailing legs and a kick to the jaw, to tickle her ribs, his face creased in laughter.

I had an idea that this definitely wasn't the sort of bedroom activity that whoever had designed this room had envisioned.

'Why don't we do that online shop later?' I asked as I stood in front of the fridge. 'Sorry, Grace, I'm going to have to renege on my pancake promise this morning; there aren't any eggs.' There wasn't much of anything in there.

'How about I take you ladies out for brunch?' suggested Nate.

'Can we go to Bluebelles?' pleaded Grace.

'That OK with you?' Nate asked me with a casual, easy smile as his daughter tugged on his hand, dancing around him as if he were her own personal maypole.

'As long as they have poached eggs, I'm easy,' I said, following his lead, laughing at Grace's antics.

'And while we're out we can stock up on some supplies for the short term.' Nate gave the pathetic contents of the fridge a rueful shake of his head. 'I don't suppose you'd like to come back for dinner? Grace and I can cook you a roast chicken, although I might ask if you could do Yorkshires.'

'Yes, yes, yes.' Grace chanted, abandoning Nate's hand and grabbing mine. 'Please, Viola.' She shot her dad a look. 'Although you make the best roast chicken in the whole wide world.'

I cocked my head at her, shooting Nate an eye roll. 'And is that based on your considerable roast chicken tasting experience? I'm sure Daddy's roast chicken is pretty good.'

She pulled a face and darted to the patio doors, pressing her nose against the glass. 'Can we make another snowman today?'

'Sorry,' said Nate in a low undertone. 'I've put you on the spot. You've probably got lots of other things you should be doing. That was a bit unfair.' He paused and gave me another one of his sweet, contrite smiles that always punched their way into my heart. 'I'm being selfish but it's . . . it's just so nice having you here. And you've done so much for us. I'd really like to make a meal for you.'

I lifted my head and stared at the corner of his mouth, wanting to kiss him for saying it. The truth was I didn't want to leave.

'I'd like that but . . . I do need to go back to my flat. I need to change and . . . I need to practise.' I waggled my fingers. 'I missed a day yesterday.'

'You could practise here.'

The idea was so tempting. My little music room was dark at the best of times and this house was so light and bright. It must have showed on my face.

'We could pick up your viola while we're out –' his eyes crinkled suddenly '– although I need to ask whether it will be safe. I hear they can be dangerous in the wrong hands.'

Everyone seemed to have had the same idea and Bluebelles was packed, with a festive air as if Christmas had already arrived. According to the news, nearly every school in London was shut and most offices were closed, with the advice not to travel unless absolutely necessary. More snow was predicted over the next twenty-four hours with temperatures dropping to minus four, so icy conditions were also anticipated.

The walk here had been strangely quiet with the cars piled with soft pillows of snow.

'Julia Roberts would have sorted that out,' Nate had said with a quick smile as we passed one of the private gated gardens, still pristine with a virgin blanket of snow begging for a stray footprint or a random snow angel.

Kensington Park Road was almost bereft of traffic, the few cars driving at a snail's pace in the heavy slush and the gorgeous stylish shops were for once sluggish and quiet, some still closed, as if the snow had spread its calming influence and decreed that today was worth taking things slow and easy. It was a little busier when we turned right onto Westbourne Park Road and there was a delighted gaggle of tourists taking pictures of the famous blue door immortalised in *Notting Hill*. Turning onto Portobello Road, we hurried on up the street and under a strangely quiet Westway, just starting to feel the cold when we arrived at Bluebelles.

'I'm going to have French toast, the Chocky Road,' announced Grace before I'd even picked up the menu. 'It's really yummy here. I don't like the other place.' She waved a dismissive arm, narrowly missing the back of the head of a woman sitting directly behind her. It was definitely cosy this morning. The three of us were wedged into a corner at a small square table.

When I looked at the menu, I could see why it was so busy in here and I realised how hungry I was. 'Ooh, the Bangers Breakfast sounds delicious, I adore caramelised onions, but then so does the Royale, I love smoked salmon.' Which put another thought into my head. I pulled out my phone and opened up the notes app. 'That's another thing I mustn't forget. Smoked salmon – we always have it on Christmas Day with cream cheese and bagels for breakfast with bucks fizz.'

'That sounds nice.'

'We have yukky green stuff,' muttered Grace, pulling a yuk face. 'And smelly stuff.'

'We had smashed avocado, smoked salmon and poached eggs on sourdough last year,' explained Nate. 'Elaine's parents were with us.'

'It was horrible,' said Grace. 'But Granny liked it and Mummy told a fib. She said she made—'

'Grace . . .' Nate's tone held a warning note.

'Well, she did.' Grace's indignation was written all over her face. 'I saw the box – the green stuff came fr—'

'I don't think Viola needs to know.'

Grace gave him a mutinous look but at his firm tone shut her mouth in a straight flat line, glaring up at him from under her lashes.

'I'm going to have a stack,' said Nate, pointing to the variation on a classic English breakfast, which sounded equally appealing.

'Hmm, now I'm torn. I'd missed that,' I said with a sudden hankering for crispy bacon and sausage.

Grace was picking at the table with her fingernail, injustice still burning in her eyes.

'What are you going to have to drink, Grace?' I asked with a kind smile. I understood how she was feeling but Nate was her dad and he was in charge. Children needed boundaries and he was responsible for setting them, not me. 'Hot chocolate, orange juice?'

'Please can I have a hot chocolate?' she asked with a sidelong glance at Nate.

'Course you can,' he said. 'I bet it won't be as good as Viola's.'

'No.' Grace beamed and all was forgotten, or so I thought until she added with a sly glance at Nate, 'You're really good at hot chocolate and cooking and everything.'

'Mmm, I'm not so sure about that,' I said. 'I can do the basics. So, what do you fancy eating next week?' I pulled out a piece of paper and together the three of us planned the following week's menu, ready for our online shopping expedition.

'Be careful,' I said to Grace as I went down, step by careful step, to my basement flat. The stairs were steep at the best of times but with the addition of a good ten inches of snow they were even more treacherous.

Although Nate had done his best to dissuade her, Grace had insisted on accompanying me back to my flat, so all three of us were now inching down the stairs.

'It's like a little cave,' said Grace delightedly, as I pushed open the front door and flicked on the light switch. The door opened straight into my front room and as I stepped in my breath puffed out in a big icy steam that immediately filled me with foreboding.

'Come in, I won't be a minute.'

Grace immediately stepped inside and, without any sense of inhibition, crossed to the mantelpiece to study the photos in the frames I had arranged there.

Nate was far more circumspect. He stood with his arms behind his back, an almost respectful pose, and gave the room a polite once-over. Following his quick gaze, I looked at the room with fresh eyes. There was nothing to be ashamed of; he might have a beautiful home but it wasn't as if I were broke or anything. I had some lovely pieces of furniture; the sofa was a particular possession of pride – I'd got it in Heal's in the sale after hankering after it for months. It was uphol-stered in deep teal silk velvet and piled with gorgeous appliquéd cushions featuring a peacock design with fabulous iridescent sequins that mirrored the teal colour. They'd cost a fortune but were worth every penny. On the pale cream walls, because white felt too stark, I had a couple of gorgeous pictures, painted by a friend of mine who'd gone to St Martin's and was now a set designer for the Old Vic.

'It's freezing in here,' said Grace, stamping her feet. 'Oh, aren't they pretty.' She darted to the peacock cushions, drawn by the sequins, which she began to stroke.

I frowned; it was like an icebox and it shouldn't be. 'I think the heating must have gone off.' That was bad news, especially for my viola. The extreme cold wasn't good for the wood or the strings.

Nate crossed to the radiator under the window. 'Not on.'

'Oh, he . . . heck. I hope the pilot light hasn't gone out or anything.'

'Want me to take a look?'

I looked at him in surprise.

'What? I do have some practical skills, you know. I'm not a complete dilettante.'

'Sorry, I didn't . . .' But I had. I'd assumed that Nate was a suited and booted professional who wouldn't know one end of a hammer from the other.

'When I had my first flat I had a very temperamental boiler. Gertie. Cantankerous creature she was.'

I stared. This again was not a side to Nate I'd suspected.

'Let's take a look. Where's your boiler?'

'In the kitchen.' I led him through to the open-plan kitchen diner. It was a lovely room and I was pleased with the new units that I'd had put in a couple of years ago, but because it was in the central part of the flat the only natural light came in from the window at the very end, so it was always quite dark.

Nate looked at the boiler while I went to my music room. My viola case was icy cold and when I opened the case the glossy body was very cold. I closed it again, latching the case and hugging it to my body as if that might warm it up, before picking up my sheet music case and my folding stand which I kept on standby because I never knew when it might come in handy. Today being a case in point.

'This is where the magic happens, is it?' asked Nate, poking his head through the doorway.

'I'm not sure about magic. But I've put quite a few hours in here.'

'It's compact.'

'It is . . . for a second bedroom.'

'Seriously, the agents tried to sell it on that?'

'They tried. But luckily it put a lot of people off. But it was perfect for me.'

'How long have you lived here?'

'Just over five years. I occasionally think about moving but this room doesn't back onto any neighbours and for some reason it's exceptionally well sound-proofed between floors, so I can practise whenever I want without disturbing anyone.'

'So what's the verdict on the boiler?'

'The pilot light has gone out and I'm afraid I can't get it back on. You're going to have to call a heating engineer. Do you have a tame plumber on tap?'

'Was that a deliberate pun?' I asked with a groan.

'No, but it can be if you like.'

'Hmm. I'll give Mike a call. He's a mate of my cousin Bella. He does the annual service for me.'

'Shall I make a cup of tea while you call him?'

'I don't think we want to hang around in here too long, do you? It's almost as cold inside as outside. God knows how long the heating's been off.' I hoped my pipes wouldn't freeze.

Mike picked up straight away and talked me through various diagnostics and possible solutions, none of which tempted the pilot light back into life.

'Think your . . .' I didn't quite catch the word '. . . has gone. It'll take me a couple of days to get the spare part. Monday.'

'Monday?' I echoed in horror. 'You can't get here any earlier?' I clutched my viola to me. I needed to practise.

'No, like I said, it needs a part. Today's Friday. With next day delivery that's Monday. They don't do weekends. And I've got emergencies stacked up. Old folks living on their own. Can't you go stay with your folks for a couple of days or Bella's? Sorry, this weather has been a killer, I'm completely chocka. At least you've got somewhere to go. I'll get to you on Monday . . . if I can but I can't promise. I'll text you Monday morning. But it might not be until Tuesday.'

'OK, if it could be Monday, I'd be so grateful.'

'You and the rest of west London, love.'

'Thanks, Mike.'

'Cheers.'

I switched off my phone.

'Not good news?'

'Nope. He reckons it needs a spare part which he can't get until Monday at the earliest and then he might not be able to get here until Tuesday.'

Nate lifted his shoulders. 'You're more than welcome to stay with us.'

'It's all right, I can go and stay at Mum's,' I said, even though the thought was already making my throat constrict. It would be fine. The neighbours were just going to have to put up with the noise. There was no way I could go another day without playing. I was probably being completely neurotic but I was sure I could already feel my fingers stiffening up.

With a raised eyebrow he studied my face. 'Is that what you really want to do? Where will you practise? There's plenty of room at ours. You can practise in a nice warm space. And if you're really worried about outstaying your welcome, you can cook for your supper. Win-win all round.'

I looked towards the lounge, where I could see Grace rearranging my candles for me on the little side table.

'I can't.'

'Why not?'

'Because . . .'

'We're two grown adults. And nothing's going to happen while Grace is under the roof, I promise you that.'

'I wasn't worried about that . . . It just feels a bit . . . soon.'

'Viola, it's bloody freezing in this flat. It's warm and cosy at mine. You'll be doing us a favour. Besides, you were coming back this afternoon anyway. And we're seeing you tomorrow, if you haven't forgotten, we're going Christmas tree shopping. That leaves Sunday, and you don't have to spend the day with us then; you can treat the place like a hotel if you like.'

The awful thing was that I was really, really tempted. I could already picture myself and my viola in the little back study room beyond the dining room, with the light pouring in through the big bay window.

'It's a sensible solution,' said Nate, his voice gentle. 'Am I worse than your mother?'

I shot a guilty startled look at him.

'Sorry, that was presumptuous of me, but I did notice she's rather a dominant character. You were a lot quieter, less Viola, when you were around her.'

'I could go to my cousin Bella's.'

'You can also be a glorified babysitter at mine.'

'Bella's all right,' I protested, but it was hard fighting a battle that I didn't really want to win.

'Or you can come to ours, where you can do as you like . . . well, apart from making Yorkshire puddings for us. Come on.' He stepped forward and lifted my chin with his hand, looking down into my eyes. 'I'd like to look after you. You've done so much for us. What have you got to lose?'

Chapter 20

We were all glowing rather rosily when we arrived back at Nate's house like a little band of Merry Men, with Nate carrying my holdall over his shoulder and a bulging Tesco bag in each hand, Grace marching along with my music stand and music portfolio bag and me carrying my viola case and another Tesco shopping bag.

Tesco had been bedlam, with empty shelves and people panic-buying as if we were about to be snowed in until after Christmas, but we'd managed to snag the all-important chicken, potatoes and a dozen eggs, so that dinner was assured as well as supplies to get us through the next few days. I have to say, Nate and Grace were dreadful shoppers. No wonder there was no decent food in the house.

It was just after two o'clock when we'd disrobed, hung all our wet things up in the utility room and put away all the shopping and I felt exhausted.

'I could do with a nap,' I said, sipping at a cup of tea, slumped at the breakfast bar. Nate was looking anxiously at his mobile phone.

'Everything all right?'

'Just work. There's a conference call in half an hour that I really ought to dial into.'

I frowned, not understanding the problem.

'I'm not expecting you to be my babysitter.'

'Nate, what would you do if I wasn't here? Grace would be perfectly happy watching *Frozen* for the ninety-nine millionth time.' I nudged her. 'Wouldn't you, trouble?'

She beamed at me. 'I've got a wobbly tooth. Look.'

I flinched as she waggled the tooth in my face. 'Eeuw,' I said as she laughed delightedly. 'Why don't you go and do your conference call and Madame Wobbly Tooth here and I will go up to the attic and check out the Christmas decoration situation? And then, when you've finished, if you could give me a couple of hours to practise that would be great.'

'What about my sheet for my costume?'

I exchanged a glance with Nate and smiled. 'I've had an idea about that. I'm calling in the cavalry.'

When Grace wrinkled her face in confusion, I added, 'I'm going to get by with a little help from some friends.'

Last night while I was having my little meltdown, when Nate had suggested making lists and breaking the tasks down, I'd had my lightbulb moment and realised that I was overlooking an obvious source of help. I worked for the London Metropolitan Opera Company, for goodness' sake, alongside world-renowned stage crew. I was friends with an extremely talented make-up artist who could face-paint donkeys, cows and sheep with one hand tied behind her back, a wardrobe lady who drove a sewing machine with the verve and speed of a Formula One racing driver and I knew any number of set and props people who could all pitch in to help. The parents of Notting Hill were in for a nativity they would never forget.

'Let's have a look and see what we've got,' I said, pulling the first big fifty-litre box marked *Xmas Decs – Blue & Silver, 2011, 2015, 2018* towards me. There were two more boxes the same size, marked *Red & Gold 2010, 2013, 2016* and *Nordic, 2012, 2014, 2017*. It seemed an awful lot of Christmas decorations. But then I guessed in this house you'd have a sizeable tree.

'Where do you have the tree normally?' I asked, opening the first box to find boxed sets of plain blue and silver glass balls in varying sizes, along with white strings of lights, dusted with what looked like ice crystals, and there were also lots of icicle-shaped decorations on silver strings. There was clearly a snow and ice theme going on here. I'd never had a themed tree in my life.

'In the hall by the stairs. It's a really big one,' said Grace, reaching for a silver ball and holding it up to the light.

'And do you have another one?'

Grace shook her head. 'No, just that one. But can I help when we get the tree?'

'Of course you can! And we could put it somewhere else, like in the snug. Then you can see it all the time, because that's where you spend the most time.'

'Can we?'

'Yes.' I smiled at her sudden enthusiasm. I loved having my tree in the lounge and at night switching the main lights off and just having the tree lights on. It seemed to make the room so much more cosy and special. At Bella's house the tree was always put up in the kitchen diner. To me it seemed a terrible waste to have a tree in the hall.

'So what happens on Christmas morning?' I asked, leaning back on my heels and studying the well organised box of decorations, loath to disturb them. If I was being cynical, the box felt like insta-tree, the sort of soulless decorated trees you see in department stores and restaurants that have been done by a team of decorators to ensure that everything co-ordinated with that year's theme.

'Father Christmas –' her eyes brightened '– comes and he leaves a stocking on the end of my bed.'

'And do you leave carrots and mince pies out for him?'

She shook her head, carefully nestling the silver ball back into its squeaky plastic packaging. 'Mummy doesn't want soot on the carpet.'

I snorted and Grace looked up in confusion. I couldn't help it, I shouldn't, but I had to laugh – it was hilarious. Making up imaginary reasons to avoid putting out food for an imaginary person.

'S-sorry,' I finally spluttered. 'I'd just never thought of that before.' I couldn't wait to tell Bella; she'd think that was funny.

'And what sort of things do you get in your stocking?' I asked. Mum had been hopelessly practical when it came to stockings: bottle openers, playing cards, pencil sharpeners and on one memorable occasional a vegetable paring knife. I was thirteen at the time. Despite the sensible bent of all my gifts,

I still remember the thrill of the lumpy stocking at the end of the bed.

'Pink things,' said Grace. Then she whispered, 'I don't really like pink.'

'Oh.' Nearly everything she wore out of school was in some shade of pink or cream or white. 'What's your favourite colour?'

'Purple,' she declared. Then, with a little frown, she added, 'And red –' followed by a pause '– and blue.'

There was plenty of scope there, suddenly I wanted to put together a stocking for her. Full of things she'd love: a couple of *Beast Quest* books, some purple ear muffs, a special Christmas tree decoration – Bella and I bought each other a new decoration every year – one of those Jelly Cat soft toys I'd seen some of the other little girls at school playing with, and that she'd had on her lap in the office that day, and perhaps some new wellies, the right size, although I wasn't sure I could stretch to Joules. There were usually some fun ones on Portobello Market. In fact there was a whole world of stocking inspiration there.

'Viola?' Grace waved at me.

'Sorry, I was busy thinking. So do you open your stocking with Mummy and Daddy?' Eek, was that wise, reminding her that things would be different this year? But I knew from staying at Bella's house – it had become a tradition because waking up there was far more fun than being on my own – that any chance of sleep after five on Christmas morning was a non-starter. Even at sixteen, Laura still climbed into bed with Mum and Dad and the two little ones to open her stocking.

Grace gave a little shrug. 'I have to wait until after breakfast.'

I did a double take and then regretted it. Every family was different; it was naughty of me to judge. But *after* breakfast – even at thirty I'd have expired with excitement and frustration.

'And what about the rest of the day – what do you do?'

'Mummy gets ready and I watch a DVD. I always get a new DVD in my stocking. Do you think Father Christmas knows there's a *Frozen II*?'

'He probably does, but I'm not sure it will be out on DVD in time for this Christmas.'

'Oh,' Grace sighed.

'But there must be other DVDs you'd like,' I said, rather pleased at this turn of conversation. I could get the inside track as to what she'd like.

'Hmm, Daddy and I saw *Toy Story 4*; I like *Toy Story* better. And have you ever seen *Finding Nemo*?'

'Yes, lots of times. With Ella and Rosa, when I babysit.'

'Can I meet them? Can they come and play one day?'

About to say a blithe yes, I suddenly paused, the question hitting me headlong in the chest, stirring up a flurry of second thoughts. It would so easy to say yes, of course, but a little thread of fear darted into my head. I was bowling along with all of this far too quickly and too easily. I'd only met Nate a couple of weeks ago and in truth I didn't really know him.

I sat back on my heels, feeling a little cold as practicality and logic intruded. There was no denying the attraction I felt for him, but had I let that blindside me? Had it given me a false sense of knowing him? Introducing Mum had been fine; she took people as she found them. She'd liked Nate but she'd exhibited no further curiosity about him or Grace. God, if I brought Bella here or introduced her kids, there'd be a thousand questions and I'd have to start thinking about things and what other people might think. Nate had made it clear that, despite the attraction between us, he couldn't and wouldn't act upon it. I understood his reasons, even if my stupid emotions weren't playing ball.

'We'll have to see,' I said, hating that I'd resorted to that miserable catch-all phrase. 'Do you have any cousins? Who else comes on Christmas Day?'

'Granny and Granddad come; they have a dog, Coco. She's cute but she sleeps a lot. I think she might be dead now.'

Her heartless deadpan tone made me laugh and ruffle her blonde curls.

'Right, well. There are plenty of decorations up here for us to raid but there are too many to bring down.' And I really didn't want to mess up the system. I was guessing that the dates on the boxes referred to the years that the decorations had had an official outing. And, to be perfectly blunt, these were the most boring Christmas decorations I'd ever seen. I had a much better plan. After lunch I'd phone my mum. Rather bizarrely, for someone so practical and unsentimental, she never threw anything away and last year she'd invested in a smaller artificial tree with new simpler decorations, saying that as I no longer lived at home it wasn't worth putting up a big tree, which meant all my childhood decorations were bound to be stored away in the storage cupboard in the basement of the apartment block.

'All done. Thanks, Viola,' said Nate, walking into the kitchen, where I was compiling the online shopping list along with my faithful assistant, who kept making very helpful suggestions as to what should go into the basket. I wasn't sure what Nate would say about the Coco Pops or the pack of Fun Size Mars Bars that she assured me were regular purchases.

'How was the conference call?' I asked quickly.

'Successful. I have a happy client and I think the other side are going to settle, which means no court case, no negative publicity and everyone can breathe easier.'

'Well, the boss and I have done the shopping list, but you might want to add some bits and bobs –' I paused and gave a quick sidelong glance to Grace and winked at her '– and check that certain things are approved items.'

Nate smiled. 'I'll do that.'

'Are you OK if I go up and . . .?' I nodded towards my viola case, which was open and lying in the dark corner of the dining area where the dining table used to reside. It was the cooler part of the room and I thought the safest place to gradually bring my viola back up to room temperature.

At his nod, I scurried forward to scoop up my baby.

'You look happier already,' teased Nate.

I shrugged, a little embarrassed, but it had been nearly two whole days now.

'Go,' he said, nodding towards the door, handing me my folding music stand and music.

'Thank you.'

As soon as I settled my chin into the chinrest and my fingers found their place on the fingerboard, I sighed and lifted my bow, making a few experimental notes and lapsing into an easy familiar piece from *La bohème*; it's a crowd-pleaser and always brings in bums on seats, so we perform it at least once a year. I played for myself for a few minutes, enjoying the lightness of the room amplified by the brilliance of the snow outside. From here I could see the communal garden and our solitary snowman, the black hat not so jaunty now that further snowfall had dimpled its brim and collapsed its crown.

After that I settled down to serious work, playing and replaying a tricky section of a new opera that I was due to perform in January. Although rehearsals didn't start until then, there wouldn't be many, three or four with the full orchestra, two Sitzprobe rehearsals with the singers and after that a few full stage rehearsals, so I needed to make sure I'd nailed the music well before we went into official rehearsal sessions. For something like *Nutcracker* or *La bohème*, I'd played them so often the music came easily, my fingers almost remembering the notes by themselves, but for this piece I needed to work hard so that by the time we got into rehearsal my playing would fit seamlessly with the rest of the strings.

When I finished, with a slight ache in my shoulder, I packed everything away, the sense of calm and all was right with the world enveloping me like a blanket. I was always like this if I went more than a day without putting in some practise hours. Now I felt so much better, the earlier panicky feelings of last night vanquished.

I pulled my phone out of my back pocket where it had been on silent and pulled faces at it, almost as if it was a little ticking time bomb in my hand. There were a slew of texts from Bella, which I'd been ignoring all morning. I was trying to justify to myself that I'd been busy rather than cowardly.

Snow day today. Do you want to come over? Ella and Rosa are desperate to build a snowman. And we're getting the tree tomorrow. Are you working? Or can you come? What time shall we go? Probably best if you come over in the morning first thing, then we can get it delivered and you can help the kids decorate it early evening if you have to go to work. I've got a ton of stuff to do so that will be perfect. Bx

I stared at the screen, irritated by what I realised was the usual subtext that she wanted me to entertain the children today and tomorrow.

Did you get my text? When are you coming over? Ella and Rosa starting to climb the walls and worried the snow will melt before you get here! Fat chance. Bx

Fun as it had been building a snowman with Grace, today I wanted to stay snug and warm and, by the looks of things, so did Bella.

Are you coming? Soup and bread for lunch? Actually could you grab one of those nice loaves from Gail's on your way? Bx

Then there were three missed calls, a minute apart from each other and one final text.

Girls very disappointed. 😟

My mouth dropped open and I stared at the screen, a white-hot flash of heat rushing through me. Cheeky cow. I actually got as far as typing in **WT** with stabby fingers before I managed to rein in my fury and thought better of it. *Breathe, Viola. Breathe.*

Part of me wanted to ignore the texts and just not reply but I also wanted to push back for a change and take a stand.

Sorry.

. . . no, not sorry. I wasn't even at the arse end of feeling vaguely sorry. Why was *I* apologising?

Busy today and tomorrow. See you soon.

Then I added **Vx** because it did look a bit bald and then looked at it again. OK, that was probably a bit abrupt but she needed to know that I was feeling aggrieved. Oh, God, was I being as passive aggressive as she'd been? So I added, **Hope the girls built their snowman.**

Maybe that was a bit snarky? I changed it to,

Hope you're all enjoying having fun in the snow. xxx

That was a bit better. Resolved, I pushed the send button and, with unusual firmness, switched my phone off.

In the meantime, I had a Yorkshire pudding batter to whip up.

Chapter 21

'This tree?' asked Nate, holding another one straight.

I shook my head. We were in the churchyard of the rather imposing St John's Church, where each year Pines and Needles set up shop bringing trees down from the Highlands. All the helpers were in jolly Santa hats, bundled up in several layers against the cold and seemed imbued with festive spirit. Today, after almost constant snow the day before, the sun had burst out as if to say *I'm back, you hadn't forgotten me had you?* The brilliant blue sky made a startling contrast against the thick layer of snow on the roofs as ice crystals twinkled in the sunshine. Lots of families were wandering around, with shiny-faced excited children dressed in thick gloves and bobble hats, darting about the paths between the piles of trees.

'This one?'

Again I shook my head and he pursed his lips but he hadn't yet reached the completely pissed-off-with-my-tree-deliberations stage, or at least I didn't think so.

There's an art to choosing a Christmas tree and, despite my parents' academic priorities, it had been one of our family traditions, including a Dad and daughter expedition to seek out exactly the right specimen, followed, when I was older, by a trip to the pub for a half of London Pride for Dad and a glass of the normally forbidden Coca Cola for me.

'After we've got the tree and before we go to get the decorations, would you like to go to the Churchill Arms? We can get a drink and something to eat. Do you know it?' I asked with a sudden touch of nostalgia; maybe I should have asked Dad to join us.

I was surprised to see incomprehension on Nate's face. Surely he'd heard of the Churchill Arms. It was a Notting Hill landmark all year round, famed for its exuberant outdoor displays of flowers, but at Christmas it came into its own. Grace would get a kick out of a visit there.

Nate shook his head. 'I don't. But I like the sound of a pint after a hard day's Christmasing. I had no idea finding a tree was going to be so much work.' He put his hands on his hips and shook his head with a mournful expression which made Grace burst into giggles.

'Daddy, you're silly. This is fun.'

'Hmph,' he said, tapping the bobble on the top of her hat. He singled out another tree. 'How about this one?'

'You're rubbish. Look.' It had a decided kink at the trunk a quarter of the way from the top, which I pointed out.

'Nate, darling. I thought it was you.' Like a hawk homing in on its prey, a woman swooped down, cutting in front of me – I'm not sure she'd even noticed me – grasping his arms and kissing him on both cheeks. 'How are you? We never see you these days!'

Oh, bums, I'd recognise that Cossack hat anywhere, even without the flowing blonde tresses cascading down her back.

'Hello, Zoe, how are you? Hello, Cassie.' Nate gave them both a good-natured smile. 'Out hunting for a tree?'

Angel-faced Cassie at her mum's side was in her own little Cossack hat and the two of them looked rather glamorous.

Zoe sighed. 'Not our main tree. Obviously that one's done professionally but Cassie and Hannah wanted one in their playroom and I thought why not. Hello, Grace, dear.

'We really must organise a play date for Grace and Cassie; it's been ages. And then you could stay for a glass of wine or something. It would be so super to catch up.

'Aren't you brave, tackling a tree on your own without a woman's touch?'

Nate beamed at me. 'Viola's in charge. I'm just doing the hunter gatherer bit and getting the tree. Decorating it is down to Viola and Grace.'

Zoe turned sharply. 'Oh . . .' there was an affected pause '. . . it's you.'

Her attempt to convey a mixture of surprise and curious enquiry failed but she nailed the hell out of Queen Bitch.

'The nativity girl. How lovely to see you.' Her sickly-sweet smile said anything but. 'I do hope it's going to come together in time.' Like heck she did.

With a coy look and a winsome smile at Nate, she added, 'You've set everyone quite a challenge on the costume front. I mean it's all right for us. I was lucky enough to find the most wonderful angel costume on a website and it was only thirty pounds. Cassie adores it; it's got the sweetest gold-trimmed wings. And we've found an adorable flashing wand that lights up with five different sequences. But I do feel for those poor children in the chorus and the animals. Just leggings and T-shirts. I think you're making a bit of a mistake there; parents are coming to see their children in the nativity. They want to see them in proper costumes.'

I nodded politely, which was quite a feat when I'd rather have scratched her eyes out.

'As long as the children enjoy themselves,' I said. 'That's the main thing.' I smiled down at Cassie, who was actually a little poppet. I wasn't sure, with a mother like this, how long that would last. 'Are you enjoying the singing?' I asked, giving Cassie a smile.

'Yeth,' she lisped. 'I really like *Away in a Manger* and I like that we all sing together. I don't like it when I have to sing on my own.'

'Don't be silly, Cassie,' snapped Zoe before turning to Nate, a malicious smile tipping at the edge of her mouth. 'And how is Elaine? Have you heard from her? Poor thing, she must be missing Grace dreadfully. The sacrifices that woman has made for her career. But she's doing it for the girls and I have to admire her.'

God, this woman was so fake. If she were Pinocchio, her nose would be about three feet long by now.

Nate gave her a tight smile. 'Nice to see you, Zoe, but we need to get on. Important work to be done; Grace here is very particular about her Christmas tree.' He winked at Grace, who beamed at him, her hands clasped together.

'I think I can see one, Daddy.' She grabbed his hand and

began dragging him to a section of trees which were a little bit smaller than the ones we'd been looking at. I followed them more slowly, feeling Zoe's narrowed eyes on my back.

'That one, Daddy.' Grace pointed, making Nate pull out a tree from the pile of trees against which it leaned.

'That looks good.' I grasped the needle-covered trunk and stood back to assess it. 'What do you think, Grace?'

She tilted her head and perused it with the grown-up concentration I'd become so familiar with. 'I think it looks perfect.'

Nate rolled his eyes and muttered something like, 'Same as the others,' under his breath. Grace gave him a dismissive look and mouthed, 'Men,' at me, which made me giggle and Nate roll his eyes again.

'We've got ourselves a winner,' I declared.

'Thank goodness for that,' said Nate but, despite his words, there was a twinkle in his eyes. 'Who knew choosing a Christmas tree was so complicated?'

'You'll thank me when you don't have to do battle with it, and the stand, trying to make it look straight or having to keep turning it round because it looks like it's leaning to the left or the right,' I said. Thank goodness I'd checked that there was a decent Christmas tree stand in the house. Before I'd convinced Dad to invest in one, I'd experienced a few too many makeshift attempts at securing trees in pots and buckets, which had invariably ended in disaster.

We took our contender to the big silver drums where a very jolly young Scot with big elf ears and the most gorgeous accent took charge and put the tree in the netting machine, tagged it with Nate's address and promised delivery in a couple of hours.

'Shall we look at the decorations?' I suggested. There was a fine selection for sale at the wooden cabin on site. Grace was captivated by the small display. 'And we could pop to Portobello Market to get some, before we go to the pub.' I glanced at Nate. This was turning into quite an expedition.

'Fine by me. It's nice to be out in the fresh air, especially in the sunshine. And we don't need to be anywhere until you go to work this evening.'

'Can we have some like that?' Grace asked, pointing to the gaudiest, fattest piece of silver tinsel.

We bought a string of coloured lights, some wooden reindeer with glitter in their horns and a pack of purple baubles dusted with fake snow. There was also a display of very beautiful hand-painted glass baubles I fell in love with but at eight pounds a pop they were a little on the expensive side.

As Nate went to the cash desk, Grace stayed by the display. 'That one's really pretty.' She pointed to a pale golden bauble with tiny snow crystals etched into the surface and then to another very pale blue bauble with a tracery of curlicues.

Leaving her there, I followed Nate to the cash desk and stopped beside him, saying quietly so that Grace couldn't hear, 'I'd like to buy a couple of the glass ones as a gift for Grace. As a memory of today. Buying the tree. The snow. The sunshine. Would that be all right?'

He shrugged. 'If you want to, but don't feel you have to spend your money on her; you've already been extraordinarily generous with your time.'

'One of my favourite things about Christmas is getting all the decorations out. When you unwrap them, special Christmas memories come flooding back.'

A sudden smile lit his face. 'You're right. I'd forgotten. I remember as a child, it was a big deal. My sister always wanted to be the one to find a glass reindeer that my gran had given us one year.'

While Grace was playing with the ends of the tinsel poking out of the paper bag, I surreptitiously paid for the two glass baubles and slipped them into my handbag, planning to give one to her later. The other I'd save for her stocking.

And then, just when I thought we were home and dry, a familiar voice said, 'Viola, fancy seeing you here.'

Shit. It was flipping Bella with Ella, Rosa and Laura. The girls came running towards me, Ella throwing her arms around my leg, Rosa hanging back, letting her more dominant sister take charge while Laura gave me a shy grin.

'Hi guys,' I said, ducking to give Ella a kiss and holding out a hand to Rosa, who sidled up to me for a kiss. Laura hugged me. 'Hey, Aunty V.'

'Hi Bella.'

'Well, hello, Little Miss Busy.' Ouch, there was a touch of snide in her voice, I was in the doghouse, but she came and kissed me on both cheeks before stepping to one side with a ridiculously arch look towards Nate. She didn't say the words, *Well, hello again, isn't this fun*, but she might as well have done.

With a sigh, I said, 'You remember Nate – this is his daughter, Grace.' I could see her totting things up with acuity, taking two plus two to fifty-five in mere seconds.

'How cool meeting you here – it was meant to be. You can help us choose a tree,' said Bella.

'We've actually just bought a tree,' I said. I could see how this might play out if she had her way.

'Excellent, that means you've got the inside track. You're already warmed up.' She herded Ella and Rosa towards me. 'What do you reckon, girls, do you want Aunty V to help you find the tree while I go and look at the wreaths and –' she paused with a sickly grin before adding '– search out the mistletoe?'

'Actually,' Nate chipped in before I could say anything, 'we've been here a while and Grace is getting a bit cold, so we need to head off.'

With those no-nonsense words, Nate earned my heartfelt gratitude.

'That's all right. V can stay and help us.' She looked down. 'Nice snow boots, by the way. Your feet look dead cosy in those.' God, Bella had absolutely no subtlety whatsoever.

'Unfortunately, we're on our way to see Phyllis,' said Nate. 'Otherwise, I'm sure Viola would have loved to stay and help. Sorry, Bella, it's nice to see you again but we've got a lot to do today and Viola's working later.'

'You're going to Viola's parents'?' Bella's sums had just tripled.

'Yes,' I said hurriedly. 'To get some old Christmas decorations out of the storage room.'

'Nice to see you,' said Nate again, putting arm around me and steering me towards the exit.

'Oh. OK. Yes. Right. Well. Nice to see you too,' said Bella, too sideswiped by Nate's decisive attitude to say any more.

'Come on, Grace,' he said.

'Wow,' I muttered, 'that was impressive. Thank you.'

'You need to stand up for yourself a bit more.' He turned out of the St John's Church yard. 'If you'll excuse me saying it, your family is rather demanding.'

'Bella's OK,' I said tentatively. 'I enjoy spending time with her and my nieces.'

'Sorry – was I being interfering?' Nate apologised.

I put an arm through his. 'Actually, no, it was rather nice having a knight in shining armour coming to my rescue.'

Portobello Market was much quieter than usual today; the weather had kept the tourists away and some of the fruit and vegetable stalls looked a bit sparse. The snow had clearly affected transport routes as there were still lots of roads closed, with some parts of the country experiencing record levels of snowfall.

There was one stall that I was particularly keen to check out, as I wanted to buy a couple of decorations for myself and the girls, Ella, Rosa and Laura as well as Tina's daughters. I thought I'd also get one for Bella as a peace offering, although, to be fair, she was so thick-skinned she probably didn't need one. It was a vintage stall, where the lady gave new life to items by decorating and embellishing them with old bits of jewellery and bric-a-brac.

Grace skipped between Nate and me as we stopped at the market stalls, the poor stall-holders in fingerless gloves, clapping their hands and blowing on them. It wasn't the weather to linger and it was a relief to track down the stall quite quickly. While I perused Verity's Vintage decorations, Grace was drawn to a stall opposite which displayed the tackier end of decorations and dragged Nate with her. They came back carrying baubles featuring rather too jolly Santa faces; with their rosy cheeks and slightly manic eyes they looked as if they'd been on the sauce since the first of December.

After twenty minutes the cold won the battle against shopping. Poor Grace's nose was quite pink and, even with my cosy borrowed snow boots, my feet were starting to get a bit chilly, so we picked up our pace to walk down to the very end of Portobello Road, our feet slipping and sliding in the slush created by the amount of traffic walking down the street.

As we got nearer to the street, I could feel my pace picking up and Grace had to skip to keep up. Nate grinned at me. 'Excited?'

'Sorry, I . . . I'm just looking forward to you seeing it.' I shook my head. 'I can't believe you don't know it. Do you actually live in Notting Hill?'

Nate frowned. 'I've spent too much time going to work, coming home and then, at the weekend, sticking to the tried and tested. Same cafés and coffee shops. That siege mentality. After a week at work you just want to batten down the hatches and enjoy being at home and not having to go anywhere or be anywhere.'

'But you might as well live in a village or in the country. There's so much to do and see here. How long have you lived here?'

'Since just before Grace was born. I guess, once you have a child, you spend more time at home.'

'Maybe – perhaps it's because I'm still footloose and fancy-free, but one of my favourite things is to pinpoint a new pub to visit and walk there or part way there. You see different things and discover different parts of London.'

We were almost there. I slowed on the corner and then pointed across the road. 'Ta-dah!'

Grace gasped.

'Whoa!' said Nate. 'That's a lot of Christmas trees.'

'I know – it was ninety-seven last year and over twenty thousand lights.'

'No!' He stared at me and then back at the building. 'That's just crazy. It's amazing.'

Every conceivable surface of The Churchill Arms was covered in Christmas trees and all of them were covered in tiny gold white lights. They were around the outside at ground level, on the first floor obscuring the windows, with more on top of the roof and around the corners, on little platforms.

Grace's eyes were on stalks.

'What do you think?' I asked, feeling a little smug.

'It's incredible.'

'It's fabtastic,' said Grace. 'Can we go inside?'

I looked at Nate, suddenly thinking that he might not want to take his seven-year-old daughter into a pub. Just because my parents had taken me everywhere at Grace's age, whether age appropriate or not, didn't mean that every parent was of the same mind.

'It's a Fuller's pub,' said Nate with a happy grin.

'London Pride man?' I asked, sensing a kindred spirit.

'Yup. You drink bitter?'

'I love a half every now and then. My dad used to bring me here every year after we'd bought our tree.' I shrugged, a little embarrassed that it looked as if I'd pressed one of my family traditions upon him and Grace.

'Can I have a Coca Cola, Viola?' she asked, her eyes wide and guileless in a way that told me this was forbidden fruit.

'Are you normally allowed to have it?' I asked, hiding a grin, keeping my voice firm. Nate had not dived in to say no, but it was important that I backed up the house rules.

Grace huffed. 'Only on special occasions.' She scuffed her foot backwards and forwards, her head bowed.

I glanced at Nate and raised my eyebrows.

'I think this probably qualifies as a special occasion,' he said gently. 'How many times do you get to see ninety . . . how many was it, Viola?'

'Ninety-seven.'

'Yes, ninety-seven Christmas trees and twenty thousand lights. I think that's quite special, don't you?'

'Yes, Daddy,' she said very importantly, in a way that elicited lots of mouth twitching from both Nate and me.

'We could have lunch here,' I said. 'My treat.' Nate went to demur and I raised a hand. 'You bought brunch yesterday. It's only fair. Mind you, they do Thai food here it might not be . . . suitable.'

I suddenly realised it wasn't that child-friendly but, to my amazement, Grace piped up, 'I love Thai food.'

'You do?'

She rolled her eyes. 'You people.' She walked ahead of us like a proud little peacock, completely sure of her welcome, and weaved through the tables towards an empty one near the back.

Nate laughed. 'She's rather partial to Nasi goreng rather than anything super spicy, although she doesn't mind hot food. Elaine didn't believe in mollycoddling her palate.'

'Great,' I said. It was a refreshing change. Tina's children only ate pizza and pasta, which severely restricted restaurant choices when we went out as a family.

'What do you want to drink?' Nate nodded towards the bar as I went to follow Grace.

'Half of London Pride, of course,' I said with a teasing wink.

'Coming up.' He paused and gave me a warm smile. 'You're definitely a girl after my own heart.' His low intimate tone set my heartbeat tripping. All morning we'd been easy in each other's company, aware, I guess, of Grace. It had felt completely natural, but here was that delicious little reminder that there was more between us.

We held each other's gazes for a couple of beats before he said, 'This is nice. I can't remember the last time I went to a pub for a pint.' Sadness touched his eyes. 'And yet I used to do it a lot with my dad before he moved to Portugal.' He nodded as if to himself rather than saying anything to me and then, with another warm, intimate smile, turned and strode towards the bar.

Chapter 22

'Where do you want to put it?' I asked a few hours later, when the tree, encased in its netting coat, was delivered. We stood in the grand hallway, looking at it.

'Where do you think?' asked Nate. 'It usually goes there.' He pointed to a spot by the stairs. Grace's mouth tightened in that familiar mutinous line.

'I'm going to be radical here,' I said. 'I think it should go downstairs, because you and Grace spend the most time in there and it's lovely to be able to see it, but it's your tree. I think you and Grace should decide.' I didn't want to be seen to be imposing Viola's perfect Christmas on the two of them. 'You could put it here or in the lounge.'

'What do you think, sweetheart?' Nate crouched down next to her. Their two heads were almost touching and Grace leaned hers on his shoulder, her blonde curls next to his dark straight hair. They couldn't have looked more different but so much a part of each other at the same time. She put her hand on his face, patting his cheek, her eyes solemn, and whispered in his ear.

I saw him squeeze her to him and had to swallow the sudden lump in my throat. This was their first Christmas on their own; there were things they needed to navigate together. I clasped my hands behind me and took a couple of steps backwards; I think it was some sort of attempt to look neutral.

Nate was nodding. 'I think that's an excellent idea.'

They both looked over towards me, identical expressions of mischief on their faces.

'We're going to have it in the kitchen, in the corner of the snug,' said Nate, rising to his feet holding his daughter's hand.

With the tree slung over his shoulder and Grace and I bringing up the rear, the three of us trooped down the stairs and then Grace ducked under the tree and weaved around Nate to take the lead, going over to the corner.

'Here, Daddy.' She pointed rather precisely to the spot. 'There's a plug for the lights and you can see them in the windows. So it will be pretty.' She meant the reflections but she had a good point; it would be pretty.

'OK. Here it is,' said Nate.

He fed the planed trunk of the tree into the stand and then lay on the floor with his head under the branches as he tightened up the four nuts on each of the sides while I held onto the prickly stem, trying to hold it straight, pine needle fronds in my face and tickling my nose as the fresh resin scent made me think of forests and the great outdoors.

'What do you think, Grace?'

She tilted her head, wandering around, stepping over the collection of decorations we'd bought and the box I'd retrieved from Mum's. 'It needs to go that way a bit.'

'Which way? Left?'

'Yes. Towards the table.'

I tilted the tree. 'Better?'

'No, that's really wonky. The other left.'

'Ladies.' There was a touch of impatience in his muffled voice. 'A decision, please.'

I pulled the tree towards me, not convinced that Grace's view was terribly accurate. And then I realised that she was seven and what did it matter?

'That's it,' she squeaked, clapping her hands and jumping up and down.

'And we have lift-off,' I said.

'Thank God for that,' muttered Nate from underneath the tree, carefully sliding his way out.

Grace already had the big sparkly piece of tinsel in her hand and was approaching the tree.

'It's best if we get the lights on first,' I said.

'Oh.' Her mouth clamped shut, the excited light in her face dimming, and I was conscious that she was used to things being rather prescriptive.

I gave her a big bright smile. 'Then you can put your tinsel on. And you can put it anywhere you like.'

Mollified, she stepped back, stroking the frothy tinsel as if it were a cat.

Together, Nate and I wound the lights around the branches with Grace, still holding her beloved tinsel, bobbing between us with helpful comments and suggestions like, 'Up a bit', 'No, higher', 'In the wiggly bit'.

Nate kept sending me conspiratorial glances, his warm brown

eyes full of mischief. For all his grumbles, he was enjoying himself and Grace's excitement and enthusiasm was contagious.

Once the lights were threaded around the tree, which at seven foot filled the corner of the room perfectly, we had the big switch-on. The lights exploded into colour, flashing with an eye-popping sequence that would put any disco to shame.

'They have colours,' squealed Grace with sudden joy.

'Wow, I'm not sure I can live with that,' said Nate. 'I'll have to get my John Travolta suit out.' He winked at me.

'You own a John Travolta suit?' I giggled.

'Who's John Revolter?' Grace was mesmerised by the lights. She touched one of the flashing bulbs with near reverence.

'Here, you can choose how the lights flash.' I showed Grace the little green box. It took another ten minutes before Nate and I were able to persuade her that the fade in and out of the blue and green to red and orange was more restful, with the suggestion that she could always change the lights at different times of the day. I had a strong suspicion that Nate would be eating his Weetabix to quite a light show each morning.

'I almost miss the old days,' said Nate. 'That moment before switch-on, when you held your breath hoping they'd work. These new LEDs take away the anticipation. Then you'd have to test each bulb until you found the duff one.'

'No, you don't,' I scolded. 'LEDs forever. Much less faff.' I rolled my eyes at the memory of sitting, fingers crossed that Dad would find the dead bulb. 'I remember my dad always, always gave me the same physics lecture about how electric circuits work.'

'And do you still know how electric circuits work?'

'Yes, it's imprinted on my brain for ever.'

He grinned at me. 'Did the trick then.'

I tutted at him.

During our conversation, Grace had been trying to work out where to put her special piece of tinsel, which she'd finally decided should go in the middle of the tree.

Sitting on the floor, I pulled the battered box, retrieved from Mum, towards me and the bag of newly purchased baubles and my handbag.

'OK, decoration time.' I glanced quickly at my watch. I had a couple of hours before I had to get changed and ready for work. Nate was on dinner duty today with a lazy menu of leftover chicken and oven chips.

'I'll make drinks. Hot chocolate all round. And I have special biscuits.' With a ta-da wave of his wrist, he produced a packet of Marks & Spencer's Extremely Chocolatey biscuits. 'Client sent a rather fancy hamper to the office.'

'With squirty cream!' begged Grace.

While he busied himself in the kitchen, I opened the box, full of carefully wrapped decorations, and Grace leaned into the box and touched the little packages, one by one, with the tips of her finger as if it were a box of chocolates and she couldn't decide which to pick up first.

'Here you go.' I handed her the first tissue-wrapped parcel, watching as she peeled away the layer to reveal a scarlet teardrop-shaped bauble with a hollowed-out front painted in silver. It was a very old one and in some places the silver paint had chipped off, but it featured in some of my earliest child-hood memories.

'Pretty. Can I put it on the tree?' Hope filled her small elfin face.

'You can put anything you like on the tree and anything you don't like can stay in the box.'

We worked our way through the box. The little wooden Scandinavian doll decorations all got the seal of approval, which I was pleased about, even the little man on his sledge with only one foot. In fact there was very little that Grace rejected. A plain silver bauble because it was dull but then reinstated because the back of the tree was 'lonely'.

Halfway through, when I had to lift Grace up to put some of the decorations on the higher branches, I pulled my handbag towards me and took out the blue bauble in its brown paper bag.

'And this is for you. This is one of your decorations for ever.'

She carefully unwrapped the blue glass ball and placed it in front of her on the floor, reaching out with a single finger and touching it before looking up at me with sheer wonderment in her eyes.

'Thank you, Viola,' she whispered, then got to her feet and put her arms around my neck and squeezed really hard, crushing my collarbone, but I didn't care.

'It's the best bauble ever, to the moon and back,' she whispered fiercely, hugging me even tighter. I closed my eyes, squeezing them shut to stop them welling up, and hugged her back.

By the time the tree was finished, it was a gaudy explosion of colour and mismatched decorations and Grace insisted on putting one of the blingier light sequences on just to celebrate completion.

'Take a picture, Daddy,' said Grace, holding out his phone and posing with one hand on her hip in front of the tree. 'It's the best tree ever.' She tugged at the silver piece of tinsel again. 'And this is my favourite, well, after the one you gave me, Viola, and the reindeer.'

That flipping reindeer had been a bone of contention with my mother for years. It was made from some sort of very dense plastic material and had a rather creepy, goofy grin, odd cross-eyes and was far too heavy because it always weighed the branches down too much. But, no matter how far Mum buried it at the bottom of the box or wherever she hid it, Dad and I would always remember it and would campaign for its inclusion on the tree. Now I kind of understood where Mum was coming from; it was hideous and I too had tried to push it back into the discarded tissue wrapping but the minute Grace had spotted its ugly little face she too had insisted it went on the tree.

'Will Father Christmas put presents under this tree? Real ones. Not the pretend ones.'

'I think he might,' said Nate.

'Can I write a letter to him?' Grace had been rather taken with the letterbox at The Churchill Arms where children could post letters to Santa. 'And can we go back to the pub to post it?'

'Definitely write to him. That's a good idea and then I can take it and pop it in the postbox on my way to work one day,' said Nate.

'On Monday,' said Grace urgently.

'On Monday,' agreed Nate and she immediately jumped up and retrieved her colouring pens and books from the kitchen drawer.

'I'm going to do it now.' She wriggled her way up into one of the bar stools. Nate and I smiled as she sat for a minute or two, her chin propped in her hand, clearly putting a great deal of thought into the letter.

'Do you think it should be Dear Santa or Dear Father Christmas?'

Nate widened his eyes as he looked at me and mouthed, 'No idea.'

'Dear Father Christmas,' I said, mouthing, 'It doesn't matter,' back at him. I preferred the formality of it.

Grace bent her head and began to write.

I began to tidy up the discarded boxes and tissue paper. 'I'll take these up to the attic and I'm going to get ready for work. Would you mind if I had a bath?' Since I'd seen the double-ended bath in the family bathroom I'd been longing to try it out and my shoulder was still aching a little. I'd managed an hour's practise first thing this morning before Nate or Grace had been up, secreting myself in Nate's study again.

'What time will you be back? I need to give you a key.'

'Probably just after eleven-thirty.'

'For some reason I thought it would be later.'

'You're joking. If we play for more than three hours, management get very twitchy. They hate having to pay us overtime. There are quite strict rules about how long we play, how long before we have a break and how long the breaks are for. Didn't you know, the intervals are for the musicians not the audience?' I joked.

Nate opened the door of a little key box. In my house spare keys, if you were lucky enough to find one, were buried under the junk in the kitchen drawer, the one filled with matches, loose change and the little packs of screwdrivers that you get in crackers.

'Here you go. Will you be OK coming back from the tube station on your own?'

'Nate, I've been doing it for years. And I quite often travel back with a couple of stage crew friends.' In fact I knew Tilly was on tonight; I was hoping to grab her and talk make-up.

He glanced at Grace, happily absorbed in her task. 'I'll give you a hand with those boxes.'

At the top of the stairs, Nate said, 'Actually, do you mind taking the boxes up to the attic? I need to do something.'

Before I could answer, he piled another box on top of mine and put a hand in the small of my back to push me along. *Charming.*

Feeling a bit miffed, I took my time on the stairs, wending my way up the next flight, passing the door to the nanny suite onto the odd-shaped attic room at the back of the house. I cleared a space on the shelf next to Elaine's carefully dated boxes of decorations, thinking the tatty box looked decidedly out of place, but then I took a second satisfied look, thinking that the box which had seen thirty years' service was more than able to hold its own.

Nate greeted me at the bottom of the stairs and took both

my hands, drawing me down the corridor before pulling me into the bathroom.

Perfume scented the air, the beautiful Diptyque candles on the shelf behind the bath had been lit and water was bubbling into a rich foam in the bath.

'I thought I'd run you a bath as a thank you for looking after us. Take your time and I'll rustle something up for dinner.'

I raised an eyebrow.

'Fish finger sandwich?' he asked. 'We've got some very nice tartare sauce in the fridge.'

I laughed. 'That would be lovely.'

'You're lovely,' he suddenly said in a low voice.

I looked up into his eyes to see an expression of longing filling them.

When he stepped forward, a hand rising to my face, his fingers feathering along my cheekbone, I froze, unable to look away.

'I shouldn't . . . but I can't . . .' His hand stilled on my skin. I held my breath. His other hand slid around my waist and gently pulled me to him. 'I want to . . .' When his eyes dropped to my mouth I felt a surge of wistful hope.

'It's no good.' With a rueful smile he dipped his head towards mine and gently kissed my lips, tightening his hold. Warm breath teased my mouth and I sank into the kiss, grateful for his arms supporting me. My legs had suddenly become decidedly wobbly.

As his mouth roved over mine, flickers of electricity sparked all over my skin and I lifted my arms to loop around his neck, feeling the softness of his hair beneath my fingers. Under his

lips my mouth opened and at the tentative touch of his tongue
I felt a small explosion in my chest.

'God, Viola.' He groaned and deepened the kiss, our
breathing loud over the running water. 'I'm sorry.' He pulled
back and rested his forehead against mine. 'I can't seem to . . .'

I stroked the skin of his neck, not wanting to hear the
inevitable words. I wanted to stay in the circle of his arms.

'I can't seem to stay away from you,' he said, almost to
himself.

'I know,' I said softly. 'It's the same for me.'

We were silent for a moment.

'It's difficult with Grace . . . I don't want to confuse her.'

'I know,' I repeated, touched by his ever present concern
for his daughter.

'But I really want to spend some time with you. On our
own. Just the two of us.' He stroked my face again, his fingers
outlining my lips. 'And not just sneaking around like this or
when she's in bed. I wish you didn't have to go to work tonight.'

From down the hall there was a sudden call. 'Daddy, Daddy,
where are you?'

Nate gave me another quick kiss and a heartfelt squeeze
before he let go of me.

'Could you do lunch this week?' He shot a quick glance
towards the door. 'Tuesday?'

I nodded as he stepped back and began to turn off the
bath taps, just as Grace pushed open the door.

'Mmm, it smells nice in here,' said Grace, sniffing with
approval and crossing to the bath. 'Bubbles. Can I have a bath?
I finished my letter.'

'This is for Viola,' said Nate, swishing the water with his hand. 'And a bit too hot for young ladies. Maybe you can have one later. Shall we go find an envelope for your letter and leave Viola in peace for a while? I think she deserves five minutes after all that Christmas tree decorating and practising her viola.'

'OK,' she replied with a happy smile. 'Have a nice bath, Viola. Daddy, come see the lights on the tree; I changed them again. Just for a little while.' She gave him a beguiling persuasive grin. 'So my LOL dolls can have a disco dance before tea.'

'Mmm –' he lifted an eyebrow '– let's see what you've chosen.' He rolled his eyes at me and took her hand.

'Enjoy your bath,' he said as they left the room, his eyes warm on mine.

I smiled back at him and when I lay in the scented water a few minutes later I allowed my mind to go back over and over his words. Tuesday felt a long way away but my skin tingled at the thought of spending time alone with Nate. I wasn't the only one that wished I didn't have to go to work this evening.

Chapter 23

'Here you go.' I handed both Leonie and Tilly a script and a cast list.

It was half past eight on Monday morning and I'd bribed them to agree to an early start at the Daily Grind with hot chocolate and one of Sally's double chocolate chip muffins. I'd been glad of the excuse to leave Nate to take Grace to school on his own, grateful not to have to run the gamut of curious playground eyes.

'Mmm,' said Leonie groggily, sipping at her drink. She'd had the furthest to come, all two miles from Shepherd's Bush, while Tilly only lived a few streets away. 'Remind me again why I said yes to this.' She narrowed her eyes and glared at Tilly.

'Because –' Tilly looked up from the page of script she was reading '– Viola needs our help and come on, Lee, it's an easy win. You said yourself you've got a ton of costumes in storage in Essex and you're going there this week.'

'OK,' grumbled Leonie.

'Oh, this is hilarious,' said Tilly, looking up. 'I love the innkeeper. He's such a grumpy sod.'

'You should see George who plays him. God, I hope's he's back from Paris today.'

Tilly had come to assist Leonie, who was going to take the measurements of the children playing the main parts and then those playing any secondary parts and then find some suitable costumes in the massive costume facility over in Billericay. Luckily, Alison Kreufeld had been in on Saturday evening and I'd nobbled her during the interval after I'd spoken to Tilly and Leonie and secured their agreement to help. When I'd explained that I was now doing a full nativity, she'd been impressed and also a tiny bit apologetic that the school's expectation had been so big. That certainly wasn't what she'd agreed with Nate's mother-in-law. I could bet it wasn't. I wondered how much Elaine took after her mother.

'Oh, this is brilliant.' Tilly nudged Leonie and pointed at the script, laughing. 'Viola, you're so clever.'

'Not really. I pinched the idea from the book, *Jesus's Christmas Party*. I can't really take the credit.'

'What the . . . You are effing joking.' Leonie dropped the script on the table. 'Did they have armadillos in downtown Bethlehem?'

'No idea . . . but I had to put one in. Long story. But do you think you might be able to find a suitable costume?'

'I'll do my best.' She screwed up her face. 'We did that really weird opera, Kafka's *Metamorphosis*. The one with all the insects. We had to build a couple of beetle carapaces. I could spray paint one of those to make them look like an armadillo's armour.'

'Whatever you can do, I'd be eternally grateful.'

Jack had dug his heels in and refused to have any other part (and refused to come to school, until it was agreed that an armadillo was written back into the play). I'd had to write in Alan the desert rat armadillo that crossed the desert following Mary and Joseph to Bethlehem, who also disturbed the innkeeper's sleep.

By the time they'd both read the script, finished their muffins and hot chocolate, we had a clear plan of action.

'I've got eleven kids to face paint, a donkey, six sheep, two oxen and two cows and an armadillo,' said Tilly. 'That's easy. If you want I can do little moustaches and a bit of face shading on the kings. For your angel I can cover her in glitter and hair dust. And we'll give your innkeeper some ruddy, apoplectic cheeks. Might as well make his wife's match if you want. And we can put some beards on the shepherds; that's just a bit of stippling with a sponge on their chins, two-second job.'

'And' Leonie added, 'I know we've got a ton of rustic tunics because we had all those kids in the gypsy camp from the last production of *Carmen*. And there were bloody loads of them. So I'll just nab all of those. And there were kids in the last production of *Tales of Hoffmann* wearing quite rich velvet capes; they'd be perfect for the three kings. Not sure if I've got a donkey costume . . . but I might have a grey horse from a ballet which might do.' Leonie was scribbling notes on her script.

'Thanks, guys, you might just have saved my bacon.'

'Any time, lovely,' said Tilly. 'It's no bother; I'm on lates next week. And I'll get Marcus to take the car into work and he can pick up the manger that the props guys are making for you, the straw bale and the backdrop. We just need to get the measurements for them today. They say they've got plenty of canvas for the backdrop. And then we're good to go.'

'You make it sound so easy,' I said.

'It is now you've got us on board.' Tilly's bracelets jingled as she folded her arms and looked at me reprovingly. 'I don't know why you didn't ask us before.'

'I think it was a case of not being able to see the wood for the trees.'

'Right, well. All sorted now. Shall we go and meet the little darlings?'

The school was back to normal today and although there was a lot of snow on the playing field and grass verges, all the paths had been cleared and heavily salted by Mr Marsh, the cheery caretaker, who admonished Tilly, Leonie and me to, 'Watch your step, young ladies,' from his position as sentry at the gates that morning. He did give Tilly a second look. Her only concessions to the snow were the Native American Indian moccasin-style boots which sort of went with her bouncy vintage yellow skirt covered in bright red cherries and her faux fur hooded jacket top. She was rocking the *Nanook of the North* meets Caro Emerald look. Thankfully Leonie's usual Goth look had been abandoned in favour of staying warm and dry, although her *Van Helsing* boots brought a raised eyebrow from the ladies in the office when we signed in.

There was a lot of whispering, giggling and nudging from Cassie and Grace, both of whom were sitting in the front row when we arrived in the hall as the rest of the school were filing out following assembly. I assumed Grace's uncharacteristic silliness was because I'd spent the weekend at her house and this was unfamiliar territory for both of us. Thankfully I spotted George straight away.

'Thank goodness,' I whispered to Tilly. 'Our innkeeper is back from Paris.'

I quickly introduced Tilly and Leonie to the teaching assistant who'd been helping me as the final stragglers from Year Six left the hall with their teachers.

'Gosh, it's really good of you to help,' she gushed with starstruck enthusiasm. 'You have such amazing jobs. Do you get to meet all those famous people? I read all about the opera singer Pietro D'Angelis last year. He's mega, although I was really shocked when I read he'd starred in porn films.'

'He was in ONE. When he was very young.' Tilly bit the words out, her mouth pinched tight like a prune. Eek, the poor woman had managed to hit a raw nerve straight off.

'We sign strict confidentiality agreements,' said Leonie, shooting a quick look at poor Tilly. This had been the scandal last year that had almost cost her her job. 'We're not allowed to talk about that sort of thing.'

'Of course not,' she said, flustered, realising rather astutely that she'd said the wrong thing. 'Yes. You must meet some interesting people. My sister is an actress. She says most of the things in the papers are made up anyway.'

'Mmm,' said Tilly, tight-lipped.

'Shall we get started?' I asked, conscious that time was ticking on.

I turned to face the children, who were sitting in two rows facing the front of the hall. 'Morning, children,' I said.

'Morning, Miss Smith,' they chorused, more loudly than usual.

I exchanged a look with the teaching assistant and she pulled a face and said in a low voice, 'They're all a bit hyper after the snow day. It might take them a while to settle.'

I looked anxiously at my watch. With less than six rehearsals to go, including the dress rehearsal, I was running out of time.

'I'd like to introduce my colleagues from the Opera House. They're going to help with the backstage bits of the nativity.

'Miss Hunter is a make-up artist. So, on the day of the show, she'll be coming to put make-up on some of you.'

'Hello, everyone.' Tilly stepped forward, her skirt bouncing slightly, and I could see all the little girls sit a little straighter with instant hero-worship.

'And this is Miss Golding; she is in charge of costumes at the Opera House. She and Miss Hunter are going to take some measurements today. So I want you all to be on your best behaviour.' They took one look at her boots – Leonie does look kind of kick-ass – and quietened.

'If I can have the principals – the people with parts,' I reminded them, 'and if the rest of you can sit around the piano to practice the carols.'

I filled the teaching assistant in with what I'd done with the music teacher in the previous week. 'They're almost there on *Away in a Manger* but *Silent Night* needs a bit of work.'

'And you're only doing the first and last verse of that one.'

'That's right.' I must have looked worried because she

patted me on the arm. 'Viola, it's all sounding great and you've done wonders on *Silent Night* with the three children singing those harmonies.' She grinned at me. 'No one will hear Cassie if she's flat.'

'Shh,' I said, making sure none of the children were in earshot. 'It took a lot of work but I think it was worth it.'

'What – to get her mother off your back? You should never listen to the parents.'

'I know but . . .' I needed to pull a few things out of the bag. The weight of responsibility to make this nativity a success was getting heavier. Having Tilly and Leonie here this morning made me feel a lot better but there was still a lot to crack through this morning.

'Grace and George, would you come up on stage and we'll go from the top with the arrival of Mary and Joseph.' Grace giggled again as Cassie smirked at her, leaning into her, cupping her hand and whispering into her ear.

It had felt a little bit weird leaving from Nate and Grace's house to go to work on Saturday night. After two nights there, I felt like a small bird being shoved out of the nest into the big wide world and I didn't really want to leave. The Christmas tree was up, the lights glowing and it looked so warm and homely. Grace had been quite put out that I had to go to work and had been a little bit sulky but the promise of an episode of *Strictly Come Dancing* had quickly cheered her up, along with my assurance that I'd be there in the morning. It might have been hard leaving, but it was a joy coming back when I let myself in just after half past eleven to find that Nate was sitting up, waiting with a glass of red wine for me.

On Sunday he and Grace came with me to my parents',
where I cooked Sunday lunch, Pork this time, and
Mum cross-examined him about his thoughts on *Game
of Thrones*. She was already on Season Five. Dad was rather
taken with Grace and read three chapters of *Harry Potter* to
her, leaving Nate and I to do the washing-up together.

As weekends went, it had been pretty perfect and this
morning, dancing in and out of each other's shadows,
preparing breakfast, getting ready for school and work, had
seemed so natural that Nate had only just stopped himself
kissing me goodbye at the door when I left to meet Tilly and
Leonie. Grace, on the other hand, had given me a big hug
and kiss, asking me for the fifth time that morning if I'd be
there to pick her up after school.

I watched as Grace, looking back at Cassie, got to her feet
and came up to the stage with a very silly walk. It seemed as
if snow fever was affecting everyone this morning, as George
copied her and the three kings fell into fits of laughter.

'Right you lot, calm down. Grace and George, can you
go from the first knock at the door with Mary and Joseph?'

As Sarah raised her hand to knock on the pretend door,
Grace pulled a face at Cassie, who pulled one back and then
started to laugh. Sarah, non-plussed, looked at me, uncertain
what to do.

'Carry on,' I said and George stepped forward to pull open
the door, his larger than life gesture suggesting a door of
gargantuan proportions. The first time he'd done that I'd been
about to suggest that he was more sensible about it, but then
realised the comic possibilities.

Despite his prolonged absence, George was word perfect and knew his lines. He delivered them perfectly and Sarah responded with a very worried, anxious Mary face. I smiled. She'd been a good choice. Of all of them, she was the most natural actor. There was a pause. It was Grace's line next. George poked her in the ribs but Grace was too busy pulling another face at Cassie.

'What?' she muttered at him. He nodded towards Mary. She slid me a quick glance, almost sly, and delivered the line with a petulant tilt to her lips.

The rest of the scene played on but Grace was uncharacteristically sulky and difficult throughout.

'Grace, you need to concentrate a bit more so that you remember your cues.' She'd missed quite a few or been slow to respond. 'George, remember to face the audience when you speak so that they can hear you. Sarah, speak up a little. Daniel, look up when you're speaking. But well done all of you; it's coming together nicely.'

We moved on to do a full run-through but Grace didn't get any better and the worst thing was that she was being deliberately awkward – slow to deliver her lines, as well as impatient and sulky with the others. By the time we'd run through the whole play, which was only half an hour long without the songs, the rest of the cast were pretty peeved with her bad behaviour and so was I.

Unwilling to take her to task in front of the other children, I was also loath to show her any preferential treatment. What had got into her this morning? She'd been fine when I'd left.

When the break bell rang, before I could say anything to

her, she'd run to Cassie's side, linked her arm through hers and was busy whispering in her ear again. Now that the rehearsal was over and everyone else had performed their parts pretty well, there didn't seem much point singling her out. I knew she could do the part, she'd shown that plenty of times before. Hopefully today was just a blip and the result of snow and overexcitement.

Grace was the last one out of her class, head down, her mouth surly and she was in her school shoes. While a lot of the snow had melted, the playground was a mass of grey slush.

'Hey, Grace,' I said. 'Do you want to pop your boots on?'

'No,' she said, looking up at me with baleful eyes.

'I think it might be a good idea. They'll keep your feet warm and dry.' Since her initial aversion to them when we'd bought them in the charity shop and then before we went out to build the snowman, practicality had won over aesthetics and she'd happily, or so I'd assumed, worn them throughout the rest of the weekend.

'Don't want to.' There was a mulish set to her face before she said, 'The cold never bothers me . . . anyway.'

I might have laughed except that she then added, 'You can't make me.' There was a pause before she added with a quick look of uncertainty, 'You're not my mum.'

'OK,' I said equably, ignoring the dart of pain in my chest. I was the adult, she was the child. 'Shall we go home?' I held out my hand but she ignored it and skipped a few steps ahead of me.

Frowning, I followed her. Had the other children been

teasing her about her mum having left? Children could be so cruel to each other.

'Did you have a good day?' I asked, hoping to divert her and let her chatter fill the odd void that had appeared between us.

She shrugged and looked away. I decided to leave her to it, hoping that as she unwound on the way home she'd confide whatever had upset her, because something clearly had. Hopefully she'd open up when she was ready and I was pretty sure, knowing Grace's usual chattiness, that it wouldn't be too long before she started to talk to me.

However, Grace's uncharacteristic sulkiness survived the journey home and when we walked into the house. She flung the carrier bag with the offending boots into one corner and took off her shoes. The feet of her tights were soaking and she must have been cold.

'Want to go and change and put some warm socks on?' I asked. 'While I make a hot chocolate?'

She gave me a mutinous glare and shook her head.

'You want to leave your wet tights on?' I mustn't smile at her stubbornness. 'Or you don't want hot chocolate?'

That made her pause. She shook her head, her mouth pressed tight.

At an impasse, I stared down at her wet feet. 'Grace, why don't you go and change? Then you can come downstairs and tell me what's wrong.' I gave her a wink. 'I'll get the squirty cream out.'

'I hate you.' Her face screwed up as the words burst out like a balloon popping.

Then she turned tail and ran up the stairs, stopping halfway up to yell, 'I hate you. I hate you,' before carrying on and slamming her bedroom door with such force that the house shook.

Too shocked to move, I stared at the stairs, the hairs on my arms standing on end. The silence of the house rang in my ears and I crept forward to sink down onto the third step. Where had that come from? What did I do now? I knew she didn't mean it. I'd seen outbursts like this with my cousins' girls over the years, although something had always triggered it.

I couldn't think of anything that had happened this morning. Grace had insisted on following me to the front door, granted a bit put out that I wasn't taking her to school, but she'd given me a big smacking kiss on the cheek and hugged me around the waist. If anything, she'd been anxious about me picking up from school. I couldn't think of any way I'd let her down.

After racking my brains, listening anxiously for any sound, I crept upstairs. Now I could hear her sobbing. I carefully opened the door. Grace was face down on her bed, crying as if her heart would break.

I carefully eased down onto the bed, sitting beside her, and reached a hand out to touch her shoulder.

She stiffened and hauled in a sharp breath, releasing it into a juddery burst of sobs.

'Grace, sweetie. I'm sorry you're so upset but I can't do anything about it if you don't tell me. Has someone upset you?'

Her whole body had gone ramrod-straight.

I rubbed her back in soothing circles. She didn't say anything and I could feel the tension in her small body.

'Sweet pea, I want to help. Is there anything I can do? You can talk to me.'

She shook her head, with her face still buried in the pillow, her hands shielding her face.

I stayed there rubbing her back and gradually I felt her relax but she didn't turn around. What else could I say? I felt helpless and frustrated. She was right, I wasn't her mum but I cared. Surely she knew that much.

With a sigh, I leaned over and placed a gentle kiss on the back of her head. 'I love you, Grace Williams. I might not be your mum –' I paused before saying fiercely '– but I'll always be your friend.'

I felt her tense again but she didn't move. I'd said as much as I could. With one final regretful rub of her back, I stood up. 'I'll be downstairs.'

My heart felt heavy and full as I took each step down to the kitchen. Nate would be home soon; perhaps he could tease out of her what was wrong. Blindly, I made a beeline for my viola, which was in the dining room area which, now I'd moved the dining table, had become a redundant space. It seemed a good place to keep my instrument while I was here. This part of the room, thanks to the toasty under-floor heating, was always warm but not too dry and didn't suffer big variations in temperature, whereas Nate's study upstairs did get very cold at night.

Taking my viola out of the case, I tucked it under my chin in a familiar and soothing automatic move born of years of muscle memory. Taking a slow calming breath, I lifted the bow, tightening my fingers to hold it just so and with the significant, almost meditative pause that had become habit before I touched the strings, I took another breath and then, as I breathed out, I stroked the bow with sure, coming home confidence. My heart bumped as the first notes, low and melodic, filled the room. I played a medley of familiar pieces for ten minutes before I settled on one of my favourites, the 1st movement from *Beethoven's String Quartet No.14*, its haunting, subtle melancholic arrangement, soaring and diving, mirroring my heartache. I was lost to everything but my bow teasing and releasing the notes, my fingers working the strings, drawing the notes into existence. There was no feeling like it, the power to make the music happen, to choose how it sounded: the speed, the intensity of the notes, the vibrato, the pressure of the bow; there were so many variables and I was the captain of this ship. The knowledge had always held a unique power that filled me with both intense happiness and a curious calm. I was meant for this.

Out of the corner of my eye I saw a movement and I shifted slightly. I'd been playing for nearly an hour and now Grace had crept into the room. She was sitting on the line that demarcated the dining area from the kitchen, her ankles crossed, her knees up to her chin and her head buried in her arms. I didn't acknowledge that I'd seen her, just carried on playing.

A few bars later and I noticed that her head lifted. Now she was watching me, her eyes following my bow.

Planning carefully, I segued into a new tune, Vivaldi, full of sunshine and joy, lifting the mood and taking a step towards Grace. I strung it out, a tiny step at a time until I was almost upon her and her head was tilted up to look at me. Moving into a sprightly polka, the exaggerated strokes and slashes of my bow were filled with gay energy. Coming to the end, I finished with a flourish and stood in front of Grace and dropped into a deep curtsy.

Grace looked up with solemn eyes. 'Cassie says you're Daddy's girlfriend.' Her lip quivered. 'And if Daddy has a girlfriend, Mummy will never come back.' Accusation filled her eyes.

My heart sank, properly sank like a heavy weight anchor. Bloody Zoe De Marco. Out of the mouths of babes and their bloody mother. I remembered Cassie's whisperings and nudgings this morning.

'Oh, sweet pea.' I dropped to the floor in front of her, resting my viola across my knees. 'Daddy and I are friends.' I sighed. Was honesty the best policy? I didn't feel I could say anything more without Nate's permission or agreement. We hadn't discussed talking to Grace. Everything was too new and all we'd done is agree a date.

'Grace, the most important thing is you. I am friends with Daddy but I'm friends with you too. I wouldn't do anything to hurt you.'

She narrowed her eyes. 'I don't want you to be Daddy's girlfriend.'

Ouch. I couldn't lie to her but I didn't know what to say. I had no idea what the situation between Nate and Elaine was.

It suddenly occurred to me that I'd been looking at this all wrong. Elaine was Grace's mother; she was all she'd ever known. Just because I had found Elaine wanting, didn't mean that Grace did. I'd got too carried away, imagining how Grace must feel, putting my emotions on her and my experience of my own parents' indifference and preoccupation with their careers.

Shame washed over me. And I reached out and touched her hand. 'I'm sorry, Grace. You must miss your mum.'

She nodded, her eyes filled with tears. 'Do you think she'll ever come back?'

'I don't know,' I said.

'I've been trying to be a really good girl. I was naughty today. My teacher told me off.'

I smiled at her. 'We all have off days,' I said. 'It's difficult to be perfect all the time.'

'Where did you learn to do that?' She pointed at my viola. 'It sounds like real music. Like on the radio or the television or in a film.' She looked curiously at the instrument lying across my lap.

'I started playing when I was your age. I practise every day.'

'Can you teach me?'

'I could but you would be better learning the violin first, which is a bit smaller and would be easier for you to hold. This is a viola, which is bigger and heavier, which is funny really because it sounds as if it should be smaller. But I can find you a teacher if you really want to learn.'

She nodded and then whispered, 'I'm sorry I was mean to you.'

I shuffled closer to her and put an arm around her shoulder. 'I can't say it's OK because it's not OK to hurt people's feelings, but I understand that you were upset and hurting.'

'I'm a bad person,' she said, looking heartbroken.

I smiled. 'No . . . no, you're not. You were sad and cross and upset.' There'd been a lot of emotional upset in her little life; she was entitled to let rip every now and then. 'And you've said sorry and that's the most important thing. Thank you.'

'I don't hate you. I really, really like you.' Her expression faltered. 'And if I do, then Daddy probably does too.' She scrunched up her eyes and I could see the conflict. 'But you can't be his girlfriend.' Something I was starting to realise myself.

Chapter 24

Nate was already there when I arrived at the restaurant. He'd chosen well; Pietro's was one of those tiny Italian restaurants owned by generation after generation of the same family. As soon as I walked in I was greeted with '*Bella, bella*, welcome,' and a big wide smile from under the bushiest moustache I'd ever seen. 'I am Pietro. You must be the *bella signorina* the gentleman is waiting for.'

Taking my coat like some royal courtier, he ushered me through the restaurant past small booths offering privacy and intimacy with rich purple velvet banquettes. Heavy brocade curtains in gold, lilac and black between each booth created clever screens. They were attached to the ceiling on brass poles, putting me in mind of old-fashioned curtained four-poster beds.

As I drew closer, Pietro gestured to the final booth and with a charming bow left me. Nate was sitting waiting for me and the second our eyes met there was an instant charge of sexual attraction between us. This was a date, a proper grown-up man, woman date in an intimate and rather sexy restaurant.

Nate watched my every step across the dimly lit restaurant

with dark hawk-like eyes, his stern gaze never leaving mine as I took the final few steps to reach him, by which time I was almost breathless, anticipation and sheer downright lust thudding through me at the unwavering look in his eyes. Nate rose and took a step towards me. Taller than me, solid and broad, he stood without saying anything, those dark eyes still locked on mine, and then his face softened into a small intimate smile that made me ache with want and my sore heart quicken a little. I managed a tremulous smile up at him, drinking in the sight of his handsome, almost too-gorgeous-to-be-true face.

He leaned forward, I felt his warm breath on my neck as he kissed the juncture of my jaw and neck, an unbelievably private and tender gesture that almost made my knees buckle. 'I can't decide whether to cancel the reservation for lunch and just take you straight to a hotel or close these curtains and ravish you right here,' he whispered as his lips feathered across my skin.

I swallowed and gazed up at him, blinking uncertainly, my nipples suddenly on alert and my nerve endings on fire.

This was not how I'd imagined our first proper date.

Over the weekend I'd got used to the stubbled, casual man with infinite depths of kindness and tenderness to his daughter. That version of Nate had completely overshadowed the man I'd first glimpsed across a crowded tube that had given a new lease of life to my dormant hormones. Said hormones which were now springing to action with attached super hero powers and urging me to do the unthinkable. That hotel room sounded so tempting, as did the idea of sinking back on the soft velvet, and I so wasn't that sort of girl . . . not normally.

Then Nate smiled, a million-dollar, heart-shivering smile of such sexiness that there was a strong possibility I might dissolve into a puddle at his feet as he said in a low tone, 'But you deserve better.'

Oh, boy, he had all the lines and all I could do was grin stupidly up at him as he took my hand and pulled me down onto the seat next to him. As soon as we sat down, cocooned in the sumptuous booth, it felt as if we were the only people in the restaurant; the sounds of the other diners seemed muted and distant. For a moment we sat looking at each other like a pair of complete idiots and I imagined that his heart was probably beating as hard as mine. I could see the pulse in his neck pumping furiously.

It was all the hearts and flowers sappy stuff that you see in a film, down to the bowl of overblown roses on the table, scenting the air with their delicate perfume . . . and it should have seemed weird in public, in a restaurant, but it didn't. It felt romantic and wonderful. Then he moved forward and slid his mouth over my lips, taking them in a kiss that went from hot to lift-off in seconds. I knew exactly why Nate had chosen this restaurant and this booth tucked away at the back. His lips eased all the hurt I'd been nurturing and I let him lead, the kiss deepening as his hands lifted to stroke my jawline, threading their way into my hair to hold the back of my head.

I sighed into his mouth and relaxed into the simple pleasure of being kissed and kissing. I adored the way his mouth moved over mine and the way his nose just tucked neatly next to mine. Sometimes kissing can be messy and awkward, nothing fits right, but, kissing Nate, everything just worked.

It was heaven and hell because, much as I let myself be led by the emotion, at the back of my head my conscience nagged. I had to talk to him.

Eventually we pulled apart and he stared into my face with a satisfied smile on his face.

'I missed you.'

I couldn't help but smile at that. 'You saw me this morning. I'm practically living with you. You can't have missed me.'

'I haven't kissed you properly since Sunday night.' We both blushed. Sunday night had been a close call, heated kisses that had threatened to get out of hand until Nate had heard – thankfully, he had bat ears or perhaps just finely tuned dad instincts – Grace's pitiful call of, 'Daddy,' before she'd appeared in the doorway of the lounge saying she'd had a bad dream. Luckily she'd still been too sleepy to notice my hastily rearranged clothes.

Thank goodness she hadn't seen anything. I winced. She really would have hated me then. I had to tell Nate what was going on in her little head.

He leaned in to kiss me again and I pulled back, wincing at his surprised expression.

'Nate, there's something I need to tell you. I didn't get chance last night or this morning.'

Circumstances had conspired against me. He'd been late in from work and I'd had to dash straight off to the theatre. There'd been a tragic incident on the line on my way home, so I'd missed him late evening. And this morning Grace had clung like a limpet to him, alternating between shooting dagger glares my way and sunny smiles. Poor kid was very confused. Adults could be shitty sometimes. I could have strangled Zoe De Marco and her vicious whisperings. What had she hoped to gain? Had she any idea the pain she was causing Grace?

'What?' he asked warily, just as the young waiter arrived to hand over the menus and offer us a glass of Prosecco each on the house.

I felt slightly sick as our drinks order was taken but as soon as the waiter left I looked at him, putting my elbow on the table.

'It's Grace.' I sighed, still feeling the kick of hurt from yesterday evening.

'What about Grace? I've never seen her so happy. This weekend she was . . . like a proper little girl. I'd got used to her being so adult and mature, which isn't right for someone her age. You've brought something into our lives, Viola.' He reached out and took my hand. 'She's been a different child this last week. Happy, relaxed, not so fearful of doing things wrong. You're a good influence.' He smiled and lifted my hand to his mouth. 'And you make me very happy.'

I leaned back in my chair. 'You're not supposed to say those things. You're supposed to warn me off again. Remember how you did when I first met you? The I'm-not-ready-for-a-relationship speech, the one you do so well.'

Nate looked a little bemused but still had that *life's good* smile on his face. 'I was wrong. I am ready. I want a relationship with you.'

I sighed and rubbed a hand across my eyes before looking up at him. 'You can't. It's not fair on Grace.'

I paused as the waiter handed us our fizzing glasses and a set of menus.

'Can you recommend anything?' I asked Nate, assuming he'd been here before.

'No,' said Nate. 'But the restaurant and food came highly recommended. They have my favourite on the menu.'

'What's that?' I asked, realising there was still so little I knew about him, even though I felt I'd known him for ever.

'Pasta, in particular spaghetti, which, according to Pietro –' he pointed to the menu '– is the food of lovers.'

'Is it?'

'Haven't you ever seen *Lady and the Tramp*?' demanded Nate with mock severity.

I almost choked on my Prosecco. 'I have but . . . I always think of spaghetti being too messy to be romantic.'

'Not the way I eat it,' he said with a teasing lift of his eyebrows as the waiter arrived to take our orders. Conscious of the burden nagging at me, as soon as we'd given our orders I snapped the menu shut, took Nate's and handed them both to him.

'Poor man –' Nate lifted his glass in toast, chinking it against mine '– I think you terrified him with your ordering competence.'

'I still need to talk to you about Grace.' I heaved out a sigh. 'People have been talking . . . she's very upset.'

'She didn't say anything to me.' He looked worried.

Tears pricked at my eyes. 'She was . . . tricky with me when

I picked her up from school yesterday.' I wasn't going to tell him exactly what she'd said to me; that would be mean and unfair. I had to keep reminding myself she was the child, I was the adult. 'Someone intimated that I might be your girl-friend.' I was, however, going to dob that harpy Zoe De Marco in. 'Cassie's mum. Apparently Cassie suggested to Grace that I'm your girlfriend.'

'Ah, the jungle drums. I should have foreseen that. Zoe was always very chummy with Elaine. But naughty to spread gossip via her own child.'

'Naughty? I'd have said grade A bitchy.'

'Yes, but do you know what, perhaps it's time that Grace knows how I feel about you.'

I raised my eyes to his. 'What do you mean?'

'I think we need to tell her that we want to spend time together. I don't want to have to sneak around in my own home, worried she might catch me kissing you.'

'Grace doesn't want you to have a girlfriend,' I blurted out. 'She's worried it will stop Elaine coming back.'

Nate froze, pulling back, withdrawing his hand and picking up his wine glass. A mixture of denial, regret and sharp consideration crossed his face as he tugged at the knot of his tie with his other hand. The silence between us grew as I waited for him to say something. Anything. Eventually he sighed and looked beyond me into the restaurant before he said heavily, 'I didn't know she felt like that. She doesn't talk about Elaine much. And I guess I've avoided talking about Elaine because I feel the weight of her rejection and I've been trying to spare Grace that.'

The sadness on his face made me reach forward to take his hand again; I needed the connection. He immediately linked his fingers through mine. 'One day she's going to realise.' His eyes darkened. 'Realise that Elaine's job was more important than . . . than her. That's too much of a burden for a little girl.'

I squeezed his hand. 'But she's got you. Do you know what? The right sort of love makes up for the wrong sort of love.'

He frowned and I realised I hadn't made much sense.

'She knows you love her and she's completely secure in that. She's not worried that if you get a girlfriend you won't love her any more. With hindsight, I should have taken that as a big plus yesterday.'

Nate gave me a weak smile.

'What I'm trying to say is I relate strongly to Grace because I feel a certain amount of empathy. My parents didn't abandon me but their work always came first. I mean, they love me in their own sort of way and if something happened to me they'd be worried and upset but –' I smiled at him to show I'd come to terms with it a long time ago '– I was an unexpected addition to the family at a time when they were both well established in their academic careers and they were determined that parenthood wouldn't impact on that.

'So I really feel for her but one thing she has, that I didn't, is a parent who does put her first, who does care about her, who does think about what she wants and needs. That's you. And that makes a huge difference. Having one parent who's present is better than two that are absent. Believe me.'

'I'm sorry, Viola, I had no idea.'

'Don't even think about it; I never knew any different at the time,' I lied. I'd always known and it had hurt for a long time, wondering why I wasn't enough for them. Wondering what more I needed to do to encourage their attention. I gave a sudden laugh. It still tickled me now, the stubbornness that had led to where I was now.

'That's how I started playing the viola,' I told him, my eyes dancing as I pushed back the sad memories. That wasn't what defined me. 'At first it was attention-seeking. Most people start playing the violin but no . . . I had to play the viola because that's what I was called. Mum and Dad thought that was quite cute and it was a good talking point. Then, because I was quite good, having a child prodigy suited them. I wasn't really, not at first, but I practised so hard to be the very best so that I'd impress them. I worked hard so that I developed a modicum of talent into real talent.

'They loved being able to say that I'd got into the Royal College of Music or that I was a finalist in Young Musician of the Year or that I played in the National Youth Orchestra. It looked as if they'd nurtured the talent and that it been born of their own academic prowess.'

'You sound as if you were quite bloody-minded about it.'

'I was to start with. Then, after I got to a certain age, I fell in love with music and that filled the hole in my heart. Sorry, that sounds completely melodramatic. But music gave me an outlet, I found a tribe where I belonged, I found something that gave me a sense of self-worth.

'And we're not supposed to be talking about me; we should

be talking about Grace. I don't want to hurt her, Nate, but I don't know what to do.'

'So what did you say to her?' Nate's voice was gentle and his fingers idly grazed the inside of my wrist.

'What could I say? I didn't want to tell her anything without talking to you first. I said that I'm friends with you but that I was friends with her too and I'd never do anything to hurt her.' My face crumpled.

'How did you leave it?'

'She couldn't have made it any plainer. She doesn't want me to be your girlfriend.'

Nate looked off into the distance again, before returning his gaze to me, thoughtful and assessing. 'Do you know what? This is all going to die down. If we hadn't bumped into Zoe De Marco at the weekend, nothing would have been said. It's just because it's been a bit intense this weekend. Once we're back on an even keel, Grace won't even be thinking about girlfriends. I suspect without Ms De Marco's helpful comments it wouldn't have occurred to her.'

I wasn't so sure about that, but Cassie's mum had certainly precipitated things.

'Once I've got a nanny sorted for Grace and you're back in your flat, we can go slowly. Take things one step at a time. See each other and Grace won't even need to know. We can go on proper dates. Like this. And I can come to your flat. Or take you to a swish hotel for afternoon sex.'

I blushed at his direct look. 'Who says I'm going to sleep with you?'

'I don't think sleep was what I had in mind,' he teased.

'One date and you think I'm going to "sleep" with you?' I asked.

'If Grace hadn't interrupted us, I think we'd have come close to christening that sofa on Sunday night.'

I narrowed my eyes at him. 'A gentleman wouldn't remind a lady of his almost conquest.'

'Viola –' his eyes went dark '– you have the most wicked hands I've ever come across.'

'It's all down to the finger work,' I said, waggling my fingers, while I gave him a secretive smile.

He lowered his voice, looking at my mouth. 'You're a very wicked woman.' Underneath the table his foot found mine. 'And I have to go back to work, so please can we change the subject, otherwise I won't be able to leave this table without shocking the other customers. What news on your plumber?'

'He texted me this morning. Sorry, the part won't be in until Wednesday. I can go and stay with my folks if you've had enough of me.'

His reproving look said it all. 'I love coming home in the evening to you and Grace chattering away; the house feels warm and lively. And there's the bonus of home-cooked food, which I'm going to miss.'

'You can cook roast chicken and I've taught you how to make Yorkshire pudding.'

'You have . . . although I'm not sure man can live on roast chicken alone.'

'He doesn't have to.' I shook my head at him. 'You can cook; you just need to be organised and with the online shopping list that we set up there's no reason for you not to have everything at hand. Even you can knock up a stir-fry and chicken and chips. That's two whole meals from one roast chicken. See, you probably don't need me at all.'

'Oh, I need you all right. Who else is going to bring sunshine and spontaneity into my life?'

We did talk about some sensible things over the amazing lunch and I updated Nate on the latest progress on the nativity. 'I saw the backdrop the props team has painted for me before rehearsal this morning; it's amazing and you should see the manger they've made.'

'With a little help from my friends,' teased Nate, waving a forkful of pasta at me, which, I had to admit, he'd twirled rather elegantly.

'Well, as long as Leonie can come up with the goods from the costume store, we're in business. George stole the show in rehearsals yesterday and . . . well, I know Grace can do better. And little Sarah who plays Mary has this quivering lip when the innkeeper tells her there's no room. Honestly, there won't be a dry eye in the house; she's a great little actress.'

'Sounds like you're feeling much happier about things.'

I nodded, chewing through a piece of very tender beef before saying, 'Yes, much. I need to get something for the teaching assistant, Jo – she's been my unsung hero. She's taught the children the carols and been so quietly supportive.'

When we finished the main course, we declined dessert or coffee as Nate needed to get back to work and I needed to get to school on time to pick up Grace.

'Thanks for lunch and . . .' as I waited for my coat in the lobby of the restaurant.

Nate touched my face. 'You don't need to worry about Grace. We'll handle things together. I know you care about her and that's what she needs to know and understand. I can't put the rest of my life on hold . . . which is what I've been doing until now.'

'Viola! God, it is you.'

I wheeled round at the sound of the familiar voice as a second voice said in one of those low, sultry, I-know-my-voice-just-oozes-sex-and-I'm-going-to-use-it-to-best-advantage-whenever-I-can tones, 'Nate Williams, how nice to see you.'

'Ingrid, how are you? It's been a while. I hear you got married.'

Married. My eyes shot to the man standing beside her. Married. The news hit me with an unwelcome punch.

Of all the people in all the world, my heart hit my boots. I should have guessed he'd move back to Notting Hill.

'Yes, this is my husband, Paul. Paul Boothroyd. Paul, this is Nate. We used to work together, until he set up on his own. Very successfully. If you're ever looking for an additional legal brain, you know where to find me.' I knew that her saccharine smile was completely misplaced by the tightness of Nate's jaw, a tell that I'd spotted when Zoe De Marco had homed in on him and when Bella was being overbearing. I also remembered him saying that no one from his previous law firm backed him up when he went out on a limb to support his client.

'Hi Paul –' Nate put his arm around my shoulders, subtly avoiding shaking Paul's outstretched hand '– this is Viola.'

'We know each other,' he said, adding a cocky, well.

'What are you up to, Vi, still playing in the orchestra?'

Seriously? He thought I'd somehow settled for mediocre obscurity *still* playing for one of the best opera houses in the world?

'Still at the beck and call of your family?'

I narrowed my eyes and stared at him as I felt the cold hard stab of outrage. *You bastard.*

Ingrid gave Paul a quick amused look. 'Viola – there can't be too many people with that name,' she said, her mouth turning down in a peculiar satisfied upside down smile. 'You must be my predecessor. Thanks for looking after Paul in the interim. I've heard a lot about you.'

Yeah, right, like she hadn't known exactly who I was from the moment Paul mentioned my name.

I don't normally do bitchy but at the sight of Paul's smirk – he'd always been a smirker – and with the reassuring stroke of Nate's hand on my arm, I said with a coolness I was so proud of, 'Sorry, you have me at a disadvantage. Paul never mentioned you . . . well, not until I realised he was having an affair.' Which wasn't strictly true but I got a hell of a lot of satisfaction out of the direct hit.

I couldn't swear to it but I thought I heard Nate snort and it was difficult to pinpoint the exact emotion on Ingrid's face. Let's just call it displeasure.

'Well, that was interesting,' said Nate, tucking the end of my scarf into my coat as we stepped out into the chilly afternoon air. 'Looks like we have similar taste in people we can't stand. And I love a woman who can go for the jugular when she needs to. Who needs a Rottweiler?'

'Oh, God, I let myself down. I shouldn't have given in to my inner bitch, but she just . . . urgh! She was so superior and so patronising.'

'Nothing's changed.'

'And I knew she had to be one of the people you talked about when you left your firm that didn't support you.'

'Yup and now she's all over me. Because I'm successful.' Nate grinned and put his arm around me as we walked round the corner onto Talbot Road. 'What's the story with Paul?'

I pulled a childish yeugh face and tried to sound blasé. This was old news. I was all cured. 'He's my ex. We lived together for sixteen months. For half of that time, he was having an affair with his ex and then he went back to her. I realise I was probably just a convenient staging post complete with a flat of my own.' I clenched my fists hard in my pockets and then went and blinked a couple of times. Shit, I thought I'd got a handle on it by now.

'More to it than that?' Nate's astute observation brought a lump to my throat. I nodded rather than risk speaking. I think he must have felt the tension in my body.

'You don't have to talk about it.'

I wasn't going to. I really wasn't going to but Paul's silent assassin dig, *Still at the beck and call of your family?* had unleashed white-hot rage burning under the surface. I was mad and angry and upset and about to boil over if I didn't let it out.

'Do you mind if we go down here?' I nodded towards one of the familiar streets away from the main road, drawn to the greenery of the central park in Powis Square, one of the many green spaces in the area

Nate nodded and we headed down the quiet street flanked by the stark branches of the winter trees.

'It's taken me a long time to figure out . . . what really happened.' I looked up at him. 'I haven't . . . talked about it to anyone. It's hard . . . realising how stupid I was. Taken in.'

'There are always two sides,' said Nate gently, stroking a piece of hair back under my woolly hat.

'You think?' Nausea gripped my stomach. He wrote the script on this one.

'When we broke up, he blamed me, said that I always put the demands of my family before him and that I kept dropping everything to run to them.' I scowled at the memory of his earnest sincerity as he'd laid the blame squarely at my feet.

'Apparently,' I said, struggling to keeping my voice calm, 'he'd turned to his ex-girlfriend for company because I was never there for him. And he was right.' My voice pitched a little higher. 'I could see it. He didn't hold back on the examples.'

My steps faltered and I paused, drawing in a laboured breath. Reacting instantly, Nate pulled me through the opening in the iron railings as if protecting me from public gaze. 'You don't have to tell me.' His gentle smile made me want to cry but I lifted my chin and said with a wan pretence of a smile, 'I've started, so I'll finish.'

I heaved in another breath, steeling myself to talk again as he led me to a bench overlooking a deserted children's playground, the swings silent and still. We huddled together, trying to protect each other from the icy wind. 'In true lawyerly fashion he'd documented every last occasion I'd put him second: the time I went to Bella's to babysit when he'd been given an official warning at work, the time I went to Sunday lunch with my parents when the ruling in a divorce case went against his client and when I did Tina's shopping for her when he was in bed with the flu. Chapter and verse, it was as if he'd noted them all down. He probably had. Was it really any wonder he'd gone back to Ingrid for solace?

'It was all completely my own fault.'

Overhead, the branches creaked as a brief gust of wind tumbled and blew around the park.

Nate's sympathetic smile as he reached for me ratcheted up my slow-burning fury. 'Except . . . it wasn't!' I snapped suddenly, making him jump with the violence of my tone, my voice discordant and loud in the serene private space. 'I spent months beating myself up about it because everything he said was true, wasn't it?'

Poor Nate – I must have looked positively wild-eyed. 'You know what my family is like. You've met them.'

He nodded, his movements careful as if he knew I could explode at any second.

'I tried to justify it. I love them. They're my family. I enjoy spending time with them. I like helping them.' I needed to slow my speech down. My words were running into each other.

'But he made me feel so bad that I'd put them first. God, I was a mess. I felt awful. No wonder he went back to his ex. I'd not really given him a choice.' My stomach hurt and I had to stop. Nate was looking quite worried now. He must have thought I was mad but seeing Paul had brought it all back and I was just so . . . so furious I couldn't stop now.

'It took me months. Months and months –' I shook my head as if that might dislodge my stupidity '– to realise that he could have come with me at any time. Any time. He was always invited. To Sunday lunches, dinners at my cousins', family meals out. He never wanted to come.' I laughed bitterly, looking at the empty playground. 'Of course he didn't – they were golden opportunities to sneak off and see her.

'It took me much longer to realise that he twisted every-thing. It was him that insisted I go and see my family. Him that said I was letting them down if I didn't go. And then he'd turn it around. For ages it was like my memories were all foggy because he'd insist I'd got things wrong.'

I whirled around and faced Nate, convinced that by now he must think I was a complete nutter. 'And do you know what . . . I've just realised he did it deliberately. The bastard said as much just now.' I clutched my stomach, the pain sharper now as I repeated the words. '*Still at the beck and call of your family?*' I swayed a little, feeling dizzy. Oh, God, any second now I was going to throw up all over Nate's shoes.

Nate took a firm grip of my shoulders and forced me to turn towards him. His face was pale and pinched and I saw anger burning in his eyes.

'Oh, Viola, I'm sorry. What a shit. If I saw him now, I'd punch the git.'

'You believe me?'

'Of course I believe you. Viola, you're the kindest-hearted person I've ever met. You do things for other people all the time. If Paul had been in bed with flu and your mother had needed you, you would have found a way to do both. I've seen the way you try to please all of the people all of the time and it's amazing how you manage to find a compromise to suit everyone.' He put an arm across my shoulders, pulling me into him. 'You're a good person.'

'It hurt, though, that he went back to his ex. As if I'd been temporary accommodation, lodgings for his emotions. A place to keep them in storage until the property he really wanted to invest in became available.'

And now I knew what I was really upset about. What would happen if Elaine ever came back?

Chapter 25

'Viola! Viola, you came!' Grace came running out of the classroom and threw herself at me with such enthusiasm I almost fell over.

I still felt slightly jittery after my emotional roller coaster lunch with Nate, so her whole-hearted delight made me even more wobbly.

'Of course I came,' I said with a huge smile on my face, feeling tearful again as she wrapped her arms around my waist and buried her head in my middle. Looking down, I could see she was wearing the slightly tatty snow boots again.

She hung on, squeezing me over and over.

'Hey, it's OK. I'm here.'

She looked up at me, her eyes shining with tears and her lip quivering. 'I was mean to you. I didn't think you'd come.'

'Of course I've come. I wouldn't let you down. I'll never let you down.' I crouched down and looked her in the eyes. 'We all say things that sometimes we don't mean. And you said sorry yesterday. It was all sorted out. Come on, it's cold, let's go home.' I took her hand and her book bag.

'But you have a nimportant job. You have to go to work. Tomorrow you can't pick me up.'

'That's right, tomorrow I have a rehearsal and then a performance in the evening. But Daddy's going to work from home so he can pick you up. But I'll be here the day after.'

'Yes, but I was really mean and I thought you might not come back because I'd been bad,' she said, falling into step beside me as we joined the last of the stragglers leaving the cold, damp playground. The snow scuffed up in most places had turned grey and the edges were covered in slush, while the school playing field was a messy patchwork of green and white with a brown scar on the small hill down to the fence where children had tried to carry on sledging even after the snow had melted.

'I said bad things.'

'You were upset and that's fine. But you need to talk to Daddy about these things as well. You need to tell him how you feel.'

'But he'll be mad at me when he knows what I said.' Her eyes grew rounder. 'My teacher says that hate is a very strong word and you shouldn't use it. And I said it to you and I didn't meant it because . . . I love you.' My heart flipped as I looked down into her guileless blue eyes. 'I'm sorry. And I'm glad that you're Daddy's friend and I . . . don't mind if you're his . . . his friend,' she finished awkwardly and began to skip beside me as if the conversation was over and done with.

'I got lots of Christmas cards today,' she announced a couple of minutes later.

'That's nice. Are they from your friends?' I remembered

seeing the big red postbox just outside the hall at school the day before.

'Yes. I got one with a robin on it from Ellie. One with a snowman from Aidan. One with . . . Do you think our snowman is still there?'

'I'm sure he will be. Shall we go and visit him quickly when we get home?' I was thinking perhaps we ought to retrieve the hat and scarf we'd left out there.

Conversation bounced around in this fashion until we reached the warmth of the house and we were peeling off all our layers in the hallway.

'Is your job really, really nimportant?' asked Grace, levering one boot from her foot and I could tell from the way she paused and waited for my answer that whatever I said held considerable significance.

I gave it careful thought, trying to figure out what the subtext to her question was; I had a strong inkling.

'It's important to me, yes, because I worked very hard, learning to play my viola so that I could get it. When I go to work, people are expecting me to be there, so I can't let them down: the people I work with and the audience that comes to see the opera or the ballet that I'm playing the music for. Everyone in the theatre can see where I sit because I sit right at the very front, just below the stage.'

'Like the front row?'

'Even closer than that.' I widened my eyes, teasing her as she scrunched her nose in a disbelieving frown.

I suddenly realised that she might not really understand what I did. 'Come on –' I shoved our coats and boots haphazardly in the cupboard and took her hand '– let me show you. You get the iPad, while I make us a hot drink.'

Pouring the milk into a pan and firing up the gas, I turned to find that Grace had switched on the iPad and was sitting on the bar stool swinging her legs. Leaving the pan to boil, I clicked onto YouTube and typed in a quick search.

'Here you go, this is the pit at the front of the theatre.' I'd found a clip put up by the Opera House, a promotional behind-the-scenes piece which had been made last year. 'That's the strings section. You can just see me – look there.'

She craned her neck and I enlarged the picture. 'That's where I sit. I share a desk with my friend Becky.'

'A desk? I can't see a desk.'

I laughed, realising that to a layman there were so many terms and traditions that I took for granted. 'That's just an orchestra term. We sit together and share the music.' I thought I'd probably get myself into trouble if I attempted to explain the hierarchy of the strings with its first and second violins, principal players and inside and outside players. I realised I was in danger of straying from the point I so desperately wanted to make.

'So when the theatre is full of people, in these seats –' I pointed to the plush red velvet seats '– they can see the orchestra playing. And that's my job to be there. People would notice if I wasn't. So it is important like that but –' I turned to her '– the thing is, Grace, when I play at the theatre, I always know when I'm going to play. It doesn't change. It's not like some jobs, where you get held up or have to do something different.'

316

She nodded, her face intent. 'So if I say I'm going to pick you up, I will pick you up. But if I'm working I'll know before, so I'll tell you I can't pick you up. Like tomorrow. Does that make sense?'

'Yes. And the people –' she pointed to the seats '– they can see you.'

'Yes, although they've come to see the opera or the ballet as well as listen to the music. So I think my job is important, because those people really want to see the opera or the ballet because they love it and I can't let those people down.' She nodded again.

I put my arm around her and gave her a squeeze. 'But it means that I won't let you down because I always know when I'm going to work and how long I will be there.'

She didn't say anything for a minute so I stood up to grab the pan of milk before it boiled over but I could see that she was processing the information. I was just pouring it into her Elsa mug when she asked, 'What if someone broke their leg? Would you be running late then?'

I blinked at her. Interesting question. 'I'm not sure anyone has ever broken a leg while I've been playing. But –' I gave it some thought '– I think we'd stop, get them off the stage, the understudy, that's another actor who can play their part or a dancer, would come on and then the show would carry on. So it might be held up for a little while but it's extremely unlikely.' And then there were the music union rules that didn't allow us to play for any longer than the agreed times. We had a maximum working day of seven hours and anything over that triggered overtime. I wasn't sure that Grace would really understand management being keen to avoid paying overtime at all costs. They were always desperate for us to finish on time. The minute the conductor takes his bow, that's the signal for us being off the clock.

'And what if the tube trains aren't working when you're at work?'

'You'd be in bed and fast asleep,' I said, tweaking her nose. 'Now, what shall we make for tea tonight?' After my big lunch I wasn't that hungry and I was a little embarrassed about seeing Nate after my meltdown, now I'd had chance to calm myself and go back over everything I'd said.

I was reading yesterday's *Metro* and just finishing my drink when I realised that it had gone very quiet. Grace had said something about going up to her bedroom to get something.

Still worrying about her, I went upstairs just in time to hear a crash coming from Nate's study.

A panic-stricken Grace was standing on a chair — oh, my God — precariously balanced on top of a footstool, stretching up on her tiptoes, reaching up to the top of the built-in cupboard, desperately holding up a haphazard pile of boxes about to cascade down on her head, like a hopeless mini Canute trying to hold back the tide. There were already a couple of boxes spilling their stationery contents across the floor.

The chair was wobbling and she looked anxiously over her shoulder at me.

I ran over and snatched her into my arms, stepping back out of the path of the avalanche of boxes as the chair fell off the stool. Bish, bash, bosh, the boxes tumbled to the ground, bouncing open and spilling out cards and envelopes, curls of ribbon, gift tags and Sellotape.

'Whoops,' I said, looking at the mess, my heart thudding furiously. 'Are you all right?'

'Mmm,' she whimpered, but I could hear her little pants of fright. I gave her a hug and gently set her down. 'What were you doing?' I asked, kneeling on the floor and starting to gather up the bits and pieces that had slid across the cream carpet.

'I was looking for Christmas cards. This is where Mummy keeps them.' She sighed. 'I'm the only one in the class who hasn't sent any.' Poor kid, another ball dropped, but at least I could help with this one. I felt like I was some kind of Caped Crusader coming to the rescue, which was kind of nice but at the same time I felt I wasn't doing a good enough job. Grace needed someone proper looking after her, who would pick all this stuff up. I really hoped that Nate found a new nanny soon.

'Oh,' I said, picking up one of the extremely expensive-looking cards that had slithered from its box. With gilt foiled lettering on very thick cardboard, I was pretty sure that sending these to every one of Grace's classmates was not what her mother had had in mind. These were so not suitable, especially when I opened one up to find that it had been pre-printed with the rather impersonal message, *Season's Greetings from Elaine, Nathan and Grace Williams*.

'Why don't you make some?' I suggested. All of my cousins' kids had art boxes with creative bits and bobs in them. 'Don't you have some art things? Some stickers or some coloured paper? You could design your own.'

'Yes!' said Grace, making a move towards the door.

'But not until you've helped me tidy up this lot. And next time ask for help. You could have hurt yourself . . . and you nearly gave me a heart attack.' I imitated her wobbling about.

'Sorry.'

'No worries. No harm done.'

We tidied up – well, shoved everything back in boxes – as I wondered if Nate had done anything about Christmas cards; these ones were definitely redundant, which reminded me I still needed to do something with the picture of Grace and Nate and the snowman.

By the time Nate came home, Grace had dragged out a very well stocked art box, which had been enthusiastically filled by Svetlana; apparently she liked drawing and watching *Neighbours*, and we had our own little production line going with me folding and cutting card and then drawing two perfect circles, one small and one large, for snowmen, with Grace adding different hats and accessories, spangling them up with liberal sprinklings of glitter glue to make Williams' copy-righted Christmas cards.

'Hi ladies – how are my favourite girls?' Nate asked as Grace clung like a monkey to his neck, covering him in glitter.

'Look at my cards,' she said. 'I'm going to put them in the postbox tomorrow.'

'They look very . . . sparkly,' said Nate. 'And so do you.' He kissed her cheek and she giggled. 'You've got sparkles on your lips, Daddy.'

'All the better to kiss you with,' he teased and started to pepper her face with kisses, making her squirm and giggle.

'Do it to Viola,' she squealed, ducking away and grabbing me and trying to jump ship into my arms. Suddenly his arm was around both of us and he was alternating between kissing her and me, with Grace giggling away.

'Stop, stop,' I cried, breathless with laughter. 'I need to get ready to go to work and I can't go all covered in glitter. Everyone will see me sparkling in the pit.'

Grace's face looked horrified. 'It will wash off, Viola.' She turned to Nate to advise him with great solemnity, 'Viola sits at the front. Everyone will see her and she's nimportant.'

Reluctant to leave the circle, I pulled away, my heart a little tender at the look in Nate's eye. This felt like being part of a family.

That golden glow lasted all through the evening's performance and a couple of people commented on the stray bits of glitter that had managed to adhere to my skin and hair. My heart was light as I let myself into the house later that night, imagining Grace tucked up in bed and hoping that Nate might still be up.

As I slipped through the door, the soft light of the lamps in the lounge were like a beacon guiding me home and I found Nate reading a book, his legs stretched out on the sofa.

'You're still up,' I whispered, taking off my coat and draping it over the nearest armchair.

'I don't like to think of you coming in on your own. I like to know you're safe.' He nodded to a bottle of red wine on the coffee table in front of him. 'I saved you a glass.' Shifting his legs off the sofa, he patted the cushion next to him. 'Come tell me about your day.'

I smiled and crossed the lounge, admiring the picture he made, looking relaxed and indolent with his open-necked shirt and the book still in his hand. 'I think you heard plenty. Thank you for listening and I'm sorry I got a bit emotional.'

'Don't you dare apologise.' He put the book face down on the arm of the sofa.

'I was worried you'd think I was a bit of a lunatic.'

'Not at all. I can't believe that people can behave like that. All it did was make me think even more of you.' He poured me a glass, which I took and sat down next to him.

'You're cold; I can feel the chill coming from you.' He touched my cheek, his warm hand almost burning. 'I don't like you walking from the tube station on your own, but thank you for texting when you leave the station.'

'It's getting icy out there. Frost on the cars already and the slush freezing.'

'It's warm in here.' Nate slipped an arm round me to highlight the point, pulling me against him and, with a this-feels-like-home sigh, I leaned in. 'So how were things after school today? Grace seemed much happier tonight. Did you say something to her?'

'No, she . . . bless her, she was still fretting about upsetting me and being bad.' Her anxiety about being bad still worried me. 'And she was really anxious about not being picked up, that I wouldn't turn up, almost as if that was what she deserved. So I explained about my job and that when I was at work I had to be there but that I always knew my schedule. I think it reassured her but . . . Any news on the nanny front?'

'Wrong time of year, apparently.' He rolled his neck as if

322

trying to ease the tension. 'But I can get a temporary nanny to start in January for a month, which isn't ideal but I'm not sure what else to do. The local childminders are all full and so is the after-school club. I can't thank you enough for stepping in these couple of weeks. I don't know what I'd have done. But I've fixed it so that next week, the last week of term, I'll wind down and just do a few hours from home each day.'

'The term is finishing really late this year. And Christmas is only three days later,' I observed.

'And?'

'Just wondering when you're going to get all your Christmas shopping done.' I hadn't seen much in the way of preparation. 'Once Grace is finished at school, what will you do? I'm going this week' I added smugly.

As I was in rehearsal from eleven every day this week, I'd planned to go into the West End first thing one morning, blitz my shopping and then go to work.

'Fuck,' he whispered. 'Oh, for—'

'Don't say it.' I put a finger on his lips.

'I . . . Elaine always did all that and I . . . I thought I'd got ages.'

'What happened to the letter she wrote to Santa?' At his blank face, I groaned quietly. 'Nate, you're rubbish. Please tell me you haven't lost it.'

'No, I think it must still be in my coat pocket.'

'If you give it to me I can have a look and do some shopping. I was going to do her a little stocking from me.'

'That's really kind of you.'

I lifted my shoulders. 'I want to . . . and I know what to put in it.'

'Come on, I'm a bloke.' My reproving glare brought a mischievous grin. 'But I know that she'd like an Elsa dress, an ice cream maker, some high heels and some purple jeans. And to appear on *Strictly*, which ain't going to happen any time soon.'

'OK –' I grinned back at him; he was looking so pleased with himself '– I'm impressed. You do know your daughter.'

'That and the fact that on Saturday night during *Strictly* she told me what she wanted because she wasn't sure that I'd have passed her letter on to Father Christmas and it was always good to have a backup plan, her words.'

I burst out laughing. 'I'll be near the Disney store this week. I could probably get the Elsa dress for you and, if you want me to, look for some purple jeans.'

'That would be amazing, because I really don't know where to start on those. The high heels she can forget and I was going to ignore the ice cream machine. And I've quite a few ideas for her; she's been quite diligent in dropping not so subtle hints.'

'She's a smart cookie.'

'She is. Very smart. She came up with a suggestion for you.'

'Me? What?'

'If I told you, it wouldn't be a surprise, would it?'

'You don't have to get me anything.'

'No, because you've done nothing for us, nothing note-worthy. You swan in, eat all our food, sleep in the guest room, using our heating and hot water . . . By the way, have you heard from your plumber . . .? Not that—'

324

'He's coming first thing tomorrow morning, seven-thirty, to fit the part. I've left him a key. And then I'll be out of your hair.' I said the words brightly, although there was a funny little wrench in my heart at the thought of going back to my empty place.

'Won't it take a long time for everything to warm up?' Nate's hold on me tightened and he kissed my cheek. 'You might want to stay here another night?'

I turned to face him. We were almost nose to nose and I couldn't look away from his intent gaze. 'Nate, I have to go back some time' Being sensible sucked. A lot. I could so get used to staying here with him and Grace.

'Do you?' he asked and I heard the plea in his voice.

'You're making this harder,' I whispered.

'I'm just being honest.' He ducked his head, studying my hand as he traced my knuckles with one careful index finger. The gentle touch sparked tiny shivers of awareness and my breath stalled. One of us had to be sensible; I always thought it would be him.

'What? You want me to move into the spare room?' I asked, trying to lighten the mood.

He sighed. 'Not exactly. I'm rushing things, aren't I? But it just . . .' his fingers skated back over my hand '. . . it feels right . . . for me. It's Grace that I worry about. I don't know what the precedent is with a young girl in the house.'

We both lapsed into silent thought before I said, turning my hand over and linking my fingers through his, 'We said we'd take it slow. I think taking up residence, even in the spare room, at this stage is moving at warp speed.'

'You're probably right, but it's so nice having you here.' He kissed the top of my head.

'Watch it, you might get covered in glitter,' I warned him, snuggling in, enjoying the warmth and comfort of his arms around me. 'I feel like one of those chimpanzees; people have been picking bits of glitter out of my hair all evening.'

He laughed and turned me in his arms and kissed me, a long, slow, languorous kiss where time seemed to slow and there was nothing in the world to do but enjoy the slow caress of skin on skin. At some point I was aware of him taking the wine glass from my hand and us sliding down the sofa, and then we were lying full length, his body pressing into mine and mine lifting in response with slow-building urgency. His hand stroked my face as we kissed and my arms wound around his neck, pulling him closer, revelling in the heavy weight of him.

I could feel the hot sweet ache between my thighs building and the hard length of him pressing into me. I moaned into his mouth and in response he groaned, 'Viola, you're driving me mad.' His hand slid beneath my dress, which had ridden up to be indecent anyway, and he stroked my thigh as I sucked in a desperate breath. 'Nate,' I breathed, struggling to be sensible. 'We can't . . . Not . . .' But his kisses were so delicious and the heaviness on top of me so warm and welcome. 'We . . . shouldn't.' His fingers trailed higher and shamelessly I pushed my hips forward in blatant invitation. I wanted his touch. 'Yes, yes, yes.'

Oh, God, that litany of pants was really me. Someone had to put the brakes on. We were in his front room. The curtains weren't even closed. There was a small child upstairs.

One of us had to be sensible. The warning voice got louder and I peeled my mouth from his and tugged at his hair. 'Nate. We have to stop.'

He winced and sighed. 'You're right. It would be bad enough if Grace saw us like this . . . let alone where we were headed. I'm sorry.' He nipped at my lip one last time and shifted, helping me to sit up.

'I think we probably need to go to bed.'

'That sounds an excellent idea.'

I poked him in the ribs. 'Don't get any ideas.'

Reluctantly, he stood up and pulled me to my feet. I took the wine glasses and bottle downstairs, while Nate checked the doors were locked and switched off the lights and then, hand in hand, we climbed the stairs, both automatically heading towards Grace's room.

Peeping in the door, we could see she was sleeping peacefully, spreadeagled in her bed, one foot hanging over the edge, poking out of her duvet. Nate tucked it back in before dropping a quick kiss on her forehead. She never stirred once, her blonde curls a halo around her pillow and her lashes brushing her cheek. My heart contracted at the sight of her, so small and slight, content and happy in her sleep.

Together we backed out of the room, pulling the door to.

Nate stopped outside my door and gave me another one of those heart-warming lingering kisses. 'Goodnight, Viola.'

'Goodnight, Nate.' I put my hand on the doorknob and we shared a rueful smile.

'This is the right thing to do,' I said, knowing it was, and patted his cheek.

'I know, but it doesn't stop me wishing otherwise.'

'Once I'm home we can do things that normal couples do when they first start dating. We seem to have jumped in right in the middle.'

'I don't know that I want to be a normal couple.' Nate frowned and lifted his hand to my face. 'You're special and this is special.'

My heart fluttered in my chest at his words and the tender look on his face.

''Night, Nate,' I said, giving him one last kiss and pushing open my bedroom door.

Chapter 26

Oxford Street in December is best avoided unless you go midweek at nine-thirty in the morning when the shops are just opening. Armed with my comprehensive shopping list, I was outside John Lewis at nine forty-five, ready to do battle.

The window displays shimmered and glittered with all manner of gorgeous things. A grand glossy wooden dining table filled one window, set with jewel-bright glassware, a white snowflake-printed runner, matching napkins tucked in crystal-covered napkin rings and fine china.

It reminded me that I still needed to think about Christmas dinner. Sort out the turkey. I could invite Nate and Grace. Two more wouldn't make a difference, not on top of fourteen. They'd have to bring chairs. It would be more fun, I was sure, than the two of them having Christmas on their own, not that Nate had mentioned Christmas Day. I ought to ask him if they had any plans.

I moved onto the next window, which was filled with angular blank-faced mannequins modelling ultra-sophisticated party-wear: dramatic lamé dresses with plunging necklines, demure little black diamanté-trimmed numbers and flowing silk palazzo pants in scarlet. Another window, my favourite, featured an old-fashioned brass bedstead with gleaming finials and rails, from which colourful stockings hung. On the bed was a plump feather duvet in a white cover decorated with silver snowflakes, and piles of soft grey throws and cashmere blankets as well as cushions and bolsters heaped in attractive groupings. This final display reminded me that I needed to add a stocking for Grace to my list.

As I stepped inside, the fierce warmth of the heaters hit me full in the face; I'd need to take my coat off in a few minutes. It was the same every year. Once through the second doors, I paused to take a moment. I loved everything about Christmas but especially the festive decorations. Everywhere I looked the make-up counters were piled high with gift sets: perfume, skincare and make-up as well as mock gift boxes wrapped with gold paper and silver ribbons. The escalators rising from the middle of the floor were covered in swags of green ivy lit up with tiny gold lights flickering among the foliage.

Within five minutes I had present number one nailed. A Thierry Mugler Angel perfume set for mum, her favourite. Then Urban Decay goodies for my older nieces. Easy-peasy. Next up, quick turn to the left. Into the accessories department. A silk scarf, a Hermes imitation, which I knew Bella would love. Leather gloves, chestnut and dark brown with little buttons for Tina. Downstairs to the home department and menswear. A Crew shirt for Dad, whisky tumblers for the cousins' husbands and a pair of gorgeous coloured gin glasses for both Tilly and Leonie. I spent a long time pondering a pricy navy blue cashmere scarf for Nate but then decided that maybe it was a bit boring.

Moving up the escalators, I headed for the toy department. I had inside information from the cousins as to what their younger daughters all wanted.

Of course, when I got to the toy department, the display was completely befuddling. Thankfully, Bella's text had been quite specific. I picked up the LOL doll sets as requested and then phoned Nate, hoping that he'd pick up.

'Hey,' he said in that soft, just-between-us tone that immediately made my pulse jump.

'Hey. How are you?'

'Better now.' Something fizzed inside me at the timbre of his voice.

I smiled, feeling deliciously warm, but pulled myself up. One of us had to be practical, otherwise this might dissolve into phone sex.

'I'm in John Lewis,' I said.

'Oh,' he said with a definite touch of disappointment.

'In front of the LOL display.'

'Scary.'

'Just a touch.'

'Did you want me to come down there and rescue you?'

I laughed. 'No, I think I'll survive but I know Grace has got some. I think she'd really love one of these sets. You wanted more present ideas.' I took a photograph of one of the sets and WhatsApped it to him.

'Viola . . . I'm a bloke. If you think they're suitable, I trust you. She does seem to love the creepy little critters. I was always more of a Barbie man myself.'

'Nate Williams, wash your mouth out.'

'When I was ten. My tastes have matured since then.'

'Forgiven. So shall I pick one of these up?'

'Yes, please, and let me know the damage so I can transfer the money into your account.'

'No problem. When do you want me to bring them round? It'll have to be one night after Grace has gone to bed.'

'How about Saturday? Grace has got a play date in the afternoon.'

'Perfect, I'm at Bella's in the morning. I'm on cake-decorating duty but I could come over at about two?'

'Oh.' I could hear the disappointment in Nate's voice. 'I thought maybe I could take you out for lunch again.'

'Sorry, but I have neglected her of late. I got a very snippy text from her when I asked her what the girls wanted for Christmas.'

'Fair enough; we have taken up quite a lot of your time.'

'Nate, I don't begrudge a minute I spend with you and Grace. You know that.'

'I know. I'm just feeling hard done by because you've gone home and I won't see you now until Saturday and . . .' His voice dropped.

I closed my eyes. I knew exactly what he was thinking.

'. . . we'll have the house to ourselves for a few hours.'

'What time's Grace's play date?'

'I'm dropping her off at twelve.'

'Lunch sounds nice.'

'I thought we could go to that nice wine bar on Elgin Avenue,' he teased and I could picture the smile on his face

'Or . . .' I paused, smiling myself now '. . . we could stay home and I could bring lunch from Mr Christian's . . .' I named a landmark Notting Hill deli '. . . and I could wear my best lingerie.'

'That . . .' he lowered his voice to the sexy tone that sent a buzz rushing through my system '. . . sounds like an excellent idea, Miss Smith.'

Shopping in a heightened state of sexual awareness and anticipation probably isn't conducive to managing your budget very sensibly. I spent a fortune on a new lacy bra and matching pants, one of those demure diamanté-trimmed little black dresses, and gaily flung twice as many gifts in my basket as I'd planned to buy for people, including the cashmere scarf for Nate because I had a sudden fantasy of him wearing nothing but that and me tugging the ends of the scarf to bring his naked body closer.

By the time I left the store, laden with bags, I felt extremely hot and bothered and it had nothing to do with the store's heating system.

Next stop the Disney Store. Oh my God, the place was mind-boggling. Who knew how hard it would be to choose an Elsa dress? There was the original shimmery iridescent aqua blue or there was the simply gorgeous deluxe dress (from *Olaf's Frozen Adventure* apparently) a deep purpley-blue velvet number with a fur-trimmed hood and a chiffon over-cape, or the new sparkly dress from *Frozen II,* which I wanted for myself.

I almost texted Nate to ask him when Grace's birthday was. Then I decided I would buy her the latest dress and Nate could buy the deluxe one, or maybe it should be the other way round. Or maybe I'd buy both and let him choose which one he wanted to give her. Yes, that was the best idea. My poor head was spinning with the weight of all the decisions by the time I finally took both dresses to the sales counter.

'Did you find everything you were looking for today in the store?' asked the shop assistant, her sparkly antlers nodding as I handed over my credit card to her fur-covered hands.

'Oh, yes,' I said, beaming at her. Thankfully, she didn't think I was a complete crazy lady, though, in that outfit, a Disney franchise mash-up where Sven the Reindeer met Chewbacca, she had nothing to complain about.

'They get such a kick out of these outfits. My daughter, she's all grown up now, but she had a Snow White dress, clean wore it out, she did.'

'I know.' A pang hit me as I imagined Grace's face when she saw the dresses and I could picture her wearing either one of them, dancing around the kitchen and blasting out *Let It Go* at the top of her voice. She was going to love them and also the little Olaf that I'd bought her, because it reminded me a little of the night we'd built Mr Snow, and a sparkly tiara that I couldn't resist and the Disney sticker book for her stocking. I hoped Nate wouldn't think I was spoiling her.

'I wish I'd known you were going to the Disney store,' said Bella as I piled my booty in her hallway on Saturday morning in readiness to hand it over to Nate. It had been stored in my lounge for the last few days. 'Ella and Rosa have gone *Frozen II* mad.'

'Sorry. I didn't think.' I pulled off my scarf and coat and hung them up on the old-fashioned coat rack on the wall.

'Oh, well, next time let me know.'

I followed her down the tastefully panelled hallway towards the kitchen.

'Actually, there's one in Covent Garden, near where you work, isn't there? I'll have to give you a list.'

'There is,' I said coolly. 'Or you could go online.'

Bella laughed. 'And that's told me.' Pouring two mugs of coffee, she handed one over and sat down on the stool next to me. 'I'm sorry, Viola.' She looked genuinely penitent and I had no idea why.

'For what?'

'I know you're a bit mad with us all.'

I shrugged and was about to deny it, when I changed my mind.

'Yeah, I was.'

She winced. 'We've hardly seen you the last couple of weeks. I spoke to Tina. She said the same. Said you cancelled going over to help with the wreath-making. I guess I kind of got used to you being so available and . . . I'm sorry, I think I probably took advantage. Tina thought something had upset you.'

I let out a mirthless laugh. 'You think?'

The truth was Grace's needs were greater than theirs. She had taken precedence. Not seeing my cousins hadn't been deliberate, even though I was cross with them.

Bella looked worried now. This was not quite how she'd expected things to go. She'd been expecting me to brush things off with my usual let's-not-rock-the-boat avoidance of confrontation. Like Grace, I'd perfected the *if I behave well and please everyone, perhaps they'll have a little more time for me* approach to life. Seeing how carefully Grace tried not to step on the cracks, her careful adult concentration to try and be perfect, had made me see how, over the years, I'd fallen into the same trap. I wanted to please all of the people all of the time and often ended up doing things for them rather than myself. The only area of my life where I'd stuck to my guns had been with my music.

I looked directly at her. 'When I asked for help with Mum, neither of you stepped up.' I felt a little bubble of anger boil up. 'You were both too busy.'

Bella swallowed and played with the handle of her mug. 'Yeah, that was a bit shitty.'

I rounded on her. 'It was a lot shitty. In the hospital not one of you offered to help, not you, not Tina or your mum, even though none of you work. I'm fed up with everyone's assumption that because I'm single and because I work irregular hours, my time is less important than anyone else's.' I was on a roll now, years of resentment spilling out.

'I never ask for help and the one time I did . . . nothing.'

'I'm sorry,' said Bella. 'It was . . . you're right; it was shitty. We're all sorry.'

I shrugged. I wasn't about to say it was OK because at the time it hadn't been OK. 'Ursula helped.'

Bella winced. 'Thanks.'

'What?' I asked. 'I was being honest. In fact she was amazing. Went out of her way to be helpful.'

'Ever heard of sparing someone's feelings?' Bella asked with an attempt at humour.

'Yes . . . but you don't deserve it.'

'OK, I've got the message. We all need to be a bit less "Call Viola" whenever we need the cavalry –' she saw my face '– or think we need the cavalry. But can I just say in our defence, you are brilliant with the kids, at being there when we need you, and that's why we call you because you're one hundred per cent reliable and never let us down.'

I rolled my eyes but smiled too. 'Flattery will get you everywhere.'

'It's not flattery but it is something that we all should have acknowledged a long time ago. So –' she looked a little coy; typical Bella, nothing held her back for long '– can I ask what's brought this . . . brutal honesty on?'

'The irony is, someone else needed me more. God, I sound like bloody Nanny McPhee.' Bella snorted and we both started to laugh.

'Nate, by any chance?'

'No, not him. His daughter. She needed someone.' And I realised that I was my own worst enemy. I couldn't resist being needed but with Grace it had been different because, in her, I'd seen so much of myself at the same age. That earnest desire to please everyone. To do the right thing. I wanted to save her from feeling that was how she had to be.

'Which reminds me, I can only stay until twelve.' I slipped a finger under the neckline of my dress to touch the silk-covered strap of my new bra.

Bella opened her mouth, about to say something, and then laughed. 'Good for you.'

'So I was thinking. Christmas Day. How would you feel about doing pudding: the works, brandy butter, cream and the pud?'

'No problem.' She smiled. 'That's a great idea. It's crazy to expect you to do it all.'

'I was thinking I'd ask Tina to bring the veg and prepare it all. Dad can do the cheeseboard and I thought I'd ask your mum to bring the port. Oh, and the crackers. That way she doesn't actually have to do anything.'

Bella sniggered. 'That'll suit Mum right down to the ground.'

'And I thought you could tell everyone.'

Bella threw back her head and let out a huge belly laugh. 'Oh, the worm has turned. Viola, I love you. We really couldn't have done without you these last few years. I don't think you appreciate how much you've been the glue that's held us all together.'

'I'm also thinking about inviting Nate and Grace.'

Bella's brows lifted and I blushed.

'Just because they'll be on their own, just the two of them, and it's much nicer, especially . . . well, it would be nicer for Grace to be with other children and I think Nate would probably like adult company.'

'Right,' she said in a teasing voice, before adding, 'What a Good Samaritan you are.'

Chapter 27

I ran lightly up the steps, my hands full of shopping bags, including a paper carrier bag from Mr Christian's, in my gorgeous new dress, butterflies leaping and dancing in my stomach with joyous abandon and a fair amount of sexual anticipation.

When Nate opened the door, I stopped dead.

It was as if he'd aged overnight, he looked so tired and worn. There was a greyness about him and I instinctively reached out a hand, he looked ill, but he backed away, staying behind the door as if it were a barrier against the plague or something.

Behind him, Grace was on the stairs and when she saw me she beamed and jumped the last two steps and came running over, pulling up short in front of me, ignoring Nate's warning hand.

'Viola! Viola! You'll never guess.' Her face turned up to me, so alight with happiness she almost glowed. 'Mummy's home! Mummy's home!' she squealed with a shudder of excitement and with that she whirled and raced away towards the back of the house.

I lifted my eyes to Nate's face. He looked at me warily.

'I tried to call you,' he said in a dull, flat voice.

'My phone . . .' I'd ignored the low battery warning and it had died. I'd meant to charge it at Bella's but we'd got into things.

Stupidly, all my brain could do was flag up the rather obvious. No sex then. I was worried I might blurt it out for the sheer lack of knowing what else to say.

Nate just looked at me.

What did he want me to do? *Give me some clues here*. Nothing had prepared me for this eventuality. I searched his face again, my heart a solid lump in my chest. His expression was blank.

'Ah, Viola.' The cool blonde of all my imaginings appeared at Nate's side. Although I'd seen pictures, her effortless elegance and gracious mannerisms were exactly as I'd envisioned. 'How lovely to meet you. Do come in. I've heard so much about you. It seems I owe you quite a debt of gratitude for looking after Grace . . .' there was an infinitesimal pause '. . . and Nate.' Her face held nothing but friendly welcome tinged with a look of enquiry. 'I'm Elaine, Nate's wife.' She held out a slim, elegant ballerina's hand, her left, in what I knew was a deliberate off-balancing tactic. I shook it, aware of my calloused fingers gracing her smooth, perfect skin.

'Hi,' I said, my voice coming out a little wheezy. 'I was . . . erm . . .' How the hell did I get out of this one?

'Come on, come in. I've got a lovely pot of Guatemalan coffee on the go. I need one, jet lag is such a bitch.' Her calm assumption that I'd come in sort of hypnotised me and I stepped inside.

'Let me take your coat. Grace, could you hang . . . Violet's coat up. Oh, what a lovely dress.' There was a loaded pause and I felt myself blush furiously. 'Are you going somewhere nice?'

Did I imagine the unspoken, *or were you planning to shag my husband?*

I smoothed down the heavy crepe fabric. 'It's for work. I'm going to work.'

'Oh.' She led the way down to the kitchen with Grace skipping ahead and Nate lagging behind. I didn't dare turn my head and look at him. I'd left the pile of bags beside the front door.

'A nice dress for work,' she said, inviting me to take a seat at the breakfast bar, her brow wrinkling in what could only be described as a light frown; it was really quite peculiar, as if she was faced with a riddle of great complexity that she wasn't terribly interested in solving but was asking out of politeness. 'I thought you worked with children.' She gave the dress which, come on, surely she couldn't find fault with, another cool glance.

I sat down in my usual seat, my heart bumping uncomfortably. 'I play in the orchestra. For the London Metropolitan Opera Company.'

Her mouth dropped open. That did surprise her and I felt I'd scored a small rather marginal point when the game was very much hers. I had no idea what was going on and I didn't dare look at Nate for any kind of reassurance. Elaine held all the cards and I was clueless as to what the game was. What had Nate told her about me?

'Guess what she plays?' asked Grace, tugging at her mother's sleeve. 'Guess, Mummy. Guess.'

'Grace, stop that.' She brushed Grace's fingers off.

'But it's really funny.' Grace grinned at me, ignoring the snap in her mother's voice. 'She plays the viola and . . . she's called . . . Viola.' She clapped her hands.

'Grace, really calm down. I don't know what's got into you. Sit down and be quiet.'

Elaine shot Nate an angry accusing look across the kitchen before turning to me. 'That must be interesting. So, I'm intrigued. How on earth did you meet *my* husband –' there was no mistaking the emphasis '– and end up looking after our daughter?' Cue tinkling laughter and coy Hollywood tilt to the head, although anyone with half a brain would know that now we were getting to the nitty-gritty. Gloves off.

'Through your mother, actually,' I said, in a jolly, isn't-this-great-fun tone because hello, lady, I had done nothing wrong. 'She approached the Opera House, wanting to know if any of our outreach programmes might include her granddaughter's school. As I live locally, I was asked to help Grove Leys School with a music project.' I beamed at her. 'When I met Mrs Roberts, the headteacher, she introduced me to Mr Williams, in his role as governor.

'Since then I've been working on the nativity with the school. One evening Grace wasn't picked up from school, I happened to be in the school office and I agreed to take her home, on the proviso that Mr Williams got home before six, so that I could go to work.

'As he was desperate and I am free between three and six most days, I agreed to help out for two weeks.'

I could see her digesting all this and I could feel Nate's eyes on me. I felt as if I were walking blind – how much had he told her? Would she know the spare room had been in use? I knew the cleaner came in twice a week. Perhaps she'd obliterated all sign of me in the master bedroom. Where was Elaine sleeping? Or, rather, where was Nate sleeping? Back in the master bedroom, in the marital bed?

My eyes strayed to the dining area. The table had been moved back and the Christmas tree had been pushed further into the corner.

'That's very generous of you.' Her eyes narrowed and she let the first arrow fly. 'My husband has always been . . . lucky that way.'

Ouch.

'I didn't do it for your husband,' I said, turning to Grace, whose eyes were a little wary and she was watching the adults with that deer-about-to-flee look about her. 'I did it for Grace. We've become quite good friends.'

'Viola's going to teach me to play the viola,' said Grace, giving a little twirl.

'Violin first.' I winked.

'Yes, because the viola's a lot bigger. You'd think it would be smaller, wouldn't you?'

I bit back a smile at her repetition of my words and took a sip of the coffee and almost gasped. Eek! It was strong. That would wake the dead. Note to self, avoid Guatemalan coffee in future.

'Grace, sit down nicely. Where's your colouring book? I don't know why you're being so giddy and silly. You're going to knock something over and break it. And I think the piano would be more suitable if you're going to learn an instrument . . . And what is my hurricane lamp doing down here!' Her mouth pinched tight and she glared at the offending ornament. 'I'm going to have strong words with the cleaner.' She turned to Nate. 'I think she's been slacking a bit. You need to stay on top of her.'

A muscle moved in Nate's cheek and I sneaked a look at him, trying to hide my sudden amusement, pushing back the red-hot memory of the weight of him on top of me on the sofa.

Elaine huffed and turned away, snatching up the hurricane lamp. Nate and I exchanged a look, his amused, apologetic and touched with longing. He remembered too.

'This needs to go back in the lounge. Nate.' She held it towards him.

As soon as he'd gone, she turned to me, all smiles, and took a step forward with the intent of a spider homing in on the fly trapped at the centre of its web.

'I am so grateful to you for looking after Grace. It was so irresponsible of the nanny to take off like that, although why Nate hasn't sorted a new one out yet . . .' She shook her head and gave me a conspiratorial roll of her eyes. 'He really shouldn't have imposed on you but –' she sighed and looked a little dreamy-eyed, which was oh, so fake '– he is rather irresistible. I made a terrible mistake –' she lowered her voice, shooting a glance at Grace, who was now quietly colouring in '– I let us drift apart. Thinking my job in New York was enough. It wasn't.'

Did she think her daughter was deaf or stupid?

'I'm back for good.' Although her voice was soft and her smile bright, there was no mistaking the implicit warning. 'And I'm so looking forward to a traditional family Christmas. There's nothing quite like it. Do you have family?'

I laughed. 'I have family. A big one.'

'I always think that must be nice.' She winked at me, all matey and chummy again, but I knew fake when I saw it. 'Nate and I need to get to work to expand ours, I think. A little brother or sister for Gracie.'

Grace's head whipped round and Elaine let out an oops giggle.

'Don't get too excited, darling. These things take time.'

'Sarah at school got two new brothers at once. Her mum had twins.'

Elaine shuddered and smoothed the jersey fabric of her expensive-looking dress across her stomach. 'I can't think of anything worse.'

I took another sip of the blood-curdling coffee and then put it down; my stomach was protesting. I looked at my watch. 'Well, I really ought to be going. I've got a rehearsal this afternoon and then work.'

'Mummy simply loves the opera. Maybe you can get me some tickets for her.' Elaine was already at my elbow, ready to show me out. 'I'm quite cross with her and Daddy. They're with friends on Christmas Day. It's just going to be the three of us and I can't get a booking for lunch anywhere for love nor money. It'll be such a fag if I have to go out and buy a turkey and everything.'

As I was ushered up the stairs – oh, yes, Elaine was keen to see me go – I was tempted to tell her that Nate had an online shopping account with Sainsbury's, but I decided against it.

Nate met us in the hall.

I looked at the bags by the door and then back at him, while Elaine got my coat from the cupboard muttering about the dreadful state of it.

'Violet is just leaving,' she said, laying a hand on his arm.

'It's Viola,' said Nate a little tersely.

'Oh, silly me, of course it is. Well, it was lovely to meet you. Grace prattled on and on about you.' She put a graceful hand to her throat. 'I have to admit to feeling quite jealous, but –' she moved her hand to touch my shoulder '– now I've met you, I can see I had nothing to worry about. You're been so kind to her. I can't tell you how grateful I am that you've been looking after my little girl for me. She's such a poppet.'

Her smile dimmed. 'I haven't always made the best decisions but I hope that . . .' she swallowed '. . . I hope that you'll give us some time and space to mend a few fences. I've got a lot of . . .' she shot Nate an embarrassed grimace, nibbling at her lip '. . . I've got a lot of work to do. To make up to Nate and Grace.' She flashed me a quick, bright smile. 'Must try harder.' Despite her glib words, I saw the shame in her body language, the tentative hand reaching out towards Nate, and I felt terribly sorry for her.

Nate's jaw tensed as he came to the door. 'Elaine, would

you mind?' he ground out, his voice like gravel. 'I'd like a private word with Viola before she leaves.'

'Grace, darling, come say goodbye to Viola,' said Elaine, blatantly putting a spoke in the wheel. She pushed her daughter in front of her and Nate and I didn't miss the symbolism. The perfect family unit. It was a challenge to me – did I really want to split that up?

Nate's eyes narrowed and I was surprised by the sudden fury in them. But it was no good. This had to be about Grace. My heart clenched. A united front. They were a pair. A pair who were trying to do the right thing for their daughter.

'I'd better go,' I said with a brittle smile at Elaine, refusing to meet Nate's eyes. 'I'm sure Grace is thrilled to have you home for Christmas.'

I looked down at the Disney and H&M bags at the door, next to the deli bag.

I picked up the bag of food and opened the front door.

'Bye,' I said and walked down the steps.

'Wait, Vi—'

'—Bye, Viole . . . Viola,' said Elaine, loudly speaking over Nate, and I could see her arm blocking his path, her other arm looped around Grace's shoulders. 'Lovely to meet you. And thank you again for everything.'

I turned and looked at the three of them standing in the doorway together.

It was a scene of family solidarity and I felt as if I'd been punched in the stomach.

Chapter 28

When the door clicked shut, with a finality that hit me hard, I lifted my head and walked, one foot in front of the other, my vision blurry. *The show must go on.* Cue Freddie Mercury lyrics in my head. They kept me going to the end of the street, keeping the tears at bay.

The show must go on. The golden rule of performing. Even more so in the orchestra. Death and heart attack were the only good reasons for not turning up to work. I'd never had a day off sick or otherwise and I wasn't about to start now, even though I felt like curling up in a ball and howling.

On the corner of the street, I was about to dump the deli bag into someone's wheelie bin when I remembered I'd passed some poor rough sleeper on the way here. With quick, angry strides I walked back to the high street and the doorway where I'd seen him. He wasn't there but his tatty sleeping bag and pile of dirty blankets suggested he hadn't gone too far. I put the bag of food on the blankets and hoped the bedraggled man I'd seen earlier would enjoy it, although a hot cup of coffee would probably be more welcome than olives, sun-dried tomatoes and prosciutto. Take that, Nate Williams. Except, of course, I had to acknowledge he hadn't looked very happy. And neither had Elaine; she'd looked sad and embarrassed. But, the absolute kicker, Grace had been glowing.

Her mum was home – and home for Christmas. That had to be a good thing, didn't it? It had to be about Grace. Despite telling myself that, I felt horribly sorry for myself.

Abandoning my original plan to walk home, ignoring the tight griping pains in my chest, my stomach, my leg muscles, in fact just about everywhere, I turned in the opposite direction, considering for a brief moment the options of popping in to see Mum and Dad or going back to Bella's. I couldn't face either but I didn't want to be on my own.

I welcomed the noise and buzz of Portobello Market, the shouts of fruit-sellers vying with each other to offer the best deals, the irate beeps of a dustcart reversing and a police siren barely a street away. Despite the cold, the streets were crammed with bobble-hatted Christmas shoppers. The fruit and veg stalls sported additional wares, with bunches of mistletoe and holly, netted fir trees and clove-covered oranges hanging from the metal frames. As I wandered along, aimless and detached, my senses were heightened. I could smell mulled wine and spices. Ginger here and cinnamon there. My eyes were drawn to the glitz and shine of dozens of stalls selling cheap wrapping paper bundled up, five for a fiver, and piled high with flimsy Christmas cards, three boxes for the price of two. Some stall-holders had paid lip service to the festivities with a few begrudging straggly strands of tinsel while others had whole-heartedly embraced the season to be jolly with everything but the kitchen sink, displaying loops and swags of tinsel, outsize baubles, fairy lights and the obligatory deer antlers on dummies heads, their own heads and their dogs' heads.

The market only provided so much of a distraction and when the cold began to seep in I turned and headed for home. There were still a couple of hours before I needed to go to work. Suddenly I wanted the solace of my viola. To lose myself in music.

Turning so quickly I barrelled into a couple coming the other way, who were luckily so full of festive cheer that they brushed aside my desperate apologies.

As soon as I got home which, thanks to magic Mike the plumber's ministrations, was now very toasty, I literally dropped my coat, hat, scarf and gloves in a Hansel and Gretel trail as I walked through to my music room. With my usual ritual I unclicked the locks of the case and reached for my viola, sliding it into place and closing my eyes as I lifted my bow. I took the breath, the familiar pause and then touched the bow to the strings. Some Vivaldi first because it was second nature, straight into Spring, familiar, easy notes that came without having to think or work. As I warmed up, thoughts of Nate began to seep in and I could feel anger itching in the tips of my fingers. I changed my tune, literally, bursting into *Ride of the Valkyries,* playing with angry intensity before moving onto the darker Holst's *Mars*, plying my bow with stealthy rage. *Bringer of War* matched my mood and, although I was only playing the strings, I could hear the full orchestration in my head, percussion, brass and woodwind. I played with a manic fervour, feeding the pent-up rage at the injustice of it all.

It took a while for the banging on the door to penetrate. If it hadn't been for the vehemence of the knocking I would have ignored it, but I could tell whoever it was wasn't going to go away. At first I thought it might be Bella; it had the hallmarks of her persistence. Then I wondered if it was Nate. No, Elaine wouldn't be letting him out of her sight any time soon. She'd marked her territory good and proper.

The banging was continuing when I got to the front door.

'OK, OK, I'm coming,' I yelled. 'Give me chance to get to the door.'

I wrenched it open, feeling like my hapless innkeeper and even very nearly shouted George's lines.

'Nate!'

'You took your time.'

'I was practising. I didn't hear you.'

'I could hear you.' His face softened. 'Are you OK?'

I blinked. He couldn't be nice to me; that wasn't fair. I wanted to be mad at him. Furious.

'Can I come in?' When I stared at him, not speaking, he prompted, 'Viola?'

With a sigh I nodded, not daring to speak. I wanted to turn away and leave him to close the door. Be detached and tough. But I wasn't built that way. Instead I waited for him to come in and closed the door behind him.

He stood in my lounge, his hair damp, with his big wool city lawyer's coat over jeans and battered tennis shoes. It struck me that he looked like my Nate . . . not Mr Nine-to-Five that I'd first seen in a crowded tube.

The expression on his face was solemn and so reminiscent

of Grace it hurt to look at him. I think that made it worse. I knew he was hurting as much as I was.

'I'm sorry that you had to arrive at the house unprepared,' he said in a ridiculous stiff tone.

'Nate . . .' I tried to interrupt but he held up his hand as if this was a rehearsed speech.

'I did try to call . . . several times.' I caught a glimpse of pain as his shoulders lifted. 'But you weren't picking up.'

'No. Didn't charge my phone.'

There was a flicker of a smile. 'What are you like?'

We stared at each other for a moment and then, taking a couple of paces, he stepped away to the other side of the room, holding himself aloof. His mouth kept opening and I could see the dip of his Adam's apple but he didn't say anything; instead his gaze kept slipping to the window as if he were desperate to escape.

'What happened?' I asked softly, wanting to relieve the burden I could see he was bowed down by.

He sighed, his eyes meeting mine. 'Can we sit down?'

As soon as he said the words, I knew it was all over. There was a telling resignation to his body language. His shoulders didn't look so broad, his chin seemed to have receded and his eyes had dulled. The fight in me simply died, without even so much as a whimper.

Like the good girl I'd always been, I sat. My knees together, my hands primly on my lap. This was going to be a grown-up talk. And he sat opposite me, like the good boy, sinking into the armchair, near enough to place a comforting hand on mine but far enough away to maintain the necessary distance and detachment. With bizarre, twisted logic this almost reassured me, the fact that he needed no-man's land, to keep himself apart from me.

I watched him take a breath, the girding of his loins. Standard preparation to deliver bad news. It reminded me of one of those episodes of *Casualty* where Charlie – it was always Charlie when I used to watch – has to go in and tell the relatives that someone has died. Nate was about to deliver the death knell.

'Elaine came home. I wasn't . . . there was no warning. The doorbell rang. I opened the door and she was there.'

I could tell from his shocked face he was reliving the moment.

'And I knew I didn't love her any more.' The quiet words were said with calm finality.

Then he looked at me. 'I love you.'

My heart skipped, missing several beats.

'And I shouldn't . . . I shouldn't say that because . . . I'm sorry, Viola, I shouldn't have said that. It's not fair. Not fair on you.'

'I know,' I said, reaching my hand out to touch his. 'I know.'

We looked at each other with sadness and understanding.

'It's Grace.' He turned his hand, palm up, our hands simply touching, a contact but nothing more.

'Of course it is,' I said.

'I read her note to Father Christmas. She wants her mum. Top of her list. What can I do?'

'It's OK.'

He swallowed and looked out of the window again.

'Elaine's back. Back from New York. Wants to try again.' He frowned. 'We've done a lot of talking. She says she realised what she's thrown away and she . . . she still loves me.' I could see that didn't sit well with him. 'I didn't tell her . . . I didn't even realise till I saw her.' His mouth curved downwards. 'But . . . Grace needs her mother. We're a family. I have to try and make my marriage work. Elaine wants to try again. I owe it to her and to Grace to try. To make that commitment. And . . . you saw Grace . . .'

I nodded, swallowing hard, and did my best to give him a reassuring smile even though my vision was completely blurred. *Mummy's home! Mummy's home!*

There was a painful silence as we stared at each other. A few tears escaped and I could see the pulse in Nate's temple, the slight sheen in his eyes and the convulsive swallow.

'Oh, Viola . . .' His fingers curled over mine, hanging on tightly to my hand. 'Don't cry, please.'

'S-sorry, I c-can't h-help it. I'm sorry.'

With one swift movement he sat down next to me and scooped me onto his lap and I began to cry in earnest while he held me, his lips buried in my hair.

This wasn't fair on him. I hauled in a breath. And then another and focused on in and out, slow and steady, before looking up at him with tearstained eyes, which I hated because it felt manipulative. I dashed my hands over my face to wipe them away.

'Sorry.' I tried to be brisk but then he stroked my face. Even though I knew it was wrong I turned and kissed his palm. He closed his eyes.

It would be so easy to reach up and kiss him and I knew he'd probably respond. One last kiss. But it would still hurt like crazy. There had to be a cut-off point and it had to be now.

As I'd always said, this wasn't about us. It was about Grace.

I wrenched myself out of his lap and stepped away.

'I think we probably need to say goodbye,' I said with a mock cheery, brave smile.

He sighed and hauled himself to his feet, looking worn-out. 'I guess we do. I can't—'

I held up a hand. 'Don't. We could make this into a really long drawn-out goodbye, with explanations, promises to see each other as friends, never see each other again. I think, to use that faithful old cliché . . . the best thing for us is a clean break. The nativity will be done on Tuesday. End of term on Wednesday and then, three days later, it will be Christmas and by the New Year Grace will have forgotten all about me. Children are resilient, they have short memories and the excitement of having her mum home is going to eclipse this last couple of weeks.' I said all this as if I had any clue.

'A clean break, Nate.' I gave him another fake smile. 'And you're a married man. I'd never have been cut out to be a scarlet woman.'

I wish I could say he looked relieved I'd made it easy for him but instead sadness clouded his eyes and he hesitated for a moment. 'God, I'm sorry. Bye, Viola.' He leaned forward and kissed my cheek. Touching my lips with one finger. 'Look after yourself.'

I watched him walk up my basement steps. Half hoping that he would look back, even though I didn't want him to.

Chapter 29

'He'll be here,' said Tilly, stopping me from my pacing and putting firm hands on my shoulders. 'There's still an hour and a half before the parents arrive.'

She kept shooting me worried looks. I'd kept myself ridiculously busy since Saturday and it showed. The bags under my eyes were big enough to pack for a three-week holiday. I'd been wreath-making with Tina on Sunday, present-wrapping with Bella on Sunday evening and I took Ella and Rosa and their cousins to see *Frozen II* after school last night, so that Bella and Tina could go Christmas shopping at Westfield, which hadn't turned out to be such a good idea because I sat and cried at all the sad bits, thinking of Grace. And suddenly it was Tuesday and the big day was here and nearly everything was in place. I felt knackered, nervous and excited. The children had worked their socks off and yesterday's dress rehearsal in front of the whole school had gone perfectly. Please let today, with the parents in the audience, go smoothly.

I looked at the empty space where the backdrop was supposed to be and then down at the stage, which was currently graced by a solitary bale of hay and the hand-built manger that Tilly's boyfriend Marcus had kindly delivered to the school. I figured he must love Tilly an awful lot to allow hay in his smart Mercedes and to unload the fifty costumes into which Leonie was currently pinning and sewing small children.

Backstage, or rather in Oak and Apple classes, thankfully several mums were helping to keep the lid on the rising hysteria.

George, like me, was pacing, his cheeks already red from his own exertion, mouthing his lines to himself a little wild-eyed. Realising my own rising panic was probably brushing off, I forced myself to take a deep breath and go over and speak to him.

'You're going to be brilliant, George.'

'I feel sick,' he mumbled.

'Stage fright. All the best actors get it,' I said. 'Seriously, I have seen the most famous opera singers . . .' I tried to think of someone he could relate to. 'You know the Go Compare man?' I didn't know the poor bloke from Adam but I didn't think he'd mind me maligning him in the name of kindness.

George nodded, his eyes still chasing all over the room, not quite meeting mine.

'He stands on the side of the stage. Quaking. Honest to God, his knees are actually shaking.'

'Honest, miss?'

'Honest,' I lied. 'It's a good thing. It means all your adrenaline is going.'

'I know what drenaline is,' piped up one of the scrawny

little lads who was one of George's mates, 'that's the stuff that makes you perform better, run faster, escape from lions.' He added with a very knowledgeable nod to show that this was gospel, 'Saw it on *Deadly Dozen*.'

'That's right,' I agreed, grateful to see that George had stopped pacing.

'Did you see the one with the tarantula?' George's mate's eyes widened to the size of dinner plates. I smiled and left them to an in-depth conversation as to which was more terrifying – finding a tarantula in your bed or coming face to face with a crocodile in the river.

I moved away and then stopped in horror, a small girl – I remembered her from the first rehearsal – demure, perfect plaits. Suggested *Away in a Manger* and had been scarily well behaved, almost like Wednesday Addams, throughout every rehearsal – was carefully and methodically opening the beautifully wrapped gift of myrrh that the props guys had made for me.

'No!' I cried and she looked up, freezing, her hands hovering over the incredibly expensive bronze paper. I snatched the prop from her and she burst into tears.

'Sorry, sorry.' I looked to one of the mums who came scurrying over with a reproving tut. 'Sorry. Very expensive prop. I have to return it to the Opera House.'

'Well, she didn't know that,' said the mum with a calm smile. 'There, there, Rebecca. It's OK, you didn't know.'

And it was OK to open a random present? I turned away, realising I was turning into a right misery.

I moved through into the other classroom, deliberately not

seeking out Grace, but a sixth sense hummed and in my peripheral vision I pinpointed exactly where she was in the room. By the window, with Cassie . . . and oh my God. I did look that way. I couldn't help it. Oh my God again. I stared at the three-foot wings, trimmed with what looked like real feathers covered in pearlized glitter and tipped with gold paint, shimmering in the weak winter sunshine coming in through the glass. Cassie lifted her head and preened as she caught my astonished gaze. On her head was a large, we're talking super large, tinsel halo complete with tiny winking fairy lights and she wore a white empire-line dress which fell in heavy folds to the gold sandals at her feet. And in her hand she held a sparkly wand.

I gave her a bland smile and would have turned around but Grace's steady stare made me stop.

'Hi Grace, how are you? All ready for today?'

Her eyes glittered and she nodded. 'Mummy's coming to watch.'

I smiled and it wasn't at all forced. 'That's lovely. She'll be so proud of you. The best, bossiest innkeeper's wife ever.'

She grinned at me and waved a teasing, nagging finger. 'And don't you forget it.'

I laughed. It was one of my favourite lines, delivered to George when he had to admit she was always right.

'My mummy's coming too,' said Cassie, tossing her hair over her shoulder and getting it a bit tangled in her wings. 'She says my costume will be the best.'

I simply nodded and hoped that Leonie wasn't within earshot. She would be horrified at the manmade fabric, the plastic feathers and the liberal use of inappropriate glitter and I could almost guarantee she'd go ballistic at the sight of the tacky wand.

I breathed a little easier. There, that hadn't been so bad. I'd seen Grace and she was happy. I wasn't going to think about Nate. Whether he was happy. The familiar stab of pain, like a stiletto sliding under my ribs, bit hard as I pictured him in my lounge. Stop doing this, I told myself. I sneaked another look at Grace, giggling at something Cassie said.

I went over to the other side of the classroom, where Tilly was doing sterling work; she had a queue of customers and had set up three stations. Two of the mums were helping, following her instructions, stippling rough beards on the shepherds with sponges, and Tilly was hard at work, her fingers deftly stroking and shading grey and white lines to create the donkey.

'That's amazing,' I said, coming to her side.

'Thanks,' she said. 'I haven't done face-painting for ages. I'd forgotten what fun it is. What do you think?' She pointed behind her to the oxen, the cows and the three kings, all of whom sported curly moustaches and exotic eye make-up.

'Fabulous.' Then I began to laugh. 'The armadillo is fabulous.' The props guys had created a little armoured vest with moving parts that clicked and creaked while Tilly had worked wonders to create a thin narrow face with anxious eyes. Jack waved an excited paw, flexing his back for me, showing off the Jacob's ladder-like movement of the pieces. 'I am the holiday armadillo. A desert armadillo.'

My eyes were drawn back to the three kings. Cassie's mum, eat your heart out. Leonie had done me proud. Each of them wore heavy swirling capes in brilliant silk fabric, one red, one yellow and one royal blue, over purple velvet robes. The design was simple but the richness and generous cut of the fabrics made them look sumptuous and luxurious. Simple, tasteful gold crowns topped their heads. They looked quite magnificent.

Next to them, my quiet stately Mary, little Sarah, looked serene and utterly perfect in her Madonna blue robes and my heart nearly broke when she lifted her head and gave me a shy smile and beckoned me over. From behind her back she brought out a small, beautifully wrapped gift.

'This is to say thank you.'

'Oh, Sarah . . .' tears pricked my eyes '. . . that's so kind of you. You didn't have to do that.'

'It's from Mummy really . . .' she whispered. 'She's really happy because I've never been anything before.'

Oh, dear, the tears were coming.

'Sweetie . . . you are something.' I gave her a swift hug. I know you're not supposed to, I've done all the child safe-guarding training, but she was just ace.

I needed to get a grip. I'd had barely any sleep since Saturday and my hormones were all over the place today. I was so bloody emotional. At this rate, I'd be blubbing before any of them got on stage.

'I'm just going to pop outside for a minute,' I said to Tilly. 'Get a breath of fresh air.'

'You all right?' she asked, shrewdly scanning my face.

'Bit emotional today,' I said, feeling my throat starting to close again. I hadn't told anyone about Nate. I couldn't bring myself to.

362

'It's your big day; of course you are. And some of this lot are so cute. Mary –' she squeezed her hands together over her heart '– just adorable. And George. I thought he was going to be funny about having his make-up done . . . By the end he was begging for more lipstick. Quite a character, that one.' She glanced over towards Cassie. 'Mascara! Seriously. No way.'

I patted her on the shoulder. 'Thanks, Tilly. You and Leonie have really made a difference. If nothing else, it's going to look spectacular.'

'Viola, the singing sounds gorgeous and the script . . . it's so funny. You've done a brilliant job. Seriously, the parents are going to love it.'

I crossed my fingers. 'I hope so.'

'You know so.'

Providing everything came together, which reminded me . . . 'Oh God, do you think that sodding backdrop has turned up yet?'

The sodding backdrop arrived in the nick of time and was just being fixed to the climbing frame as a few parents started to file into the hall. The music teacher was at the piano playing a few carols very softly.

I crossed and stood behind her, tapping her lightly on the shoulder. 'Everything OK?'

'Yes,' she said, continuing to play without fudging a note, 'and that backdrop is awesome . . . as is the very tasty piece of hot stuff putting it up. If you can get his number, I'll be your best friend forever.'

I laughed. 'I can certainly try.'

'But seriously, Viola, it's been amazing working with you. You've made it fun for the children, kept it simple, but it's really come together. You should be really proud of yourself. If I weren't playing . . . consider yourself hugged.'

'Oh, don't you set me off. I'm a mess this morning.'

'That's working with kids for you. Wait until the end. You'll be sobbing. And that's way embarrassing in front of the parents. Although most of the mums cry.'

Parents. My heart thudded uncomfortably in my chest. Oh God, Nate would be arriving at any moment. But I'd known that. Prepared myself. It would probably be the last time I'd ever see him and I wouldn't have to talk to him.

I hastily looked around; more parents were starting to fill the seats in the front few rows. Thankfully no sign of Nate or Elaine. A few curious eyes looked my way and I slipped back into the classroom, calling for everyone to come through from the other classroom.

'OK, guys.' I clapped my hands together. 'The parents are starting to arrive and they're just through those doors, so we need to be quiet now. Just a few things to remember. You've all worked really hard and you're going to be . . . fab . . .'

'U . . . lous,' they all chorused back at me.

'Remember, chins up when you're singing and speaking. Smile when you're singing. Except for George; you can stay grumpy.'

He gave me a double thumbs up.

'And just enjoy yourselves. Thank you all for working so hard and it's been lovely.'

Bless them, they all started clapping, which made me get all emotional again. Thank God for waterproof mascara.

The head teacher popped her head around the door. 'All set?' She beamed at all the children. 'I know you're going to be wonderful. All the mummies and daddies are here. I'm just going to say a few words and then you can start.'

She withdrew her head and excited chatter began to rise.

'Shh,' I said. 'Everyone needs to be quiet now.'

The children crept through the door, the choir to the left of the stage, the cast staying behind except for George who, carrying his duvet, climbed onto the stage and lay down in the middle.

Sarah in her Madonna blue gazed up at me with terror-stricken eyes, clutching Joseph's hand. Behind them, Jack the armadillo paced in readiness.

'OK, Mary and Joseph, off you go. Jack just behind them. Remember, speak loudly.' God, I hoped Sarah would remember; she had a natural tendency to quietness.

I needn't have worried; that girl had star quality. The minute she stepped on stage, she was Mary. My heart almost burst with pride, especially when I saw – it had to be – her mother leaning forward, almost gasping with amazement.

Joseph rapped tentatively on the door, exactly as we'd rehearsed.

George snored. The audience giggled. George snored louder.

Joseph knocked a little louder.

Jack the armadillo stepped in front of him and barged open the door.

And they were off. It took a little while for the cast and the chorus to settle down; there was a lot of neck-craning and searching as the children tried to spot their parents and a few surreptitious waves but eventually they forgot about that.

It was gratifying that the audience laughed in all the right places and even in some of the wrong ones, especially when one of the kings presented his gift of *Frankenstein*. There was a near mishap when one of Cassie's wings got caught on the edge of the manger but, with her usual quiet efficiency, Mary unhooked her and with a gentle pat sent her on her way.

George and Grace stole the show with their comic bickering and her line, 'And don't you forget it,' almost brought the house down. Although Joseph with his to 'Affinity and Bethlehem,' came a close second.

I kept my concentration focused on the children and the stage, even though I knew Nate was probably somewhere in the audience. I did pretty well until the final carol. I spotted him sitting next to Zoe De Marco and, despite all my good intentions, I couldn't stop my eyes straying towards him or the flip of my heart at the sight of those broad shoulders and the sleek dark hair. Strangely, there was no sign of Elaine. Perhaps she was sitting somewhere else.

As the music teacher played the piano louder and gave the children a quick signal, they belted out the final verse of *Hark the Herald* – or Harold as it would forever be known to me – *Angels*. I'd baulked at any solos but one little boy had such a heavenly voice I had given him the final two lines to sing by himself to bring the show to a close. As his clear piping voice sang *Glory to the newborn king* I felt those bloody tears leaking out again. But then the parents were on their feet, clapping with genuine rapturous applause. I gestured to the children to all come towards the front of the stage, to take their bows as we'd practised.

I beamed at them all and George cheekily winked at me. I rolled my eyes at him, unable to stop smiling.

Mrs Roberts stepped on stage and it took a minute or two for the applause to die down. Those parents were really enthusiastic but I was delighted for the children; they looked so pleased with themselves, congratulating and hugging each other. From the piano the music teacher grinned at me.

'Well, wasn't that splendid? Children, you were all brilliant. And mums and dads, I'm sure you'll agree they've all done brilliantly.' She paused and there was another spontaneous round of applause. I had to give it to her, she knew how to work an audience. 'We'd like to invite you to stay for a cup of coffee and a mince pie but, in the meantime, I have a few thank yous.

'Of course I am particularly grateful to the London Metropolitan Opera Company, who very kindly loaned us the services of Miss Viola Smith as part of their primary schools outreach programme. Miss Smith plays in the orchestra and for the last few weeks she has been working with the children to put together what I'm sure you'll all agree was a superb nativity play.' From the edge of the stage George appeared with a huge bouquet of flowers which he presented to me.

Oh God, the tears were back again. 'Here you go, miss,' he said gruffly, thrusting them at me with little ceremony, which thankfully stopped the would-be tears in their tracks.

'Thanks, George.'

He grinned at me.

'Perhaps you'd like to say a few words, Miss Smith?'

Perhaps I wouldn't! But Mrs Roberts was inviting me up onto the stage. Oh, hell!

Once on the stage, I could see all the parents . . . Nate, Zoe, some other familiar faces.

'Er . . . well . . .' Nate smiled at me but his eyes were shadowed. I swallowed hard. 'I was . . .' I was about to deliver a diplomatic speech but then decided honesty was the best policy.

'I have to admit, I've never produced a nativity play in my life before. I think it went quite well.' The parents laughed and the children cheered. Nate's smile widened and I saw a mixture of pride and sadness. I felt a funny wobble in my chest. This hurt. It hurt so much.

I sucked in a harsh breath. *Don't look at him. Don't look at him.* I focused on the back of the hall. 'It was quite daunting at first but . . . the children made it fun. Talented, interesting, they were brilliant to work with. You should all be very proud of your children, no matter the role they played. They all worked together so well and it's been a joy to spend time with them.' I turned to face them, behind me on the stage. 'Well done, guys. You did good.'

'I have a few thank yous of my own, the biggest one of which goes to Mrs Ames, the class teaching assistant, who has literally been my lifesaver. Thanks, Jo.' I nodded at Sarah who, as primed, produced a bouquet of flowers, sadly not quite as big as mine but certainly much prettier. I'd chosen it myself that morning from Harper & Tom's on Elgin Crescent, taking a detour especially. 'Also my wonderful colleagues from the Opera House, Tilly Hunter and Leonie Golding. Thanks to them, we had these wonderful costumes and the incredible make-up. Can we give them a round of applause?'

And the applause was heartfelt, although not surprising. Tilly and Leonie had raised my average little production into something special. I was so grateful to them.

'I'd also like to thank the props team at the LMOC. They made our props and painted this fabulous backdrop. And that's it; thank you all for coming. I hope you enjoyed it and had as much fun as we did putting it on.'

I lifted my flowers in salute and stepped off the stage to a hug from Tilly and even one from Leonie.

'That was fantastic,' Tilly said.

'Awesome,' added Leonie.

'It worked out OK,' I said with a hearty sigh of relief. It was all over.

Mrs Roberts gave some magical signal and the room went quiet.

'The children will take their costumes and make-up off and join you all for mince pies and coffee.'

It took a while to round all the children up and clean off their make-up and collect up all the costumes. George was grinning from ear to ear as he stood in line. 'My mum came. She never comes to nuffink. She got time off work.'

'That's lovely. Was she impressed?' I asked, pulling another wet wipe out of the packet to rub off one of the twins' moustaches.

'She cried! My mum never cries. Not even when one of her old ladies dies.'

'George's mum works in a care home,' interjected one of the other mums as she scrubbed at his rosy cheeks. 'I bet she was really proud of you, George.'

He went off looking a few inches taller.

Eventually the queue had dwindled and Leonie's clothes rail was almost full.

I looked up, a fresh wipe in my hand, to find a rather subdued Grace in front of me, her rosy innkeeper's wife cheeks at decided odds with her woebegone face.

'Hey, Grace, what's the matter? You were wonderful and did you hear how much everyone laughed when you delivered your line? The audience loved you. Everyone loved you.' Even George had given her a self-conscious little hug when they'd taken their bows.

With one of her trademark indifferent shrugs, she lifted her face for me to clean off her make-up, her mouth pinched tight. I carefully dabbed at her skin, marvelling at how soft it was. She was so small and delicate. I wanted to scoop her up in a hug, tell her everything was all right. I missed her. My wipe was fairly ineffectual against the red face-paint, so I added a dollop of make-up remover for good measure. Poor George's cheeks were still quite stained. Grace bore my ministrations with quiet stillness, her eyes downcast, her lashes resting on her cheeks.

'Is everything OK?' I asked softly, aware that she wouldn't want to attract any attention.

She lifted her head to reveal suspiciously bloodshot eyes.

'Oh, sweet pea, what's the matter?'

'Mummy's not here. She didn't come.'

My heart went out to her. 'Maybe she had to go to work,' I said, sounding reasonable and sympathetic.

'She promised.' Grace's mouth pinched tighter.

'Sometimes . . . things happen that adults don't anticipate, that they can't help.'

With another lift of her shoulders, she looked out of the window, in the same way that Nate had done in my flat. I recognised that same reluctance to share the pain, the attempt to stay detached.

I could have killed Elaine. At least my parents had never promised; they'd been far too vague to make that much of a commitment. It still stung that they'd never come to see the nativity when I was Mary, but I hadn't expected anything else.

Elaine's loss. Sadly, Grace would always remember this.

'Did you like the costumes?' I asked, looking at Grace's striped robe in blues, purples and greens; it was a lot nicer than a belted sheet would have been. Grace brought her gaze back to focus on me.

'She promised.' Grace sniffed and then wiped a hand across her eyes. I ached to hug her. 'But she didn't come.' There was a sad acceptance to her words, as if it was what she'd expected all along.

With another Grace-like change of tack, she said, 'Your job is nimportant, but you come when you say you're going to.'

Ouch. How did I get out of this one?

'Mummy's job is important too. But Daddy came, didn't

he? Did he like your performance? I bet he was really proud of you.'

'Daddy likes everything,' she said wearily, before adding with one of her random tangential changes of tack, 'I have new boots. With flowers on them. Joules ones.'

'That's nice. Mummy bought them? You see, she's thinking about you,' I said, injecting a positive, upbeat note into my voice. I wanted Grace to be happy.

'Yes. She's been doing a lot of shopping. I have new clothes.'

I wondered if Elaine had bought Grace the purple jeans she craved and whether the H&M ones I'd bought as a Christmas present would have to go back. I couldn't remember if I'd given them to Nate or not. There was still a pile of abandoned shopping bags in my music room that I'd not looked at since that abortive visit to the house. And in the corner of my bedroom a black lace bra and matching pants tossed behind the laundry basket, too scorned to even merit being washed. I would probably never wear them again.

I finished rubbing at her cheek; it was still a little red. 'Sorry, Grace, that's the best I can do. When you get home a bit of soap and water should do the trick. Or maybe some of Mummy's make-up remover.'

Mrs Roberts appeared and clapped her hands. 'Is everyone ready? Follow me to the dining room. No running or silliness.'

Despite her words, like unleashed puppies, the children rushed through the hall towards the dining room. I followed more slowly, arriving in time to see them all being reunited with their parents and grandparents amid lots of hugging and squealing. It was a touching sight, especially George throwing himself at his tiny mum, dwarfing her with his enthusiastic hug. Sarah's mum gave me a shy teary smile as she held Sarah's hand and came straight over.

'I just wanted to say thank you. This has been –' she glanced down at her daughter '– a wonderful experience for Sarah.'

Sarah beamed at me. 'Mum cried. I saw her.'

Her mother and I both laughed.

'They were happy tears.' Sarah's mum dropped a kiss on her daughter. 'Why don't you go and get some squash and biscuits?' As Sarah skipped off her mum turned back to me. 'You have no idea how much confidence having this part has given her. I had no idea she was capable of this. She's never wanted to do anything before and she loved it.'

'You're not crying again, are you?' asked a man coming up to take her hand. He shook his head and tutted before saying in a soft voice, 'Although I have to admit I might have shed a couple of tears. Wonderful production and . . . our Sarah, what a revelation! Thank you so much.' The two of them turned to each other and smiled. My heart contracted at the sight of them, both timid and unassuming but so united in their pride for their daughter.

'She's a little star. I hope she does some more things.' I smiled at them as they walked away towards their daughter.

Standing alone for a moment among the sea of children and parents, I felt a little lost and then I caught Nate's eye over Grace's head, buried in his stomach, her arms wrapped around his middle. Compared to the other parents in the room who were all smiles, congratulations and animated conversations, he looked stern and sad as he gazed back at me, those dark brown eyes looking both haunted and stoic at the same time.

Oh God, there was that lump in my throat again. It hurt when I tried to smile back at him. This was too painful. I'd be glad after today that our paths wouldn't cross again. When he dropped his head to look down at his daughter and turned away, I felt grateful and sick at the same time.

Chapter 30

'Hi Miss Smith, it's Grove Leys School here.'

'Hello,' I said cautiously, putting my viola down into its case, my heart taking a nose-dive to my boots. I wasn't expecting to hear from the school again . . . well, not for a while. Now the head had a direct line to the Opera House, I suspected that string would be tugged a time or two more. And I genuinely wouldn't have minded, if it could be guaranteed that I wouldn't run into any of the Williams family.

Yesterday morning had felt like goodbye to Grace and Nate. The end of the nativity bringing with it a clean break.

After tidying up at school, saying my farewells to the staff and children, clutching my bouquet of flowers, sniffing at the roses periodically to hide threatening tears, I'd thrown myself into Christmas preparation with manic desperation. Unable to stay in my flat, I'd carted all my presents, wrapping paper, tags and scissors to my parents' and spent the afternoon wrapping, making shopping lists and working out cooking times for Saturday. Christmas Day was just three days away. The panicked preparation helped, almost stopping me thinking about Grace and Nate, apart from when I'd wrapped their presents, putting the stocking together for Grace and the cashmere scarf for Nate, admittedly dropping a few tears on the soft blue wool which I would give to Dad instead. I'd decided to deliver Grace's stocking some time in the next couple of days, perhaps dumping it on the doorstep with a cowardly knock and run. I couldn't bear the thought of seeing Nate again.

'I'm really sorry to bother you, Miss Smith.' The secretary's hesitant voice brought me back to the present. 'I can't get hold of anyone else.' Like a fox scenting dinner, all my senses went on alert; I even think I stood on tiptoe.

'It's just . . . no one's picked Grace up. We finish early on the last day of term. School officially closed at two-thirty. I wouldn't have called but we can't get hold of anyone . . . Mr Williams isn't answering his phone, there's no answer at the house and Mrs Williams' mobile is permanently engaged.'

I looked at my watch; it was nearly four o'clock. Late by normal pick-up standards.

'I . . . I'm . . . er . . .' My voice dried up, silenced by uncertainty. *Don't get involved, Viola. It's over. You have to leave them alone.*

'Miss Smith?'

'Yes?'

'I didn't like to call . . . not when Mrs Williams is . . .' her pause said it all '. . . but . . . well, the head says the next call is to –' she lowered her voice and whispered, 'social services.'

'Social services?' I squeaked, horrified.

'I know; it sounds drastic . . . but it's procedure.'

'I'll be right there. I'm not far,' I said, dropping to my knees and latching my viola case. Grabbing it and my coat, still talking to her, I waved a goodbye to Mum, mouthed I'd call later and dashed out of the door. 'See you in five.'

Taking off at a run with my coat flapping and my viola case swinging, I couldn't get the image of Grace sitting swinging her legs underneath the clock in the office out of my head.

I could barely speak when I burst through the doors and the secretary buzzed me straight through with a grateful smile. I glanced beyond her to where Grace was sitting, exactly as I'd imagined, her expression inscrutable.

'Hey, sweet pea. Fancy seeing you here,' I said breathlessly, trying to be upbeat. Mary Poppins would have been proud of me.

'Are you going to take me home?' she asked in a cool, almost disinterested tone that was far too adult by half.

'That's the plan. Have you still got a key in your bag?'

She nodded.

'OK,' I said, still trying to pretend everything was fine as I held out a hand. 'Shall we go?'

'Don't you have to go to work?' There was a little quiver to her lips. 'Will you have to leave me on my own?'

I sucked in a quiet painful breath. 'Absolutely not,' I said stoutly. 'But I'm not working tonight. So hot chocolate all round.'

'What if you had to go to work?' she persisted, eyeing me gravely.

'I'd have taken you to my mum's or my cousin's house. Do you remember Bella and her two little girls? They love *Frozen* just like you – I'd have arranged for you to go there and watch it with them. Come on, let's pop your coat on. It's really cold out there. I think it's going to snow again.'

Reassured, Grace lifted her head, her eyes sharpening. 'If it does, can we build Olaf? Like we did with Mr Snow.'

I hesitated. It would have been so easy to say yes but too much had changed; there was no way I could lie to her. 'Let's see if it snows first. Shall we go?' I raised a hand in farewell to the office secretary.

'Thank you, Miss Smith . . . Viola. I've left a message with Mr Williams telling him you've picked up Grace and that she's safe. He has your mobile number, doesn't he?'

'Yes.' Unless he'd been stronger than me and deleted my number.

As soon as we left the school Grace tucked her hand into mine and I squeezed it, conscious of her unconditional trust as we set off back to her house in the gloomy twilight.

The roads were busy with the start of rush hour traffic, car headlights like moonbeams reflected on the slick, wet roads, their tyres hissing like malevolent snakes as they passed us. I realised Grace's grip had tightened as if she were worried I might let go.

'How was your day?' I asked brightly, trying to disguise the heaviness of my heart. Why hadn't she been picked up? An hour and a half sitting waiting. I wanted to hug her tight; I'd missed her so much and this uncharacteristic quietness really worried me.

'OK.'

'What did you do?' I asked in a sparkly voice, still rocking the Julie Andrews impersonation.

'We watched a DVD.'

'What did you watch?'

She shrugged. 'Can't remember.'

'A Christmas film?' I persisted.

Another shrug.

'Are you looking forward to the holidays? To Christmas?'

She shook her head in quick, vehement denial, her small mouth pursed as she looked up at me with guarded suspicion.

'Why not?' I asked.

She gave yet another listless shrug.

Christmas was supposed to be magical, full of sparkle and happiness, especially when you were seven. I looked down at her closed, shuttered face, feeling helpless.

The house was in complete darkness as we climbed the front steps. When I switched on the lights the first thing I noticed was the huge Christmas tree, dwarfing the grand staircase, decked out in co-ordinating blue and silver balls.

'New tree,' I said, addressing the fir in the room.

Grace inclined her head and made no comment but as we walked past, heading for our usual sanctuary of the kitchen, I saw her reach out and touch a bauble tucked away towards the back, almost out of sight. Something squeezed my heart. It was the glass decoration I'd given her.

'Would you like something to eat? Shall I make some tea?'

Grace nodded.

'Or you could wait for Mummy and Daddy?'

She shook her head. 'They have grown-up dinner together.'

It was a sharp reminder that things had gone back to a

previous status quo that I knew nothing of. This was reinforced by the new contents of the fridge: cartons of goji berry
juice, glass bottles of wheatgrass, packs of lactose-free cheese
and jars of tahini paste and kimchi. None of which was either
snack or child-friendly.

'How about beans on toast?' I asked Grace, closing the
fridge door. It felt like a beans on toast sort of day.

When she didn't respond I turned to find her standing
forlornly in the kitchen looking out of the patio window or
rather at the empty space beside it.

'Where's . . .' I stopped myself. 'Where's the tin opener?'

The tree had gone.

'Mummy didn't like it.'

I couldn't pretend I didn't know what she was talking
about.

'That's a shame,' I said, laying a hand on her shoulder,
feeling the tension in the muscles beneath her skin, my voice
pleasant as I clenched my other hand in a tight fist, willing
myself not to say a word.

Grace sniffed. 'She said it was . . .' she frowned '. . . naff.'

My throat was so tight I couldn't speak. 'She said my sparkly
tinsel was tasteless and grass. And what would people think
if they saw it in her house? I liked my tree. Did you like it,
Viola?' Silent tears were trickling down her face.

'Oh, sweet pea.' I scooped her up and hugged her as she
wound her thin arms around me, burying her face in my neck.
I could feel the warmth of her tears on my skin.

'M-m-u-u-mmy took it down. P-put all the d-decorations
in a b-box. F-for the charity shop.' She lifted her chin. 'Daddy

said they were yours and we had to give them back. Then she got really cross and said, "I might have guessed". But some of them are ours. Mine and Daddy's. We bought them. Remember? The Santa ones. At the stall in the market.'

I pinched my lips tight together as images of that perfect sparkling Saturday – walking in the snow, brunch, tree-hunting and putting the tree up – flashed in my brain like a favourite movie.

'Maybe,' I said, struggling to hold it together, 'you could put your decorations up in your bedroom or even have a little tree in there?'

'Then Daddy wouldn't see it,' said Grace sadly, patting my face. 'He liked our tree. I think he was sad when Mummy took it down.'

As I spooned Grace's beans onto her toast, my mobile rang.

I grabbed it without looking, my heart pinching, knowing it would be Nate.

'Hi, just a sec,' I said in a stupid attempt at delay, putting the phone down and setting the plate in front of Grace along with the glass of orange juice I'd just poured, knowing that hearing the timbre of his voice would hurt. 'There you go. Be careful, the beans are very hot.'

I picked up my phone. 'Hi!' I said in my best sparkly, *we're just friends and speaking to you is quite normal* voice.

'Viola, I take it that's my daughter you're speaking to.' He sounded stern and distant.

I closed my eyes briefly and focused on my next breath before speaking. 'Yes. I'm really sorry. I didn't know what else to do. The office sounded desperate and it was already so late. I couldn't leave . . .' My words spilled out, tumbling over one another before I realised that Grace was listening avidly. 'I couldn't not.'

'God, don't apologise. I should be apologising. I'm so sorry. And mortified that they had to call you. Thank you so much for going. I've only just picked up the message from the school office; otherwise I'd have been in touch before. Elaine was supposed to be picking Grace up. I've no idea where she is. She's not answering her phone. Anyway, I was ringing to say I'm on my way, but are you going to be all right? Getting to work?'

'It's fine, luckily I'm not working tonight.'

Nate sighed. 'I'm very grateful. I'll be there as soon as I can, probably another hour. Again, I'm really sorry.'

'Don't worry. Grace and I are having a . . . lovely time.' I smiled at her, conscious that she was sitting very still, listening to every word.

Except, if I were completely honest, we weren't having a lovely time because we were both on our best behaviour. She was back to being that too careful small adult and I was guarding every word I said, fearful of betraying too many things: being critical of Elaine, revealing how I felt about Nate, being furious on Grace's behalf.

After tea I checked my watch; there were still another forty-five minutes before Nate would be home. 'What do you want to do?' I asked. 'Some colouring?'

'Can we watch *Frozen*?'

'Of course you can.'

'No –' there it was again, that adult watchfulness '– will you watch it with me? In the snug?'

'Go set it up and I'll just load the dishwasher.'

Grace was draped comfortably over me like a sprawling indolent cat completely at ease, lying on her stomach across my lap, one elbow digging into one of my thighs, when we heard the door slam upstairs. Nate had made good time.

She didn't move, totally absorbed, even though she must have seen the DVD a thousand times before, but I felt her stiffen as we both heard the clip clop of high heels coming down the stairs.

When the footsteps hit the kitchen she wriggled off the sofa and stood up, awkward and stiff, making tiny movements, almost as if not sure which way to run.

Elaine came in, the lights catching the blonde highlights in her hair, wearing a gorgeous dress which emphasised her beautiful figure and the colour complementing the big Cameron Diaz blue eyes.

'Oh my goodness, thank heaven. Grace, you're home. Daddy's just sent me a text. I completely . . .'

Then she caught sight of me. 'Oh! Violet.' She looked around the room. 'Where's Nate?'

'He's on his way back from work.'

She looked delighted at that news, clearly pleased that he wasn't here hanging out with me.

'I had to go into the London office, small problem in the New York office with a deal we've been working on for months. They needed me to step in and sort a few things out. Honestly,

I've only been gone a couple of days and they can't cope without me.'

'So . . .' her smooth forehead didn't shift even though I could tell she trying to do one of those frowny make-me-understand-this-curious-situation smiles '. . . what are you doing here?'

Then she added after a five-second beat, 'Not that it isn't lovely to see you.' She ha-ha-ha ed. Had someone once told her that her tinkling laugh was attractive or something? 'Grace, can you turn that off?' Her quickfire bite and glare in the direction of the television had me clenching my fists again.

'I picked Grace up from school,' I said, being super pleasant back to her. 'The office phoned me in a panic. No one had collected her.'

'Oh . . .' she winced '. . . that's . . . sort of my fault. I got the call . . . and, well, you know what it's like. Suddenly you're running on adrenaline and caffeine again. It looked as if this merger was about to go tits up. We've been negotiating with the West Coast since this morning; you can imagine the time difference played havoc. I thought at one point we'd lost it. But –' she gave me a relieved smile '– everything's back on track. There was a lot of money at stake.' She grinned suddenly, her face transforming. She looked genuinely happy. 'But that's why they pay me the big bucks.' With another grin she crossed to the kettle. 'Too early to celebrate and I'm already running on pure caffeine but I don't suppose another will hurt. Today was one of those days that will go down in company history. Do you want one?' She indicated the cafetière she'd taken out of the cupboard.

I shook my head. 'I'd better head off.'

'Oh God, listen to me. I haven't even said thank you to you. I'm still buzzing. What a day! But thank you. It's such a good job you were on hand.' She beamed at me. 'You must make sure Nate reimburses you for your time and doesn't take advantage.' She tipped in two large spoonfuls of fragrant coffee grounds before turning to me, her eyes softening. 'Perhaps you should think about becoming a nanny. You're very good at . . .' she looked up now, her eyes a little too guileless '. . . coming to our rescue.'

'I did it for Grace,' I said as pleasantly as I could manage.

'And Nate, no doubt.' She lifted an eyebrow, still all smiles, but I had no doubt what she was getting at.

'No,' I insisted, 'just Grace.'

Then I realised that Grace was watching us, like a pair of combatants about to do battle. I sent her a reassuring smile, to which she responded with a very uncertain frown.

'Anyway, I ought to be going –' I gave Grace another smile '– now I've had my *Frozen* fix.' I winked at her.

There was a sound upstairs.

'Daddy's home,' said Grace as she went running towards the stairs. 'Daddy, Daddy.'

I heard her stockinged feet pad up the steps.

Elaine's mouth tightened fractionally and then she turned to me, a pleading look on her face that took me aback. 'Viola, I really am very grateful for all your help, please don't think I'm not but . . . I know how . . . oh, this is awkward.'

She came over to my side, bringing a waft of Jo Malone lime, basil and mandarin, and perched on the sofa arm. 'I know . . . Nate is gorgeous and I really don't blame you . . . but we really want to make this work.' Her voice broke a little. 'I'm trying but it's hard . . . especially when I've made . . .' she held out her hands, palms upwards '. . . so many mistakes. You have to understand, Nate and I, we've had our problems, but at the end of the day . . . there's too much here for us to throw away.' Now there was a touch of shame in her demeanour and I felt guilty. 'I've not been the best wife or mother but . . .' she gave me an earnest look '. . . you have to give Nate and me space to rebuild things. For Grace's sake more than anything.' The beseeching look she gave me made me feel hot with shame.

She was right. I needed to butt out and leave them to sort things out.

I swallowed and gave her a wan smile. 'I'm on Grace's side. I understand.'

'Thank you, Viola.' Her sad smile tugged at my heart and then she looked up as Nate walked into the room, her eyes shadowed with chagrin.

'Where were you?' he asked.

'Sorry, darling. I'm terrible . . . but New York called. It was such a mess. Whitby was desperate and if I hadn't gone we'd have lost the deal. Everything.'

'You were supposed to pick up Grace.' There was a tic in his cheek and I could see the tightness in his jaw.

'Oh, Nate –' Elaine stood up and faced him '– do we have to do this now?'

'Our daughter was left waiting for an hour and a half. If it hadn't been for Viola, the school would have called social services.'

'Don't be so silly; they wouldn't have done that.'

'Yes, they would.'

Elaine rolled her eyes. 'It was unprecedented circumstances. Seriously, deals like that are once in a lifetime opportunities. Besides, as soon as we've got a nanny we won't need to worry.'

'Won't we?' Nate's tone was dangerous and low.

'You're overreacting, darling. All's well that ends well. This was an absolute emergency. We would have lost the deal and nearly a year's work would have gone up in smoke. It's hardly the end of the world.'

Nate's eyes widened and I thought of Grace, looking lost and defeated in the school office.

Elaine shook her head in frustration and huffed. 'I hate to remind you, but you've managed childcare arrangements perfectly well without me for the last eleven months. Just because I'm home, do you seriously expect me to drop everything? I am still working for the New York office.'

'You're supposed to be on vacation,' Nate's voice ground out, fury shimmering in the quiet, restrained words. 'And we agreed this morning that you would pick Grace up. I told you school finished early today.'

'I got caught up. It was important. No one else could sort it out. I had to be there.' She lifted her chin with a defiant look. 'It's not as if someone else couldn't pick Grace up. And –' she looked my way '– they did.'

Nate eyed her and I was glad I wasn't on the other end of that look, his mouth tightened but what he was about to say was swallowed as Grace appeared in the doorway, clutching a piece of silver tinsel and the blue snow boots I'd bought her to her chest, looking with suspicious distrust at her mother.

'Oh, Grace!' Elaine moved forward to take them from Grace's hands. 'They're to go to the charity shop.'

'But they're mine.'

Like some small street urchin from a musical film, Grace ducked under her arms and ran to the other side of the room.

'They're mine,' she yelled. 'You can't have them.'

Elaine frowned and looked over at Nate in confusion. 'But you have lovely new ones. From Joules.'

'They're mine.' Grace's mouth folded into an implacable, mutinous line and she held the boots and the froth of tinsel tight to her chest.

'Grace, I bought you beautiful brand-new boots. Those are horrible, ugly things. They need to go.' She turned her back on Grace and was about to say something to Nate when Grace burst out, 'They keep my feet warm. And this is my decoration for my tree. You can't take them away. You're horrible and I hate you.'

'Grace Anna Williams. Don't you speak to me like that. Go to your room. Now!' snapped Elaine.

Even I jumped at her furious bark.

'They're mine and you're just mean. You're not having them,' said Grace, so furious herself that she was unfazed by Elaine's bristling, ugly anger.

'I don't want them, you stupid ch—'

'Enough!' barked Nate, glaring at both Elaine and Grace. Then, gentling his tone, he said, 'Grace I'd like you to go up to your room. I know you're upset but that's no excuse for being rude.'

Grace stood still and looked up at her father, her face

working with mutinous calculation as she figured out whether it was worth doing as she was told.

With a shuddery in-drawn breath, Grace plunked down on the floor, rammed her feet into the boots and wrapped the tinsel around her neck with Miss Piggy bravura that would have made me want to cheer if it wasn't all so sad, before getting to her feet and sticking her nose up in the air as she stalked out of the kitchen.

I shouldn't be witness to this; it was private family business.

'I think I'd better go,' I said hurriedly.

'Yes,' agreed Elaine, her face crumpling, her eyes shining with tears. 'I think you probably should.'

Nate's expression was thoughtful and as I gathered up my coat he stopped me. 'Wait. Actually, Viola, I've got a massive favour to ask you.'

'Oh?' I glanced at Elaine.

'Would you stay and babysit so that I can take Elaine out for dinner? I think we need some time to . . . to talk on our own.' His brown eyes were unblinking as he held my startled gaze.

What? He wanted to fix his marriage on my time? I started to shake my head. I wanted out of here.

'Please.' The quiet heartfelt word scored a direct hit and I felt the hopeless flutter in my chest. 'I need your help.'

I narrowed my eyes: *need*. He knew I couldn't resist that word. We'd talked about it. Bastard.

'This will be the last time,' I said, lifting my chin and staring back at him. 'There'll be no more *needing* me.'

'Thank you,' he said again, holding my gaze as if he wanted

to say something else. I could kill him for using my Achilles heel, especially in front of his wife. 'Elaine, we'll go in five minutes. I just want to talk to Grace.'

'Good luck with that. I think she needs a firm hand and some proper discipline. Things have slipped while I've been away.' Her voice was tight and angry. She'd dabbed away those brief tears but the upset had left her looking strained and subdued.

'Why don't you go and get ready, Elaine?' Nate's even, patient tone drew my gaze. There was something different about him. 'We'll leave in five minutes.'

'Five minutes.' She snatched up her handbag and with a return of her usual confidence stalked across the kitchen. 'See you later, Viole-la.'

Nate waited until she'd gone and then came over to me. I wanted to step back but couldn't.

'Sorry about that. Are you OK?' His face softened.

'I'm fine.' Inside I seized up, stiff and unyielding. I couldn't let him affect me. We were done.

'Thanks for staying, Viola.' He cupped my elbow and looked into my eyes as if he were trying to say a lot more.

I stepped back, frightened by the sudden hungry leap of my pulse. I wanted to do something dangerous like kiss him.

He was standing so close I could hear his breathing, smell his cologne and see the black pepper bristles shadowing his chin. Hopeless longing gripped me. I shouldn't be here. It was made worse by the answering hunger mirrored on his face. I couldn't do this again. After today, this really was it.

'Viola,' he said softly, the timbre of his voice playing across my skin, 'I won't be long. Can you put Grace to bed? Look after her for me.'

I nodded, my heart twisting in my chest as his eyes sought mine, a strange urgency in them.

'Thank you for being there for her.'

He ran a barely-there finger across the tops of my knuckles, a gesture that echoed one less than a week ago on my last night here, reminding me of all that we had lost. I pulled my hand away.

'Don't,' I whispered, feeling the familiar clouds of despair start to gather, black, rain-filled and full of misery, but I couldn't move away.

His eyes glimmered and he leaned forward, pressing a kiss onto my lips, coaxing them with infinite gentleness to move beneath his. I closed my eyes, the kiss like coming home, before wrenching back. This was wrong. His wife was upstairs.

He touched my lips with his finger and whispered, 'Thank you, Viola.'

I watched as he walked away, just like he had at my flat. Then he'd moved like an old man. Now . . . weirdly, there was almost a spring in his step. He looked back over his shoulder and smiled.

Turning away, unable to bear the pain, I watched his reflection in the patio windows disappear up the stairs and then closed my eyes, an uneasy feeling in my chest.

Chapter 31

After Nate and Elaine had left, I went upstairs to find Grace. Tearstained and subdued, she was lying on her bed staring up at the ceiling, holding onto the blue boots and the tinsel.

'You OK?' I asked, coming to sit on the side of her bed.

With a half-hearted nod she sat up, drawing her knees to her chest, still hanging onto the boots.

'Want to come downstairs and watch some television?'

She shook her head. It was quite restful in the dark cocoon of her bedroom, lit by the fairy lights around the bed head.

'Tell you what? Why don't you pop your PJs on, I'll go and make a hot chocolate and I'll read you some more *Harry Potter*?'

'Yes, please,' she said, so quickly that I felt quite pleased with my child whispering skills.

'OK, you got yourself a deal. Be back in two ticks.'

When I returned with two mugs of hot chocolate, she was already tucked beneath the covers, one of the boots poking out of the duvet by her pillow.

With a bit of juggling and wriggling, the two of us managed

to accommodate the boots, the tinsel and our hot chocolates without spilling a drop, and settle into a comfortable position just under the little reading lamp attached to the bedstead.

Determined to cheer Grace up, I went to town on the voices with a performance worthy of my own audio book contract, although I suspected I probably wasn't a patch on Stephen Fry.

Before long I could feel her body, nestled in next to mine, start to soften, and her breathing deepen. I kept reading for another minute but I knew from the weight of her head now slumped against my ribs that she was fast asleep. With a delicate bit of manoeuvring I wriggled my way out of the bed without disturbing her. I pulled the boots out and laid them neatly by the bed and slid the tinsel from beneath her pillows and draped it along the top of her bookshelf.

Touching my lips to her cheek, I backed out of the room, standing at the doorway watching her sleep for a long, long time, tears shimmering in my eyes. I had to face it, this might be the last time I saw her.

It hurt too much to see her and Nate.

At last I tore myself away and picked my way down the stairs. The insipid Christmas tree was level with the top of the stairs and as I came down each step, I looked at it with greater and greater pity, as if the tree were a real entity and knew that it had been short-changed.

Back in the kitchen, I tidied up, even though it wasn't my house. It was like a farewell tour as I put the tea towels back on their hooks, straightened the chopping block and turned off the dripping tap. Things I'd done so many times before. I ran a hand over the Roberts radio, still plugged in by the draining board. It had managed a stay of execution and retained its place on the worktop, although I noticed sadly that the chicken tablecloth had gone and so had the ugly placemats.

I looked at my watch. The silence in the house, heavy and still, felt oppressive but I didn't feel like watching television or putting any music on. Why, oh why, couldn't I have said no to Nate? With a heavy sigh, regret writhing through me with sinuous spite, reminding me with unkind persistence of what I'd lost, I walked up the stairs to the entrance hall. The despised Christmas tree gloated down at me. Turning away, I picked up my viola from the hall table where I'd left it earlier, a defiant thought making me smile. Even if it was only momentary, at least with my music I could leave an echo of myself on the silent house.

I'm not sure how long I played for, but my body had relaxed and I'd breathed into the rhythm of the music, my muscles supple and responsive. I finished the particularly tricky piece I'd been practising off and on for the last few weeks, feeling happier with it than I had to date when I heard enthusiastic clapping.

Whirling round, I realised that I'd been so absorbed I hadn't heard Grace come downstairs. I was a terrible babysitter. She had curled up on the end of the sofa in the living room.

'You should be in bed,' I said quietly. 'Did I disturb you?'

'No.' She shook her head, sounding wide awake. 'I needed a wee. And then I heard you and wanted to listen.' She sighed. 'You're very good.'

'Thank you but it is bedtime.'

'I don't have school tomorrow.' She folded her hands on her lap and looked far too innocent. 'And I'm not tired now.'

I tutted. 'What are you like? You can stay up for half an hour. Do you want me to read some more *Harry Potter* to you?'

'No.' She shuffled off the sofa and came towards me. With a careful hand she touched the bridge of my viola. 'Will you teach me something?'

I was about to say no, the viola really wasn't the instrument to start learning with, but she'd been said no to a lot in her short life.

'OK,' I said, sitting her down on the armchair, standing in front of her. 'I'll teach you how to make the sounds with the bow.'

Carefully, I placed the viola under her chin and arranged her hand to support the neck, holding my hand over hers. The room felt cold for an instant as I checked that she was holding my precious instrument.

'Now, hold the bow in this hand. And draw it very gently over the strings.' I stood back to watch as she tentatively moved the bow.

Her eyes widened at the horrible screech and she tensed. I almost stepped forward, worried she might drop the viola, but forced myself to stand still. Instead I smiled reassuringly at her.

'That's fine,' I said, fighting the urge to take it back. Grace needed to learn that not everything in life had to be perfect. 'Everyone makes that noise when they start.' Her brow furrowed with instant suspicion.

'Everyone,' I reiterated. 'How will you know if you've got it right? You have to make mistakes first. You have to get it wrong to know what that feels like, so you'll know what it feels like when it's right.'

She frowned again.

'Honest.' I held up my hands in mock surrender. I took the viola and bow from her. 'Watch.' I played, not quite sawing at the strings but certainly abandoning years of training and technique to make the point and added a little jig to further make the point. 'How bad is this?'

She giggled, so I played louder and added a few hip wriggles and shook my booty in time to the raucous noise. 'Can you be this bad?' I asked, still dancing. Her eyes lit up and she nodded, putting her hands over her ears.

'That's horrible, Viola.'

'I know.' I gave her a broad smile and stopped. 'Now, you try. Be as bad as you can, be really, really bad,' I teased before adding a little cautiously, 'but gently.'

She got up from the sofa and I arranged the viola in her hands and stepped back. She stood a little straighter and with a lot more confidence lifted the bow, flashing me a quick naughty grin. There were several more awful screeches and she faltered, looking anxiously at me. 'Keep going,' I encouraged.

She managed to wreak some truly horrible sounds out of my poor viola before I said, 'OK, now, feel it with me.' I sat down opposite her and stretched my legs out. 'Come sit here between my legs with your back to me.'

She nestled in front of me, her back to my chest. I helped

her support the viola with one hand, conscious it was quite heavy for her, and then covered her bow hand with mine. Very gently I helped guide her hand over the strings, showing her the correct positioning.

'You want to glide the bow over the strings as if you were easing the music out of them. The strings and the bow are best friends; they love each other. Neither one is more important,' I said as I steered her hand and the bow over the strings, eliciting a few scratchy notes, the resulting sound a distinct improvement. 'Can you feel that?'

She nodded, her face screwed up in concentration. I eased my touch on her hand, letting her guide the bow herself. This time, although far from perfect, the sound was almost mellow and musical. I took my hand away completely from her bow hand. There were still a lot of screeches but in between there was the odd note.

She turned round and looked up at me, wonderment dawning on her delicate face. 'I did it.'

'You did, sweet pea.'

Lifting the bow, she tried again and I looked down at the blonde curls, resisting the urge to bury my noise in her soft clean hair and squidge her tight to me. My throat tightened at the thought of letting her go.

A movement caught my eye and I looked up to see Nate stepping out from the shadows in the hall into a beam of light coming in through the window from the outside street lights. He stood with his jacket hooked over one finger on his shoulder and leaned against the door jamb. How long had he been home? I'd not heard the front door.

A slow, tender smile lit his face as his eyes roved over my face. Mute, I stared back at him, taking in every feature. Those warm expressive eyes, the soft curve of his kind mouth and the shadowed jawline that I wanted to press soft kisses against. My throat tightened and I could feel tears rising. I loved him so much it hurt. It was impossible to tear my eyes away from his, from that intent solemn stare. The air between us felt heavy and silent; the rest of the world had stopped, leaving the three of us in a private tableau.

'I love you,' he mouthed. I felt hot and then cold and hot again as my heart stopped and stuttered.

My eyes flickered over his shoulder, beyond him to the hall.

He shook his head.

Elaine had gone.

With a swallow I blinked; a tear escaped and slid down my cheek as I stared back at him, my feelings reflected in every movement of my face.

Grace, sensing something stopped and looked up. 'Daddy! You're home. Viola's teaching me.'

'So I see,' he said dryly, with a wink at me. 'Or rather heard.'

'Did you hear me being really *baad*?' she asked, scrambling to her feet, the bow and viola still in her hands. I put my hands on her waist to steady her.

'I did indeed. You were terrible.'

'So was Viola,' she said, flashing a look of mischief at me. She crossed to the nearby case and with reverent care laid the viola and bow into the lining. 'I think I'll go to bed now.'

Nate raised an eyebrow. I wiped a surreptitious hand at my face.

''Night, Viola.'

I rose to my feet and she hugged my waist before tugging at my sleeve to whisper something in my ear. Before I could say anything, she turned and went over to Nate, who bent down to kiss her.

''Night, Daddy.'

She shot me one beatific smile before she padded off to the stairs, leaving Nate and me staring at each other with bemusement.

We both stood perfectly still, listening to her as she climbed the stairs.

Then Nate took a step into the room. Fireflies of hope and excitement winked in and out, dancing low in my stomach.

I took a matching step forward, my knees suddenly not very sure of themselves. My heart thudded so hard I was sure he must be able to hear it and I could feel the throb of its urgent pulse in my ears, at my throat, my wrists.

Anticipation buzzed in the small space between us, almost as if we were savouring this final moment before the die was cast one way or the other. Then Nate took three quick strides to me, his hands reaching forward to grasp my wrists, his fingers pressing on the furious pulse there, pulling me to him to close the gap more quickly. With his arms encircling me, I let out a gasp of breath, not realising I'd been holding onto it so tightly.

'Viola,' he murmured, even as he lowered his head to kiss me. It was a desperate, possessive kiss, the like of which made my mouth curve into an involuntary smile under the delicious onslaught of his lips as my heart melted. My hands slid around his waist, relishing the solid feel of him and the delicious warmth of his skin through his shirt.

I laid my head against his chest, hearing the thud, thud, thud of his heart. My arms tightened around him as I felt a curious sense of contentment and ease. The sort that came from the touch of someone you know with bone-deep awareness is the other half of your soul.

We stood for a while in the pool of light, Nate's chin brushing my head, before we finally moved over to sit on the sofa for the serious stuff.

He smiled at me. 'I knew I'd made the right decision as soon as I walked in tonight and saw you with Grace –' his eyes twinkled '– showing her how to play badly.' He lifted a hand to my face, smoothing away a strand of hair. 'Showing her that she can be human. That she doesn't need to be perfect. You . . .' His voice cracked and my eyes darted to his. I saw him swallow and press his lips tight together before he said in a whisper, 'You're so good with her, it almost breaks my heart. You understand her. But you don't do it for me, you do it for her and for you. That's what I love about you, that huge compassion and understanding you have. Your quiet awareness of the things we, Grace and I, keep below the surface.'

I reached up and touched his face, my heart contracting at his words as he carried on.

'You never pushed, not once. You let me come to you,' he said in a low fierce voice. 'I'm not the best bet, you know. Failed marriage, single dad.' With a sad smile he pulled back slightly.

In response I reached up to trace his mouth with my fingers, my heart full to bursting, too choked with emotion to frame the words. I poured my love into that touch as I explored his face, my eyes never leaving his.

'Viola?'

The brief touch of uncertainty in his eyes shocked me into speech. 'I love you, Nate. Married man or not, I couldn't seem to stop myself falling for you. My heart didn't seem to understand that you were out of bounds.'

'Married in name only. I love you, Viola. More than I thought possible. With heart and soul in a way that I never ...' His fingers toyed with the skin behind my hair almost as if he were unaware of it.

I leaned forward and kissed him. God, I loved him.

'And I know you love Grace.' He paused, a smile touching his lips. 'Of course you do know she comes as part of the package.'

I groaned. 'Oh God, I'm not going to have to teach you the viola as well.'

Nate gave a shout of laughter as he pulled me into his arms and we fell back against the sofa, his lips finding mine as we kissed, or tried to kiss, in between giggles. Then the kisses moved up a gear and, mindless, I sank into the feel of his body against mine, the electric touch of his tongue toying with mine and the fireworks that fizzed and exploded in every last part of me.

When I came to, my blood settling as I lay nose to nose with Nate on the sofa, I stared into his solemn eyes. Practicalities now after the fizz and flush of love, lust and sheer joy.

'Elaine?'

'She's gone.' His quiet statement of fact suddenly made everything seem so much simpler. 'Going back to New York.'

'I'm sorry. For Grace.' I winced.

'Don't be.' He touched my cheek. 'Seeing you teaching her to play your – I dread to think how expensive viola – it just cemented everything. You give Grace so much more. Elaine might be her biological mother but . . . we talked it all through. She accepts that she can't be what Grace needs or deserves.' Sadness glowed in his eyes and his hand drifted down to hold mine. 'We both cried. For Grace. For our marriage. But I realise now, Elaine was very generous there, she said that neither of us failed, we were just the wrong people together. And Elaine's the wrong person to be a mother. She's a brilliant, talented, beautiful woman. Today I suspect she really did save the day. Made millions of dollars for her clients. I admire her for being a trailblazer. I'm proud of her and the daughter we made together but . . . for her that's not enough. And she's not enough for me, not when I've seen what could be.' He kissed me, a tender caress with his mouth, and then his lips drifted to press tiny kisses along my jawline before stopping and holding my gaze again, telling me everything he needed to without words. That intent insistent regard would never get old.

'I understand her in a lot of ways,' I said quietly, squeezing his hand. 'If I couldn't play my music . . . it's part of me. Part of who I am.'

'But you have the capacity for more as well. You have love to give. So much empathy.' He paused. 'I'm not sure I deserve you.'

I kissed him softly on the mouth. 'Luckily for you, I'm the one that gets to make that choice.'

'Will you have me?' The quiet simple words dropped into the silence of the room.

My eyes locked on his as I made my promise. 'Yes.'

'And Grace?'

I raised an indignant eyebrow. 'You even have to ask?'

'No . . . you know what you're taking on.'

'What about Grace? How are you going to tell her –' my voice broke '– that Elaine is leaving again?'

'It's sad –' I felt his body sag slightly with a touch of defeat '– but Grace knows; in her heart of hearts she knows. I think having Elaine back for this last week hasn't been quite the fairy tale family moment she'd hoped for. Grace is too adult for her years.' He shook his head. 'I'm going to tell her the truth . . . that it's Daddy's fault . . . he doesn't love Mummy any more.' He laced his fingers through mine and held them against his chest.

'She'll be upset but I'm hoping that we can build a home that's happy enough to make her realise that she's loved, to compensate for what she's lost. It will hurt to start with but . . . when you're here this house is a home. When you're here I want to be here. It's the sort of place I want Grace to grow up in. A home rather than a house. A home where she's loved and where she comes first, within reason. A proper family.'

His intent gaze made me swallow. 'Of course, if you hate this house we can move.'

'This is Grace's home. I don't think it would be fair to impose too much change on her, although there are things

404

I'd change,' I said with a sudden teasing grin. 'That wallpaper, for a start. And tomorrow we have to go out and get another tree.'

'Yes, we must.' He sobered. 'I could have killed Elaine when I realised the tree had gone. All I could think of was you and me putting the lights on the tree with Grace giving us those useless instructions, "up a bit", "no, higher", "in the wiggly bit". And you laughing at me. And then I couldn't stop thinking of you . . . in the snow, at brunch, tickling Grace in bed, remembering how happy I was that morning when I woke up and remembered you were in the house, and so many other things. When I looked at that empty space in the kitchen I missed you. That's when I realised I couldn't play happy families even for the sake of Grace. I just wanted you to be here.'

'I missed you too. Mum can't understand why I've been at her and Dad's so much . . . I just couldn't bear to be on my own in the flat. I'm actually almost organised for Christmas, I've been so busy trying to keep myself occupied for the last few days. Although –' I gave him a mischievous look '– you're going to have to help me with the food shopping tomorrow . . . looks like there'll be two extra mouths to feed at Mum's.'

'You're inviting us to lunch with your family?'

'I am . . .' I laughed '. . . I *need* the moral support, although they have all been given strict instructions that they have to pitch in and help.'

'I'm glad to hear it. I think they're going to have to get used to the idea that Grace and I need you far more than they do.' He brushed my lips again. 'But remember this, you're allowed to *need* us. From now on, you have us and I'll be here for you.'

He lifted my hand and kissed each knuckle in a tender promise that had the rest of my heart pooling into nothing more than a puddle.

'By the way, what did Grace say to you?'

I laughed. 'She's decided that she doesn't mind if Daddy has a girlfriend after all.'

Nate gave me a brilliant smile. 'I think that should be amended to: she doesn't mind if Daddy has a girlfriend as long as it's you.'

'I agree with that.'

'I've got a horrible feeling from now on I'm going to be outnumbered and the two of you are going to gang up on me.'

I grinned up at him. 'You'd better believe it and there are going to be a few changes around here.'

'There are?'

I sobered and nodded, thinking of Grace. 'Perhaps we can begin with introducing some Christmas traditions of our own. Make our own perfect Christmas for Grace. This year, I think Santa and Rudolph should get a mince pie and carrot and that someone should wake up with a stocking on their bed on Christmas morning.'

'That's an excellent idea.' A wicked twinkle lit up his eyes. 'And I think if it's going to be the perfect Christmas I should wake up with something in my bed on Christmas morning. Any suggestions?' he asked as his hands slid down my body.

'You don't want a stocking as well, do you?' I sighed with mock weariness.

'No,' he growled, 'I want you.' He kissed me on the mouth. 'On Christmas Day.' He kissed me again and this time I sighed with happiness and smiled up at him. 'That sounds perfect.' In fact it looked as if this Christmas might just be the best one ever.

THE END

Acknowledgements

Some books are easier to write than others and some are closer to an author's heart than others, this one was very much a labour of love as I completely fell for my characters, especially Viola my viola playing heroine. I needed to do considerable research and as most people who know me will attest, I do not have a single musical bone in my body and I have to thank Alan Garner and Julie Price who talked me through the inner workings of being in an orchestra and introduced me to a brand new word, Sitzeprobe[1]. I'm honoured to count these renowned classical musicians as friends and any mistakes I've made are all mine, in spite of their patient teachings.

With any book, no matter how much you fall in love with it, there are points where you never believe it will be good enough. My much loved agent, Broo Doherty, gave me the vital belief, support and encouragement exactly when I needed it for this book, also providing her usual wise owl brilliant

---

1 Sitzprobe is a rehearsal where the singers sit in with the orchestra and often it's the first time the two groups have rehearsed together.

suggestions to help improve the story. The icing on the cake bits are all down to the fabulous skills of my wonderful editor, Charlotte Ledger, who like a heat seeking missile homes in on what needs to be done to make a book the best it can be. I can't thank either of these two wonderful women enough. I'm also extremely grateful to copyeditor extraordinaire, Sheila Turner, who added the final bit of sparkle.

I also have the most amazing behind the scenes cheer-leading team of author friends, who help me with plot ideas and problems, Donna Ashcroft (and her partner, Chris Cardoza, who puts up with me constantly invading his kitchen) and those who cheer me on when the word count gets sticky; Sarah Bennett, Darcie Boleyn, Philippa Ashley and Bella Osborne. Being friends with all of them has enriched my writing life no end. Thanks also go to fellow author, Sue Moorcroft, as I wrote part of this book in Italy (not necessarily conducive to writing about snow) on a writing retreat and we had several invaluable chats which helped me to resolve a couple of thorny plot issues.

Special thanks to Paulene Le Floche, schoolfriend and champion proof reader, who swooped in to the rescue when I needed some help and is a wonderful supporter.

Last and never least are you the readers. Thank you for choosing to read my book when there are thousands out there, thank you to those who get in touch, it's always lovely to hear from you and thank you to all those who leave reviews . . . even its only a one liner, they make the world of difference. I hope you enjoy Viola's story as much as I enjoyed writing it.